LIE TO ME

JOANNE RYAN

Tamarillas Press

This book is a work of fiction. All characters, locations, businesses, organisations and situations in this publication are either a product of the author's imagination or used factiously. Any resemblance to real persons, living or dead, is purely coincidental.

Cover Design: © Joanne Ryan
ISBN: 978-1-913807-17-7

Other books by Joanne Ryan:

Without Reason
All The Lost Years
Not Your Average Girl
The Lodger
The Double
One Night

Writing as Marina Johnson:

Fat Girl Slim
Fat Girl Slim Returns
Fat Girl Slim Three
A Confusion of Murders
So Talk To Me
The Herb Sisters
Say Hello & Wave Goodbye
The Harriet Way

CHAPTER ONE

I've known since I was five-years-old that I was adopted and I'm fine with it, honestly. I've never felt the yearning to know anything about my parents because my birth mother is dead and my father, well, who knows?

I don't mean that statement to sound callous but I've always assumed that my father was very much alive when I was adopted but he made no attempt to look after me, so why should I be interested in him? I don't know if my birth mother had any family but if she did, they didn't want me either so I have no desire to find any of them.

When Mum and Dad sat me down and told me that I was adopted, I wasn't surprised or upset because I had such a happy life that it really didn't matter. And I was only five, so I didn't really grasp what they were telling me. In my mind it was all mixed up and I likened it to the Tom Thumb story; I thought that I'd been chosen by them especially because they couldn't have a child of their own, which I suppose, is sort of right. Of course, as I grew older, I began to understand the truth of it but to me, Mum and Dad are my real parents and no one else.

Mum has asked me many times over the years if there's anything that I want to know about my birth parents. She always said that she'd tell me everything that she knows, although the details that she has are scant. The only thing I wanted to know as I got older, was how old I was when I came to live with Mum and Dad, because I wondered if I had any memories from before that. I was about twelve when I asked and Mum looked sad and told me that my birth mother died when I was eleven months old. I didn't really want to know if she was alive or dead but I remember being relieved that I couldn't remember anything about her. The furthest back that I could recall was when I must have been older than that. I was walking properly on my own and I was able to talk so I must have been around two-years-old and I was crying because my pram was being sold and I didn't want it to go. I wasn't sure, you see, who was there, whether it was Mum or my other mother, because the only bit I remember is the pram. It was yellow with a square hood and big wheels and a funny squiggly pattern on the side. How bizarre is that – remembering something so trivial? I told Mum about remembering the pram then, because I'd never told her before in case it was my birth mother and I hurt Mum's feelings by telling her about it. Mum laughed and said that I was right, I was just past my second birthday. She didn't say it but I've often wondered if they were waiting to adopt a brother or sister for me and that's why they hung onto the pram for so long. Anyway, Mum told me then not to be silly and worry about upsetting her because if I wanted to talk about my birth parents, it was fine.

I did worry though, and I still do, because it seems really ungrateful to want to know about them when Mum and Dad have been such fantastic parents.

I didn't ask how my birth mother died, but I always assumed that it was in a car accident or something similar because she must have been quite young. Or maybe it was cancer because that can strike at any age. As to my birth father, Mum *thinks* that he's still alive, as he would only be in his forties now, but she didn't really know. I stopped her from saying any more because I honestly didn't want to know. I was perfectly happy as I was and had no intention of trying to find my father and opening up something that's best left alone. He didn't want me then and I don't want him now, I don't even think of him as my father. As Mum and Dad were issued with a new birth certificate when they adopted me, I had no idea of my birth name. Layla is the name that they chose for me and I wasn't interested in the name I went by in my previous life.

I may only be nineteen-years-old but I've

learned that when things are good, you should leave them be and not do anything to change them. Stupidly, on several occasions, I've said and done things that I shouldn't have and have massively regretted it so now, as Mum says, I keep my own counsel. I also think it will be hugely hurtful to Mum – and Dad, although he's no longer with us – because she's the most perfect mother than anyone could wish for. We're best friends as well as mother and daughter and even though she's said that she'd be perfectly fine if I *did* suddenly decide that I wanted to know more, I had no intention of ever finding out.

I didn't *need* to know.

Funnily enough, Mum and I do actually look alike; we have the same fair, wavy hair and blue eyes and the same slender figure. People comment on our similarities; we were *meant* to be mother and daughter. We love the same things too, art and music, nature, and of course, cooking.

When Dad died when I was eight, it was the absolute bond between Mum and I that made our grief bearable. Mum said that she couldn't bear to stay in London because without Dad she felt adrift and unable to cope with the noise and grime and constant bustle. In no time at all she'd sold the London flat and we moved further south to the outskirts of a large village. We love the countryside and the slower pace of life. Mum and I like to forage a little, not through necessity but because we love to do it. Mum knows every mushroom and fungi that grow around here and although we go shopping at supermarkets like everyone else, we also like to take from the land. No one here knows that Mum and I aren't blood relatives and why should they? It's no one's business but ours. I'm not ashamed of being adopted but I know that the questions would start once people knew; who are your real parents, what happened to them, don't you want to find them? On and on and on because people are nosey and think they have a right to know every single thing about you.

No. I've learned my lesson; keep your own counsel.

And my life would be just perfect if it wasn't for the fact that, by complete accident, I've found out who my birth mother was. Mum and I tell each other everything but I haven't told her that I've discovered the truth and that I *know*. I could tell her, because I know she'd be absolutely fine about it and not cross at all, but I'm keeping it to myself. Because I don't want to talk about it, I don't want to know any more details, and I wish with all my heart that I'd never found out.

Because once you know something, you can't un-know it.

And honestly, I wasn't even looking, all I wanted was a photograph of Mum, Dad and I together so I could make a copy of it and put it in a nice frame for Mum's birthday. We always like to make gifts for each other rather than buy things because it means so much more. I'd been wondering what I could make her when I realised that although we had lots of pictures of us all around the house, we didn't have one of the three of us. There are lots of Dad and I and Mum and I, but none of us all together. I suppose one or other of them would have always been taking the photograph but I reasoned that there must be one of the all of us somewhere.

I thought the best place to look was in the old photograph box that Mum keeps in the huge sideboard in the lounge. So, the day before yesterday, I decided to get it out and have a good root through. I thought I was being so clever when I waited until Mum had gone into her art studio at the end of the garden before I even attempted to look. I knew that once she started painting, she'd be in there for hours and I'd be quite safe. There'd be no chance of her catching me and spoiling her birthday surprise. I went into the lounge and dragged the box out of the back of the sideboard and onto the floor. I sat down and made myself comfortable and began to go through the contents. There were so many photographs of me it was almost embarrassing. Do all parents take so many photographs of their children? I suppose they do but as I have no siblings, I have no way of telling. I did feel a little tearful looking at the ones of Dad and to my shame, I struggled to remember very much about him. Maybe that's why I was crying.

Anyway, halfway down the box I was already feeling disappointed because I hadn't found a photograph of the three of us when I noticed the corner of a piece of paper was poking out at the bottom. Curious, I pulled it and the paper came out, ripping slightly in the process. Yellowed and faded, it was an old page from a newspaper, an article with a mottled black and white picture of a young woman next to it. I turned the page over in my hand and wondered why on earth Mum had kept it.

How I wish I'd never found it, or at least never read it.

But no, my interest piqued, I began to read and as I took in the words, I realised that the dates were very relevant and with mounting horror, I discovered two things.

The first was that I look nothing like my birth mother.

And the second was that she didn't die in an accident or of cancer, or of any illness at all.

She was murdered.

CHAPTER TWO

'Penny for them?' Mum asks, as we walk along the side of the road.

'Just thinking what a lovely day it is,' I say. It is a lovely day, hot and sunny and it's only the end of May, so hopefully we have a good summer ahead of us. But I'm not being completely honest; I was thinking about the newspaper cutting again. It's been on my mind and I can't seem to make myself forget about it. I'm usually very good at compartmentalising things that upset me but this is refusing to go away and keeps popping into my head when I least expect it.

'Is something bothering you, Layla?' Mum stops and takes hold of my hand and I stop too.

'You know you can tell me anything, right?' She smiles and grips hold of my hand tightly and her eyes search my face.

'No, I'm fine, honestly.' I gently shake her hand free and resume walking. Mum falls back into step beside me.

'Are you sure?' She persists. 'Because you've been very quiet for the last few days.'

'No,' I say, laughing. 'I'm fine.'

I don't look at her but I hear Mum sigh and I know that she won't leave it, she's going to keep on asking until she finds out what's wrong. That's the trouble with being so close; she always knows when something is bothering me.

'Is it the posing thing again?' she asks, after a moment. 'Because I'm not forcing you, you know. It's entirely up to you.'

I say nothing but carry on walking. This is one of the few topics that Mum and I have *nearly* argued about. Every Friday – today, we're on our way there now – Mum teaches a drawing class at the local community hall. Each week the same eight loyal pupils turn up to learn how to sketch from Mum. New ones come for a few weeks or months but the *steadfast eight* as Mum calls them, have been coming for years. Some weeks it'll be an arrangement of ornaments or pieces of pottery to paint, sometimes wild flowers, sometimes a life model.

'It's not that,' I say, in an attempt to put a stop to the conversation.

'It's quite natural to be shy.' She stops again and takes hold of my hand and I fight the urge to shake myself free of her grip. How I wish a car would come by so we would both have to step onto the grass bank to let them pass. Anything to stop this conversation. Again.

'I'm not shy.'

'Darling, you have to forget about what happened at school, that's just immature teenagers for you. You're beautiful and your body is beautiful. If you could just find the courage to do this, I think it would really help you get over your hang ups.'

'I don't have any hang ups.'

'Darling.' Mum drops my hand and links her hands around my waist and pulls me close, resting her head on my shoulder. 'If you want to get over something, you have to face it, yes?'

I swallow down the tears that threaten and I know that it's not the posing nude that's bothering me, I honestly don't have a hang up about my body, I just don't want to do it. It's the newspaper clipping, ever since I found it, I can't stop thinking about what I've discovered, but what's even worse, is the things that I *don't* know. The thought has taken root that my father has never contacted me because *he* killed my mother. It's perfectly possible because the newspaper report only stated that my mother had been found battered to death whilst I slept upstairs in my cot; there was no mention of the murderer. The more I think about it, the more I've become convinced that it was my father who murdered my mother because that would explain his absence from my life. A normal man wouldn't abandon their only child, would they? Mum has always told me that she assumes he's still alive and I'm the one who's stopped her from telling me anything more about him. If he is still alive, he'd still be in prison. I could find out for sure simply by asking Mum or googling my mother's name, but I'm too afraid of the truth.

Why can't I be like Mum, why do I have to be such a coward?

'A body is just skin, bone and fat, Layla. The art class artists are *adults*, not silly boys,' Mum says, oblivious to the real reason for my silence. 'No one will laugh at you, I promise. Mr Jones was fine when he posed and I've done it several times and no one laughed at me, did they? Not even so much as a snigger.'

'I'll think about it,' I say.

'That's the spirit,' Mum says, standing back and gently pushing a tendril of hair from my face. 'It's not like you haven't sat before, is it?'

'No. But I had clothes on then.'

'There's really no difference.' She turns and takes hold of my hand and we start to walk again. 'Truthfully, Layla, you'll feel so empowered afterwards that you'll wish you could do it again straight away. You'll feel absolutely wonderful, I guarantee it.'

I manage a smile and Mum starts to talk about the items that she's chosen for today's lesson and I feel relief that we don't have to talk about it anymore. As well as what I've learned about my birth mother, it's all too much and today I want to blank everything out and think about nothing. Mum talks about the collection of knicks knacks in her carrier bag which she will no doubt arrange with something she finds in the community hall kitchen. I wonder how much longer I can put off posing nude; it's my choice, of course it is, Mum wouldn't force me. But I know if I don't do it then she's going to think I have a serious hang up about it. She'll probably suggest that I have some sort of counselling or something because she'll see my refusal to strip off and pose nude for an art class as a serious mental health problem.

Maybe I should just do it and get it over with, it would be easier than actually talking about my feelings to a perfect stranger because where would it end? Who knows what I'd end up saying once the floodgates were opened. I feel that if I relinquish even the slightest control, there'll be no holding me back. Besides which, I'm in no way ashamed of my body and I don't have any hang ups about it but I just don't want to pose naked. I can't see that it's necessary. I cringe at the thought of sitting naked in the dusty, fusty, community hall while a load of old people peer at me and attempt to draw me. All of the people in the class are ancient except for Dylan, who's young. He's not much older than me and he stares at me all of the time when he thinks that I'm not looking. He gives me the creeps. He's like an old man in a young person's body. The thought of being naked in front of him feels almost as bad as the memory of my practically non-existent breasts being *WhatsApped* to the whole of year ten.

Although that was totally my own fault.

I shake the thought off, stow it back in its mental security box and refuse to think about it. I'll just have to do it and get it over with because Mum won't let up. If I tell her that it's because Dylan gives me the creeps, she'll be convinced that it's really to do with what happened at school. She already thinks that it's high time I had a boyfriend and even asked me if I liked girls instead. I don't; I just can't see myself meeting anyone. Mum says I have to stop dwelling on the past and she's right, but I don't think that posing nude is going to be empowering, it's just going to be embarrassing.

I was mortified the first time Mum stripped off and posed and I truthfully wanted to curl up and die I felt so embarrassed. She sees these people in the shops and in the street, at the Christmas fayre, everywhere, for God's sake, and she let them see every part of her. Mr Jones kept putting his glasses on and taking them off again and wiping them with a cloth as if he couldn't believe what he was seeing. Mum made a makeshift sofa by pushing three chairs together, threw a velvet throw over them with a couple of cushions and then lay across them. She even asked the class which pose was best, putting her legs up on the chairs and putting them down again and making no attempt to keep her legs closed. I didn't know where to look. It's not as if I haven't seen her naked hundreds of times before because I have, we're very relaxed about nudity at home. I'm comfortable in front of Mum, but that's different. I can go topless on a beach with no problem but that's with strangers and everyone does it. The thought of Dylan ogling every bit of me makes me feel sick. I bet he's never seen a naked woman before. Apart from Mum.

'So, what do you think?' Mum asks.

I haven't been listening but I can't tell her this so I take a chance and assume she's asking my opinion on today's collection for sketching in the class.

'Sounds perfect,' I say.

Mum smiles and I know I've said the right thing.

'We'd better hurry,' she says, picking up the pace. 'We don't want to be late.'

I glance at my watch to see that it's nearly ten-to-two. We march along until the grass verge peters out and we're walking on a proper pavement. The road is quiet today and only one car has passed us, although the school bus from the nearby town will drop its passengers outside the community hall at four-thirty. The class will be over by then and we'll already be home unless we stop on the way to forage for berries. The thought of the school bus makes me feel anxious and I push the feelings down. Even if I was here when the bus went by no one on there would know me; I left school years ago.

So why do I feel anxious about it?

Because I'm feeling anxious about everything today and I have done since I found that piece of newspaper. It's stirred it all up, all the things that have ever made me unhappy or anxious, just as I knew it would. This is why I don't like change; I like everything to stay exactly the same.

Because if it stays exactly the same, I can cope.

'Mr Jones!' I hear Mum trill as if she's greeting a long-lost friend. He's sitting outside the hall on the wooden bench that the teenagers congregate around at night with their bottles of cider and cigarettes. Mr Jones looks about to fall asleep but when he spots Mum, he smiles and with a lot of grunting and groaning, hauls himself slowly to his feet. I don't know how old he is but he's so wrinkled that he reminds me of an old elephant from one of the wildlife programmes that Mum and I watch on TV. The week that he posed nude for the still life still haunts me, whatever possessed him to do it, I have no idea. Why he imagines anyone would want a picture of his body is beyond me. Thankfully, he's so old and wrinkled that I didn't have to look at his penis because it was hidden underneath the elephantine folds of grey, floppy, skin.

'And how's young Layla?' he asks, as he plods towards us.

'Very well, thank you.' I move swiftly to one side to stop him from touching me. 'And you?'

'Same old, same old,' he says, puffing heavily as he utters each word.

Mum unlocks the hall door and we step inside to the smell of old wood and plimsolls. Everything that goes on in the village is done here; ballet lessons, boy scouts, girl guides, keep fit, *everything*. Some people even choose to get married here and most of the children have their birthday parties here, apart from the ones who have defected to the *McDonalds* in the nearby town of Wellerton. I walk straight through to the kitchen and put my bag on the counter. I pick up the ancient kettle and take it to the sink and fill it from the tap. The sound of voices and tables and chairs being moved across the floor carries through from the hall and I know that the rest of the class are arriving.

I stay in the kitchen.

I take cups and saucers from the cupboard in readiness for the tea break that we have after forty-five minutes and line them up neatly on the counter top.

I do everything very slowly and methodically.

That way I can stay in here for as long as possible.

* * *

I have to come out eventually, because Mum would think there was something wrong with me. I sit at one of the spare tables and begin to sketch the arrangement that Mum has placed in the centre of the room. I can draw and have some talent, but nothing on the scale of Mum's. Her drawings and paintings sell very well in the bijou art galleries in the nearby towns, and artwork by Debs Trevellyn has become quite sought after. Even though she could, Mum doesn't charge anyone for her art lessons, she sees it as *giving back* and truthfully, Dad left us very well provided for so she has no need of the income. I've barely started when it's time to put the kettle on for the break, so I escape to the kitchen again. I throw teabags into the big teapot and when the kettle's boiled, I make the tea. I pour the tea out and put the cups through the serving hatch with the sugar pot for everyone to help themselves. I stay in the kitchen and drink my own tea, and fill the sink with hot soapy water ready to wash up. After everyone's drunk their tea, I wash up the cups and saucers and slowly dry them. I make this job last as long as possible. Once I've finished putting everything away, I have no choice but to go back to my table and resume my sketch. I feel, rather than see, Dylan look up at me as I walk by. I ignore him. I sit down and pick up my pencil and sweep it across the paper and focus on the edges of the pretty cups and saucers that Mum has bought from home. Mum could capture the tableau with a few strokes of her pencil but my style is more measured and careful.

Like me.

Sometimes I think that I should have been the mother and Mum, the daughter, because she is much younger and freer in heart than I. The girls at school used to make fun of me, saying I was boring like an old woman. I wish I were different but I am what I am. Maybe I'm a victim, like my birth mother. The thought pops into my head before I can stop it and once there, it begins to take root. I think I've always been a victim and now it sort of makes sense, because I've obviously inherited it. It's in the genes.

Or maybe I'm like my father.

Maybe I'm a killer.

I push the thoughts away because they're becoming ridiculous and I try to concentrate on shading the handle of the cup. As I press the pencil into the paper the back of my neck starts to tingle and I know that I'm being watched. I have a sixth sense for when people are looking at me and I wish I didn't; life would be much easier if I was oblivious. I turn my head slightly and glance sideways to see Dylan gazing at me. He sees that I've caught him and hurriedly looks down at his paper, scribbling furiously with his pencil.

Now that he's no longer looking at me, I take the opportunity to scrutinise him and see the flush of red racing from his neck up to his cheeks. Tall and gangly, his trainer clad feet jut out from the table in front of him. His mousey brown hair is overlong but not in a fashionable way, but rather that of an old man with a short back and sides who's overdue a haircut. It looks like his mother cuts it. It's not that he's ugly, his features are even and he has quite nice skin but there's something lacking about him, something not attractive or *attracting*. He looks like an overgrown schoolboy rather than the twenty-four-year-old that I know he is; he's always clean, smart, tidy and polite and totally sexless. He works in the local newsagents which is owned by his father and which will one day be his. He's allowed an hour-and-a-half off every Friday so that he can come to this art class because he loves art. He really wanted to go to university to study it but felt obliged to continue in the family business. Every weekday evening, he works until seven o'clock when the shop closes, except for Saturdays when it closes at five and Sundays when it closes at one.

I know all this because he tells me. Whenever he has the opportunity, he talks to me, his words coming out in a rush as if he's on a timer and he has to get it all out before the buzzer goes off. Or he tells me about his hobby; bird-watching, the feathered type. Or he talks about newspapers and magazines and sale-or-return and the complexities of selling sweets from jars and the problems of under-age cigarette smokers who come into the shop and pretend to be over eighteen. He's seriously uncool as the girls at my old school would say – just as I am – but will no doubt make a very good, faithful and boring husband to someone one day.

I'm not fashionable or cool and I wear the same clothes as Mum, long floaty dresses and colourful jingle-jangle jewellery as she calls it. I have no style of my own but simply copy hers. My hair is down to my waist and Mum cuts it and I wear it parted in the middle and I do nothing with it except wash it and let it dry naturally. But I quite like it.

I quite like how I look, actually, despite my aversion to showing my body off to the art class because objectively, I know that I'm very pretty. I'm slim, almost blonde, have good skin and teeth and although Mum says I'm beautiful, I don't think that I am. But I am pretty. I have no idea if I'm attractive, or attracting, to men, because so far, as far as I know, I haven't attracted anyone.

Except for Dylan, and he doesn't count because I don't find *him* attractive or attracting in any way at all.

The screech of chair legs across the dusty wooden floorboards breaks my daydream and I realise that the class is finishing. Dylan stares straight at me and smiles, again flushing red to the roots of his hair. I realise that I'm still staring at him. I quickly look away but it's too late, he's standing up and pushing his sketch book into his leather folder and I can just tell that he's going to walk over to me. I stand up and look around for Mum to see her deep in conversation with Lorna Botham, the local gossip, their heads close together as Lorna whispers the latest scandal in Mum's ear. I can hardly go and gate crash their conversation so I'll have to make my escape to the kitchen.

But it's no good, before I can move Dylan is by my side, beaming down at me.

'Hi, Layla,' he says.

'Hi,' I say, gathering up my paper and pencils and pushing them into my folder. I make to move away but Dylan steps sideways, blocking me. I stare down at his impossibly clean trainers and will him to move.

'Layla,' he says, softly. 'I was wondering, would you like to go out with me one evening?'

CHAPTER THREE

'I see you were talking to Dylan.'

We've stopped on the way home and Mum and I are picking blackberries to make a crumble for tonight's dessert. We have to stretch to reach the berries as all of the lower branches are picked clean. The spikes keep sticking into my fingers and I wonder why we're bothering; neither Mum or I are really dessert people.

'I wasn't talking to him,' I say, throwing a handful of berries into the basket. 'He was talking to me.'

'Anything interesting?'

'No,' I snort. 'Same old boring stuff.'

I don't tell her that he asked me out. I basically blanked him and turned and walked away without even answering. I was rude to him and Mum wouldn't approve.

'I think he likes you.' Mum throws a handful of berries into the basket and looks at it. 'I think that's plenty, any more would be wasteful.'

I pick the basket up in readiness to leave but Mum stops me.

'Let's sit on the grass for a while, enjoy the last of the sunshine before it gets dark.'

I flop down onto the grass and draw my legs up underneath my chin and wrap my arms around them. Mum sits down opposite me.

'He seems like a nice boy, Dylan.' She looks at me meaningfully and I realise that she knows, she knows he asked me out because she never misses a thing.

'He asked me out,' I say, with a shrug. 'But I don't want to go out with him.'

'Why not?'

'He goes on and on about sweets and newspapers and blue tits.'

Mum looks at me and we laugh.

'I think he's just nervous,' Mum says. 'Maybe a bit shy. If you got to know him, he's probably much more interesting.'

'He's dull, boring and not even remotely attractive,' I say, picking at the grass. 'I honestly wish that he'd just leave me alone and go and pester someone else.'

'He's quite nice looking. Good teeth and skin,' Mum says, with a smile.

I shrug.

'But he is quite ordinary and a bit reserved, and maybe a bit old-fashioned, too. Not the sort that girls chase after. Nothing like that Darius boy or Mr Evans.' She softens the remark with a smile but

I still wince at her words.

Why would she bring them up? The school heart-throb who pretended to like me just so I'd send him a topless picture and the hot English teacher who I had a massive, embarrassing, crush on?

'I'm sorry, darling.' Mum puts her hand on my arm. 'I just wanted to point out that you shouldn't judge by looks alone. Dylan is a very nice boy; he just hasn't found his confidence yet. He's still finding out who he is.'

We sit in silence and I wonder how long is long enough before I suggest we go home. I feel that there's something different about Mum lately; or maybe I'm imagining it, maybe finding that newspaper has unsettled me more than I thought. I should just tell her, talk about it and get it out in the open and then I'll feel better. It'll be fine to tell her as long as she doesn't tell me any more about my dead mother because I don't want to know. The article that I read about her death is already haunting me and I'm trying desperately to block it from my mind. No one should have to die like that. I'm going to tell Mum, I suddenly decide, because once I've told her it'll be out of my head and not going around and around on a loop. I open my mouth to confide in her but before I can say anything, she starts to speak.

'Layla, I've been thinking.'

I look up at her and wait. Is it going to be the nude posing conversation again? I feel that it is.

'I think,' she says, slowly. 'That you should get yourself a job.'

I stare at her in shock.

'What?'

'Yes, a job. You have good grades in your exams and although you don't have any experience you could easily get something in a shop. Just for a start. To get you into the swing of working.'

'But you've always said we don't need to join the rat race, we're fine as we are. You've *always* said that. We have lots and lots of things to do and working for someone else for eight hours every day for ever and ever is not a good thing to do. *You* say that, Mum, *all* of the time.'

'I know.' Mum looks down at her hands. 'And it's very selfish of me. I've been thinking only of myself when I should have been thinking of you. I've had lots of jobs and now I'm doing what I always wanted to do but that's me; I haven't given *you* the opportunity of working outside of the home and I should have. You might find a job that you love as much as I love painting.'

'I don't want a job, Mum. I'm quite happy as I am. If you think I'm not doing enough to help you, I can do more, all you have to do is ask.'

'Oh, darling.' Mum sighs. 'It's not that, you do more than your fair share of looking after the house and garden and you *never* complain when I ask you to do anything. No, it's most definitely not that. The truth is that I think you need to get a job to find out what *you* want, not what I want.

Maybe it'll make you realise what you want to do; you could decide to go back into education, find a career that you like. What I'm saying is that you need to try things to find out what you want to do, the world is your oyster, Layla. You're nineteen-years-old and there's a great big world out there and you need to go out and discover it.'

I shake my head. I can't believe what I'm hearing; this is the complete opposite of everything that she's always told me.

'Layla, trust me,' Mum says. 'This will be a good thing for you to do. It may seem frightening now but you'll thank me later on. You will.'

'Will I?' I snap. 'Like I'll thank you for making me pose naked?'

Mum flinches and I can see that I've hurt her but for once I don't care; I don't want to get a job.

'I'm not forcing you to do anything, Layla, but you do need to think seriously about what I'm saying. I have to think about your future for when I'm not here.'

'What do you mean, when you're not here? You're young, Mum, you're only fifty-five.'

'Fifty-six, darling. I'm not old but I'm not going to live forever, no one does. You need a proper life; you need friends and to at least try working away from me. I've been very selfish by keeping you all to myself.'

'I have friends,' I mutter. 'And I have a life.'

'All of your friends are old people, Layla, my age or older, and you only know them because they're my friends. How many of them do you truly like or ever have any meaningful conversation with?'

I feel my cheeks flush and I don't answer. Mum's right; I only speak to people when I have to and I don't have any friends my own age. I never have, even when I was at school I was the odd one out.

'I'm not saying this to hurt you or embarrass you, Layla, but it needs to be said. You know, deep down, that I'm right.'

I stand up without answering her and brush my dress down. My legs feel damp from the grass and I have the beginnings of a headache.

'Shall we go?' I ask. 'It's starting to chill off, now.'

Mum gets up and stands next to me and attempts to take hold of my hand but I move away from her and start to walk. She falls into step beside me and we walk in silence. Why do things have to change, why can't everything stay the same? Why is Mum suddenly being so cruel to me? But underneath my fear of change, I know the truth; she's not being cruel, she's doing it for my own good. She's trying to give me a normal life where I'll fit into society and not be the outsider that I've always been. But I don't think it's going to work because I've been a loner all my life. For as long as I can remember I've felt as if I was on the outside looking in, the spectator watching the game but not allowed to play.

Except for at home with Mum, where I belong.

And although it's irrational and not even true because I could feel that change was in the air before I even found it, I blame it all on the newspaper cutting.

I curse myself for having found it.

* * *

We walk home in silence, and Mum makes no attempt to talk to me. By the time we emerge from the wood into our lane, I feel disgusted with myself for behaving like a sulking child. We both come to a halt at the end of the lane and stare in surprise; a huge removal lorry is parked across the front of our garden. It's blocking the path and the little patch of scrubby driveway where we park our battered Ford Fiesta.

'Looks like someone is moving in,' Mum says, stating the obvious.

There are only two other cottages in the lane apart from ours, a young, professional couple who we rarely see live in the one nearest to us, but the cottage on the opposite side of the lane has been empty for years. Ninety-eight-year-old Mrs Patterson lived there for all of her life but moved into a nursing home five years ago when she was no longer able to cope. Except for the occasional visit by a gardener to tidy the overgrown garden, no one has lived in the cottage since she moved out. Mrs Patterson died last year and the house has been up for sale ever since. We rarely saw her even when she lived there, as she never ventured outside. Mum and I took some homemade bread over there soon after we moved in but were met with barely concealed amusement by one of the carers who visited four times a day. She told us that 'Edith' could only manage to eat mashed-up food and we'd best take it back home with us. We did visit again on several occasions after that but it was awkward and embarrassing; Mrs Patterson was frail beyond belief and sat staring at us blankly, making no effort to engage in conversation. She'd sometimes smile and nod but I'm not sure that she ever really knew who we were or what we were talking about. Her husband had been dead for many years and Mum said she thought that maybe she'd forgotten how to talk to people. The lounge was filled with huge, dark, ancient furniture that loomed over us and I found it oppressive and depressing, not like our colourful, cosy cottage.

According to Lorna Botham, Mrs Patterson had no living relatives and her inheritance has gone to the state as she left no will. Mum said Lorna was most put out about this because she'd been one of her carers at one time and seemed to think that she should have been left something, even though she got paid for looking after her.

Mum and I watch as two men appear from the back of the lorry carrying a large leather sofa between them. They bring it to the edge of the lorry and lower it onto the platform, press a button on the side and descend to the ground with it.

'Oh, hello,' the taller of the two says, seeing us

standing watching them. 'D'you live 'ere? Sorry we're blocking your driveway; closest we could get to the house without blocking the whole lane.'

'That's okay,' Mum says. 'We can squeeze by.'

'Shouldn't be too much longer, love,' the other, shorter man says, with a wink. 'Cup of tea would go down a treat.'

I bristle at his cheekiness but Mum simply asks if they'd like milk and sugar. I don't like the way the shorter one is looking at Mum, either, he's practically leering at her.

'Are you moving in?' I ask.

The two look at each other and laugh loudly.

'Nah, we're just the removal men, chick. Bit too much work wants doing on it for my liking, not that we could afford to buy it, anyway.'

They pick up each end of the sofa and carry it across the lane as if it weighs nothing. They deftly manhandle it through the small gateway into the garden and then through the front door and into the cottage. The wrought iron gate is rusting and hanging off its hinges and I imagine that the inside of the cottage is as unwelcoming and dark as when we last visited. A home clearance company visited shortly after Mrs Patterson died and removed all of the contents of the house and took them to a second-hand shop. Lorna Botham said that she'd seen a photograph album in one of the junk shops in Wellerton and Mrs Patterson was definitely in a lot of them. The house clearance company must have taken everything, personal possessions included, and sold them, too. I found that really sad, that her whole life had been sold to a second-hand shop because there was not one relative or anyone who cared about her, to leave them to.

Maybe that's what Mum thinks will happen to me when she dies and I'm all alone until *I* die.

We squeeze past the lorry and go round to the back door of our cottage. As we open the door, our dog, Benny, leaps from his basket and hurtles towards us. I bend down and cuddle him and try to calm him down and stop him from jumping around in excitement. He's only been alone for a few hours but anyone would think he'd been abandoned for days. He may be a ten-year-old cocker spaniel but he still behaves like a puppy. Mum pats him on the head and then sets about putting the kettle on and placing cups and saucers onto a tray.

'Do you think I should make a pot?' she asks. 'Because I expect the new owners are inside, sorting everything out.' She doesn't wait for me to answer but puts the teapot on the tray and adds two more cups along with a plate of home-made oatmeal biscuits.

I watch her and try to quell the uneasiness that I'm feeling. It seems that everything is changing and it's too much to cope with, all at once. A new neighbour won't make any difference to me, we rarely see the ones we have next door, so we're hardly likely to see the new ones in Mrs Patterson's old cottage.

So why am I nervous?

Am I afraid that it will be someone from school, someone who remembers what an outsider I was? It's unlikely, the sensible part of me acknowledges, mostly because the cottage will have sold for a small fortune, despite it's near falling-down condition. No one of my age around here will be able to afford it. Most likely it will have been sold to some *London-type*s, as us villagers call them. Whoever has bought it will spend a huge amount of money having it rebuilt and modernised, and in no time at all, it'll be put back on the market and resold for at least double the price they paid. *London-types* rarely stick around here for very long because the lack of bright lights and decent shops soon puts paid to their romanticised idea of living in the country.

'Are you coming?' Mum asks, picking up the tray.

'Of course.' I remove two of the teacups and the plate of biscuits from the tray and carry them, afraid that they'll fall off the overloaded tray. We walk across the lane and the air is starting to chill now, the late May sunshine having lost its power. The two removal men are sitting on the brick wall that runs around the garden, one of them drawing deeply on a roll-up cigarette. Mum puts the tray on the floor and pours them both a cup of tea and they take the cups with a *thank you* along with a handful of biscuits from the plate that I'm holding. Mum picks up the tray and I stand back and let her go into the house first. She calls out *hello* as she enters and I follow behind.

We enter the old kitchen which seems bigger and lighter now that Mrs Patterson's dark, heavy furniture is gone. A man who is standing with his back to us at the front window, turns to say *hello*. It looks as if he's in the process of attempting to pull down the ancient, metal curtain rail.

'Hello,' Mum says, putting the tray down onto a nearby packing case. 'I'm Debs from across the lane and this is my daughter, Layla. We thought you might appreciate a cup of tea.'

He smiles and walks towards us, hand outstretched to shake Mum's hand.

'Will,' he says. 'Pleasure to meet you and so kind of you to bring tea.'

I stare at him; tall and muscular, he's handsome in a casual, no effort kind of way. Fair hair flops into his eyes and he has stubble on his chin, as if he's been too busy to shave. I stand awkwardly as he shakes Mum's hand before he turns to me.

'Nice to meet you, Layla,' he says, with a smile, thrusting his hand towards me.

I reach out and he closes his hand over mine, his skin dry and warm. I try not to stare at him but can't help myself.

He's attractive and attracting.

He's the most beautiful man I've ever seen.

CHAPTER FOUR

I have a job interview.

I can't believe it's happened so quickly, I thought it would take weeks or months, and maybe not even happen at all, given my lack of supermarket experience. But no, I applied online on Saturday and here I am attending an interview for a job and it's only Tuesday afternoon. I'm in a grubby room behind the goods inward entrance at the Chiverson's on the outskirts of Wellerton, waiting to be called through for my interview for a position as a *store colleague*.

I only did it to appease Mum. I thought if I got on with it and showed willing then it would give me some breathing space to get used to the idea. I secretly hoped that my lack of experience would stop anyone from wanting to employ me. When I had to fill in the online form where it asked for experience, Mum said to put that I was employed by her as an assistant in her art business. She listed all of the skills that I used to help her and it actually made it sound as if I'd *had* a job. Going around the art galleries with Mum became *marketing*, helping at her weekly art class became *class facilitator* and even going to the supermarket for food became *assisting with housekeeping and supplies*. Mum impressed me with the way she worded things and I realised that there's much more to Mum than I'm aware of; she had a career and a life, long before I arrived.

Unluckily for me, supermarkets and the hospitality industry are struggling to recruit staff at the moment so bar not turning up, I think the job is pretty much mine. No one has told me this, obviously, but after searching through several job-hunting forums the general opinion seems to be that they're desperate for staff and if you get an interview, you're in. I had to do an online test to get to the interview stage but I can't claim any credit for it as it was simple in the extreme. All that I think it actually proved was that I can use a computer or a mobile phone.

I sneak a look at my watch; ten minutes to go. There are three other people waiting here as well as me and I guess that they've all come for their interviews, too. There's a lad who looks barely older than sixteen and has been glued to his phone from the minute he arrived, an elderly man who looks to be well past retirement age and a middle-aged woman wearing a smart business suit who looks totally over-dressed. Mum told me to dress smart but casually so I borrowed a pair of her beige linen trousers and a white cotton top. I've tied my hair up into a pony-tail so that it looks tidy and Mum suggested that I apply some make-up so that I look business-like.

The job was advertised as twenty-one-hours a week and I wonder if I'll have to work weekends. Not that it matters, because it's not as if I have a hectic social life, is it? A weekend is pretty much the same as every other day of the week to me. I do hope it's a Friday, though, because if I have to do this – and it looks like I do – I would like not to have to go to Mum's art class anymore because then I can avoid posing naked. I can also avoid seeing Dylan, which will save him embarrassing himself further by asking me out again.

The middle-aged woman next to me has started to hum and I wonder if she's nervous. She could be; this job could be really important to her, she could be desperate for the money and here's me, hoping I don't get it. To stop myself from feeling bad about that, I think back over the weekend, and, more importantly, I think about Will. I feel my cheeks grow hot just thinking about him, he is *so* gorgeous. On Sunday, I watched him from my bedroom window as he tackled the enormous weeds in the front garden. Stripped to the waist, he already has a great tan and his pair of tatty old shorts showed his physique off to perfection. He's seriously hot but doesn't seem aware of it, unlike the good-looking boys at school who were all too full of themselves and always showing off. Will was oblivious to my scrutiny as he pulled weeds and bagged-up rubbish and ferried it around the cottage into the back garden. I stood to one side of the window so there was no chance of him noticing me and after a while I wandered down the lane on the pretext of taking Benny for a walk. I stopped at the front of his cottage and said *hello* and asked how he was getting on and we chatted. He's so easy to talk to and seemed genuinely interested in what I had to say. He asked where I worked or if I was at university and I lied a little – but it was only a white lie - and said that I hadn't yet decided what I wanted to do so was going to get myself a shop job while I considered my options. I actually said that; *considered my options.* As soon as I'd said it, I felt stupid but he nodded thoughtfully and said that *was a very good idea* because I shouldn't rush into anything when I have my whole life ahead of me. He said that I needed to make sure that I didn't get trapped into doing something that I didn't like. I swear he looked right into my eyes when he said it, and for a moment I wondered if *he* was trapped, because of course, he's married, because how in the world could a gorgeous man like him still be single?

I couldn't stay talking to him for too long because that would be odd, wouldn't it? So, I carried on down the lane but I'm sure I felt a tingle on the back of my neck, which meant that he was watching me as I walked away. Why does he have to be married? She's beautiful, too, his wife. Tall and slim with glossy dark hair that always looks just-stepped-out-of-a-salon perfect. Mum says she works away a lot, in London, and has a very important job in finance, apparently, so won't be around very much. Will has taken a sabbatical from his job for six months to fix the cottage up. It turns out that the company Will works for is in the next street to where Mum worked when we lived in London. Well, before I came along, obviously. Mum found this out when she was chatting to Will on the day they moved in and I never heard anything she was saying because I was too fixated on gawping at Will. I hope he didn't notice me looking at him. Will is thirty-eight and his wife, Lucinda is thirty-two, He didn't tell Mum this, because she wouldn't be so rude to have asked, that information came from Lorna Botham because that's the sort of stuff she finds out about people. Lucinda is the one who earns the big money, too, and gets a massive bonus every year. So Will is nearly twice my age, but he doesn't seem that old.

Why does he have to be married?

I was sad when he'd finished clearing the front garden and I couldn't watch him anymore. I smelled smoke that evening and guess that he'd made a bonfire in the back garden but there was no way of seeing from our cottage. Unless I went into the field behind his house; there are lots and trees and bushes there so I could have watched him, unseen, but I stopped myself because, well, it's not healthy.

Mum would call it a crush, obviously, but it's nothing like Darius Curran or Mr Evans, this is different. Even though we've haven't spoken very much I can feel that there's a connection between us and if he wasn't married, well, who knows?

'Would you all like to come through?' A woman wearing a Chiverson's uniform has appeared in the doorway and without waiting for a reply, she turns and goes back into the office. I assume we're to follow. Everyone gets up, unsure of what to do so I take the plunge and head straight for the doorway and follow the woman into the office.

It seems it's going to be a joint interview.

* * *

I got the job.

Wednesday, Thursday and Friday from seven until three, so no more helping at Mum's art class, so that, as they say, is a result. No more dreary Dylan. It wasn't even an interview, as such, Susan, the day-shift manager, told us what was required and told us that we could be asked to do a range of duties from sitting on the checkout to stacking the shelves. She emphasised that we wouldn't be able to ask for a particular job, it would all be on a basis of what was needed most. The woman in the smart suit didn't look very impressed and said she only wanted to work on the till. There was an awkward moment of silence before Susan replied that, as she'd already said, it wasn't possible to choose so she needed to consider whether Chiverson's was the right choice for her.

Susan didn't sound very enthusiastic or happy and I had the feeling that the turnover of staff was quite high and she was fed up with interviewing people. She raced through it all and after less than twenty minutes she said that if we wanted to take up the offer of employment, she would give us a contract to sign and we could collect our uniforms from the wages office. She then asked if anyone had any questions – no one did – and then asked who wanted to take *the offer of employment*. We all accepted, even the woman in the smart suit, so I guess that she really needed the job. Susan then took us all to the wages office and left us there, without even saying *goodbye*, which I thought was a bit rude, but maybe rudeness is something that I'm going to have to get used to.

I told the woman in the office my size and she gave me a couple of t-shirts, a horrible nylon zip-up jacket and a pair of black trousers. It'll be strange wearing a uniform after wearing whatever I want for so long, it'll be a bit like being back at school. I start on Friday, which seems a bit strange but I have to be 'inducted' and this is the day they do their inductions so it'll be a short first working week for me.

I'm not sure how I feel about having a job, it's new and strange but perhaps it won't be that bad. At least I'll get paid instead of Mum having to give me money all of the time. Although I don't really spend anything because I don't go anywhere.

As I drive home, I realise that Mum could be right about getting a job, because the very fact that I'm able to drive home is because she insisted that I learned to drive and pass my test the minute I turned eighteen. She was right about that, although I never did take driving lessons as she wanted me to, she taught me herself. But she taught me well, because I passed my test first time.

When I get home, I walk into the kitchen and Mum is sitting at the kitchen table. She has her sketch pad in front of her but it's blank and I know that she's been waiting for me to come back. I keep my expression impassive and sit down opposite her and try to stop Benny from sitting on top of me.

'How did you get on, darling?'

'Awful.' I intend to keep my face straight but I can't help grinning.

Mum's face breaks into a smile and even though I don't want the job, I feel so happy that I've pleased her.

'Well done.' She jumps up and comes around the table and hugs me. 'I'm so proud of you.'

'I don't think the bar was very high, Mum. I think all I had to do was turn up.'

'Nonsense! Don't do yourself down, they wouldn't give you the job if they didn't think you were capable.'

I smile but I'm not sure she's right.

'Wednesdays, Thursdays and Friday, from seven

until three, so I won't be able to come to art class anymore.'

Mum waves her hand. 'Not a problem, Mr Jones is always itching to get in the kitchen and make tea, he can take over and everyone is quite capable of washing up after themselves.'

'And I'll have to use the car too, so you won't be able to go anywhere while I'm at work.'

'Well, it's not as if we use it much anyway, is it? It'll probably do it good to give it regular use, clear out the engine or whatever.'

We only use it to go to shopping and to go around the different galleries for Mum's paintings and of course, doctors and dentist because they're a bus ride away.

'But what if you need to take your new paintings to the galleries?'

'I'll do it on a Monday or Tuesday or a Saturday. It's nothing that we can't get around.'

She's right. And if she really needs the car, she can take me to work and drop me off and pick me up later. It'll also give me the opportunity to drive more because I don't drive very often and I'm a bit nervous on the road.

Mum places a glass of her homemade apple juice on the table and I gulp it down and then go upstairs and get changed. I take the band out of my hair and let it loose and put on my favourite cream cotton dress. I slip my feet into my flip flops and immediately feel more relaxed. My Chiverson's uniform is still in the car and the thought of wearing it doesn't fill me with joy. Never mind, that's two days away so for now, I'm still free. I run down the stairs and go into the kitchen and take Benny's lead down from the peg.

'Thought I'd take Benny for a walk,' I say, snapping the lead onto his collar as he jumps around in excitement. 'Stretch my legs. I feel as if I've been sitting around all day.'

'Good idea, get some fresh air. I'll be in my studio for a while until dinner. Have a few things I need to finish.'

'Okay, I'll see you later.'

We both go out of the back door, Mum heads down to the end of the garden and I drag Benny along to the front of the house and onto the lane. We walk along the lane and I'm disappointed to see that Will isn't outside his cottage. Their cottage. I'd already looked out of the window to see if he was there and even though he wasn't, I was hoping that he'd come outside. I walk past his cottage and along the road and then cut through the trees and onto the fields that run along the edge of the road. Once we're safely away from the road I unclip Benny's lead and he bounds off, stopping at each tussock of grass to sniff it. I wander after him and head back down towards the direction of Will's cottage.

I've noticed over the last couple of days that I've not been thinking so much about my birth mother. Perhaps I'm adjusting to the knowledge now that things are sinking in, maybe I'm getting used to the idea of how my mother died. This must be a good thing. I'm feeling more accepting of it although I still don't like to dwell on the circumstances of my mother's death. But I'm not thinking about it as much as I did when I first found out.

Because I keep thinking about Will.

I know that he's married and there's no chance for me but that doesn't stop me from thinking about him and watching him from my bedroom window. It's nothing like a crush, nothing like that at all. I'm just appreciating a handsome man and I think that there is a connection between us although obviously nothing can come of it.

But it doesn't hurt to look, does it? I'm not doing anyone any harm.

As I reach the back of Will's cottage, there's no possibility of Will or Lucinda seeing me as I'm hidden from view by trees and a high hedgerow. If I stand close to the hedge, I can look through the gaps in the foliage into their garden, but they won't be able to see me. I walk slowly along and then stop where the hedge is highest. The garden is long and overgrown and as I peek through the hedge, I can see that Will has started clearing the weeds and overgrown plants away as he did in the front garden. I peer through the gap to see if I can see him, and jump back when I spot him close to the other side of the hedge. He's bare-chested like before, wearing the same tatty shorts, but he's not working, because Lucinda is standing in front of him. They're arguing.

I should go but I don't; I stand still, hold my breath and eavesdrop.

'Not this again.' Will sounds annoyed, irritated.

'I can't go through it again, Will.' Lucinda sounds upset and I creep closer to the hedge. She's dressed in a business-like way, in high heels, with her hair pulled up into a smart bun. I guess that she's dressed for work. Her face is perfectly made up but her cheeks are flushed and I wonder if she's been crying.

'Look,' his voice softens. 'There's nothing to worry about, Lucy, you're letting your imagination run away with you. We've talked about this, haven't we?'

He strides over to her and she turns and starts to walk down the garden towards the cottage but he steps in front of her and prevents her from moving.

'Come on, let's not argue, eh? We've got the home of our dreams and everything we've ever wanted. Don't spoil it with your paranoia.'

They stand looking at each other for a moment and then Will takes her in his arms and, after a moment's resistance, she wraps her arms around his waist and clings to him. He takes hold of her chin and tilts her head up and they kiss. I want to turn away but I can't, even though the sight of them kissing twists my insides so that I can't breathe. After what seems like forever, they break for air and she nestles her head into his shoulder.

'Sorry.' I hear her mumble.

Will rubs her back.

'It's fine,' he says. 'It's just your imagination getting the better of you, you know you have nothing to worry about. I'll be busy working here and counting the days until you're back from London. Think of poor old me all alone in the wild countryside.'

The words are loving and reassuring and Lucina mumbles something but I can't hear her because her face is buried in Will's chest. But I can see Will's face over her head and his expression doesn't match the words he's just spoken. His mouth is set in a straight line and he looks angry and I wonder what Lucinda has done to him. I step silently back from the hedge and walk slowly across the field towards Benny. I don't know what I've just witnessed but I know one thing.

He doesn't love her.

CHAPTER FIVE

Benny and I emerge from the field onto the road just in time to see Lucinda pulling away from their cottage in her brand-new BMW. As I head down the lane, I see that Will is standing in the garden waving her goodbye. I put up a hand as she drives by but she doesn't acknowledge me; maybe she didn't see me. Or maybe she's just rude.

I quicken my pace and tug Benny's lead to drag him away from his incessant sniffing of every blade of grass and he reluctantly trots along beside me. I want to get to Will before he goes back inside the house or into the back garden. Luckily, he sees me walking up the lane and makes no move to go into the house. He smiles and waves at me as I approach and I wave back, praying that the red flush that I can feel shooting up my face will have subsided by the time I reach him.

'Hi, Layla.' He leans on the half broken down garden wall and smiles at me as I draw closer to him.

'Hi Will,' I say, surprised at my own composure. 'How are you?'

'Oh, you know, not so bad. How are you?'

I see a shadow cross his features and even if I hadn't witnessed the argument with Lucinda, I would know that something was wrong.

'I'm good, thanks. Actually, I just got myself a job this morning, at Chiverson's. Just part-time though, as I'm not sure what I want to do yet. It'll give me time to think about what I really want, whether I should go to uni or not.'

He smiles and I wonder if he can tell that I'm lying and that I'm trying to impress him. I have no intention of going to university, the very thought of it fills me with horror. This is the second time I've told the same lie to him and I suddenly feel stupid for trying to make myself sound even remotely interesting.

'Good idea.' He looks at me, his pale blue eyes holding my gaze. 'The last thing you want to do is rush into something that you'll regret and you can't get out of. Think carefully before you jump.'

There it is again, I'm certain that he's hinting that he's trapped, because what else could he mean? We stand for a moment in silence and I can't look away from him. Does he mean Lucinda, does he mean that he regrets marrying her?

I think he does.

'That must be,' he says, after a moment. 'Why you look different today.'

'Different?' I echo.

He nods. 'Make up. You're wearing make-up.'

Oh, yes.' I laugh, remembering that I deliberately didn't take it off, in case I saw him. 'I thought I'd better make the effort, try and look sort of professional, even if it was only for a supermarket job.'

Inside I'm doing cartwheels of delight, he's actually noticed me, noticed that I'm wearing make-up. He's properly looked at me.

'It looks nice.' The smile is gone now and he looks serious. 'But you really don't need it.'

He lowers his gaze and I hold my breath as his eyes slowly travel up my body, finally reaching my face. We stare at each other for a moment and the air is filled with promise. I'm not imagining it, nor the way he's looked over every inch of me with his eyes.

'Listen, Layla, I was...'

He doesn't get a chance to finish what he's saying because Benny starts barking. Someone is cycling down the lane towards us and Benny is doing his guard dog routine that he does every time someone appears in the lane. The moment broken, Will and I both turn to watch as the cyclist grows nearer and whatever it was that we were sharing, is gone. I feel anger rise in me as the cyclist comes to a juddering, shingle-spraying halt in front of Benny, dismounts the bike and removes his helmet.

'Hi, Layla.'

It's Dylan.

In that moment, I hate him, because now I'll never know what Will was going to say. Dylan beams a smile at me and I stare back unsmilingly at him and wonder why he's here. Will looks at me expectantly and I begrudgingly introduce him to Dylan who says a brief *hello* and then ignores Will completely as he turns and asks me if Mum's in. Will moves away from the wall and gives a little wave as he heads towards the side of the cottage and disappears around into the back garden. I ignore Dylan and cross the lane towards our cottage and he follows beside me, pushing his bike.

'Look,' Dylan says, as we cross the lane. 'About last week, I know you're a bit shy but if you'd like to come out one evening, I thought we could go for a drink or something?'

I stop and stare at him. I'm amazed that he didn't take the hint when I totally blanked him on Friday. I'm not shy, I just don't want to go out with him.

'Or a meal?' he adds. 'Or the cinema? Although I'm not a fan of these modern films, I prefer the classics.' He laughs a honking laugh and I stare at him with dislike.

'Dylan?' His eyes light up with hope when I say his name and a part of me feels delight at what I'm about to say, because it's his fault that I never got to hear what Will was going to say and I feel it was something important.

'I don't want to go out with you, for a drink or to

the cinema, or anywhere, actually.'

He looks surprised and I wonder how desperate he thinks I am.

I start walking towards our cottage but he quickens his pace with his gangly legs until he's ahead of me. He turns and steps in front of me, blocking my path.

'Layla, I meant just as friends. To start with, anyway.' He smiles. 'I know you haven't had a boyfriend before so there's no need to be nervous. I'll be the perfect gentleman.'

I stare up at him for a moment and try to walk around him but he dodges to one side and laughs his stupid laugh again, as if we're playing a game.

'Dylan,' I say, slowly, enunciating every word so that there is no possibility of him misunderstanding me. 'Please. Do me a favour and fuck off.'

* * *

I spent most of yesterday evening in my bedroom, watching out of the window for a glimpse of Will. He never came around to the front garden again and I cursed Dylan repeatedly for turning up when he did. I behaved like a spoilt brat when I came in with him to the kitchen. I took Benny's lead off and then left the kitchen and went straight upstairs without a word and didn't go back downstairs again until I was quite sure he'd gone. Mum said he'd come round to ask her what the best art pencils were to buy and wanted her advice on art materials but I know it was only a pretext so that he could see me. Perhaps he'll get the message now because I don't think I could have been any blunter about it. I was rude and vile and I should be ashamed of myself but I'm not, because he's thick-skinned and I wanted him to know that there's absolutely no possibility of me ever going out with him. I never use language like that but I'm sure it's had the desired effect; Dylan looked stunned and made no further attempt to talk to me.

When I went to bed last night, I fantasised about what Will might have been going to say and it took me ages to get to sleep. I kept remembering how his eyes had travelled up my body; I definitely didn't imagine *that.* When I woke up this morning, I'd decided that I was going to take Benny out for a morning walk so that I'd have a chance of seeing Will. Unfortunately, Mum had other plans. She needs to take one of her new paintings to the art gallery in Wellerton because they've sold several of hers and have space for another. Apparently, I need to go with her because I should buy myself some comfortable shoes for my new job. I tried desperately to think of an excuse but I couldn't think of one single reason why I couldn't go with her. Then I realised that it doesn't matter, because Will and I are *meant* to be together and it will happen, I just know it. Besides, Mum's right, I can hardly wear flip flops with my Chiverson's uniform and the sheet of information they gave me did advise suitable footwear. Black, flat shoes or trainers as long as they are all black with no markings on them. I don't have anything like that; aside from flip flops in the summer, I wear ankle boots in the winter and the only trainers I have are white. Mum said to try lots on to make sure they're comfy because I'll be on my feet for hours. I realise that the thought of starting a new job doesn't seem so bad now, maybe taking the first step has been a good thing and Mum was right.

Although even if I wasn't going to be working on Fridays in future, I still wouldn't want to pose naked at the art class, not with Dylan there gawping at me.

Although it wouldn't be a problem if Will was there.

The thought pops into my head from nowhere and I'm shocked at myself for even thinking it. I put the thought out of my mind and try to ignore the thrill of excitement that I feel at the thought of Will. I make myself concentrate on what Mum is saying, what I have to tell the gallery about her new theme of paintings.

When we go out and get in the car, I look over at Will's cottage but there's no sign of him. It's only nine o'clock, so quite early, far earlier than Mum and I normally go out. Lucinda's car isn't parked on their drive and I wonder how long she's away for. If I had a husband like Will I'd never go away and leave him. She can't love him very much, can she?

'What I thought,' Mum says, as she starts the car

up and reverses off the drive. 'Is that you could take my painting into Fothergills while I pop and visit Annie on the other side of Wellerton. I could drop you off on the High Street and after you've taken the painting in you can go and get your shoes and have a look around. I'll only be a couple of hours.'

Annie is one of Mum's friends and I don't usually go with her because Annie is a total bore, God knows how Mum puts up with her. No one else can get a word in with Annie; Mum says it's because she's lonely and has no one to talk to so when someone visits, it's off-load time. I try not to feel fed up and remind myself that buying a pair of shoes won't stop fate. Mum, thankfully, has no idea that all I want to do is hang around the cottage so I can watch Will.

'Okay,' I say, because how can I argue?

'This is part of your marketing skills,' Mum jokes.

I laugh, because taking a painting into a shop is hardly marketing when they're the ones asking for more. We pull up in the car park behind the High Street and I get out and go around to the boot and take the bubble-wrapped painting out. It's quite light as it's not one of Mum's larger works and I hold it carefully in front of me so as not to damage it. I smile at Mum and she zooms off with a toot-toot and I set off towards the art gallery. I like a trip into town, although Mum and I usually go together and have a good look around the shops. We rarely buy anything because we're not massive consumers but we do like to window shop. Maybe this is part of her plan to get me out into the world, I wouldn't be surprised. Although now I think of it, lately she's dropped me off and visited Annie quite a few times.

I drop the painting off at the gallery where they're thrilled with the picture of colourful houses and boats at night. Mum has a quirky style and uses acrylics in bright colours and adds things to her pictures, sometimes even pages of print from books to create her artwork. It's quite unique and her distinctive style sells well. I chat with Sally, the manager of the gallery, until a customer comes in and then I leave and head down the street to the first shoe shop that I reach. Luckily, there are lots of places for shoes in Wellerton, and if all else fails I can probably get a pair from *Next*. Mum's given me a hundred pounds which I know is way more than I'm going to need but she said to spend it on whatever I like. When I get my first pay packet from Chiverson's I'm going to buy Mum a really nice present, although I'll have to wait a whole month before I can do that.

I go into Baileys Shoes and scan the shelves; the flat, black lace-ups are beyond hideous. Clumpy and old-fashioned, I can't imagine ever being so old that I'd even consider wearing them. I might not be fashionable but there are limits. I think that it's going to be black trainers unless by some miracle I can find something else. I come out of Baileys and go into a sports shop where they have trainers galore. But at a price; I baulk at paying nearly a hundred pounds for a pair of obviously plastic trainers. I realise that buying a pair of shoes is not as easy as I thought it was going to be. I come out of the sports shop and head down the street to *Next,* convinced that I'll find something there. As I'm browsing the shoe section, I try to ignore the screaming baby in the buggy being pushed through the aisles of shoes. I glance over to see a girl bending over the buggy trying to persuade the red-in-the-face baby to take the offered dummy. The crying finally stops and the girl stands up and as she drags her hand across her face, I realise that I know her. I was at school with her, we were in the same class together and she was one of the prettiest and most popular girls in the school. Petite, slim and always perfectly presented, Alicia was never without a boyfriend and they were always one of the popular boys that all of the other girls hankered after. By the time I left school, Alicia Maunsell and Darius Curran, the boy who humiliated me in year ten, were the golden couple. I heard that they even applied to the same university so they could study together. English for Alicia and Sports Science for Darius, as I recall, because Darius was the sporty type. Everyone knew that they were going to have the most perfect lives because they had it all; looks, intelligence and good families.

But Alicia isn't in university now, is she?

I turn my back so that she can't see me but I

can see her reflection in one of the mirrors. She doesn't look quite so perfect now, her skin looks blotchy and there are dark circles underneath her eyes and she's put weight on. All perfectly normal after having a baby, I would think, but I can't help being shocked. I compare my own reflection to hers and can't help feeling a little smug. I'm slim yet shapely and my skin has a glow to it and my eyes sparkle. It's because of Will; I feel so alive since he's moved into the lane. I doubt Alicia is studying now; she can hardly get a degree with a baby to look after, can she? I wonder if Darius is still at university, living the single life. I could go over and talk to her and find out, but I won't, not least because we weren't exactly friends at school. I can still remember her raucous laughter at the picture of me that Darius sent around the school. The jibes that she made about my small breasts and my ridiculous notion that Darius Curran would take a first look at me, let alone a second, are still imprinted on my memory. I debate whether to walk past her and let her see that it's me, without talking to her, but the decision is taken from me because when I look again, she's gone.

I resume my search for shoes and decide on a pair of black, fabric lace-ups. I sit down on the bench and slip my bare feet into them making sure that no assistant is watching me in case they come and tell me off for having no socks on. The shoes fit perfectly and I stand up and walk around in them and even without socks, they feel fine. I sit back down and take them off and put my flip flops back on and turn the shoes over; thirty-five-pounds. Perfect, because I've seen something else that I'd like to buy, too. Holding the shoes in one hand, I head towards the lingerie section and browse the matching sets. They're lacy and expensive, but so gorgeous. The thongs are so skimpy that they're barely there at all.

Not the sort of thing that I usually buy.

I decide on a cream satin, balcony bra with a matching lacy thong and then pick up the same set in red. They're thirty-two-pounds for each set, far more than I'd usually pay but I want them and I'm going to have them. I make my way to the till and hand over my items and she rings them up and I pay. A small part of me wishes that Alicia was here to see what I'm buying so she can see that now I have proper breasts and a good figure. Purchases made, I emerge onto the street and wonder when Mum is going to ring to tell me she's picking me up.

I window shop up and down the street enjoying the sunshine. It's June the first today and it feels like the start of something, as if the first day of the month has real significance. The only thing that mars the day is that as I'm peering into the window of a candle shop admiring the display, I think that I see the reflection of Dylan cycling by. The back of my neck tingles and I think that perhaps I'm being paranoid, because Dylan will be at work in his father's newsagents, not cycling around Wellerton. I stop myself from turning around to look properly because it *can't* be him and I'm not going to allow the thought of him to spoil today.

But my neck definitely tingled.

Maybe it's paranoia.

Or guilt.

Because when I bought that underwear, I wasn't thinking of myself.

I was thinking of Will.

CHAPTER SIX

My first week at Chiverson's is done.

It wasn't so bad; the day that I had to go in for my induction consisted of being shown where the fire exits and toilets were. That and a ten-minute health and safety talk and that was pretty much it. Jack and I – he's the spotty teenager who was at the interview on Tuesday – were put on shelf stacking and we had to follow one of the *lifers* around and stack the shelves with the goods as directed. Jack called the middle-aged woman a *lifer* – not to her face, obviously, but behind her back – because she'd proudly informed us that she'd been at Chiverson's for over twenty years. According to Jack, there are a lot like that working here, although I don't know how he knows this as he only started on the same day as me.

Jack is very funny, chatty and outspoken and he's made the rather boring days more bearable, fun, even. He's not sixteen as I thought, but eighteen, and he's only working here because he's been forced into it by *the social*. He was quite happy as he was, he says, just hanging out and playing on his *PlayStation* but *the social* don't like you loafing around for too long, he says, because it makes the figures look bad. Jack reckons than he can work at Chiverson's for a few months and then get himself sacked or *let go* and then he can have some time off again. Jack is one of those people who like to talk but unlike most talkers, he does like to listen as well. When we were first put together, I trotted out the *I'm not sure what I want but I might go to university* line but since then we've become mates, and I've told him the truth; that I don't have any plans to go to university at all.

When lunchtime came around on that first day, the induction day, I was unsure what to do because Jack disappeared as soon as it was twelve o'clock. He said he was off to meet his boyfriend and would see me later. I was undecided what to do on my own; I had an hour to kill when I'd much rather have worked straight through and gone home an hour earlier. I wasn't particularly hungry and it only takes ten minutes to eat a sandwich so I don't know why we have to take an hour for our lunch. There was nothing else for it so I went back to my locker, got my purse and headed to the staff cafeteria. If the store had been in the town centre, I wouldn't have bothered, I'd have gone window shopping instead but I didn't have that option as there are no other shops near to the store.

The cafeteria was busy so I bought myself a sandwich and sat down at one of the few spare tables next to a table with a bunch of girls who looked around my age. A couple of them looked up at me as I sat down and I smiled at them but they both stared at me blankly, sweeping their eyes over me from head to toe before resuming their conversation with each other. I wasn't bothered, it was just like being back at school, really, and pretty much what I expected. Even so, I was pleased when lunchtime was over and Jack came back and I had someone to talk to. We continued following Betty-the-lifer around and spent the rest of the afternoon cutting open boxes and putting out pasta and baked beans onto the shelves and shoving the empty boxes into huge cages on wheels.

When I came out and got in the car to go home, I felt quite pleased with myself. I also felt a bit embarrassed for my over-reaction that I wouldn't be able to cope with any sort of change. It seems ridiculous now and even slightly hysterical. I need to stop seeing myself as an outcast schoolgirl and realise that I'm a grown woman and that there's nothing to be afraid of. I think that maybe I've lived in my head far too much, building things up out of all proportion. I need to get out there and start living and that's what I'm doing, even if it is only as a shelf stacker in Chiverson's.

I have a job and I have a new friend – Jack. We may have only known each other for just over a week but we get on so well that I think I can definitely call him a friend. As we were leaving work that first day, he said that he didn't mind having to get a job now that he had someone decent to talk to. It took me a moment to realise he meant me. He also asked me what I did for lunch and when I told him about the staff restaurant and sitting on my own, he was horrified. He said he only went to meet his boyfriend, Marcus, because he didn't want to be sitting around like *a spare dick*. After that we spent every break and lunchtime together and I don't think that I've ever laughed so much. My life is definitely looking up, a new job, a new friend and there's Will, too; I have a feeling about him because we get on well together. Life feels good.

I've seen Will several times and we chat so easily, and for ages, too, but I've never found out what he was going to say before Dylan ended our conversation that day, because either Mum or Lucinda are always in earshot. Yesterday, Mum and I were taking Benny for a walk and we stopped to chat to Will. Mum was telling him all about the different activities and clubs at the community hall that he and Lucinda could go to. Will sounded interested and said all of the right things but I'm sure he doesn't mean it. I can't imagine him going to gardening club or Lucinda joining the aerobics class. I'm sure Lucinda will be a member of a fancy, expensive gym in London. As Will was talking I was surreptitiously watching him and I *know* that

I didn't imagine the expression on his face when I saw him arguing with Lucinda in the garden. So, my life is changing and I feel optimistic about the future and there's only one thing spoiling it.

I wish Will wasn't married.

Because I want him for myself.

* * *

When I arrive home from work, Lucinda's car is parked at the front of their cottage and I feel immediate disappointment. Of course, she's going to be there, isn't she? Because it's Friday afternoon and it's not as if she has a job in a shop and has to stay in London to work on a Saturday.

I unlock the back door and go in and Benny launches himself at me. Mum won't be home for a while from her art class so he's been on his own for a few hours although from his greeting anyone would think he hadn't seen a human being for weeks. I sit down on the floor and cuddle him until he calms down and then go upstairs to get out of my uniform. I throw the hideous nylon t-shirt and the trousers into the wash basket and decide I'll take a shower before taking Benny for a walk. I tell myself it's because I feel hot and sweaty from the physical work of stacking shelves, but I know that I'm just lying to myself. I want to look and feel fresh in case I bump into Will.

Once showered, I go back into my bedroom and am about to get dressed when I catch sight of the bag from *Next* in the bottom of the wardrobe. It's been sitting there for over a week. I take it out of the wardrobe and pull out the new underwear. It's so pretty and I decide that I might as well wear it instead of leaving it lying in the bag. I pull the thong on and the silk feels cool against my skin, so much nicer than my usual cotton underwear. I slip the bra on and do it up and then can't resist looking at myself in the full length mirror. The girl staring back at me with hair wet from the shower doesn't look like me at all; in fact, she doesn't look like a girl at all.

She looks like a woman.

The thong makes my legs look impossibly long and the bra makes my boobs look much bigger and I turn this way and that, admiring myself. I walk over to the window and pull the edge of the closed curtain aside and look over to Will's cottage. I'm surprised to see him standing in the garden, leaning on the wall, staring across the lane. He looks pensive and deep in thought and without thinking, I slowly pull the curtain away from the window. We don't have net curtains and I know that I'm in full view of Will but I suddenly don't care, I *want* him to see me. The movement of the curtain must have caught his eye because he looks up and I can tell by his expression that he can see me. I don't move but stand completely still and stare at him and hold my breath. He doesn't smile, or acknowledge that he's seen me, but simply stares. After what seems like forever but is surely only seconds, he suddenly looks away and I feel crushing disappointment until I see why. Mum has appeared at the end of the lane and is heading towards the cottage. I hurriedly step back and away from the window.

Did she see me?

Making sure the curtain is closed, I quickly grab the dress that I'd taken out of the wardrobe and pull it over my head and tug it down my body. I run across the room to the door and let myself out onto the landing and listen. I can't hear anything so I dash downstairs and Mum isn't there, she must be talking to Will. My cheeks are on fire, what was I thinking? Suppose Will is telling Mum right now what I've done? He could be telling her, and Lucinda, too. Or what if Lucinda saw me? Will could be telling Mum she needs to get help for me because I obviously need it, standing in front of my bedroom window in my underwear for all the world to see.

I slip my feet into my flip flops and grab Benny's lead from the peg and snap it onto his collar. I'll take Benny out the back way so I don't have to walk down the lane. I can get into the fields from the end of our back garden and avoid seeing Mum and Will. I can't stay out forever but at least it'll give me some time to calm down. I tuck my mobile into my bra strap and head down towards the end of the garden. I don't want to speak to Mum but I know if I leave my mobile at home and she rings me and I don't answer, she'll send a search party out for me.

We're never out of touch and it wouldn't be fair to do that to her.

I'm relieved to reach the end of the garden without Mum appearing but equally, I become more convinced that Will is telling her that I've been exposing myself at my bedroom window. As I drag Benny along in my efforts to get as far away from the cottage as quickly as possible, ever worsening scenarios fill my head. Lucinda has now appeared and she's angry because she saw me too and she wants to know what Mum's going to do about it. Will's unsmiling stare at me is no longer his longing for me, but shock that I could flaunt myself in that way at a married man. My head in a whirl, I tramp through the fields dragging a bewildered Benny behind me, totally forgetting to let him off the lead. It's only when I reach the main road that cuts through the countryside to Wellerton that I realise how far I've walked. I pull out my mobile to see that it's half-past-five. I've been walking for over an hour.

I turn and start to walk back home, letting Benny off his lead when we're a safe distance from the road. Mum hasn't rung, which is strange, because she'd be expecting me to be there when she arrived home. I tell myself that she'll know I've taken Benny out because he's not there so there's no need to ring me. But I also know that although this is true, it's still odd that she hasn't rung because we always check in with each other

As I make my way slowly home, Benny running

around in circles in front of me, I'm expecting the worst and I begin to feel disgusted with myself. Will has told Mum about my pathetic parading in my underwear and she's not rung because she wants to speak to me face to face. Your daughter making an exhibition of herself is hardly a subject for a telephone call. Why did I do it? What on earth was I thinking? Why did I think that a man like Will could possibly be interested in me? I feel ridiculous and stupid and it's Mr Evans and Darius Curran all over again. I'm going to throw the stupid underwear away when I get back because no one except me is ever going to see it.

I walk as slowly as I possibly can but in what seems like no time at all, the familiar sight of our cottage greets me. I step through the gap in the tumbledown fence at the end of our garden and Benny gallops in front of me, making a bee-line towards the cottage. I walk up to the house on leaden legs and push open the back door. Mum is seated at the kitchen table and as I walk in, she turns to face me and I know that the worst has happened. She's been crying and is clutching a tissue in her hand.

'Hi,' I say, hanging Benny's lead up on the peg as if everything is normal.

There is silence for a moment and then Mum speaks and her words confirm the worst.

'Sit down, Layla, I need to talk to you.'

CHAPTER SEVEN

I pull out the kitchen chair and slowly sit down. Mum has her hands in front of her and she looks very serious. I feel so bad and ask myself why I've done this to her. I remember the way I spoke to Dylan, too, and I wonder if he's told her. She's probably ashamed of me and who could blame her? I decide to get it all over with and apologise straight away but as I open my mouth to speak, she beats me to it.

'So,' Mum says, looking up at me. 'There's something that I need to tell you.'

I look at her in surprise, this isn't what I was expecting.

'What?' I say, the word coming out loud and blunt.

Fear clutches at my stomach as I suddenly know that this is going to be much worse that I thought. I stare at her in confusion.

'I have to go into hospital, Layla.'

'What?'

'I've been having some tests done and I need an operation, but it's nothing serious. I'm sorry that I haven't told you before now but I didn't want to worry you.'

The tears start before I can stop them and all I can think is that Mum is going to die.

'Layla.' Mum reaches across the table and takes hold of both my hands in hers and grips them tightly. 'Please don't cry, it's nothing serious, it's just a benign lump, I'm going to be absolutely fine.'

'But you've been crying,' I wail. 'So, it's obviously not fine.'

'There were tears of relief, Layla, honestly, I'm absolutely elated that it's not cancer.'

'Where's the lump?' I ask.

'In my left breast, but it's benign and they're going to remove it, but only because it could become unsightly if it doesn't stop growing.'

I stand up, take a deep breath to calm myself and walk across the kitchen to the worktop. I put the kettle on to boil and take two mugs down from the cupboard and throw a teabag into each. I take the milk from the fridge and then stare at the kettle, waiting for it to boil. Once I've made the tea, I take both mugs over and put them on the table and then sit down opposite Mum. She looks pale and tired and I ask myself how I failed to realise that something was wrong with her.

'How long have you known about this operation?' I ask, gently, determined not to sound accusing.

'I only found out today when they rang,' she replies. 'That Wednesday morning when I said I was visiting Annie, I was really going to the hospital for a biopsy. I was so afraid that it was cancer, especially with my family history. I'm sorry I lied about where I was going but I didn't want to frighten you for nothing and as it turned out, I was right not to. When they rang, about half-an-hour ago, to tell me it was benign I was so relieved. It was sheer relief that made me cry. They've booked me in for a lumpectomy to remove it.'

Wednesday, the morning I went shopping for shoes and bought that stupid underwear. Whilst I was wandering around the shops enjoying some silly fantasy about Will, Mum was having a biopsy to see if she had cancer.

'I'm sorry I didn't tell you, Layla,' Mum says, quietly.

'No, Mum, I'm sorry. Sorry that you had to go there on your own, sorry that I wasn't there for you when you needed me most. Sorry that you didn't think I'd be able to cope. Please promise me that you won't try and protect me anymore. I'm not a child and you don't need to shield me from the world. I'm an adult.'

Mum doesn't speak but gazes down at the table. I try not to feel angry that she assumed I wouldn't be able to cope, that she needed to keep it a secret from me. Am I that pathetic? Obviously, Mum thinks that I am.

'When did you first think something was wrong?' I ask, because I need to know everything and if we talk about it, maybe I can get past the hurt about Mum feeling that she has to lie to me.

'A few months ago. I found a lump and I tried to convince myself it was a cyst, something trivial. But I was sick with worry, Layla, because your grandmother died from breast cancer and I wondered if it would come for me. I've always checked my breasts and I was so frightened when I found the lump.'

I never met my grandmother because she died long before Mum and Dad adopted me. Mum told me why she died so young but until now, I'd forgotten, because it hadn't seemed important to me. It was just a fact about someone that I'd never met and that I never would meet.

'I have to go into hospital next week, they're going to do the lumpectomy. I should only be in there for a night, you'll hardly notice I've gone.'

'If it's benign, why can't they just leave it where it is?' I ask.

'It's grown, even since I first found it, I can feel that it's got bigger. If it wasn't a fast growing lump, they would leave it and wait and see but as it's not, it's better that they remove it. I don't want to end up with lop-sided boobs.' Mum laughs.

I laugh with her but inside I can't stop the bitterness that Mum thinks so little of me. She thinks I'm unable to cope with anything and couldn't even confide in me that she was terrified that she had cancer. So, this is how we continue our evening as we cook dinner together and watch Mum's favourite quiz show, with my false laughter and an outward show of not caring that she didn't tell me. The only reference we make to her operation is when she tells me what day her surgery is; other than that, we don't talk of it. Her operation is next Tuesday because there's been a cancellation, otherwise she would have been waiting for months. That's provided they still have a bed for her and there are no emergencies and they have to cancel her, and then who knows when it will be. Mum seems more concerned that I still go to work and don't lose my job than she does about the surgery. I humour her and agree that I'll go but there's no way I'll be going to work once she comes home. I'm guessing that she'll be sore from the surgery so will need looking after. I'll go to work on Wednesday if she's still in hospital but if she's coming out early, then I won't. I'll let them know that my mother is ill and I'll need to take time off. I don't care if I lose the job or not. I don't tell Mum this because I know it will stress her and there's no point. Now it makes sense why she was so intent on me getting a job; it's because she thought she was going to die.

By the time we go upstairs to bed I feel exhausted from the effort of pretending that I'm not hurt and upset that Mum thinks I would have made her cancer scare all about me. And although I'm so tired I can barely brush my teeth, I'm quite sure that I won't sleep at all but somehow, I fall into a deep sleep almost immediately.

* * *

I awake with a start. I don't know what it is that's woken me and I lie in the darkness and listen but the room is silent and near black with only a glimmer of moonlight shining through the curtains. In these first waking moments, I've forgotten about Mum's impending operation. But the peace doesn't last; the events of yesterday come rushing back and I begin to turn them over and over in my mind and I know that there's no possibility of going back to sleep. I pick up my mobile phone from the bedside table to see that it's just gone one o'clock in the morning. The night stretches before me and the thought of lying here thinking about everything going around and around in my head is more than I can bear. I feel so sad that Mum didn't feel able to confide in me and the irony isn't lost on me that even now, I *am* somehow making it about me. I think, no, I *know*, that I need to grow up. Mum thought I would fall to pieces and she obviously still thinks of me as a child and who can blame her? Because the way I've behaved lately only confirms that. The way I flaunted myself in front of Will yesterday, what sort of behaviour is that?

Very bizarre, not normal behaviour, that's what.

There's no chance of going back to sleep now so

I climb quietly out of bed, take off the oversized T-shirt that I wear as a nightdress, and slip yesterday's dress over my head, not even bothering to put on a bra. Picking up my flip-flops, I carefully open my bedroom door and listen; there's no light or sound coming from Mum's room so she must be asleep. I pad silently down the stairs, through the hallway and into the kitchen. Benny is asleep in his basket, snoring contentedly, and I tip-toe past him, quietly unlock the back door, take the key out of the lock and slip outside, locking the door behind me. Not so many years ago Benny would have woken at the slightest sound but he's getting deafer by the week, his hearing deteriorating the older he gets.

The night is fresh and I shiver as I slip my flip-flops onto my feet and walk down the lane. Perhaps the silence will calm me, perhaps some fresh air and time away from my bed will help me to sleep when I return. I know that if I'd stayed in bed I would have tossed and turned until morning, the events of yesterday on an unending loop.

I walk slowly down the lane as my eyes adjust to the dim light from the moon. I'm not afraid to be out on my own in the countryside because there's never anyone around, except for the odd owl or fox. There's hardly any traffic on this lane in the daytime, let alone in the early hours of the morning. I reach the end of the lane and meander along the road by the trees when I smell the unmistakable aroma of cigarette smoke. I stop and stand immobile for a moment, suddenly afraid, because there is someone else here and I have no idea why or who they could be. Why would there be someone smoking in the middle of a country lane at past one o'clock in the morning? There aren't any pubs for miles so why would someone come to a lane in the middle of nowhere to smoke? I want to run back to our cottage but the noise would draw attention so I turn very slowly, intent on making my way back home as silently as possible. My heart is pounding and in my near panic I put my foot on a twig and it snaps underfoot, sounding like a gunshot in the silence. I freeze.

'Hello?' a voice says. 'Who's there?'

'Will?' I ask, tentatively, praying that it's not wishful thinking that the voice sounds like his.

'Layla.' He laughs quietly, and relief floods through me. The shadows move and he appears in front of me in the moonlight. 'What are you doing out here at this time of night?'

'I could ask the same of you,' I whisper.

'I just needed some air.' He moves closer to me and I look up at him and wonder how a man can be so beautiful.

'I didn't know you smoked.'

He sighs and throws the cigarette onto the ground and grinds it into the gravel with his shoe.

'I don't. Usually. Disgusting habit, I quit years ago but sometimes, when I'm stressed, I can't help myself. Stupid really, because it doesn't help. Why are you out here?'

'Couldn't sleep,' I say.

'Any particular reason?'

I feel my cheeks grow hot as I remember standing in front of my bedroom window in skimpy underwear.

'Layla?' he whispers.

'I'm sorry,' I say. 'For what I did. For embarrassing you.'

There's absolute silence and I force myself to continue.

'Standing at the window like that, I don't know what I was thinking.'

There, I've said it. I turn to leave, but the feel of Will's hand on my arm stops me.

'There's no need to apologise.' His voice is soft and he doesn't sound angry and I feel such relief. Although I know that realistically, I'll never stop and talk to him again because of what I've done. If I see him in the lane, it'll be a quick hello because I'll be too embarrassed to speak to him ever again. I feel his fingers moving and he gently grips my arm and pulls me towards him and I'm afraid to breathe in case I spoil the moment. We stand immobile, facing each other and he looks down at me and smiles. I smile back and he lowers his head and I think that he's going to say something but he doesn't, he kisses me gently on the lips, lingering for just a moment. I taste tobacco and toothpaste and it tastes wonderful; *he* tastes wonderful. There's a moment of absolute stillness between us, and neither of us move at all. It feels like a test almost, of whether we should stop. I reach up and put my arms around his neck and we kiss again, long and deep this time and when we finally come up for air, Will wraps his arms around me and holds me to him tightly.

'I shouldn't have done that,' he murmurs, into my hair. 'But I've been wanting to since the moment I first saw you.'

I lean back and gaze up at him in wonder; this is really happening.

'So, you're not angry with me for yesterday, in my bedroom?'

'Angry?' He laughs, tracing the outline of my lips with his finger. 'God, no. You have no idea what you do to me.' He lips find mine and he kisses me again, more hungrily this time. I hold him tightly and the only coherent thought in my mind is that I didn't imagine our connection at all.

CHAPTER EIGHT

Mum is at the hospital; she's waiting for her surgery which is scheduled for this morning. They couldn't give a definite time – she had to be there for seven o'clock but her procedure could be at any time up until twelve-thirty. I wasn't allowed to stay with her but the nurses have assured me that they'll ring me as soon she's had the procedure and let me know when she's ready for a visit. It's only seven-thirty now and it could be hours until I hear anything and I wonder what to do with myself. I know that it's routine and it's not cancer but I can't help worrying because operations go wrong, don't they? Even routine ones. I drive back to the cottage and think about having some breakfast but just make a coffee instead, I don't think I'm capable of eating at the moment.

Mum had to be nil-by-mouth from last night so I didn't haven't anything either, because I didn't think it would be fair on her but quite honestly, the thought of food made me feel sick. Even telling myself that this is the very reason that she didn't tell me about her hospital appointments doesn't stop me from imagining the worst case scenario. I pace around the kitchen while the mug of coffee that I've made goes cold, getting more and more agitated as I pace. I just want today to be over and for Mum to be okay. My mind starts to go into a loop of worry and in an effort to stop myself from descending into a pit of anxiousness and fretting, I grab Benny's lead from the peg and head out of the back door. He follows behind me and when we get to the gate, I snap his lead on and we walk down the lane, past Will's house and into the fields behind. There's no sign of Will because he's not here, he's gone to London with Lucinda. They went yesterday morning and I miss him so much. He'll be back tonight but I wish he hadn't had to go. With *her*. He said that it's just routine and that he has to go into work every now and again and he sometimes stays over. I didn't ask where he was staying, but of course it'll be with *her*. He may have taken a sabbatical from his job but like he says, he has to show his face now and then and check in because if there's a special project on, they need his expertise. Will laughed and said that he also needs to be sure that they can't do without him because he needs a job to go back to once the cottage is finished. I asked him what he actually does and he said it was to do with funds and acquisitions and quite honestly, it meant nothing to me. He usually spends a couple of hours in the office and then lines up a meeting elsewhere so that he's not stuck there all day. Because, like he says, he's not getting paid while he's taking time off so he doesn't want to be too available. Despite my worry over Mum and missing Will, I couldn't help but feel excited when I knew that we'd be able to see each other tonight without Lucinda being around to spoil it.

I know now that I didn't imagine our connection; when Will was watching me in the window, he said that he'd never felt such longing for anyone in his whole life. We lingered outside for hours that night, kissing and talking, although we moved into the field behind the trees in case someone, unlikely as it was, should see us. I've never felt like this about anyone before; every time Will kissed me, I never wanted it to end and I know he felt the same way. When he pressed his body against mine, I wanted more and I know he did, too, because he whispered that he wanted me so badly that it hurt. But we should wait, he said, because making love in a field would feel somehow sordid, and he didn't want it to be like that.

Making love. I think that means he loves me; he didn't say the words but I'm sure that's how he feels because that's how I feel about him and we have an almost telepathic connection. It proves that there is such a thing as love at first sight, that loving someone doesn't depend on how long you've known them. Some things are meant to be; it's fate. We met in the field again the following night and the night after that, and we kissed and talked and as our kisses became more urgent, I reminded myself that tonight, we'll be properly together. Our secret meetings have been quite wonderful and the only thing that has marred them is Lucinda.

I couldn't stop myself from asking about her, because if he was in love with her, he wouldn't be meeting me in secret, would he? I feel I have a right to ask, because he's with me now, even though he has to live with her. Will was very quiet after I asked and I thought that he wasn't going to answer because he was silent for so long. Eventually, when he spoke, he said that she's not well, but that he can't leave her because he's worried what she might do to herself. I asked him in what way she wasn't well and he said she has *some issues* with her mental health but is getting treatment. He didn't actually *say* that he didn't love her but I could tell that he doesn't, he's just too loyal to utter the words. And although I want him for myself, it shows what a good man he is that he feels he can't abandon her. He has to stay with her until she's better, which will hopefully be soon. I feel less guilty about being in love with a married man now because I'm not a bad person and I like to think that I try to do the right thing. And actually, it's not even cheating because their marriage was over before he even met me. He also told me that he didn't really want to buy the cottage but was forced into it by her father, who's domineering and overpowering and seems to think that he should have a say in everything. Will seemed angry when he told me this so I didn't ask any more questions because I didn't want to spoil our time together. I can't wait until he's back from London tonight.

Benny and I walk into the fields behind Will's cottage and I stand and stare through the hedge. I think of Will, stripped to the waist, clearing the garden and my stomach flips as I think about seeing him next. It's only when I notice that Benny is sitting down next to me that I realise I've been daydreaming. I clip his lead on and drag him home, he's tired and wants me to carry him so when we get to lane, I pick him and he licks my face and puts his head on my shoulder as if he were a child. Once we're in the cottage, I decide that I can't sit around until I hear from the hospital or I'll drive myself mad. I set about vacuuming and dusting, giving every room a good clean. Once I've done that, I get the ironing board out and catch up on all the clothes that are languishing in the bottom of the ironing basket because they're difficult to iron. I concentrate on getting every crease out and by the time I've finished, it's four o'clock.

I thought the hospital would have rung by now.

I'm starting to worry and imagining all kinds of complications when my mobile rings. I pick it up and when I see that the number is withheld, I know that it's the hospital. I answer the call and my voice comes out as a squeak because I'm so nervous. The calm voice on the other end of the line informs me that she's Ward Sister Stephens and that Mum is awake and sitting up in bed having a cup of tea. I can visit if I want to. She assures me that Mum is absolutely fine. As soon as I finish the call, I grab the chocolates and get well card that I've bought in readiness and stuff them into my bag. I wanted to buy Mum a big bouquet of flowers but she won't be allowed to have them on the ward so I'm going to wait until she comes home tomorrow. Despite Mum not wanting me to, I telephoned Chiverson's and spoke to the store manager, Colin, and told him that I needed some time off because Mum is ill. I fully expected him to tell me that I needn't bother coming back but he surprised me by being very sympathetic. He did add though, that unfortunately Chiverson's wouldn't be able to pay me as I'd only worked there for such a short time. I didn't think he needed to say that because I obviously wouldn't expect to get paid. Although maybe some people do, so perhaps he did need to say it. Anyway, I told Colin that I'll come in to work when I can and he seemed happy with that.

Despite not being at all alike, Jack and I are already firm friends because we get on so well. Somehow, we just clicked. I rang him and we were on the phone for ages. I told him about Mum's operation and how she couldn't tell me and he was so sympathetic and understanding, and I realised that there's a lot more to him underneath his flippant exterior. We've been messaging each other a lot and it feels so good to have a friend of my own age at last. I feel that I can be myself with Jack and not have to pretend to be someone else like I did when I was at school.

With a last look around the kitchen, I feel pleased with my productive day. Mum will be pleased when she gets home that everything looks so fresh and tidy. I give Benny a treat, lock the back door and set off for the hospital.

* * *

Mum's sitting up in bed when I arrive on the ward and she looks fine, she has colour in her cheeks and there are no signs of any ill effects from the anaesthetic. She was concerned that she might be sick with it as she had her tonsils out when she was a child and was vomiting for the entire day when she came round.

We hug and I give her the chocolates – her favourites – and she opens her card. I made it myself with wild flowers that I picked from the fields behind our cottage. Mum smiles and runs her fingers over the front of it and puts it on the cabinet next to her. I sit down in the chair next to the bed, which makes an awful puffing sound as the air escapes from the vinyl padding covering. I lean on the counterpane, closer to Mum.

'How have you been?' she asks, as if I haven't seen her for weeks, rather than just this morning.

'I'm fine, Mum.' I grin. 'More importantly, how

are you?' I wish I could share my feelings about Will with Mum, but I can't, at the moment. Once Lucinda's well and we can be together things will be different, there'll be no secrets between us then.

'I feel okay, actually. Hardly any pain at all, although I am dosed up to the gills with painkillers so it may be a different story tomorrow. But right now, I feel fine. And I haven't been sick at all, so that's a bonus.'

'So, you're coming home tomorrow?'

We're interrupted by a nurse who's come to take Mum's temperature and blood pressure. I sit quietly and watch as the nurse moves around with quiet confidence and I see that she's not very much older than me. For the first time, I wonder if maybe I should get a career, or some training. Once Mum is better and fully recovered, maybe I'll look into it, consider my options, as they say. The nurse removes the blood pressure cuff, makes a note on her clipboard and disappears back to the nurses' station.

'They're very nice, here,' Mum says.

'They are,' I agree. 'But you'll be home tomorrow, won't you? Because I'm going to cook you a special dinner because hospital food's supposed to be awful and Benny's missing you dreadfully, too.'

Mum hesitates and I know, then, that the worst has happened, that the lump wasn't benign at all, it's cancer.

'Mum?'

'I'm not sure. I might have to stay in a bit longer.'

'Why?' My heart starts to pound and I feel the saliva dry up in my mouth.

'Well, for some reason my blood pressure is high which can be a sign of infection. They had to make a bigger incision than they thought so they need to keep an eye on the wound and make sure it doesn't get infected. It's quite common and nothing to worry about.'

I stare at her in silence, willing myself not to burst into tears.

'But not for long,' she adds, hurriedly. 'As soon as my blood pressure is back to normal and the wound is healing, I'll be coming home. It might even be tomorrow, they're just forewarning me; erring on the side of caution, that's all.'

I bite my lip and try not to cry; Mum doesn't need me turning into a cry baby.

But I can't help wondering if we're really going to get back to normal. Swallowing down my emotions, I smile and start to chat about work as if I'm not worried at all.

Time to grow up, Layla.

* * *

All visitors were made to leave the ward
at eight o'clock when visiting time ended
and I came home and left Mum there.

I wonder how many more
nights she'll be staying.

I was so preoccupied on the way home that I can't remember one single thing about the journey home. I remained calm whilst I was with Mum and tried to talk of practicalities but the worry was always there, underneath. I have to stop thinking worse-case scenario and letting my imagination run away with me. I left the hospital with a list of things to take in for her tomorrow because she only took enough things in with her for one night. I'm going to take her some clean nightdresses and more underwear along with some food, because the hospital food isn't the best. Although it'll have to be cold food because there's nowhere to heat it up. I'll make her some really tasty sandwiches and we have pasties and cakes so I'll put them in a cool box and she can eat them when she feels like it.

I give Benny his dinner and then go upstairs and into Mum's bedroom which is at the back of the house and has a view over the back garden. The evening sunlight is filtering through the windows, making dappled patterns on the rose-patterned and trellis wallpaper that's been on the walls for as long as I can remember. I've spent many a night sleeping in Mum's old double bed with her. When I was young if I had a bad dream or there was a thunderstorm, Mum and I would snuggle up under the duvet and read her old *Broon*'s albums. I remember being fascinated by the language in them and the words that I didn't understand. She still has them, stacked on top of her dresser and I take one of them down and flick through the pages. How simple life is when you're a child.

I put the album back on top of the pile and open the top drawer of the dresser and take out a nightdress and then take one more to be on the safe side. There isn't a lot of room to keep stuff in the hospital but I can bring her dirty washing home with me when I take her clean stuff in. I try not to think about Mum being in hospital for more than a few days. The doctors like to get patients home, now, don't they? They don't want people jamming up the wards when they can be looked after at home. I can look after Mum and get her well again; she'll be on her feet and back to normal in no time. I start to feel anxious at the thought of Mum not being home soon.

Stop panicking and stop catastrophising and think about something else.

I think about our visit and how I told Mum about being able to take time off from Chiverson's. I wanted her to know that it wasn't a problem because I didn't want her fretting about it. Mum thought that was very good of them, and I couldn't help agreeing with her and actually, I don't really want to lose the job because I don't mind going there because I get to see Jack. Stacking shelves isn't exactly exciting but when you work with someone you like and can have a good laugh with it makes the time go very quickly.

I take some underwear out of one of the drawers and put it in the holdall I've brought from downstairs and try to think if there's anything else that she'll need. She has her dressing gown with her but the heat in that hospital is near tropical; it was so hot that I was sweating by the time I left. The dressing gown she took with her was a quilted satin one that she wears at home because even though it's June, our cottage is old and is still chilly in the mornings sometimes. That dressing gown is far too warm for the heat in that hospital and I know she has a thin cotton wrap around here somewhere which would be far more suitable. I decide I'll take it in for her because Mum likes to look and feel nice, and frankly, it's about the only thing I can do for her at the moment.

I pull out the drawers and look in the ottoman but it's not there. I pull open the wardrobe doors and stand and stare at the hangers and am about to close the doors when I spot the familiar lavender sprigged material on the top shelf. Too lazy to go and get the folding steps from the kitchen to stand on, I stand on tiptoe, stretch upwards and grab the edge of the dressing gown and pull. The whole pile comes toppling down with it and I stand and watch as it all falls around me onto the floor. Now I've made myself the job of putting it all back because I couldn't be bothered to go and get something to stand on, which I'll have to get now anyway.

Annoyed with myself, I start picking everything up. I'm folding it and putting it on the bed in a neat pile when I notice an envelope lying amongst the clothes. I pick it up and look at it and am surprised to see that it's addressed to me.

It's been opened.

I turn it over in my hand and look at it; my name and address are typed and the paper and envelope are official looking. I don't understand why it's in Mum's bedroom or why she's opened it when it's addressed to me. Mum never opens my post, not that I get very much. I sit down on the bed and pull the letter out of the envelope. The heading along the top of the paper states that it's from *The Adoption Intermediary Service* and the date underneath the address is January 27th this year. Confused, I begin to read:

Dear Layla

We are writing to you at the request of your birth mother. She would very much like to contact you and this is an opening letter to see if this is something that you would like to do. She would like to write to you in the first instance but we would not give her your address but would be the intermediary for any correspondence. You do not have to accept any correspondence from her if you don't want to.

Please take as much time as you wish to make a decision and if we do not hear from you, we will not contact you again but will wait until you are ready to contact us.

Yours sincerely

CJ Brierley

I read the letter again and check the name to make sure that there is no mistake. There isn't, it's definitely my name and my address.

The letter is for me.
But how can it be?
Because my birth mother is dead.

CHAPTER NINE

Robot-like, I go downstairs and get the folding steps, take them into Mum's room and put everything back onto the top shelf of the wardrobe.

Except for the letter.

I take that into my bedroom and tuck it into the top drawer of my dressing table and then sit on the bed and try to figure out what on earth is going on. After a while I get up from the bed, go downstairs into the lounge and drag the photograph box out of the dresser. I root through until I find the newspaper cutting. I hold it in my hand and reread it carefully, even though every word is already imprinted on my brain.

As I reread it, I realise that I've obviously got it all wrong and jumped to completely the wrong conclusion; this clipping isn't about me at all. Just because the dates tallied up with my birth, it doesn't mean that the woman battered to death while her baby slept upstairs in her cot is *my* mother. I am *not* that baby. This is just a random piece of old newspaper that happened to be lying around and I've put two and two together and made five. Mum probably used it to wrap something in and it's somehow found its way into our photograph box.

What an idiot I am.

But something isn't right.

Because Mum has always told me that my birth mother is dead and that letter states very clearly that she's not. Mum wouldn't lie to me; I know she wouldn't because Mum *never* lies. She's asked me many times over the years if I wanted to know anything at all about my birth mother so why would she lie? It just doesn't make any sense.

It *must* be a mistake, the adoption tracing company or whatever it is have made an error and sent this letter to the wrong person. There must be thousands of people looking for adopted children and they've simply got me mixed up with someone else.

But that doesn't explain why Mum opened it.

But I'm over-thinking it; she opened it by mistake because she didn't read it properly. Our surname is the same, it's only our initials that are different so it would be easy to do. Perhaps once she'd opened it, she didn't want to tell me and stir everything up. She knows how I hate talking about my birth parents, she knows that I don't want to know anything about them.

I pick up all of the photographs and shove them

back into the box and put it back in the dresser. I take the clipping upstairs and put it in the drawer with the letter. I'm going to ask Mum and find out what's going on but I'll wait until she's fully recovered from her surgery. I don't want it to sound as if I'm accusing her. I don't want to sound like a whiny brat demanding answers for a genuine mistake. I'll wait until she comes home before asking her because I'm sure that there's a perfectly logical explanation for it.

I stand and stare at the dressing table for a while and then pull the drawer open again and stare at the clipping. I could Google it and find more information about the woman in the newspaper. Or I could ring the adoption agency for them to confirm that they've made a mistake. That way I wouldn't have to bother Mum at all. I reach for my phone; I know the adoption agency will be closed now but I could put their telephone number in my phone ready so I can ring them tomorrow. I open my phone and hover over the screen, not sure whether to open the Google app or the telephone keypad. As I stand there staring at the screen, a message pops up from Will.

I'm home.

I catch my breath and my stomach flips with excitement. I quickly close the drawer so that I can't see the newspaper clipping or the letter. I don't want to see them or think about either of them. Not now. I tap a reply to Will and press *send*.

Come over. I'm on my own.

I run down the stairs and into the lounge and watch through the window as Will comes out of his cottage and makes his way across the lane. I can see that there are no lights on in the cottage next door so I know that the young couple who live there are out. There's no one to see Will coming here except for me. The light is fading and it's that peculiar time between evening and night, a time of stillness and the end of the day. A time of infinite possibilities.

I go and stand by the front door, looking through the small side window as Will walks up the driveway. He's unaware that I'm watching him and I feel a shiver of anticipation as he strides towards the front door. He's so gorgeous and handsome. I watch as his hair flops over his eyes and he brushes it back, completely unaware of how hot he is. As he reaches the porch and puts his hand up to tap on the door, I open the door, take hold of his hand and pull him inside. I slam the door closed and quickly lock it behind him, push him up against the door and stand on tiptoes and kiss him hungrily. When we break for air, he laughs.

'Wow, that was some welcome.'

I put my hands on each side of his face and kiss him again, grinding my body into him and I can feel that he wants me as much as I want him.

'Woah,' he says, with a smile, taking hold of the top of my arms and pulling me gently away from him. 'Let a guy get through the door, eh?'

I stare up at him unsmilingly and his face is suddenly serious as he remembers what's happening today.

'Oh God, how is your Mum? Did her surgery go okay?'

'She's fine.' I say, after a moment. 'Everything went very well.'

'Well, that's great,' he says. 'You must be relieved.'

'I am.' I step away from him and he drops his hold of my arms. I take his hand and lead him through the hallway. 'But if you don't mind, I'd rather not talk about it now.' I'm not going to think about any of it; Mum, the newspaper clipping, the letter. None of it.

I hear a low growl from Benny as he bounds towards us, stopping in his tracks in front of Will. He barks at him, his tail down and Will steps back in alarm. I laugh and tell Benny not to be silly and I marvel at my composure when mere minutes before Will arrived, I was in turmoil over what I've found.

'Don't worry, he'll only lick you to death, he's a big baby, all growl and no bite.'

I ruffle Benny's ears and Will pats him gingerly on the head. Satisfied that Will isn't going to attack me, Benny pads back to his basket and flops into it with a sigh.

'Drink?' I ask, as I walk into the kitchen.

'Please,' he answers, perching on the edge of the table and folding his arms.

'I thought we'd have wine,' I say, talking a bottle from the fridge. It's a bottle that Mum bought ages ago although neither of us really drink. I wonder why I'm doing it now, am I trying to look grown up and sophisticated to Will, as if having a glass of wine is a normal occurrence? Maybe I am.

'White, okay?' I ask, as I take wine glasses down from the wall cupboard.

'Great,' Will answers.

I pour the wine and carry both glasses over to him, giving him his glass and taking a sip from mine.

'So, how did London go?'

'Okay. Did what I had to do and left. Showed my face. Showed willing, made sure there's going to be a job for me when I go back.'

'And Lucinda?' I don't know why I asked, I don't even like saying her name so why the hell am I asking him?

'Let's not talk about her.' Will takes another sip of his wine and I feel I've made a mistake; I shouldn't have asked him. I need to control myself, control my jealousy.

'Let's go in the lounge,' I say. 'It'll be more comfortable.'

Will smiles and I walk through to the lounge and he gets up and follows me. The moonlight is coming through the lounge window, giving the room an ethereal, other-worldly feel. I place my glass on the coffee table and switch on the small lamp by the sofa. I don't close the curtains because

I like the way it feels in the room, I like the moonlight. I close the lounge door to keep Benny from coming in. Will sits on the sofa and then places his glass next to mine on the table and I sit down next to him.

'I've missed you,' he says, stroking my hair.

'Not as much as I've missed you.'

He puts his arm around me and we kiss gently.

'You know I'm obsessed with you, don't you?' Will murmurs, kissing my neck. My stomach does a lazy roll and I gasp as he nuzzles my neck, working his way downwards.

'I think about you all of the time, Layla, I can't get enough of you.'

I pull away from him and get up from the sofa and stand in front of him. He looks up at me in alarm.

'What's wrong, Layla?' Will looks so worried and in that moment, I love him even more.

'Nothing,' I say, pulling my dress over my head and throwing it onto the floor. 'Absolutely nothing.'

* * *

'What time does visiting start?' Will asks, biting into his toast and marmalade.

'Three o'clock. I'll get there as soon as it starts. I'm taking Mum's mobile phone up with me too, as well as the other bits and pieces she asked for.'

'Hasn't she got it with her?' Will asks, in

surprise.

'No, she was only going in for one night and she was afraid it might get stolen. The nurses gave her the whole *we can't guarantee your property* talk and I think it spooked Mum. But I think it's worth the risk because without it, we have no contact at all.'

Will nods through a mouthful of toast and I sit and watch him eat. I love everything about him, even the fact that he's a bit of a noisy eater. He's not a pig though, he doesn't eat with his mouth open or anything, he just enjoys his food. He sees me watching him and he winks at me and grins. I feel my face flush scarlet because I know what he's thinking; he's remembering last night.

It was wonderful, more than wonderful, perfect, in fact.

Will and I made love on the floor of the lounge, the moon bathing our bodies in soft light and it wasn't possible for it to be more perfect. We lay in each other's arms afterwards and Will held me close and told me how beautiful I was. I *nearly* told him that I loved him but stopped myself because I want him to say it first. I know that he loves me because he's already told me he's obsessed with me but I think he needs to actually say the words before I confess my own feelings to him.

Although he must have guessed.

We lay in each other's arms and talked; he said that he never dreamed that I would want him as much as he wanted me. He said that I must have hundreds of young, virile men chasing after me and never imagined that I would want an old man like him. I laughed then and said he wasn't old, because he's not, although he is twice as old as I am. I didn't tell him that he was the first man that I've slept with because I think he assumed that I've had boyfriends before. I didn't want to tell him; I don't want Will thinking that I'm some sort of odd nineteen-year-old virgin, even though I am.

Or was.

As the night drew on, the house cooled down and the lounge grew colder. I shivered and suggested we go upstairs to my bedroom and Will agreed. I got up from the floor and Will sat up and watched me as I drew the lounge curtains closed. As I was closing them, just for a moment I thought that there was someone outside Will's cottage watching us. My breath caught in my throat and I turned to Will in panic but then quickly turned my face back to the window. I didn't want anything to spoil our perfect night and it didn't, because when I looked out of the window again, there was nothing.

It was the shadow of a tree, or a stray branch waving in the wind.

Or maybe just my guilty conscience for sleeping with another woman's husband.

'I love that you're not shy about your body,' Will said, as he watched me picking up our discarded clothes from the floor.

I laughed when he said it, not least because of the fuss I made about posing nude for Mum's art class. I'm not shy, I'm just choosy about who sees me naked. I'm not shy in front of Will; why would I be when he's seen and loved every inch of my body?

'You're smiling.' Will says, from across the table, bringing me back to the present.

'Just thinking about last night.'

Will smiles and I feel his toes touch mine beneath the table. We're still not dressed; Will is wearing his boxers and I'm wearing the shirt that he wore last night. He strokes the top of my foot with his toes and I marvel that even his feet can feel so sensual and arousing.

'I should probably get showered and dressed,' I say. 'Because it's a quarter to two and I want to get to the hospital for three.'

'You should,' he agrees, taking my plate and putting it on top of his. 'You go ahead and I'll clear up down here.'

I reluctantly get up from the table and go out into the hallway. The journey to the hospital will take at least twenty minutes and that's without parking. I should have got ready earlier but time went on and neither of us wanted to break the spell and come downstairs. It was only when Benny started howling that we got up. My poor dog was desperate to go outside and he'd been so patient, waiting for me to let him out when normally he'd have been outside at eight o'clock.

I go into the bathroom and turn on the shower. It always takes a few minutes to warm up and I never get straight in. I strip off Will's shirt and hold it to my nose. It has his distinctive citrus smell; it must be the aftershave he uses. Since that first night I've not seen him smoking again and I remember that he only smokes when he's stressed. He's not stressed now because he has me. I breathe in the smell from his shirt and close my eyes; everything is so perfect now. I silently pray that Mum is going to be fine and home soon.

And that there's a perfectly logical explanation for the letter.

I fold Will's shirt carefully and lay it the basket chair in the corner of the bathroom and then turn to get into the shower. I jump when I realise that Will is standing there.

'I've come to help you,' he says, with a grin, as his arms encircle my waist and he pulls me to him.

* * *

I'm late.

Visiting starts at three and it's already twenty past. Guilt engulfs me as I drive around and around the hospital car park looking for a space. Mum will be wondering where I am, thinking that something has happened to me or that I've had an accident whilst in reality, Will and I were making love in the shower. Even the thought of it makes me shiver; we simply cannot get enough of each other and despite my guilt at being late to visit Mum, I allow myself a moment to think of Will.

Is it like this for everyone when they fall in love? I have no idea because I've never been in love before, or had sex, or even talked about boys with girlfriends like other girls do. I'm sure Mum would tell me if I asked, but for now, Will and I have to remain a secret.

I spot an empty space and zoom into it, making a man in a Volvo toot his horn at me in the process. I deliberately don't make eye contact even though I was here before him and the space is, by rights, mine. I've no wish to get into an argument about a parking space and make myself even later getting to see Mum.

Making sure I have the ticket with me, I pick up the bag with all of Mum's stuff in, get out of the car and march across the car park as fast as I can towards the hospital entrance. I decide not to take the lift because there are crowds of people waiting and I don't want to waste any more time. Slinging the bag over my shoulder, I head towards the door to the stairs and practically run up the first two flights. Mum is on the fifth floor so there are three more to go. For some reason, I'm starting to feel panicked and, in my haste to get up the stairs, I catch my toe on the step and fall forward. Thankfully, the only thing hurt is my pride but I take a deep breath and stand still for a moment. I need to calm down, taking the stairs at a normal pace will be much safer and make hardly any difference to the amount of time it takes to get up them.

I reach the fifth floor and push through the double doors into the corridor. I look at my watch as I walk along to Linnet Ward; three-thirty-five. What excuse am I going to give for being so late? Not that Mum will ask, she'll be happy to see me no matter what time I get here. I stand outside the ward, cleanse my hands with the gel provided as the sign suggests, press the door release button and enter the ward. Once inside, there's another corridor and I head straight down it then turn to the left and into the first door on the left where Mum is. There are six beds in the ward and she's at the far end, nearest the window.

Except that she's not there.

I walk down the ward, and some of the visitors sitting around the beds look up at me as I pass by. I reach Mum's bed and wonder where she is, she could be in the toilet or maybe she's using the payphone at the entrance to the ward to ring me and ask me where I am. I'll blame the traffic, I decide, and then immediately feel guilty for my intention of lying to her.

'Can I help you?'

A young girl is standing in front of me in a white uniform. She looks even younger than me and I wonder what she wants.

'Can I help you?' she repeats.

'I'm just waiting for my mother,' I say.

'And where is she?' she asks, slowly, as if I'm having trouble understanding her.

'The loo, probably,' I say. 'This is her bed. I'm

waiting for her to come back.'

She looks alarmed and then tries unsuccessfully to hide it.

'Deborah Trevellyn,' I state.

'Oh, but she's gone,' she says. 'Did nobody tell you?'

'Gone?' I demand. 'What do you mean, gone?'

That's when I notice the bed, Mum's bed. It's no longer made up with linen but has been stripped and the only thing left on it is a clear plastic mattress cover.

'I'm very sorry...' she begins to say, but I don't hear the rest because all I can think as my head starts to swim and my legs crumble beneath me, is that while Will and I were making love without a care in the world, Mum was dying.

And it's all my fault.

CHAPTER TEN

I slowly open my eyes to see the concerned face of the young girl in the white uniform leaning over me. I'm lying on the bed that used to be Mum's and another nurse is standing on the other side of the bed holding my wrist as she takes my pulse.

'How are you feeling?' white-uniformed girl asks.

'Okay. I think,' I say, after thinking about it for a moment.

'You fainted.' The nurse holding my wrist lowers my hand to the bed and studies me. 'Were you feeling unwell? Are you pregnant, perhaps?'

'No, neither! I was fine. I don't quite know what happened. I remember feeling a bit panicked and then the light started to fade and everything got darker and darker.'

The nurse looks across at the girl in the white uniform – *Anna, student nurse*, according to the name badge pinned to her breast pocket - and frowns.

'You were asking where your mum was,' Anna says. 'And I was just about to tell you she'd been moved to a side ward when you fainted.'

I remember my panic at the empty bed and my fear that Anna was going to tell me that Mum was dead. It seems absolutely ridiculous now but then, in my panic at Mum not being here and my guilt at being late, it seemed perfectly possible.

'I'm sorry,' Anna says, quietly. 'If I implied that something was wrong with your mother.'

I look at the nurse. She's appraising Anna, a serious expression on her face. I think that Anna is somehow getting the blame for my fainting, as if in some way, it's her fault.

'No, I'm the one that should be sorry,' I say. 'It's completely my own fault. I've skipped a few meals, what with worrying about Mum and then I ran up five flights of stairs so it's no wonder I felt light-headed. I'm really sorry to have put you to any trouble.'

It's the truth; I've barely eaten for the last two days. One slice of toast with Will at lunchtime today is all that I've eaten since the night before Mum went into hospital. I've hardly drunk anything either so I'm probably dehydrated, too. It's hardly surprising that I passed out.

And of course, Mum isn't dead, she's simply been moved to a side room. Lack of food, guilt, running up five flights of stairs and near hysteria over a simple bed move caused me to faint. I feel ridiculous and have managed to get the poor student nurse into trouble for absolutely nothing.

The nurse looks slightly placated at my reply and Anna smiles hesitantly at me. I start to sit up and then wince. My elbow hurts and when I try to put any weight on it, it's painful. I think I'm going to have a massive bruise there by tonight.

'You might want to get that checked out,' the nurse says. 'You must have banged it when you fell. You were lucky, considering how hard the floor is.'

'I will.' I struggle and manage to sit upright on the bed. My mouth feels dry and I have the beginnings of a headache.

'Anna will get you a cup of tea.' The nurse turns to leave. 'Just sit quietly for a while and make sure that you get something to eat fairly soon.' She stalks off down the ward and Anna follows while I stay on the bed. I want to go and see Mum but equally, I don't want to get Anna into more trouble. I lay back down on the bed and decide to wait for the tea, another ten minutes won't make any difference because I'm already late. Besides which, I don't know which side room she's been moved to and this hospital is like a maze, so I need to ask Anna. I can hardly go around opening doors and nosing around until I find Mum.

I'm not going to tell Mum what's happened because she'll just worry that I'm not looking after myself properly, which realistically, I haven't been. I need to eat properly and stay fit and well because I can hardly look after her when she gets home if I'm starving myself.

Anna appears with a cup of tea and places it on the bed table and swings it over the bed. I thank her and then haul myself upright and push the pillows against the headboard so that I can sit up. The plastic cover squeaks as I move and sticks to the back of my legs.

'You can just leave the cup there when you're finished.' Anna turns to leave.

'Thank you,' I say. 'And I'm sorry if I got you into trouble.'

'No, no, you didn't. That's just Sister Andrews way. She's a sweetheart really.'

She didn't look like a sweetheart, she looked like a bully to me but of course I don't say this but simply smile.

'Can you tell me which room my mum's been moved to?'

'Oh, yes, of course. Room twelve, straight out of the door, turn left and it's the third door along.'

'Thank you.'

Anna smiles and walks down the ward towards the door and I pick up my tea and sip it. It's boiling hot and tasteless but I can hardly complain. I blow on it in an attempt to cool it down but realistically, I have no choice but to wait. I lay my head back and close my eyes for a moment and a memory from last night pops into my mind. I see Will's face above mine, his eyes glistening in the moonlight that's coming through the lounge window. It was so wonderful and romantic and

I'm thankful that Will is such a thoughtful lover. I had a fear of seeming awkward and having no idea what to do but somehow, with Will, everything came naturally. I allow myself a few minutes to remember our night together and when I open my eyes again, I'm disorientated and not sure if I've been asleep. I sit up and take a sip of the tea; it's stone cold. I look at my watch to see that it's a quarter-past-four. I must have fallen asleep because I would only have been out for a matter of minutes when I fainted.

I drink down the tea, even though it's cold, and then push the bed tray away and swing my legs off the bed and stand up. I feel better. I still have a headache but nothing that a couple of paracetamols won't fix. I pick up the holdall with all of Mum's bits and pieces in and head down the ward. Once outside, I turn left and walk down the corridor, counting the doors as I go. I'm going to have to lie to Mum about why I'm so late and I'm still trying desperately to think of something as I arrive outside room number twelve. There's also the letter to consider, do I ask her today or leave it and ask her when she's home? I'd planned to wait until she gets home but am I just putting it off because I'm afraid? Despite being unsure about what to do, I fix a big smile on my face because I'm looking forward to seeing her and equally, I don't want her to see me as anything but happy because she'll only fret. I push open the door to her room and my smile slips as I take in the scene before me.

Dylan is sitting in a chair at the side of the bed.

'Hello,' I manage.

Hello, darling,' Mum smiles but she looks pale to me, and not her usual perky self.

'Hi Layla.' Dylan makes no secret of the fact that he's looking me up and down and I choke down the anger that's building in me. What the hell is he doing here?

'I just popped in to see how your mum is,' he says, reading my mind. 'See if there is anything I can do to help.'

'It's all under control,' I say, tight-lipped. I walk over and hug Mum and then walk over to the corner and pull one of the chairs that are sitting against the wall to the opposite side of the bed to Dylan. 'I visit every day so I can bring Mum anything she needs.'

'Of course.' He smirks. 'Although we were starting to think you weren't coming, weren't we, Debs?'

I stare across the bed at him and I want to punch him; he shouldn't even be here and he definitely shouldn't be saying something like that. I open my mouth to explain and then close it again. No way am I explaining myself to him, I'll tell Mum when he's gone because he must have been here for a while so he'll be going soon.

But he doesn't.

He sits there while I take out Mum's dirty washing from the little cupboard at the side of the bed and replace it with clean clothes. He watches whilst I exchange her quilted dressing gown for the thin cotton wrap.

'So, Mum,' I ask, settling down in the chair again. 'Why did they move you to this room?'

Mum shrugs. 'I don't really know. They discharged the patient out of this room and then moved me down here. I don't mind though, because some of the other patients do snore a bit.'

Dylan is paying close attention to every word and I don't feel that I can talk freely in front of him. I can't talk to her properly with him sitting there. Why is he here? It's not as if he's a personal friend of hers, he just happens to attend her art class.

'And how are you feeling, Mum?'

'I'm fine, just tired.'

She doesn't look as well as she did yesterday, she looks flushed and slightly sweaty. I make a mental note to ask the nurse in charge a few questions on my way out.

'You should go into work tomorrow,' Mum says. 'Don't take any more time off.'

'Well, if they discharge you tomorrow, I'll be picking you up so I'll have to take another day off.' I say. 'Anyway, Mum, I've told you, don't worry because they've been very understanding about me taking time off even though I haven't been there for long.'

'Very understanding,' Dylan chips in. 'You'll only worked, what, one week?' He laughs and again I have the urge to hit him. GO, I mentally urge him, take the hint and leave me and Mum alone.

'But if I'm not coming home tomorrow it'll take your mind off things and stop you worrying,' Mum persists.

'I'm fine, Mum, you honestly don't need to worry.'

'Yes, no need to worry, Debs,' Dylan says, with a smirk. 'I'll look out for Layla, keep an eye on her for you.'

I glare at him; how dare he speak about me as if I'm a child. I'm saved from replying when a nurse bustles into the room.

'Time for your obvs, Ms Trevellyn,' she says, looking pointedly at Dylan and I, which I take it means that we have to vacate the room.

'We'll wait outside if that's okay,' I say. She nods and smiles and I walk out of the room, Dylan close behind me.

The door clangs shut and I stand against the wall and Dylan stands next to me. I realise that he intends staying here until the nurse has finished and will then go back in to see Mum.

'Shouldn't you be looking after the shop?' I ask. 'Or is your dad working there today? I thought you told me that you never get any time off.'

'Dad hardly works at all, now, spends most of his time on the golf course. And I've got an apprentice working for me so I don't have to do so many hours. Have to leave him on his own now and then so he can get used to it. It's called man management, Layla.'

I stare ahead and don't look at him. What a pompous prick, anyone would think that he was fifty, not twenty-four. And he's so stupid that he thinks it's acceptable to stay here and encroach on mine and Mum's visit. He's obviously not going to leave. How can he be so thick-skinned and stupid?

'The thing is, Dylan,' I say, as calmy as I can. 'I really want to visit Mum on her own, just her and me. Because you've already been here for quite a while, haven't you?'

'You mean you want me to go?' he asks.

'If you don't mind.'

He taps his lip with his finger and turns and stares at me as he thinks about what I've asked.

'At least you're a bit politer this time, not like when you told me to F off.'

I suddenly want to laugh. He's such a stuffed shirt that he can't even bring himself to swear. He's an old-aged-pensioner in a twenty-four-year-olds body.

'Something funny about that?' he asks, and I realise that I must have been smiling.

'Absolutely nothing,' I say. 'But I would rather you went so I can visit Mum on my own.'

'I bet you would.' He steps away from the wall and stands in front of me. 'Because you wouldn't want her to know what you've been up to, would you?'

'Sorry?'

'You and that neighbour of yours. You wouldn't want Debs to know about that, would you?'

How could he know?

When he saw me talking to Will the day he cycled to see Mum, he must have put two and two together. He's just guessing, there's no way he could know. I've just convinced myself of this when his next words dispel any doubt.

'A married man, too. You should be ashamed of yourself, flaunting yourself like that.'

I feel colour flood my face, was he watching us through the lounge window? Was the shadow that I thought I saw as I drew the curtains, him? Did he see everything that Will and I did? I feel suddenly sick at the thought of the unwitting floor show that we put on for him as we explored each other's bodies. I stay silent, it's best I say nothing and hopefully, he'll go.

Dylan suddenly turns and paces to the end of the corridor and I'm elated, thinking that he's leaving, until he stops and stands still in front of the window. He stands looking out over the car park before suddenly turning around and stomping back towards me. In seconds he's looming over me and I flinch involuntarily as he leans in close to me, his face inches from mine. I find myself unable to look away as he spits his next words at me.

'I thought you were different, Layla, but you're just like all the rest. You're a disgusting slut.'

CHAPTER ELEVEN

Jack and are putting sachets of dog food on the shelves and Jack is not happy. Luckily, the pet food section is located at the far end of the store and for the moment we're alone and out of sight of Ron, the supervisor. Although Jack is obviously disgruntled and pissed off, I can't help feeling pleased that I have a job and that I've met him. He sees me as a proper friend even though we haven't known each other for very long and I think of him the same way. It's so nice to have a friend to talk to and Jack is good company, even when he's pissed off. Coming to work has kept my mind from constantly looping around Mum's illness, the letter and Will. I spoke to the nurse when visiting time ended and she said that Mum's infection isn't responding very well so they're going to put her on intravenous antibiotics. She'll have to stay in hospital for a bit longer but the nurse assured me that there's absolutely nothing to worry about. It's very common after surgery and Mum will be fine once the antibiotics have kicked in. Being with Jack helps me to think about other things and not keep dwelling on the worst case scenario of everything.

'What's happened now?' I ask, although he's already filled me in on most of what I missed on Wednesday.

'Just more of the same. That Ron's a piece of shit and a homophobe. He's got it in for me, keeps picking on me and finding fault with everything I do and you wouldn't believe the stuff he says to me. I quite liked working here until we got put on his section. Would have been so much better if we could have stayed with the lifer they put us with first.'

When I came back to work yesterday, I found that I'd been moved, along with Jack, onto Ron's section. Jack had already endured a day of Ron and he was beyond disgusted by him. Ron is tall, thin, miserable and old. If there are other people in earshot, he treats Jack in the same way as he treats me – blunt and to the point, foul-mouthed and with no niceties – but when no one is watching him, he'll sidle up to Jack and make snipes about being gay and a *nancy boy*, *taking it up the arse* and other totally vile comments.

'You should report him to the manager,' I say, not for the first time. 'And the police, because that's hate speech and there's a law against that.

No way should he be getting away with it.'

'Yeah, but he only does it when no one else is around, or says it so quietly that only I can hear. I don't have any witnesses.'

'You don't need witnesses,' I insist. 'They'll listen to you because there's no way they'll tolerate that sort of behaviour from one of their staff. And if he's saying it to you, I'm sure you can't be the only one he's doing it to. He'll be giving others the same treatment and why should he be allowed to treat people like it?'

Jack doesn't answer but continues practically throwing the sachets onto the shelf.

'I could say I heard him saying stuff to you, I could be a witness,' I say, surprising myself at my willingness to lie. But it would be a white lie and a totally justified one.

Jack turns to me in surprise. 'Thanks, mate, that means a lot, that you'd do that for me but no, I'm not going to report him. I can't be arsed with all the fuss and I'll end up getting moved onto another section and having to work with someone else while they investigate him. We'll get split up and I'll be stuck with a lifer and why should I suffer because of him, why should him being such a bastard impact my life?' He slams his fist onto the shelf in frustration. 'He wants to be careful, that fucking Ron,' he mutters. 'Because I *know* people.'

I can't help laughing and Jack turns and looks at me.

'I'm not joking, I do,' he says, his face serious. 'Or

at least Marcus does.'

Marcus is Jack's boyfriend. He's quite a lot older than Jack – though not as big an age difference as Will and I, and from what Jack's told me about him, not to be messed with.

'Are you going to get a contract out on Ron?' I say it with a smile so Jack knows that I'm joking but he doesn't give me his trademark grin. 'Get him taken out, make him disappear?' I add, because the conversation suddenly seems to be getting way too serious and I need to lighten the mood.

'Maybe,' Jack says, his expression grim. 'Marcus can arrange for someone to teach him a lesson, make him realise that he can't go around insulting people and fucking bullying them.'

I hear the sound of footsteps and glance towards the end of the aisle to see Ron clomping towards us. Jack and I immediately fall silent and concentrate on stacking the shelves and pretending that we haven't seen him.

'Not done, yet?' Ron barks, as he draws closer.

I don't answer and nor does Jack because I don't think it was an actual question.

'Thought you'd be done by now. There's a whole pallet of tinned dog food to go out yet so you'd better get a fucking move on. Going to have to split you two up if you can't shut your fucking gobs and speed it up a bit.' Ron folds his arms and stands, legs akimbo, and watches us. I don't want to give him the satisfaction of squirming under his scrutiny but it takes a huge effort, because he makes my skin crawl. After several moments, he moves a few steps until he's on the other side of Jack and then steps forward until he's standing really close to him. I see him lean down and mutter something before turning on his heel and marching off with a nasty smirk on his face.

'Definitely talking to Marcus about him,' Jack says, quietly, when Ron's gone. 'Not going to tolerate that wanker anymore.'

'What did he say?' I ask.

'Usual shit. Hope he enjoyed it because it's the last time he's getting away with it.'

We continue loading the sachets onto the shelves and I wonder why there are such people as Ron, and Dylan, in the world. Why do they think they have a right to say whatever they want to people who are nothing to do with them? Why is Ron so hateful to Jack when Jack has done nothing to him? I don't understand any of it. Why does Dylan think that he can say whatever he likes to me? I know that he asked me out but that doesn't give him any right to comment on my life. I've told him I'm not interested so why doesn't he just leave me alone?

'Anyway, enough about me,' Jack says. 'You don't want to listen to my going on. How's your Mum?'

'She's okay,' I say. 'She's going to have to stay in a bit longer because of the infection but they've assured me she'll be fine.'

'Better to keep her in than discharge her too early.'

'That's what I thought,' I say. At least that's what I keep telling myself in an attempt to stop my mind from going down a catastrophic rabbit hole where the infection worsens and Mum ends up in a coma. I could give classes on worst-case scenarios with an imagination like mine. I've also confided in Jack about Will; not everything, obviously, not actual *details,* but he does know how I feel about him.

And that he's married.

I thought about lying or just not mentioning that Will was married because I didn't want Jack to think badly of me. But as well as being wrong, lying is difficult, because where does it end? And I think Jack would've guessed anyway. He didn't judge me, just said that marriage was outdated and that he didn't actually believe in it anyway, because it's like a life-sentence. He said that he and Marcus weren't exclusive, that they could see someone else if they wanted to. He didn't really get why people tied themselves to one person for the rest of their lives. His outlook is that life's a very long time to stay with one person forever. I sort of agreed with him but it did get me thinking that if you've met the right person, why wouldn't you want to stay with them? I can't ever imagine not loving Will, he's perfect and I'll always want to be with him. He's the one. I can't actually bear the thought of Will with Lucinda and I try very hard not to think about it. He's only with her because she's ill but once she's better he can leave her and be with me. He's loyal, which is a good thing to be but bad in this instance because he won't abandon her while she's ill. The thought of Will having sex with Lucinda makes my insides twist painfully and I catch my breath at the thought of it; I can't stand it.

'You okay?' Jack asks. 'You look really pale.'

'Just thinking about Mum,' I lie, then immediately feel bad for lying in case fate pays me back and the infection turns into something worse. I mentally shake away the fear.

'She'll be fine, from what you've told me,' Jack reassures me and I feel even worse for lying. Yesterday I told him all about my disastrous hospital visit and it made me feel so much better, sharing it with him. When I told him about my fainting, he laughed and said I really ought to look after myself better. Like me, he finds it incredible that Dylan had the cheek to visit Mum and stay at her bedside once I'd arrived.

'Do you think that dork will visit your mum again?' he asks.

'No,' I say. 'I think he's got the message now.'

Mum and I had a lovely visit after Dylan had gone, although I didn't ask her about the letter. I didn't want to stress her out when she's stuck in there and, despite her saying the opposite, I know she doesn't feel very well.

'You been out with this Dylan or something?' Jack asks. 'Shagged him?'

'Definitely not.' I shudder and Jack laughs. 'Although he has asked me out but there's no way

I'd go out with him, he's completely sexless and boring.' I feel grown up and clever when I say it, as if I get asked out every week and have my pick of men.

'If he turns up again, you should lay it on the line, tell him to do one.'

'I already have,' I say. 'Told him I'd never go out with him and to fuck off but he still came back for more and that was before he gate crashed at the hospital.'

Jack blows his cheeks out and shakes his head. When I told him what happened once Mum was taken for her scan, he found it incredible. The way that Dylan leaned in close to me and almost spat in my face when he spoke. I didn't tell Jack that for a moment I almost felt afraid of him; afraid of tall, skinny, Dylan who couldn't fight his way out of a paper bag. And then, much like Jack, anger got the better of me at the things he said and I stared at Dylan's face, inches from mine and I thought, how dare you, how dare you judge me as if you have anything to do with my life. I'm not quite sure what happened, I think I must have pushed him to get his face away from mine because the next thing I knew, Dylan went sprawling across the corridor floor and ended up on his backside. I stood and watched as he scrambled to his feet and maybe I was slightly hysterical with his accusation but I started laughing at him and I couldn't stop. He looked up at me and his face was a picture of shock and bemusement. I shouted at him that *he* was the disgusting one for snooping around my cottage and watching me through the window. He looked at me and said that he didn't know what I was talking about, so maybe he didn't see us. Or maybe he was lying. It could be that the day that he cycled down the lane and saw me talking to Will, he somehow guessed. I don't know, but telling him to F off, as he put it, probably confirmed to Dylan that I was angry at him for interrupting us. Once he got himself up off the floor he left, and when the nurse came out and I went back in to see Mum and she asked where he was, I told her that he had to get back to the shop.

As Jack and I resumed our shelf-stacking, taking our time putting out the sachets, we talked and laughed about Dylan and Ron, and felt better for it. There was no one near us to hear what we were saying and after a while, Jack said that he's definitely going to get Marcus to *sort Ron out* or even make him *disappear*. He says if I wanted, he could get Dylan *disappeared* too and we laughed some more. I said that he'd have to find him first, because I'm sure that at the first sign of trouble Dylan would run away and hide somewhere that he'd never be found. And then Jack became all serious and he said, *mate, my Marcus is good at what he does. He can find people, no matter where they run to.* And when he said that, for some reason, and I have no idea why, I felt a little bit afraid.

* * *

In the afternoon I sneak off to the goods bay where we keep all of the goods to go out on the shelves and hide behind a tall cage of bread to ring Mum. She takes a while to answer and I think I might have woken her up. She says that she's not feeling great and that the intravenous antibiotics are upsetting her stomach. Apparently, this is a well-known side-effect for that particular antibiotic and they've now given her an anti-sickness drug to combat it. She says she doesn't really feel up to a visit tonight if I don't mind and when I sound disappointed, she says it will be too much for me after working all day, anyway. I don't argue with her because I can tell by her voice that she's tired so I tell her to take it easy and promise to visit her tomorrow.

I could have asked Ron if it was okay to phone her and he wouldn't have been able to say no, but I didn't want to ask. He's not very pleasant to talk to and knowing how he treats Jack; I don't want to speak to him unless I have to. I can't help wondering if Jack's boyfriend Marcus really is as bad as he says, if something bad will happen to Ron or if it's all just wishful thinking.

I slip my phone back into my pocket and peek out from the bread cage to make sure the coast is clear and then head towards the double doors that lead back into the supermarket. I have only half-an-hour until I finish work and Jack and I are now putting out tinned dog food onto the shelves. It's a laborious process as we have to take off all of the tins that are already on the shelf and put them back on in front of the new tins. This is so that those with the oldest sell by date get sold first but when I look at the dates, they're both the same. I would tell Ron this, but I know it would make no difference and that he already knows. He likes to make things as difficult as possible and for us to waste our time doing pointless tasks.

The double doors are made of soft plastic and they swish along the floor as I push them open and exit into the bakery section. I walk along by the sliced bread and am heading towards the pet section when I stop dead in my tracks. Straight ahead of me, browsing the French sticks and uncut loaves, are Will and Lucinda. They're standing in front of the baguettes and Lucinda is holding one in her hand and looking at Will. She's wearing a navy suit with heels and her hair is pinned up so I guess she's picked Will up on her way back from London and come straight here. As always, she looks immaculate, her hair glossy, her make-up perfect. I watch them for a moment and try to quell the feeling that bubbles up in me as I watch them.

Absolute longing for Will, a physical ache to be in his arms, to be with him.

And hatred for Lucinda, for her pathetic refusal to let him go.

I intend to turn and walk back the way that I came but it's too late, Lucinda has seen me and she puts her hand up in a wave. Will turns as he sees her acknowledge me and his face betrays his shock at seeing me. I can't turn now because it would look obvious; I have to continue down the aisle and past them. I carry on walking and wish that I were wearing anything but the hideous Chiverson's uniform and the flat, black shoes.

'Hi!' Lucinda says, with a smile. 'Will and I were just talking about you.'

'Were you?' I ask, accusingly. I've barely spoken to Lucinda apart from *hello* and I can't understand why she's suddenly being so friendly. Normally if she can avoid acknowledging me, she does. Or I *think* she does; maybe all of the times I think she's been ignoring me, she hasn't actually seen me. Or maybe it's part of her illness, over-friendly one minute, ice-cold the next. And why have they been talking about me? The sudden, irrational thought strikes me that he's told her all about me and asked for her forgiveness.

'Yes, we were wondering how your mother is.'

She's looking at me, waiting for an answer. I feel jealousy at the way she says *we;* as if she and Will are actually together, as if they have a proper marriage and he's not forced to stay with her.

'She's still in hospital,' I snap. I don't look at her but at Will. He looks uncomfortable and can't meet my eyes. 'They're keeping her in for a bit longer.'

Lucinda puts her hand on my arm. 'And if there's anything we can do to help, just let us know.'

I stare down at her arm. *We*, she keeps saying *we*, *us*. How can she be so selfish, hanging onto him when he doesn't want her, she must know that he's only staying with her out of pity. She should get some pride. If she only knew how Will and I have spent every single minute together while she's been away. Every second that I haven't been at the hospital or at work, I've been with Will, in my bed, in his arms. If only she knew the things we've been doing, that we can't get enough of each other. He's obsessed with me and thinks about me all of the time and she's still clinging onto him like a limpet. It's pathetic. After a moment she takes her hand off my arm and I look at and wonder if she knows how much I hate her.

'Well,' Will says. 'We must let Layla get back to work, Lucy.'

He still won't look at me.

'Of course. Please give your mother our best wishes, Layla.' Lucinda smiles at me and I stare back at her impassively. Somehow, I manage to mutter *thanks* and walk away from them both, my stomach churning. As I make my way through the aisle, all that's going through my mind is how Marcus can *disappear* people and how perfect it would be if Lucinda were to disappear. And then I realise what I'm thinking and I begin to wonder if this is how it starts; that I might actually be going mad.

CHAPTER TWELVE

I wait underneath the oak tree at the end of the lane and shiver. I'm wearing only a thin cotton dress which is fine for a June day but not the middle of the night. The night has turned cold and there's a hint of rain in the air. Where is Will? It's gone one o'clock and he should be here by now. I messaged him when I got home from work and he took ages to reply.

I was the one who suggested we meet, not him. I wanted him to come to the cottage but he said no, it was too risky with Lucinda being at home. I don't think it's risky at all; surely it's riskier meeting out in the open?

I can't help fearing that he doesn't want to come to the cottage because he wants to end things with me. What if he's going off me? What if he doesn't want me anymore? I tell myself I'm being ridiculous, that he couldn't keep away from me whilst Lucinda was away and that we've spent every available minute together. Will begged me to take time off from Chiverson's he was so desperate to spend every second with me. And every day since Will came back from London, if I haven't been at work or visiting Mum, we've been together and it's been wonderful, like living together. I need to stop overreacting because he's probably just overslept. It's not as if he can set the alarm, is it?

An owl hoots and I jump. I try not to feel spooked at being out alone when it's pitch black, but I can't help it because there's no moon at all tonight and the only light is the glimmer from my phone screen. I hear the sound of footsteps, so loud in the silence of the night, coming down the lane. I peer into the darkness but can't see a thing.

'It's me.' I hear Will whisper as he draws nearer. I turn on my phone torch and shine it down at the ground so he can see where I am. When he reaches me, I step towards him and fling my arms around him and hold him tightly. He doesn't return my embrace. After a moment he takes hold of my arms and pushes me backwards, behind the tree, out of sight.

'What's wrong?' I wrap my arms around his waist and hold him tightly, resting my head on his chest, willing him to embrace me. He sighs and I fight down the feeling of panic that he doesn't want me anymore. He's had his fill of me and *she's* back now and maybe she's being extra nice to him.

Maybe he's had sex with her.

'Layla, you made it very awkward for me this afternoon.'

'Did I?' I whisper. He's had sex with her, I know he has. She's seduced him.

'Yes, you did. You were very rude to Lucinda and wouldn't even look at her but couldn't take your eyes off me.'

'Was I?' I knew I was rude to her but I didn't realise I was staring at Will.

'You were. I didn't know where to look, you couldn't have been any more obvious if you'd tried. Now Lucinda has got it into her head that you have a crush on me and I had to pretend to agree with her and laugh about it. Can you imagine how that made me feel?'

'I'm sorry,' I whisper. They were laughing at me as if I'm a silly little schoolgirl. *She* was laughing at me. I hate her.

He sighs and then wraps his arms around me and strokes my back.

'No, I'm sorry, I'm expecting too much of you. You're so young and I've put you in this terrible situation and I'm expecting you to behave as if this is all perfectly normal. I should never have started this, you deserve better. I'm being selfish. I should have kept my feelings about you to myself. I should have left you alone.'

'Don't say that, please.'

'It's not fair on you. I'm a married man, Layla, and I'm behaving like an absolute bastard.'

'No, you're not,' I protest. 'You've made me so happy, please don't say that, we're so good together. I was jealous and I behaved like a stupid spoilt brat when I saw you together. I couldn't bear to look at her I was so jealous.'

'You've don't need to be jealous.'

'I can't help it,' I whisper, slipping my hand underneath his shirt to feel the warm of his skin. 'Because she's with you in your bed and I'm not. The thought of you touching her instead of me makes me feel sick.'

I look up at him and our lips find each other's in the darkness and as we breathe each other in, I feel his hand slowly travel up my leg and underneath my dress.

'You're not wearing any underwear.' He can't hide the delight from his voice.

'I'm not,' I whisper, as I feel the warmth of his fingers on my skin. 'We could go back to the cottage now, sneak in the back way, no one will see us.'

Will presses his body into mine and I feel the rough bark of the oak tree pushing into my back through the thin material of my dress.

'Later,' he says, with a groan, as he lifts my dress up. 'We'll go there later.'

And I know then that everything is going to be alright.

* * *

Before I leave for the hospital, I make myself some scrambled eggs on toast – no more fainting for me – and I wonder if Mum will be coming home today. If she's still on the intravenous drip she won't be able to and I try not to get my hopes up. I force down the scrambled eggs and a cup of tea but I feel as if I'm eating cardboard. After I've loaded the dishwasher, I wander through to the lounge and stare out of the window. Lucinda's car is parked outside their cottage and I look up at their bedroom window to see that their curtains are still closed. It's only eight o'clock and it's a Saturday so why would they be up this early? Lots of people have a lie in at the weekend. I try to block the vision of Will lying in bed with Lucinda but I can't help wondering if he sleeps naked as he does with me. The thought of him with Lucinda makes me feel physically sick with jealousy and I clench my fists and close my eyes and try to stop my mind from creating pictures of them making love. Of course they won't be, I tell myself; why would he when we had our fill of each other last night in the field? Will's need for me was so urgent that he couldn't wait to come back here.

We never did make it back here.

I never knew I could feel like this; I may have only known Will for a matter of weeks but I know it's true love; when it's true love, you just know. Loving Will is the most wonderful feeling in the world but the flip side of that is a jealousy of Lucinda which is almost more than I can bear. I feel such rage when I think of Lucinda, rage that she won't let Will go when he obviously doesn't love her.

Would I cling onto him if he stopped loving me?

I dismiss the thought; Will loves me, even if he hasn't actually said the words. He's obsessed with me; he wants to spend every minute possible with me. I think that he's wary of telling me that he loves me because Lucinda is still here, like a dark cloud hanging over us. Why won't she do the decent thing and leave him alone?

Determined not to dwell, I turn from the window and leave the lounge and go upstairs and into the bathroom. There's no point moping around, Will and I will see other tonight and although it's not ideal, at least we can be together for a few hours. I've persuaded him to come here; I'll leave the back door open and he can come straight up to my room. Maybe he'll fall asleep with me in his arms and Lucinda will find out about us and she'll let him go, because what's the point of trying to keep someone who doesn't love you?

I know it's a fantasy and that it won't happen but I can't help my wishful dreaming. When Lucinda leaves for London on Monday we'll be free to see each other whenever we like while she's away, although of course we'll have to keep our secret from Mum.

I strip my clothes off and climb into the shower and while I wash my hair I wonder when Mum will be allowed home. Once she's off the drip there'll be no reason to keep her in. I feel bad for not telling her about Will but I can't, yet. Mum wouldn't be happy about it because of Lucinda and I know she'd be disappointed in me. Even the fact that Lucinda is using emotional blackmail to hang onto Will wouldn't sway Mum; she believes that marriage is forever.

I climb out of the shower and dry myself and wrap a towel around my head and walk across the landing and into my bedroom. I pull the corner of the curtain aside and look out onto the street to see Lucinda coming out of the front door of the cottage. She's dressed for running; shiny black sports leggings with bright pink stripes with a matching top and white trainers. Her hair is tied up in a pony-tail and she looks different without her usual face full of make-up. Younger and fresher and not so severe. I watch as she runs up the lane, past our tree, the tall oak where Will and I always meet. She runs past the field and straight on to where the lane turns into a road. She's running on the side of the road with the traffic coming towards her but this road is quiet, there are very few cars that drive along here although once she hits the crossroad it'll be a different story if she takes the route into Wellerton.

I quickly pull a dress over my head, slip my feet into my flip-flops and run downstairs. Benny looks up at me from his basket and I go over to him and pat him on the head.

'Won't be long, boy. I'll give you your breakfast

when I get back.'

I slip out of the back door and walk quickly across the road and through the gate to Will's front garden. I don't knock at the front door but slip down the side path of the cottage and into the back garden. I try the door handle of the back door and am thrilled to find that it's open. When I open the door and step into the kitchen, the house is silent, Will must still be in bed. I quickly walk through the kitchen, noting how different it is to when Mrs Patterson lived here. Instead of the old dark furniture there is a huge light oak dresser with a matching table and chairs that makes the room feel modern and airy. Even though Will hasn't yet decorated, the walls have been plastered in places in readiness and the old, gloomy pictures are gone from the walls. This could be our home, I think, as I slip my flip-flops off and holding them in my hand, run lightly up the stairs.

I reach the landing and there's silence, the bathroom door is open and Will's not in there. I walk along the landing to their bedroom and the door is ajar and when I push it fully open, I see the mound of Will's body underneath the duvet. His mop of hair is poking out from the top and I feel a rush of love for him. He has his back to me and doesn't even know that I'm here and I feel a thrill of excitement for surprising him. I silently pull my dress over my head and throw it onto the floor, lift up the duvet and climb into bed behind him. I slip my arms around his waist and press myself into his back, stroking the calf of his leg with my toes. He murmurs something that I don't catch and after a moment, turns around to face me, slipping his arms around me. He slowly rubs my back for a moment and then opens his eyes.

'Fuck!' He stares at me in shock. 'What are you doing here?'

'I thought I'd surprise you.' I smile.

Will stares at me for a moment and then throws the duvet off himself and leaps out of bed. He pulls the corner of the curtain away from the window and peers outside.

'You have to go,' he says, dropping the curtain and turning to me. 'NOW.'

I stare up at him.

'It's fine,' I say. 'She's gone for a run, come back to bed.' I pat the mattress. 'It's nice and warm and we should make the most of it.'

'No.' Will walks around the bed and picks my dress up from the floor. 'You have to go; she could be back any minute.'

I sit up. This isn't how I thought it would be, I thought Will would be delighted by my surprise.

'Layla,' Will hisses at me. 'Put this on and go. What the fuck where you thinking?'

He sounds angry and I scramble out of bed and pull my dress over my head. I reach out to Will but he avoids my arms and pushes me towards the bedroom door and hustles me along the landing and down the stairs.

'Hurry up, before she comes back and catches

us,' he says, as we hurry down the stairs.

'Maybe she needs to catch us.' We've reached the kitchen and I say the words without thinking. Or maybe I am thinking; maybe that's why I've done this. Maybe I want Lucinda to find out.

'What the fuck, Layla?' Will looks at me in shock and I reach towards him to put my arms around him but he takes hold of my arms and pushes me away.

'Just go, Layla. GO.' His eyes are blazing with anger.

'But…'

He marches over to the back door and pulls it open and stands there, naked, waiting for me to leave. It's almost laughable but I want to cry because it's all gone so wrong. I walk towards him and start to speak but he takes hold of my arm and pushes me through the doorway.

'Go home, Layla,' he says, as I step into the garden. 'And fucking grow up.'

* * *

'I feel much better, Layla.' Mum looks better, not so pale, but the drip is still in her arm. 'They've changed the antibiotics now,' she says, following the direction of my gaze. 'These ones don't make me feel sick and I should be out of here in a couple of days.

'So is the wound healing?' I ask.

'As far as I know, darling. I haven't actually

managed to get a look at it but it's starting to itch, now, which is apparently a good sign.'

'That's good,' I agree.

'I just wish.' Mum takes my hand and holds it. 'That I'd confided in you in the first place. I haven't given you enough credit, you're no longer a little girl but a grown up, responsible woman and I'm sorry that I haven't treated you that way.'

I smile but her words sting, because Will's parting words of *grow up*, come back to me. My stupid idea to surprise him turned into disaster and I wish that I'd never gone over there. I haven't heard from him since, which isn't unusual because we don't constantly text each other because Will can't when *she's* with him, but I can't help thinking that he's going off me. When I slipped into bed and put my arms around him, he turned and embraced me but he didn't know it was me, did he?

He must have thought I was Lucinda.

And he was naked. He sleeps with her *naked*.

'They're talking about letting me out on Tuesday,' Mum says. 'I can get back home and we can get back to normal, can't we? I'm so looking forward to sleeping in my own bed again.'

Mum's been in hospital for less than a week but it feels as if my life has completely changed in that time.

I've completely changed.

So next week Mum will be home and then I can ask her about the letter and whether it's a mistake, and why she opened it. It's a mistake, I know it, because no way can I believe that Mum has lied to me for all of my life, it's just not possible. She's not a liar.

Not like me.

But there's that doubt; what if she has lied?

I have to face the possibility that for reasons unknown to me, Mum has been lying to me for all of my life and if this is so, then that can only mean one thing.

My birth mother is out there looking for me.

CHAPTER THIRTEEN

By the time Monday morning dawns, I'm in absolute despair.

Will never replied to my increasingly desperate *WhatsApp* messages over the weekend and I can see that he never even read the last three that I sent. Since Saturday I've veered between heartbreak that Will and I are over and rage at Lucinda for hanging onto him when he clearly doesn't love her.

And rage at my own stupidity for going to see him on Saturday.

I've hardly slept all night, again, and the first thing I do when I get out of bed is to look out of the bedroom window to see if Lucinda's car is there. I'm praying that she's going to London to work today; she normally does but I have a fear that she's going to stay home and I'll have no opportunity at all to see Will. When I see her coming out of their cottage dragging her wheelie suitcase behind her at just gone eight o'clock, I'm elated.

Until I remember Will's anger at me and the way he pushed me down the stairs and practically threw me out of the house. It felt, in that moment, as if he hated me.

I watch as Lucinda's car zooms up the lane and onto the main road. Satisfied that she's actually gone, I open the window to let some fresh air in and then go to the bathroom. As I shower and wash my hair, I argue with myself endlessly over what to do. Yes, I should go over and see him and talk to him about Saturday. Apologise for doing something so risky and stupid. The very minute that I've made the decision, I change my mind and decide that it would be best if I waited for him to contact me because he's ignored my messages, which surely means we're over. By the time I'm dressed and downstairs I'm still in an agony of indecision and am no further forward. I desperately want to see Will but the thought of him angrily rebuffing me and telling me he doesn't want me is more than I can bear.

But part of me still hopes.

I force myself to eat some toast and then set about cleaning and tidying the kitchen. Mum is supposed to be coming home from hospital tomorrow, because they'll be taking the drip out of her arm as long as her blood pressure and temperature are normal and the infection is under control. I want the house to be warm, welcoming and tidy because there's no way I want her attempting to do anything other than rest. She needs to recuperate and take things easy, even though she assures me that she'll be fine. She's insisting that I go to work on Wednesday because she says there's absolutely no need for me to stay home because she's perfectly capable of spending seven hours without me. Besides, she says, it'll give her an opportunity to catch up on all of the telephone calls and messages from her friends that she hasn't felt like replying to. I've told her that I'll go in but she's to ring me the very minute she feels she can't cope. She laughed and said to stop fussing; she says if it hadn't been for the infection, she'd have been home and back to normal already.

If only I hadn't found that stupid letter; I have to ask her about it but it would have been so much better if I'd never found it.

My life seems to be full of *if onlys* at the moment.

Once the kitchen is spick and span, I check the lounge. It looks fine but I flick the duster around to make sure that Mum doesn't get any ideas about housework.

Nine-forty-five.

Benny whines from his basket and I know that he wants his morning walk but I feel frozen with indecision; if I take him out, I'm afraid that I won't be able to stop myself from going to Will's. Once I see him there'll be no going back. I'll have to face the truth that he doesn't want me anymore and then I don't know what I'll do. At least now I have a tiny sliver of hope that I haven't ruined everything, even though realistically, I know that I have.

I sit down next to Benny's basket and he climbs onto my lap. I stroke him and bury my face in his fur and drink in the biscuity smell of him. He snuggles into my arms and I feel a surge of love for him; you've never let me down, have you, Benny, not ever. The day stretches ahead of me and as I'm wondering how I'm going to get through it until I visit Mum at three, there's a tap at the front door. I lift Benny off me, jump up and dash to the door, my heart pounding, praying that it's Will. The disappointment crashes into me like a physical force as I pull open the door to see the postman standing there. He holds out a parcel towards me – regular art supplies for Mum – and I take it from him, barely managing to say *thank you*. After I've closed the door on him, I carry the parcel through to the kitchen, cursing myself yet again for ruining everything with my stupid idea to surprise Will on Saturday. As I put the parcel on the counter top there's another tap at the front door and I trudge back and pull it open, giving the postman my best miserable face.

But it's not the postman, it's Will.

We stare at each other in silence and I can't believe how awful he looks. He's unshaven, pale, and his eyes are red-rimmed and he looks as if he's had as little sleep as I have.

'Will,' I gasp. 'What's wrong?'

'Me,' he says, stepping into the hallway and closing the door behind him. 'I'm wrong. I'm a complete fucking idiot.'

* * *

We lie in each other's arms and the June sunlight streams through the curtains chasing light patterns on the ceiling. I half-sit up and smile and then lean over and kiss Will's chest and he laughs.

'What was that for?' he asks.

'Nothing,' I say. 'Just because.'

'I don't deserve you.' He strokes my hair and I close my eyes and savour the moment. 'I'm so sorry for being such an absolute pig. I wouldn't blame you if you never wanted to see me again after the way I've behaved.'

'Ssh, it doesn't matter now.' I kiss his chest again. 'Let's just forget about it.'

Once Will had closed the front door, he was distraught and close to tears. He said that he'd spent the weekend feeling so bad about the way he'd treated me that he'd decided to end it – not because he didn't care or because I'd done anything wrong, but because I deserve better. The reason he never read my messages was because he couldn't bear to read how upset I was. He'd decided that the best thing for me was to never see him again because then I'd be able to meet someone else, someone who could put me first, someone my own age who'd be able to give me a future. He said that he hadn't slept a wink since he saw me on Saturday morning. When he woke up this morning, he knew that he had to come and tell me in person, instead of taking the coward's way out and ignoring me. And that's what he intended to do, he said, until I opened the door and he saw me.

He knew then that he couldn't.

And he begged me for another chance, even though he has nothing to offer me – because Lucinda had been *difficult* all weekend. I started to cry and he took me in his arms, murmuring how sorry he was and I felt as if a miracle had happened. I wanted to pinch myself to make sure that I wasn't having a wonderful dream.

'What are you thinking about?' Will asks.

'You,' I say.

'I don't deserve you.'

'Will?' I sit up and turn to look down at him. 'When you say Lucinda was being difficult, what do you mean?'

'You don't want to know.' He laughs but can't hide the sadness in his eyes.

'I do. But only if you want to tell me. If it's too private, I understand if you don't feel you should share it with me.'

Will sits up and swings his legs out of bed and stands up. He picks his clothes up from the floor and starts to put them on.

'Will, stop, please, I've upset you, forget I asked.'

I feel panicked and wish that I'd kept my mouth shut and never asked him. Yet again, I've ruined everything.

Will turns to me and puts his hand on my face, stroking my cheek. 'Don't be silly, you'd done nothing wrong. I'm getting up because I'm going to cook you some lunch, I want to look after you. And then I'll tell you about Lucinda.'

'You don't have to.'

'I do. Because you need to know, but not here, in your bed. I don't want her intruding in that way. Come over to the cottage when you're dressed and we'll talk. And eat.'

Will goes downstairs and I get out of bed and go into the bathroom and quickly shower again and get dressed. When I get downstairs and into the kitchen, Benny stares at me reproachfully from his basket and I promise him that I'll take him for a walk later as I leave the cottage. I cross the lane to will's cottage and go around to the back garden and open the back door. Will is standing by the cooker, a frying pan in one hand, his mobile phone in the other.

'Bye,' I hear him say, cheerfully, and as I look at him, he looks so much better than he did when he arrived at my cottage this morning. He's still unshaven but he looks happy, no sign of red, tired eyes or pale skin.

He looks so much better because of *me*.

'Work,' he says, tossing his mobile phone onto the counter top. 'They needed a bit of advice, which is good to know because I want them to miss me a bit so I have a job to go back to.'

'Work on a Saturday?' I ask.

'No rest for the wicked,' he says, with a grin.

I smile and sit down at the table.

'Bacon and eggs?' he asks.

'Please.'

Will puts the pan on the hob and turns it on before using a spatula to take a large blob of butter from the butter dish and drop it into the pan. He then takes a large, brown paper wrapped parcel from the fridge and removes several rashers of bacon from it. He drops the bacon into the frying pan where it immediately starts to sizzle, releasing the irresistible aroma of frying bacon.

'Anything I can do?' I ask.

'You can cut some bread and butter it, if you like.'

I go and stand next to him and cut several slices from the crusty loaf that's sitting on the bread board and then butter them and put them onto plates. I fill the kettle and put it on to boil.

'Tea or coffee?' I ask, realising that I have no idea what Will drinks, or how.

'Tea, milk no sugar.'

'Same as me.' I open several cupboards before finding a shelf full of mugs. I take out two, putting one of them back and changing it when I see it has *Lucy* written on the side of it. I wait until the kettle boils, make the tea and then take them over to the table and sit down. I watch Will as he cooks, the way his hands deftly crack the eggs, the way he turns the bacon without splashing. I could watch him all day. This will be us when Lucinda is gone, living together, making our home together. He dishes up the bacon and eggs onto the plates and brings them over and places them on the table before sitting down.

'Don't know about you but I'm starving,' he says, with a grin. 'It must be all that exercise.'

I blush and tuck into my bacon. I am hungry, despite the fact that I had breakfast this morning, and I clear the plate in no time. When I put my knife and fork down for the final time, I look over to see Will watching me, a smile on his face. Luckily, he's finished too, so I don't look like a complete pig.

'That was delicious,' I say.

'Glad you liked it. I do a mean fry up, even though I say so myself.'

'You do.' I pick up my mug of tea and take a sip.

'So.' Will looks suddenly serious. 'Lucinda.'

'Will, honestly, you don't have to tell me anything. It's private and nothing to do with me.' Even though I'm saying the words, they're a lie; I'm desperate to know. I seem to be lying more and more lately.

Will shakes his head.

'No, I need to tell you. You need to know, if only to make you understand why I behaved in such an unforgiveable way when you came here on Saturday morning.'

I don't say anything. I don't want to be reminded of Will on Saturday morning, that's not the Will that I know. And love. That man was a cold, unpleasant stranger.

Will is looking at me intently.

'Okay,' I say. 'Tell me.'

'Right, okay. As I've told you before, Lucinda's been having problems. Mental health problems, quite severe ones. This weekend was particularly bad, and when she's bad she gets very suspicious and jealous and demands my undivided attention. She doesn't even like me watching television when she's having a bad episode because she thinks I'm not listening to her, she thinks I don't want to talk to her. She gets particularly jealous of any women that are on TV because she's convinced that I'm comparing her to them. She works herself up into a frenzy until she's almost hysterical. It's exhausting.'

Will picks up the plates, gets up from the table and carries them over to the sink.

'It's not your fault, but seeing you in the supermarket on Friday afternoon started it. She got it into her head that I was having an affair with you.'

'Oh God.' My hand flies to my mouth. 'I'm so sorry, Will, I didn't mean to make her think that.' Or did I?

'It's not your fault, don't ever think that. She's the same with anyone who talks to me, she can't help it, it's the illness. Honestly, if it had been your mum, she'd have reacted in exactly the same way.'

'But she seemed so normal when she spoke to me,' I say. 'So friendly, so happy.'

Will shrugs and sits back down in the chair.

'I know, and that makes it worse, in a way, because I feel so alone with it all. She appears perfectly normal when she's at work, too, and they have no idea what she's really like. Fortunately for me, her job is so busy and full on with social events in the evening that she has little time to contact me. Except if she's really bad, and then once she gets back to the hotel at the end of the evening, she'll message me constantly throughout the night. She knows she shouldn't because part of her therapy is not to do it but sometimes, she can't help herself. And even if she's been calm during the week and managed to stop herself, it all builds up and by the time she comes home on Friday she's like an unexploded bomb. That's why this weekend was bad, because she'd stopped herself from constantly badgering me and then, well, we saw you and that was it really. Although if we hadn't seen you it would have been something else that triggered it. God knows how but I managed to persuade her to go out for a run early on Saturday morning, I told her it would do her good and for once, she listened. She'd been screaming at me all night and I honestly just wanted some peace, so I could sleep. And then you came in.'

'Oh, Will, I'm so sorry.'

He rubs his hand over his eyes.

'I was so afraid she'd come back and catch us, that's why I was so horrible to you, because I had to get you out of the house.'

'What would she have done, if she'd come back?'

Will doesn't answer and he won't look at me.

'Is she violent?'

He shrugs and I know that means *yes*.

'How long has she been like this?' I ask.

'Pretty much since we got together, but she never used to be so bad. I thought she'd get better but she's got worse, even with all the counselling and therapy.'

'Maybe you should leave her,' I say.

'I can't.'

'She might never get better; she can't expect you to look after her and put up with her jealousy forever.'

Will looks at me.

'I can't leave her, Layla, because I'm afraid of what she'll do.'

'You can't be responsible for her actions, Will, no matter how ill she might be. She needs help and maybe leaving her is the only way she'll get it. She can't threaten you with suicide to keep you, that's just not fair.'

Will shakes his head.

'No, you don't understand. It's not what she'll do to herself, it's what she'll do to me.'

I look at him in shock and he takes hold of my hand and laces his fingers through mine.

'Or you,' he says, quietly. 'If she finds out about

us.'

CHAPTER FOURTEEN

Mum came home from hospital yesterday and quite honestly; she seems totally back to her old self. She said she feels fine and I'm to stop fussing around her because she's perfectly capable of making herself a cup of tea and a sandwich. She says she has no intention of sitting on her backside all day when she feels so well and today, while I'm at work, she's thinking about going into her studio to try a little painting. She said that where they removed the lump there's a little sore spot but aside from that, she feels no ill effects at all. The infection is totally gone and the antibiotics have done the trick. And I have to agree that she does look well; she has colour in her cheeks and I could tell that she was itching to do things yesterday even though I wouldn't let her. I've told her not to overdo it and to take things easy and made her promise to pace herself. Some of her friends are coming round to visit this morning so that'll make her sit down if nothing else will.

I wondered if she was putting on a brave face, to make sure that I go to work this morning, but I watched her as she bustled round the kitchen and she seems fine. I planned on doing all of the cooking and clearing up but Mum's insisted on helping because she's one of those people who can't keep still. Of course, now that she's back, Will and I have had to go back to meeting in the early hours of the morning. Luckily, Mum sleeps like a log so I slip out the back door at about one o'clock and I'm back by the time she wakes up so she has no idea that I've even been gone.

We haven't been meeting by the tree, though, I've been going to Will's cottage.

In Will and Lucinda's bed.

It wasn't the first time; we spent the night together there on Monday and Tuesday night because Lucinda's away in London, and we know that we're safe. I wasn't sure at first and Will must have seen my hesitation because he told me that he's changed the sheets and there was *nothing of Lucinda in the room*. I was a bit puzzled by that and he confessed then, that he and Lucinda hadn't had sex for a long time, not for months. Apparently, the medication that she takes kills her sex drive but Will said that actually, it's a relief, because he doesn't want to have sex with her anymore. I felt ecstatic when he told me, and any guilt that was still hanging around about my having an affair with a married man dissipated with his words, because it's not really a marriage at all, is it, if they're not having sex? They're more like brother and sister than husband and wife.

I smile and feel a thrill go through me as I remember our love-making in Will's bed, so much more comfortable than the field and no need to rush at all. Will's assertion that love-making in the field would be sordid was soon forgotten when passion overtook us; it just wasn't possible for us to wait until we were in my room. It *was* exciting, and rather romantic too, out in the open air. And if I'm honest, there was always the underlying thrill of the fear of being caught. Although that was extremely unlikely in the middle of the night in the middle of nowhere. I sometimes wonder if we'll ever tire of each other's bodies but I can't imagine that I ever will. I can't imagine ever tiring of Will or not wanting him anymore, because he's perfect.

The power of my feelings for him frightens me sometimes, especially when I think of him with Lucinda. To prevent the unbearable jealousy, I have to keep reminding myself that they're barely married at all. The thought of Lucinda brings hatred bubbling up inside me and although I remind myself that she's ill and can't help it, the uncharitable side of me tells me that she's also not stupid; she must *know* that he doesn't love her anymore. And is she really ill or just super-jealous and trying desperately to hang onto him? I don't feel in control of my feelings when I think of Lucinda.

Maybe that's how *she* feels whenever she sees Will looking at another woman.

I push the thought from my mind as I open my bedroom curtains and stare across the lane at Will's cottage. His curtains are closed and there's no movement, Will must still be asleep and I imagine him lying in bed and I wish the hours away until we meet again tonight. The hours stretch ahead endlessly and with a sigh, I turn from the window and pull on the hideous Chiverson's nylon jacket and then walk across the landing to Mum's bedroom. I slowly open the door to see if she's awake; it's not even seven o'clock yet so if she's still sleeping, I won't wake her, I'll text her later on.

'Morning, darling.' She's sitting up in bed, a book open on her lap.

'Mum, why are you awake so early? You're supposed to be resting.'

'Pah!' Mum snorts. 'I've spent nearly a week lying around in hospital, how can I possibly be tired? Besides, I *am* resting, I'm lying in bed reading.'

I cross the room, lean over the bed and kiss her on the cheek.

'I'm off now, I'll be back about half-three.'

'Enjoy your day.'

I laugh. 'It's Chiverson's, Mum, it's not like I

actually have any interest in it.'

I go down into the kitchen and say hello to Benny before picking up the car keys and letting myself out of the back door. It's far too early to eat breakfast so I'll pick something up in my break. One of the perks of working at Chiverson's is that they have a very good staff cafeteria. As I start the car and reverse off the drive, I think to myself how well everything is working out. It's only a matter of time before Will and I are together properly, despite his fears over what Lucinda might do. She has to face up to the fact that Will doesn't love her anymore, whether she's ill or not. And now Mum is back home and back to normal, she's going to be fine.

So, the nagging voice in my head asks, if that's so why haven't you asked Mum about the letter, yet? If I'm so sure that it's a silly mistake by the tracing agency, why haven't I just got it over with and come right out and asked her about it?

I don't know.

Or maybe I do.

Maybe it's because I'm afraid.

Afraid of what she might tell me.

* * *

Jack and I are unloading a pallet of granulated sugar and putting it on the shelves. The bags are heavy and awkward to hold properly and we're doing it slowly because neither of us wants a bag splitting because it'll make so much mess. Even though we've haven't broken any of the bags, every time we move, we make a crunching sound so there must be a broken bag on the pallet somewhere but we haven't found it yet.

There's a more relaxed atmosphere today and this is because there was no sign of Ron when we arrived this morning. Brenda, one of the *lifers*, told us that he's *off sick* and that she's standing in for him. She's much pleasanter than Ron, although a bit eager to prove that she can do his job. She insists on coming over and checking that we're getting on okay every time she passes the aisle. It seems that every time I'm about to ask Jack if he knows where Ron is, Brenda pops up yet again to ask us if we're okay. It's barely nine o'clock and she must have been over to us four times already.

'We're fine, Bren,' Jack says, as Brenda appears in front of us, yet again. 'Honestly, if we have any probs, we'll be sure to ask.'

Brenda smiles and bobs about, crunching around on the sugar and watching us for a while before skittering along to the next aisle to pester someone else.

'Fuck's sake,' Jack says, rolling his eyes. 'Worse than my mum.'

I laugh and am about to ask him about Ron when a tall, gangly figure loitering at the end of the aisle draws my attention.

Dylan.

He's standing still, as if he's been there for a

while, and he's watching me. He doesn't wave or try to attract my attention, but simply stands, unsmilingly, staring at me.

'Who's the lanky dude?' Jack asks, following my gaze.

'Dylan,' I say, quietly. 'The one who visited Mum in hospital.'

'What?' Jack turns his head and stares at Dylan, who stares right back at him unflinchingly. 'Want me to sort him out, tell him to do one?'

I giggle at Jack's confidence; Dylan may be tall and gangly but he's still twice the size of Jack.

'No, it's okay, just ignore him.' I turn back to the shelf and resume my stacking, determined not to give Dylan the satisfaction of seeing that I'm bothered by him. Jack takes my cue, shrugs his shoulders and does the same and we carry on as if Dylan isn't even there. He'll get tired eventually and go, I tell myself, but I can't help feeling uncomfortable. Dylan no longer seems like the same person that I sat next to in Mum's art class; he's not the eager to please, boring geek that I took him for. This new version of Dylan makes me nervous and I wish he'd just leave me alone.

'So, this is where you've been hiding.'

The voice comes from right behind me and I jump and turn around. Dylan is towering over me and standing far too close to me. I step back but can put hardly any distance between us as the shelf digs into my back. I look up at him and try not to feel threatened.

'I'm not hiding anywhere,' I say, haughtily. 'I work here.'

'Is that right,' Dylan sneers. 'Is this another of your boyfriends?' He looks at the back of Jack and sniggers. 'You're slipping, Layla, he's not much to look at, is he? Although he is more your age.'

'Fuck off, mate,' Jack says, without even turning around from the shelf. 'She's not interested in a lanky streak of piss like you, so do one.'

Dylan bursts out laughing and I glance around, hoping that Brenda will come and check on us like she has for the whole morning so that the situation doesn't escalate out of control. I don't want Jack to lose his job because of Dylan.

'Go away, Dylan,' I say, calmly. 'Who I see is none of your business so just fuck off.'

Dylan stops laughing and suddenly grabs hold of my arm and grips it tightly. He pushes his face close to mine.

'There's no need to use that language to me, you disrespectful slut. You've made a fool of me, Layla,' he hisses. 'And I can't forgive that, so just remember that other people have feelings the next time you decide to behave like a cheating slag and drop your knickers for someone else.'

'I haven't cheated on anyone,' I gabble, as I stare at him in confusion.

'We had something good and you threw it away.' Dylan shakes his head, his expression grim. 'You treated me like dirt. I thought you were a nice girl, Layla, not a whore.'

'And you, mate, are a fucking nutjob,' I hear Jack say as he turns quickly from the shelving, grabs hold of both of Dylan's arms and pulls him off me and pushes him with force down the aisle. I watch in surprise as Dylan trips and then tumbles along the aisle, amazed at Jack, who's obviously much stronger than he looks. Dylan looks dazed at what's happened and is attempting to scramble to his feet when Brenda appears at the end of the aisle. She makes a bee-line for Dylan and puts out her hand in an attempt to help him to his feet but he shrugs her off angrily before standing up. He brushes the sleeves of his jacket down and glares at Jack and I before turning and storming down to the end of the aisle. He stands there for a moment, and with a last glare at us, he's gone.

Brenda stands watching him with a shocked look and when he's gone, she makes her way hurriedly down to us.

'Too much to drink,' Jack says, with a shake of the head as she comes nearer.

'Do you think so?' she asks. 'At this time of the morning?'

'It's all the same to pissheads like that. He was asking where the booze aisle was just before he fell over. Could hardly stand up he was so wasted. Couldn't you smell it on him?'

'No.' Brenda shakes her head. She furrows her brow, a worried look on her face. 'Do you think I should call security, get them to throw him out?'

'Nah,' Jack says. 'Don't waste your time, he'll be

long gone by the time they manage to get down here.'

'I think I should inform them.' Brenda pulls her mobile phone out of her jacket pocket. 'Just in case he hangs around and causes trouble. I don't want to get in trouble for not reporting it.'

'Your choice,' Jack says nonchalantly, as he picks up a bag of sugar and holds it in his hand. 'Old Greg won't be happy that you've got him out of his cubby hole and away from his telly for nothing. Don't worry though, I'll back you up if he slags you off to the manager.'

Brenda stares at the mobile phone in her hand, biting her lip as she considers Jack's words. After a moment she slips the phone back into her pocket.

'I'll just have a wander around, make sure he's gone before I call Greg, don't want to bother him for nothing.' She ambles towards the end of the aisle and Jack winks at me. 'Carry on with what you're doing,' she calls, and with a distracted wave, she's gone.

'I hope he has gone, because if he tells her what you did you could lose your job,' I say.

'Got to prove it,' he says, with a shrug. 'And I've got a witness to say I didn't do it.' He grins at me and I smile back.

'Thanks for getting rid of him, I don't know why he thinks he has a claim on me, I've never even been out with him.'

'He's a nutjob, I've met his sort before. Not right in the head. Imagine what he'd be like if you had gone out with him. Seriously, Layla, you need to do something about him because he thinks you belong to him or something. You need to send him a message he can't ignore.'

I think Jack's right, I don't think Dylan is going to leave me alone and I just know that he's going to cause trouble. I should tell Mum what Dylan is like but I can't, because then I'll have to tell her about Will. Although Dylan might tell Mum himself, he might decide to tell Lucinda, too.

But if he told Lucinda would that really be so bad?

'I could get Marcus to scare him off,' Jack says.

'Oh God, don't say that!' I laugh but Jack doesn't join in, and I realise that he's not joking.

'Has something happened to Ron, Jack? Why isn't he at work?'

'Don't know.' He shrugs and grins.

'So why are you smiling?'

'Layla.' He moves closer to me and drops his voice. 'I honestly don't know because as Marcus says, *ask me no questions and I'll tell you no lies.* It's better that I don't know because then I don't have to lie if the police come calling.'

'But you told Marcus you'd had enough of Ron?'

'Course I did. He'd been wanting to get his hands on him since the first time I told him but I'd stopped him. And then when he was such a vile prick last week, I thought, why not? The world will be a better place without an old bastard like that.'

'Do you do know or not?'

'No details. It's all about the details. Hearsay's not admissible.'

'You mean he's dead?' I whisper.

'Like I say, I don't know, I just know that I don't have to put up with him anymore. I could put a word in for you, if you like. It'd be free 'cos you're a mate and because Marcus quite likes his job, if you know what I mean, so he doesn't always want paying especially if it's a mate of mine.'

We stare at each other and I think what a bizarre conversation this is to be having in the sugar aisle of Chiverson's.

'I'm not afraid of Dylan,' I say, not quite convincing myself. 'I don't think we need to do anything like that.'

'You sure? Could just rough him up a bit, give him a black eye, maybe break a bone or two, scare him off, stop him bothering you?'

'No, honestly, Jack.' I say. 'It's fine.'

'No problem.' He turns to resume his shelf stacking. 'But if you change your mind, just let me know.'

Dylan's a creep and his behaviour is becoming more and more weird but I can't imagine myself asking Jack to scare him off or make him disappear. The idea of it seems so weird and unbelievable.

But not so weird when I think of Lucinda, because if she were to disappear, my life would be just perfect.

CHAPTER FIFTEEN

By the time I leave work at three o'clock, the rumour mill is spinning like a top. Although Brenda had told us that Ron was off sick, someone on the tills, whose daughter works at the hospital, had some interesting gossip about Ron and it was spreading around the store like wild-fire. Ron is apparently in intensive care in a coma and he isn't expected to survive. He hasn't been beaten up or disappeared, but hit by a car on his way back home from his nightly trip to the local pub.

The car that hit him never stopped and the police are treating it as rather more than a hit and run due to the extent of Ron's injuries. From the extent of Ron's injuries and the marks on the road, it seems that after Ron had been knocked over, the car reversed back over him and then ran over him once more before driving off. Although the pub he'd left only minutes earlier has CCTV cameras installed outside, the incident, as the police are calling it, wasn't recorded as the cameras had been smashed the previous night and weren't working. There were several smokers having a cigarette outside the pub when Ron was hit but unfortunately none of them were any use as witnesses. They couldn't identify the car or give the police any details at all because they were all looking in the other direction at the time. I looked at Jack when Susie from the warehouse told us this and Jack had the tiniest hint of a smile on his face.

When Susie had gone, I asked Jack how he thought it was possible that not one of the smokers noticed a car hitting Ron when it happened right in front of them. Even if they really were looking the other way when he was hit, the noise of the car reversing over him would have drawn their attention. Jack shrugged and said that people don't like to get involved in police investigations; he said no one wants to be called as a witness because it just ends up as hassle. Wasn't it lucky, he said, that they noticed him lying in the road afterwards because they were able to call an ambulance for him really quickly.

Not really, I said, because Ron isn't expected to survive and if by some miracle he *does*, his brain damage is so severe he'll likely be in a coma for the rest of his life. Jack just shrugged and muttered something about *karma being a bitch* and all the while he still had that hint of a smile on his face.

As I drove home, I mulled it all over. Before we found out about Ron, when Jack was talking about people *disappearing* and being *warned off*, it all seemed a bit unreal and the tiniest bit thrilling.

But it doesn't now.

This is real; Jack's boyfriend Marcus is an actual criminal and not to be messed with. Ron's accident is too much of a coincidence for it not to have been instigated by Marcus. I feel ashamed at my silly thought about having Lucinda *disappeared*, I wasn't seriously wishing that something would happen to her because I didn't really think Marcus could make anything happen. It all seemed like a bit of a make-believe. A convenient fantasy. I know that it was totally wrong to think something like that about Lucinda but I can't help it if it popped into my head, can I? It's not as if I would ever *do* anything, having a bad thought doesn't make me a bad person, does it?

I can't make myself feel too sorry about Ron either, because I do believe in karma and the way he behaved towards Jack was totally unacceptable. Whether he deserved the brutal treatment that he received, I'm not so sure, but there's not anything I can do so I'm not going to start worrying about it. I did feel a bit sad when I heard that Ron lived with his elderly mother and she was in absolute pieces about his accident, though. She's suffering now, as well. Although I do wonder what sort of mother she's been to produce someone like Ron.

What's happened has made me think, though, that Jack had better not do anything to upset Marcus or have a really bad argument with him, because he just might find himself *disappeared*.

As I pull up onto the driveway of our cottage, I see that there's a bike leaning up against the wall underneath the porch. I know straight away that it belongs to Dylan. I turn the ignition off and remain in the car while I think what I'm going to do. He could be sitting in there now telling Mum all about Will and I. I could just drive off and text Mum and tell her I'm working late and avoid him. But I'd feel bad doing that because I should be at home with her. Besides, Dylan will probably hang around until I get home so I'd still have to see him. I don't know how he has the nerve to come here after what happened this morning. I feel angry at the thought of him but also a bit anxious, he's not dangerous, is he? Jack's words that Dylan is a nut-job come back to me but I shake them off. I'm not going to allow Dylan to stop me from going into my own home.

I get out of the car and go around to the back garden and let myself into the kitchen. I can hear Mum and Dylan's voices from the lounge so I take a deep breath and, before I can think about it too much, I walk through the kitchen and straight through into the lounge. Dylan is sitting on the sofa with a mug of tea in his hand and Mum is sitting opposite him in the rocking chair.

'Hi, darling.' Mum looks up at me and smiles.

'Good day at work?'

'All good.' I smile at her and then look at Dylan, who beams at me as if this morning never happened.

'Hi, Layla, nice to see you.'

I stare at him and force myself to smile.

'Hi, Dylan.'

As I walk past Dylan and sit down in the chair opposite Mum, I notice Benny sitting on his bed in the corner next to the fireplace. He looks bedraggled and grubby, with burrs and twigs snarled onto his usual glossy coat.

'Benny's in the doghouse.' Mum laughs, seeing me looking at him. 'Somehow, he managed to get out this morning and run off. I was quite frantic when I came downstairs and couldn't find him. I wasn't sure what to do but luckily Dylan was out on his bike and happened to see him wandering around on his own. He picked him up and bought him home. You can imagine my relief when I opened the front door to see Dylan standing there with Benny in his arms.'

'He was miles away from here,' Dylan says, quietly. 'Completely lost. It's fortunate that I recognised him otherwise you might never have seen him again. Not that he cared much for being tucked underneath my arm while I cycled back one-handed.'

He looks so sure of himself, so pleased with his good deed.

'How could Benny have got out?' I ask. 'He was

fast asleep when I left this morning.'

Mum shrugs and doesn't answer and she won't meet my eyes.

'Well,' Dylan smiles at me and I want to punch him. 'You couldn't have shut the back door properly when you went to work. He must have sneaked out after you.'

'It's my fault darling,' Mum says, hurriedly. 'I laid in bed for far too long, Benny was probably desperate to go out while I was being totally selfish, lazing around in bed, reading my book.'

I'm sure that I locked the back door behind me.

'Oh God, how stupid of me,' I say, even though I'm certain that it wasn't my fault. 'I thought I'd locked it. I'm so sorry Mum.'

'Oh, don't worry, darling, these things happen, no harm done. Benny's going to have to have a bath now so maybe he'll think twice the next time he decides to go off on an adventure on his own. You know how much he hates water.' Mum laughs and I join in, determined not to let Dylan see how much he's bothered me.

'You need to be careful, though, Layla.' Dylan places his mug on the coffee table and stands up. 'Because it was just sheer luck that I happened to find him. Next time you might not be so lucky.' He walks over to Mum and leans down and kisses her on the cheek and then walks towards Benny and pats him on the head. Benny cringes under Dylan's touch and I hear a low growl coming from him. Dylan laughs.

'Is that the thanks I get for saving your life, Benny?' He ruffles his ears and Benny shrinks into his bed. 'You should be more grateful or maybe I won't bother next time.' He laughs as he stands up and Mum joins in and as Dylan turns to leave, he stares at me for a moment.

'You were lucky he didn't get run over, because he'd got all the way up by the main road and the cars rip along there. I've seen many a dead cat and dog by the side of the road.' He holds my gaze for a moment and smiles and then turns, walks out of the lounge and lets himself out of the front door.

As I watch him leave, I know for sure that I didn't leave the back door unlocked, or open, and that Dylan is lying. I'm not careless, I always lock the door behind me, especially if Mum is still in bed. Dylan came here after our encounter in Chiverson's and somehow managed to get into the kitchen and take Benny. He didn't find him in the forest at all, he took him from our kitchen.

And everything he said just now was a threat.

He was letting me know that he can take my dog and kill him any time he likes.

* * *

I wake with a start; daylight is filtering through the curtains and for a moment I'm disorientated and have no idea where I am. The heat from Will's body next to mine brings me to my senses and I remember that I'm in Will's bed, with him.

I stretch out my arm and grab my mobile phone from the bedside table and hold it up in front of my eyes to see that it's five-thirty.

I don't usually spend the night with will, I go back to our cottage in the early hours of the morning and sleep in my own bed. Even though I know that there's no way that Mum will be awake yet, I pull the quilt back, intending to get up. In that moment, Will turns over in his sleep and flings his arm over me, pinning me to the bed. I lie back down, savouring the closeness of his body next to mine. A few more minutes won't hurt.

After we'd made love last night, I told Will about Dylan, about his appearance in Chiverson's and how he turned up at the cottage. I hadn't intended telling him anything about it, mostly because I didn't want Dylan to intrude on our time together. But the thought of harm coming to Benny wouldn't stop from going through my mind and I felt helpless and distraught at the thought of any harm coming to him.

At first, Will didn't take it too seriously and even struggled to remember who Dylan was. When he realised he *was the boy on the bike*, as Will put it, he laughed and said that Dylan looked as if he'd blow over with a good puff of wind. I told him that I'd always thought the same but now I wasn't so sure. The more I told Will about what had happened and what Dylan had said to me, the more annoyed he became. He asked if I'd gone out with Dylan for a long time and I said of course not, I'd never been out with him at all. Then he asked if I'd had sex with him and I was shocked and said no, that it wasn't like that. Then he became very quiet and when I asked him what was wrong, he said that I didn't have to lie, it was perfectly alright for me to have had boyfriends before him. I repeated that Dylan wasn't a boyfriend and I hadn't had sex with him but I had the feeling that he didn't believe me. Will asked why Dylan would say such things to me if I hadn't been his girlfriend. I said I had no idea but that I thought Dylan wasn't quite right in the head and had become a bit obsessed with me. By that time, I was beginning to regret even mentioning it because Will seemed a bit irritated with me and talking about Dylan was spoiling our time together. I couldn't figure out why Will was being so off because I hadn't done anything wrong. And then it suddenly hit me; Will was jealous.

I felt elated when I realised because that confirms, surely, that he loves me. Will still hasn't said the actual words to me and I haven't said them to him either because he should definitely say them first. He says that he can't get enough of me and thinks about me all of the time and that I'm beautiful, but has never actually said *I love you*. I'm sure he does love me but I would like to hear him say it. I didn't say anything but I enjoyed Will being jealous as I lay there and after a while, I heard the regular sound of his breathing so I knew that he'd fallen asleep. I lay there thinking about things for a while and I must have been tired because the next thing I knew was when I woke this morning. Will's obviously not annoyed with me anymore because he's cuddled up to me.

'Will,' I whisper. 'I have to go.'

He murmurs something intelligible and I stroke his cheek and think how gorgeous he is. How I wish I could stay here with him and we could be together properly.

'Will.'

He opens his eyes and stares at me and I smile.

'I have to get up. I've got work today.'

He slips his hand underneath the duvet and around my waist and pulls me closer.

'Sorry about last night.' He kisses me softly on the lips and I feel the warmth of his fingers as they travel down my body. 'I was just being a jealous idiot at the thought of another man touching you. I know I have no right to feel that way.'

'You have every right because I'm yours,' I whisper. 'But there's no need for you to feel that way because before you, there was no one. At all. Ever.'

He looks at me in puzzlement and then comprehension dawns. 'What, you mean...?'

I smile and kiss him and he pulls me closer and I gasp as I feel how much he wants me and all thoughts of Dylan are forgotten as we lose ourselves in each other. By the time I get out of bed and finally leave to go back to the cottage, it's already past six o'clock and I know I have to hurry now or I'll be late for work. I let myself out of the back door and run lightly across the lane. I smile at the thought of Will's passionate love-making as I walk up the path to our back door and long to be back in his arms. I could tell that Will was delighted at the thought of being the first man that I'd ever slept with and our love-making was unbelievably passionate and urgent this morning, even more so than usual. I wonder why it matters so much to him. We didn't talk any more about Dylan this morning and I can't help feeling that Will's not taking his threat seriously. He thinks that Dylan's just trying to rattle me and to ignore him and that of course he wouldn't hurt Benny. This is the back of beyond, he reminded me, not some rough part of London where gangsters' rule. Things like that don't happen here.

I almost told Will about Ron when he said that but stopped myself. Would he believe that Marcus had made something happen to Ron or think that Jack was some sort of teenage fantasist too? Because it does sound crazy when I think about it in the cold light of day.

I slip my key into the back door lock and turn it and then quietly open the door.

'Where have you been, Layla?'

Mum's voice is uncharacteristically loud, not her usual soft tones. She's sitting at the kitchen table, a cup of tea and a book in front of her on the table.

'Mum! What are you doing up so early?'

'I couldn't sleep,' she says. 'One of the drawbacks

of not really doing anything all day is that I'm not tired. But never mind me, where on earth have you been?'

'Same as you,' I lie. 'I couldn't sleep. I thought I'd go out for an early morning walk. Clear my head.'

Mum doesn't smile but simply looks me up and down.

'In a man's t-shirt and a pair of flip-flops?'

I look down at Will's t-shirt. I was in a hurry to get back home and picked it up and slipped it on after we'd made love, leaving my dress behind on the bedroom floor.

I look at Mum. I want to tell her the truth, I *should* tell her, but I can't, because I know she won't approve and will make me feel guilty. Struggling to know what to say I decide that attack is the best form of defence.

Besides, I *need* to know and I've been putting off asking her for long enough. Now is as good a time as any.

'Never mind where I've been, 'I say, my voice suddenly loud. 'How about you tell me why you opened a letter that was addressed to me?'

'What letter? What are you talking about?'

Mum's face belies her words; she's trying to hide it but I can see panic in her eyes. She knows exactly what I'm talking about.

'The letter from the adoption intermediary service. It was addressed to me and you opened it and hid it; I found it when I was looking for your dressing gown.'

Mum's hand flies to cover her mouth and her eyes are fixed on my face but she doesn't speak. I walk over to her and stand in front of her, anger bubbling up inside.

'Tell me Mum, why does the letter say that my birth mother wants to see me when you've been telling me for all of my life that she's dead?'

CHAPTER SIXTEEN

As I stand and wait for Mum to answer me, I'm glad that it's out in the open at last. She can tell me that it's all a mistake and then we can forget about it and put it behind us and there'll be no need for me to think about it anymore. Perhaps it's a good thing that she caught me this morning, because I've been putting off asking her for far too long.

Mum stares up at me, her eyes wide, and then after a moment she lowers her hand from her mouth and stands up. I watch as she picks up her cup from the table and carries it over to the sink. She turns the tap on and holds the cup underneath the water and rinses it.

'Well?' I demand, when the silence has stretched to breaking point and I realise that she's not going to answer me. 'Don't you think you should tell me?'

I see her body stiffen for a moment and then she turns the tap off, puts the cup on the draining board and takes the tea-towel from the rail on the cooker and carefully dries the cup. She puts the cup in the cupboard and I watch her with growing impatience until she turns and walks towards me. At last, I think, now she'll tell me. When she reaches me, she puts her arms around me and hugs me tightly and I stand stiffly in her embrace and wait for her to speak. After a moment she releases me and smiles, pushing a stray strand of hair back from my face.

'I'm going back to bed now, darling. I'm feeling a little tired.'

I stare at her. It's as if I haven't asked her to explain the letter, as if I've never spoken about it.

'Aren't you going to answer my question?'

Mum looks at me blankly for a moment and then pats me on the arm before turning to leave the kitchen.

'Have a good day at work, darling, and I'll see you when you get home. I thought I'd do a lasagne for dinner with some mince out of the freezer.'

'Mum…'

'You'd better get a move on or else you'll be late,' she says, walking out into the hallway. 'I'll see you later.'

I follow behind her and watch as she climbs the stairs. She's not going to talk to me about it. She's not going to tell me the truth, she's not even going to acknowledge it, she's totally ignoring it.

If only she knew.

I don't *want* the truth; I wanted her to tell me that she opened the letter by mistake, I wanted her to tell me that the agency had made an error and got it all wrong. I would have gladly believed her and never asked her anything about it ever again.

I *wanted* her to lie to me.

* * *

'You're quiet today.' Jack takes a deep drag of his cigarette and blows the smoke up into the sky in a long stream.

I shrug, not sure if I'm even capable of speaking. We're on our lunch break, sitting at the far end of the car park on the bank of grass that surrounds it. The sun is hot and it's the perfect June day; or it would be if my life didn't feel as if it were in tatters.

'Not bothered about Ron, are you?' Jack asks, flicking his cigarette end high into the air before it falls into the car park.

I wonder what he's talking about for a moment and then remember; Ron is dead. The doctors switched off the life support machine last night and the news of his death has been flying around Chiverson's all morning. Rumours are abounding, getting more outrageous with each telling, but none of them are anywhere near the truth. Ron was involved in drug-running and the mob have got him because he stole from them. He had a secret girlfriend whose husband found out and killed him. A drunk driver hit him and the police are fast closing in on him. On and on, more and more theories and not one person seemed sad that he was dead, not one. The very opposite, actually, there seemed to be real enjoyment as each new theory was mooted and spread around and discussed endlessly. Which tells you something about Ron, and also something about people who love to gossip.

'God, no,' I say. 'Good riddance.' I feel immediately bad once I've said it because that means that I'm no better than the gossips who devour each new story with gusto.

'Karma,' Jack says. 'Karma got him. The only sad thing is that I wasn't there to see the bastard draw his last breath.'

Not really karma, though, because you had him killed, Jack. But I don't say it, not least because Ron deserved what happened to him. We sit in silence for a while and I think that maybe I should make myself talk to Jack, because I've been silent for most of the morning and he knows that there's something wrong. He's my friend so I shouldn't shut him out.

I will tell him about what happened with Mum, but not yet, because I'm still trying to process it myself. I need to get my head around it before I can even think about talking about it with anyone else. But I am going to find out the truth and have already taken the first steps towards doing so. On the pretext of going to the toilet this morning, I sat in a stall in the ladies' toilets and googled the number for the Adoption Intermediary Service. As soon as I found it, I pressed the call button before I could change my mind. My hopes were soon dashed that I would find any answers today, or any time soon. The crushing disappointment that I felt when after answering numerous questions about my identity, I was refused any information at all, was unbearable.

Why couldn't they tell me? Why do I have to wait? Surely I have a right to know.

When I asked for my birth mother's details, they wouldn't give me any information at all, although their reply did confirm at least, that she is alive. I have to write to her, apparently, and they will act as intermediary. It was for my own benefit, the officious woman told me, to protect mine and my birth mother's privacy and mental health. I pressed the *end call* button on her last words when she informed me *that these things take time and cannot be rushed.* I don't tell Jack any of this, of course, instead I tell him about Dylan.

'Dylan was at my house when I got home from work yesterday,' I say. Because I need to talk about something or else Jack might start to think that I don't want to talk to him anymore. I wonder if Jack will think that I'm overreacting, as Will does.

'I knew something was wrong.' Jack frowns. 'What happened?'

I tell him about Benny and how Dylan said that he's found him wandering around in the forest. I don't hold back in telling Jack that I think Dylan was threatening me.

'You're sure that you locked the back door?'

I think about it for a while and yet again, I retrace my movements of yesterday morning.

'Yes, I'm sure. I'm very particular about locking doors. Don't believe all of this nonsense about people leaving their doors unlocked in the country – it's quite the opposite, especially with it being just me and Mum living together. I definitely locked the door because there's no way I'd go out and leave Mum asleep in bed with the door unlocked.'

'So how would Dylan have a key?'

'I don't know. It's an old door, not one of the new multi-lock ones. I don't think Mum changed the locks when we moved in, so who knows, perhaps there were other keys floating around. Or maybe it's easy to pick because it's so old.'

Jack fumbles for his cigarette packet, pulls out another cigarette and pops it into his mouth and lights it.

'You know.' He blows a plume of smoke straight ahead. 'You're going to have to do something about him.'

'You don't think I'm overreacting?'

'Fuck no. He's threatened you.'

I nod my head, pleased that he's not doubting me. My head feels full; Mum refusing to tell me anything, my birth mother being out there somewhere, my intense need for Will and my growing hatred for Lucinda. Dylan is one more problem that I don't need, one more thing to be thought about and dealt with.

'I was hoping that he'd get the message and just leave me alone,' I say. 'But he's getting worse because him taking Benny isn't the only thing.'

Jack looks at me sharply.

'What do you mean?'

I take a deep breath. 'I think he's been following me.'

'When?'

I sigh and admit what I've suspected for a while, that I'm sure someone's watching me and that it must be Dylan, because who else would it be?

'Lots of times, I think,' I say, slowly. 'And I know it sounds stupid, but I get this tingle on the back of my neck when someone is watching me. I can sense it. I've always had it and I'm not usually wrong. I've felt it loads lately but I can't catch who it is. But it's obviously Dylan.'

'It doesn't sound stupid to me, you can feel it, can't you, when someone's got eyes on you. Makes you turn around and look at everyone and you can usually spot who it is when they suddenly turn away.'

'That's exactly it, but I can't catch him out, he's being too clever. But I get a glimpse in a shop window or on the opposite side of the street, or a quick movement but by the time I look, he's gone. But it's him, I think.'

'Course it's him.' Jack turns to look at me, his

face serious. 'You need to do something about him Layla, because you don't know what he's capable of. Watching you and threatening you, what's he going to do next?'

I shiver as I remember his threat about Benny. Was he just trying to frighten me or is he capable of more than just words?

'I have to think about it,' I say, standing up and brushing down my trousers. 'Think about what to do. I don't want to make any rash decisions.'

Jack looks at his watch and then hauls himself to his feet.

'Alright, think about it,' he says. 'But mate, don't think about it for too long. Don't make the mistake of not taking him seriously. Like I told you before, he's a nut-job and nut-jobs aren't rational.'

'I know.'

We amble across the car park towards the store entrance and I think about Jack's words. Is Dylan dangerous? I'm not sure, but I know one thing.

I'm afraid of what he might do next.

* * *

When I get home after work it's as if this morning never happened; Mum is her old self, bustling around and asking me about my day and I marvel at her ability to totally ignore what's going on.

Although isn't that what I've been doing for all of my life?

I think it is; my absolute refusal when I was

growing up to know anything at all about my birth parents when I could have asked all the questions I wanted.

But would Mum have told me the truth?

I don't know. And honestly, this morning I didn't even *want* the truth. I wanted to carry on believing what I've always believed because it was easier than facing the truth and having to deal with my feelings. Mum could have lied to me and I would have gladly believed her.

But now I can't. I have to find out about my birth mother because if I don't, it's going to eat away at me underneath everything else in my life.

It seems almost surreal that Mum and I eat our dinner as if nothing has happened. I don't ask her again because I know that she'll totally ignore the question. I tried when I got home and she did the same as she did this morning. I talk about work – not about Ron, of course, and Mum chats about her latest painting as if she doesn't have a care in the world and our life is just as it's always been.

I wish I could be like her; I wish I could go back to not wanting to know. But I can't; from wanting to know nothing, I now have a burning desire to find out the truth.

After dinner, Mum goes down the garden to her art studio and I'm left alone. She hasn't asked me again where I was last night, because she can't, can she? Because then I'll ask her about the letter again and she won't want that. I have a sudden yearning for Will, for the feel of his strong arms around me, his body next to mine. I could go and see him now, Mum wouldn't know because she's in her studio and even if she guesses where I am, what does it matter? Lucinda is away, so why not?

I go into the lounge and look out of the window and feel immediate disappointment. Will's car isn't there, which means that he's out. I could message him and find out where he is, find out when he'll be back, but I stop myself. I don't want to be like Lucinda, constantly messaging him and wanting to know where he is, checking on him, demanding to know what he's doing. I'll wait until tonight, when he'll be waiting in bed for me. I try to ignore the fact that I'm afraid to ask too much of him, afraid that he might react with the same coldness as the day he threw me out of his house.

I should take Benny for a walk, just down the lane, because he hasn't been out today. Since Dylan's threat, I've decided not to take him up to the field, I want to stay close to our cottage where it's safer. I wonder if Dylan watches me at night as I cross the lane to Will's cottage, if he loiters around the lane at night to see what I'm doing.

Jack's right; I need to do something about him.

I walk through the lounge intent on taking Benny out when I notice the dresser and it reminds me of the box of photographs. The intermediary service wasn't interested that I was impatient to find out about my birth mother, their attitude is that these things shouldn't be rushed. I can write to her but it could be months before I find out anything about her. Could the newspaper clipping have something to do with my birth mother or is it in the box by chance and of no relevance at all?

I go to the dresser, open the door and pull the photograph box out onto the floor. I open it and begin to look through. The clipping is still in the same place that I left it and as I pull it free, I realise that it can't be anything to do with me, because if it was, Mum would have taken it out of the box after this morning, wouldn't she? But maybe she doesn't know that it's there. Either way, I have nothing to lose by looking, absolutely nothing. I put all of the photographs back in the box and return it to the back of the dresser and then take the clipping and go upstairs to my bedroom.

I sit on my bed and read it again even though I remember it all. I reread it carefully in case I've missed some tiny detail, but of course I haven't. Could the murdered woman be a relative of my birth mother? It's not very likely, this is just a random piece of paper that has absolutely no significance at all. But there is a way I can find out for sure, and then I can stop thinking about it. I pick up my mobile and open Google and type in the murdered woman's name. *Janice Caddell* brings up pages and pages of hits immediately, the entries all referencing her murder eighteen years ago. I click on one and begin to read, scrolling down the screen to reveal other photographs of her, colour photographs that are much clearer and sharper than the mottled black and white one in the newspaper clipping. As I scroll further down the article, my fingers become still as I read more slowly, rereading each word to try and understand what I'm seeing. I stare at the screen in disbelief, my heart pounding, my breath coming in gasps as I start to hyperventilate.

It can't be, my brain screams at me, *it can't be.*

But it is.

CHAPTER SEVENTEEN

'Jack, you said Marcus can find anyone, right? Even if they don't want to be found?'

'Yeah, pretty much. Except if they've left the country, it's not so easy then. Do-able, but takes a bit longer. Why?'

We're on our lunch break in our favourite spot, sitting on the grass bank at the end of the car park. We like it here because Jack can smoke to his heart's content and no one comes here except us. Most of the staff prefer to sit in the staff cafeteria or loiter around the smoking shelter. Neither Jack nor I talk much to anyone else, or them to us. Somehow, we've never fitted in like the other new starters; it's not deliberate, it's just turned out that way. Maybe it's because Jack and I hit it off straight away and have never made any effort to befriend anyone else. I don't mind at all, because Jack is a proper friend and even when I've left here, I know that we'll still be friends and see each other.

'I need someone found,' I say. 'I need an address.'

'O-k-a-y.' He turns to look at me, a quizzical look on his face.

'My mother,' I say, as if that explains everything.

'But you live with your mother.' He frowns.

'I'm adopted.'

'Really? Wow, that's a surprise, I wasn't expecting that.'

'Why not?'

'Dunno.' He shrugs. 'Just thought that you and your mum were really tight. The way you talk about her, like you're best mates, almost.'

'We are, I just want to meet my birth mother, that's all, natural curiosity, you know?'

Jack narrows his eyes and I stare at him.

'Is that a problem?'

Jack shrugs. 'Just don't know why you'd want to find her, from what you've told me you and your mum have a great relationship, so why spoil it? How does your mum feel about it, what with her having been in hospital and everything? Bit of a kick in the guts for her to know that you want to meet your real mother after she's brought you up.'

'I haven't told her.'

'Oh. I see, look, I don't mean to sound harsh, Layla, but your birth mother fucked you off once so why bother with her now? Why ruin what you've got with your mum to trace a woman who couldn't give a shit about you?'

I stare at Jack in shock and he turns his head away and looks down at his feet. The skin on his cheeks has flushed a deep red and we sit in silence.

'Jack?'

He doesn't answer but fumbles in his jacket pocket and pulls out his cigarettes, takes the last one out of the packet and puts it in his mouth. He crumples the empty packet up into a tight ball and throws it with force across the car park before lighting his cigarette with a plastic lighter. He takes a deep drag and after he's exhaled, he turns to face me, his expression grim.

'Sorry,' he says. 'Not your fault and it's none of my business. It's a touchy subject.'

'You're adopted?'

'Fuck, no.' He laughs, harshly. 'Wish I was. No, my mother wouldn't let me go, I was much too valuable for getting benefits off the social. She didn't want me though and she never did, cared more about her latest boyfriend than she ever did about me. Always took their side, too, no matter what they'd done to me. She never believed me. I think she quite enjoyed it when I got in the way and they gave me a good belting. Or worse. As soon as the money stopped when I left school, she kicked me out.'

'Oh, Jack, I'm so sorry.'

'Don't be, you weren't to know. But it just guts me, you know, because if I'd been adopted like you were, I might have had a fighting chance, instead of being stuck in a shit life with a bitch for a mother.'

''You haven't got a shit life.' I put my hand on his arm. 'You've got Marcus now and you're working here and you've got a job, so you're just the same as me, aren't you? You have your whole life ahead of you.'

'Not the same though, is it, Layla? You're not going to be staying here, are you? It's just a stop gap for you, you'll end up with a career and a real life because you come from a proper, decent family. You've got a future. Not like me.'

'Don't talk like that, Jack. You're only eighteen, you've got plenty of time to get a good life. You're clever, you can do anything you put your mind to.'

Jack smiles and shakes his head.

'It's too late for me, Layla, there's a lot about me that you don't know and I wouldn't want you to know. As for Marcus, I'm one of many. I just happen to be the favourite at the moment because I look so young. Marcus likes them young. You thought I was sixteen, didn't you? That's what he likes, Layla, *boys*. No, as soon as I start looking older, I'll be kicked into touch.'

'How can it be too late for you at eighteen, Jack? That's just madness, you could get a career, do anything you like.'

Jack laughs, bitterly. 'No, I've grown up way too fast and there's no going back when you've done the things I have. I've hardly been to school since I was thirteen and I haven't got any qualifications. I'd have to go back to school and do the basics before I could even think of doing anything else. I missed so much; even the teachers pretended not to notice that I was never there. Makes for a quieter life, especially at the shithole school I went to. Do you know, for a while I had the fucking stupid idea that I wanted to be taken into care because I thought I'd have a better life. That was until I found out from mates what it was really like. I move in a different world to you, Layla, and I always will. But it's okay, I'm okay with it, and I'm sorry that I sounded nasty because it's up to you what you do about your birth mother, it's none of my business.'

He stares across the car park, and I reach over and put my arms around his shoulders and hug him tightly. He stays still for a moment before shrugging me off.

'Enough of the sloppy stuff. If you want to meet the bitch who abandoned you, text me whatever details you have and I'll give them to Marcus and ask him to find her for you.'

'Thank you.'

'Although I thought you had a right to meet her if you want to. Don't the adoption people have to put you in touch with her or something?'

'Well, yes, they do, but it takes forever. We have to write to each other first and I don't want to wait, I want to find her now.'

'Oh. Right. And what about that streak of piss, Dylan? Have you decided what you're going to do about him?'

I sigh. When I came back from Will's this morning, I felt the familiar tingle on the back of my neck and I'm almost sure that Dylan was watching me from the oak tree at the end of the lane. I couldn't actually see him but the light seemed to be flickering as if someone was moving about in the shadows.

'Hey, don't cry,' Jack says, softly. 'I didn't mean to upset you.'

I wipe my hand across my face and I'm shocked to see it come away wet. I had no idea I was crying.

'Honestly, it's not you,' I say. 'I'm just a mess at the moment.'

I dry my face in my sleeve and pull my phone out of my pocket. I open WhatsApp and press *send* on the message that I typed in readiness this morning before I came to work.

'Are these the details for your birth mum?' he asks, as his phone pings.

'Yep.'

I stare out across the car park while Jack opens the message and reads it and then clicks on the link that I sent him. Out of the corner of my eye I see him turn and stare at me, open-mouthed in shock, before returning to his phone and rereading my message.

'Fucking hell, Layla.'

'I know,' I say, quietly. 'I know.'

'You sure this is her?'

'Yep.'

'And you definitely want to do this?'

'Positive.'

'Okay, I'll get Marcus on it. She'll be easy enough to find, I think.'

'Good. I just need her address, that's all.' I stand up. 'I think I'll head back now. I need to go to the loo before our shift starts. See you on the shop floor, yeah?'

'Defo. You alright?'

'Not really.' I walk down the bank and am about to head across the car park when Jack's voice stops me.

'And that other thing?' he calls. 'What do you want me to do about him?'

I pause for a moment, remembering the fear that I felt at the thought of Dylan watching me from the shadows. The fear that made me break into a run as I left Will's garden and dash across the lane to our cottage as fast as I could. The fear that's making me double check that I've locked the back door every time I go out, even though I know that it wouldn't stop him from getting in. The fear of arriving home and Benny not being there. The terror of what Dylan might do to him.

'I want him to stop following me.' I turn around.

'So, you want Marcus to get him scared off?'

'I don't know, Jack. I just want him to leave me alone.'

He shrugs. 'It's your call but I know what I'd do if it was me. He's a nut-job.'

'I know.' I bite my lip; another decision to make, another thing to have to think about. It's all too much.

'You decide for me, Jack,' I blurt out. 'I trust you. Whatever you think best is fine by me.'

Jack nods, his expression grim. I'm asking too much of him; expecting him to make a decision about something that I don't want to. I turn away and walk across the car park, knowing that I'm being unfair.

But I don't care.

* * *

Jack knows everything that I know about my birth mother.

I feel guilty about that; guilty that Jack knows and not Will. I soothe my guilt with the reasoning that I need Jack to find her, so he needed to know. And I didn't actually speak about her to him; he read it, the same as I did.

But Will should have known first, he's my partner, even if we're still keeping our relationship a secret. I could have told him last night; I *should* have told him last night when I was in his arms and in his bed. He could have comforted me, and maybe, I would have felt better for actually uttering the words out loud. But even though it was whirling around in my head constantly, I couldn't bring myself to tell him. I wanted to lose myself in him and not have to think about what I'd discovered.

I'll tell him tonight.

Although it'll be difficult to talk very much because we have to meet down the lane. Lucinda will be back from London. I try to stop the feeling of hatred that wells up in me when I think of her but I don't succeed. Why does she insist on clinging onto Will when he so obviously doesn't love her? She's not stupid, she must realise that he's only staying with her because he's forced to. Because of her we'll have to meet outside in the dark and our love-making will be hurried and perfunctory, tainted by having to be quiet to make sure there's no possibility of anyone hearing or seeing us. We should be able to tell the whole world how we feel about one another, not have to hide away as if we're doing something wrong. I should be living in Will's cottage and sharing his bed and life with him, not her.

And what if Dylan is sneaking around, what if he's standing in the shadows, watching us as we make love?

I shudder at the thought. Is Jack going to arrange for something to happen to Dylan? I'm still not sure if I really believe that Ron's death was organised by Marcus; it could easily have been a totally unconnected hit-and-run. According to the Chiverson's grapevine, Ron was very drunk when he left the pub. He was an alcoholic who got wasted every single night before making his meandering way home along the road, making no attempt to stay on the path.

Or maybe I'm just telling myself this so that I

don't have to feel guilty about throwing Dylan to the wolves. I know that I'm being a coward by telling Jack to decide; have I done this so that if Marcus really does do something to Dylan, then I'm not to blame? Is it so I don't have to feel guilty because Jack is making the decision?

I think it is, but I'm just fooling myself because if something happens to Dylan, I'm the one to blame, I'm the one who's made it happen.

One thing I do know for sure is that nothing will happen to Dylan tonight, nothing will be arranged that quickly. Which means that to be safe, Will and I should wait until Monday to meet because Dylan could be watching me. If we wait until then I can be sure that Dylan won't be able to watch us because we'll be safely inside Will's bedroom, away from prying eyes. Perhaps I could move in with Will while *she's* gone, we could be together properly while she's away. Will has to go to London on Wednesday for work but I could cook for him and look after him and spend all of the other days with him.

Play house.

Maybe he could take me with him on Wednesday; after he's been into work we could spend the day together. I could take the day off work; it wouldn't be a problem.

Except that I know that I'm fooling myself; Will won't want to risk being seen out with me and he won't let me stay at his cottage all week because the neighbours would notice. And what about

Mum? Despite everything that I've found out, am I ready to tell her yet? And what about Lucinda? If she finds out, who knows what she'd do to Will – and me. I also know that I won't be able to stop myself from seeing Will until Monday because I can't bear the thought of a weekend without him. Will's all that's keeping me sane at the moment.

I need him so much.

After what I discovered yesterday, I don't know how I could go on if I didn't have Will. I wish I could talk to Mum about it but she won't even acknowledge anything at all about my birth mother. I've tried, but she refuses to engage and totally blanks me.

It's her way of coping and I can't blame her for it.

I see now why Mum lied to me and the only thing that I blame her for is not continuing that lie.

Because the truth hurts.

If only I hadn't found the newspaper clipping, if only I hadn't found the letter from the adoption service, if only I'd never asked Mum to tell me the truth.

If only, if only.

It's too late now, because once you know something, you can't un-know it, no matter how much you wish you could.

The shock of finding out the truth about my birth mother has made me look at myself in a new light. I've had so many dark thoughts lately; mad imaginings about Lucinda and Dylan that surely a normal person wouldn't have. And even though I'm pretending to myself that I'm leaving the decision about Dylan being *warned off* or *disappeared* to Jack, I know, really, that by saying *you decide*, if Marcus is really all that Jack says he is, then I've sealed Dylan's fate. He'll be beaten up or possibly murdered and yet even knowing this, I've still done it.

What does that say about me, what sort of person does that make me?

A bad one.

Maybe it's all in the genes, nature, not nurture.

Maybe I always knew that there was a darkness inside me, and maybe that's why I never asked Mum the questions about my birth mother that any normal person would want to know.

Maybe, I'm just like my mother.

CHAPTER EIGHTEEN

I look at my phone for what feels like the millionth time.

Two-thirty-five in the morning.

I finally face the fact the Will isn't coming. I've been waiting here for over an hour-and-a-half and he's not here. He's never been this late before.

Something must have happened.

I shiver in the night air and pull my dress tightly around me and wrap my arms around my body with my arms. My dress is made of flimsy cotton and I'm not wearing any underwear – I never do when we meet – and I'm amazed that I've never noticed the chill night air before. When we lay together on the damp grass, I've never once felt cold.

I shiver.

Go home, Layla.

I check my phone one more time to see if he's replied to any of my increasingly frantic messages. He hasn't, and what's more, the one solitary tick next to each message shows that he hasn't even read them. I try to quell the rising panic that I'm feeling, the fear that something terrible has happened. Has Lucinda found out about us and attacked him? Is he lying injured, or worse, in their cottage?

I step out from behind our tree and slowly make my way down the lane, the pale moonlight guiding my way. Something's wrong, I know it. I can feel it. Although strangely, tonight, I don't feel as if I'm being watched, I don't have the tingle on the back of my neck that tells me someone is looking over me. Perhaps Dylan has finally tired of pestering me and is going to leave me alone. I feel a pang of guilt; what if he's already decided to stop following and harassing me? There's no need for Marcus to scare him off now, I should tell Jack, tell him to call Marcus off.

But what if tonight is a one off? What if Dylan decided to do something tomorrow or the day after? What if he takes Benny and tortures him? If I tell Jack to have him left alone, I won't be able to go back on that. No, I'll leave things as they are; it's in Jack's hands now and, a small part of me thinks, Dylan deserves to be punished.

With a mind of their own, my steps take me to the front of Will's cottage and I look up at their bedroom window. The curtains are closed and there are no lights on either upstairs or down, the cottage is in darkness. I quietly open the gate and walk around to the back garden to see if there are any lights on at the back but it's in darkness, too. I stand in the garden and stare at the back door as if it will tell me what to do. What if Lucinda has attacked him and Will is lying inside the cottage, injured, or dead?

I should do something.

I know that there's a key to the back door hidden in the shed. It's out of sight on the wooden ledge that runs around the inside underneath the roof. Will put it there because he said that if he locks himself out, he'd never be able to get back into the cottage without a key. Both of the exterior doors are new with triple-locks made of tough composite, much stronger than wood. All of the cottage doors and windows are new and have safety glass and locks on them. They may look old-fashioned and appear to be traditional sash-windows but they're not. Will told me that he locked himself out of their London flat once and had to get a locksmith out. He still winces at the memory of the amount of money it cost to break into his own house.

I pick my way through the rough ground towards the shed and once there, I open the shed door slowly, cringing at the noise that the hinges make as I open it. It sounds as loud as a gunshot in the silence. Once the door is open, I stand perfectly still for a moment, expecting lights to start going on in the house.

After a minute there's nothing, no lights, no noise, no sign of anyone having heard, so I step into the shed. I leave the door open to avoid the ear-splitting noise and point my phone torch upwards and feel around the ledge with my fingers until I find the familiar shape of a key. As I come out of the shed with the key and head towards the house, I tell myself that everything is fine and that Will has simply fallen into a deep sleep. The house is in darkness because it's the early hours of the morning and they're both asleep. There's absolutely no need to panic; I'll simply go into the house and reassure myself that he's okay. I can then return the key to the shed and go home to bed and no one will ever know that I've been here.

I put the key in the back door lock and slowly turn it. It turns easily and silently, not like our old back door which protests at every turn. Leaving the key in the lock, I pull the handle down and quietly open the door and step into the kitchen. There's a smell of food in the air, spicy and pungent, a curry perhaps. I slip my feet out of my flip-flops and leave them by the door then cross the kitchen and pad through into the lounge. Once in the lounge, I turn on my phone torch and partly cover the beam with my hand and point it at the floor. I stand still for a moment and listen but the only thing I can hear is my own breathing. I cross the lounge and go through the open doorway into the hallway and stand at the bottom of the stairs.

Keeping the half-beam of the light low on the floor, I shine it on the stairs. They're in total darkness and I step forward and begin to slowly climb the steps.

So far, so good, I tell myself as I reach the landing, there's no need to panic. There are no signs of any violence, no knocked over furniture, everything looks ordered and tidy and I begin to feel foolish for letting my imagination run away with me. My vision of blood-spattered walls and a deranged Lucinda having killed Will is just a hysterical nightmare of my over-active mind. Will has simply fallen into a deep sleep and didn't wake up to come and meet me. It's not as if he can set an alarm call to wake himself up. He's going to be so cross with himself when he wakes up in the morning and realises that he missed our time together.

By the time I reach the bedroom door, I'm already mentally planning my journey back out of the cottage. Their bedroom door is slightly ajar and I stand outside and listen, sure that I can hear the sound of breathing, although perhaps it's my own. I touch the door lightly with my fingertips and gently push it open. I don't want to wake them, but I've come all the way here so I might as well check Will is okay. Already in my mind, I know that he is.

I stare into the room and let my eyes adjust to the darkness.

I clamp my hand over my mouth to stop myself

from crying out as I stand and stare at the bed, my eyes wide, unable to believe what I'm seeing.

This is so much worse than anything I ever imagined.

* * *

'You look tired darling.' Mum is sitting across the table from me and is looking at me with concern.

I don't answer her but take a bite of my toast, as if this will convince her that I'm fine. I feel like death and I never slept at all.

'Is there something troubling you, Layla?'

I nearly choke on my toast.

'Do you mean something other than the mother you told me was dead being very much alive?'

As soon as the words are out of my mouth, I feel disgusted with myself. Mum's face crumples and I want to reach over and put my arms around her but the selfish part of me won't allow it. She gets up from her chair, picks up her plate and walks slowly across the kitchen to the dishwasher, opens the door and carefully places the plate in the rack. By the time she turns around, she's regained her composure and comes and sits back down.

'I understand why you lied to me, Mum,' I say. 'About my mother. I'm not angry with you. I know all about her.'

She stares at me for a moment and then begins to cry. I reach across the table and take her hand in mine. I hold her hand tightly, as if she'll know how sorry *I* am. She's been in hospital and had to cope with the cancer scare all on her own and I feel another wave of disgust for my lack of attention to her; lately, it's all been about me. On some level I become aware that she's going to talk to me about my birth mother and not ignore it any longer.

'I'm sorry, Layla, so, so sorry,' Mum sobs. 'I wanted to tell you the truth and then time went by and it seemed more and more unreal. And you never wanted to know anything about her, so I convinced myself that I was doing the right thing. I know that's no excuse; what I did was unforgiveable but once I'd said it, I couldn't face telling you that I'd lied. It was such a stupid, spur of the moment lie and I'm not even sure why I lied because you didn't ever want any details. I always told myself that if you asked me, I'd tell you, even though I'd lied to you for all these years. But when that letter arrived, I just panicked.'

'I wish I'd never found it, Mum. I wish I didn't know.'

'I'm so sorry.'

'Don't be. I'm sorry I ever found out because I was better off not knowing. What's the point of knowing the truth when it's so awful? A lie is much better. You were only trying to protect me; I can't blame you for that.'

Mum's sobs gradually subside and I let go of her hand and get up from the table and walk to the countertop and turn the kettle on. I make us both another cup of tea and take them over to the table and then sit down again.

'I won't lie to you anymore,' Mum says. 'Ask me anything, and if I know, I'll tell you.'

'No, it's fine. I know all that I need to. I've read all about her on the internet. There's nothing more *to* know about Tamsin Greenton.'

'She was very young,' Mum says, after a moment.

'Don't make excuses for her, Mum, because there are none.'

'Sorry.'

'I look just like her, don't I? The absolute image of her. I wish I didn't.'

'Don't say that, darling, you're so beautiful, don't hate the way you look.'

If there was the slightest doubt about who my birth mother is – and there isn't, because the facts speak for themselves – the photographs of her alone would have convinced me that she's my mother. We look like twins.

'Are you going to meet her?' Mum asks.

'No,' I lie, shaking my head.

'Really?' I see relief in her eyes and I'm glad I've lied to her, because she doesn't deserve to be hurt. I would have lied to me, too, if I'd been Mum, she was only trying to protect me.

'I don't want to meet her,' I lie. 'You're my mother and I don't need anyone else.'

'Was she the reason that you didn't sleep last night?'

'No,' I say, surprising myself. 'It was something

else.'

'You can talk to me,' she says, softly. 'About anything.'

She knows. I badly want to confide in her about Will, I want to talk about it all. I feel as if I'm going mad with everything whirling around in my head. I couldn't sleep last night because my brain wouldn't stop with everything, it was on a constant loop that made me feel as if I was going insane.

'I've been seeing someone,' I say. 'Will. From across the cottage opposite.'

She nods and smiles and reaches across the table and takes hold of my hand.

'How long have you known?' I ask.

'A little while. I guessed. I watched you going to his cottage when you thought I was asleep.'

This time, I'm the one who cries and I tell her about last night, and how much I love Will. How every time I close my eyes, the same picture of Will's bedroom is imprinted on my eyelids. I've tried to tell myself that I'm overreacting but it's not working, I can't erase what I saw last night.

Will and Lucinda were both asleep as I stood in their bedroom doorway looking at them. They didn't stir at all; they had no idea that I was standing there. I think I'd know; I think even if I was asleep, I'd still have that sixth sense that tells me someone is spying on me.

Not that it matters.

The duvet was thrown back from the bed

because it was warm inside their bedroom, despite the slight chill outside. They were lying together on Will's side of the bed, Lucinda's pillow remained on her side of the bed and was undented by any imprint of her head. Will was lying on his back and Lucinda was nestled into his chest and his arm was over her body, holding her close. One of Lucinda's legs was resting on Will's leg and they looked like any normal, loving couple, sleeping together.

And they were both naked.

I confide all of this to Mum but I don't tell her about the pure rage that engulfed me as I watched them. Or the compulsion I had to pick up Lucinda's pillow and hold it over her face and press down with all of my strength until she wasn't a problem anymore. That, I keep to myself.

I don't know how long I stood there but I was brought to my senses when Lucinda murmured in her sleep and moved closer to Will. I don't know how but I made myself walk out of the room. I walked down those stairs and into the kitchen, making no attempt to be quiet. I slipped my flip-flops on and let myself out of the back door and locked it behind me. I don't remember walking across the lane and coming home, although obviously I did. I found myself standing in my bedroom, wondering how I'd got here and I couldn't stop shaking. I was still holding the key to Will's back door in my hand – but I don't tell Mum this, either.

When I've finished speaking there's silence and

Mum has such a sad expression on her face. She reaches her hand up to my face and gently pushes the hair from my eyes, just as she did when I was a child.

'Oh, Layla,' she says, softly. 'Not again.'

'What?' I demand.

I think she's going to cry again.

'What do you mean, Mum?' I ask, more softly, because I hate to see her cry.

She's silent for a moment and then takes a deep breath.

'It's like before, Layla, and you know how that ended.'

I want to shout at her but I stop myself, behaving like a chid will just make her think that she's right.

'It's nothing like before.' My voice is measured and calm. 'Will and I love each other, it's not a stupid crush.'

'He's married, Layla.'

'He doesn't love her, he's told me. He wants to leave her but she won't let him.' I don't tell her that Lucinda's ill and that's why Will can't leave her because what would she think of me then?

'If he doesn't love her, why was he lying naked in bed with her?'

I stare at Mum for a moment.

'She forced him, tricked him somehow.' There must be a reason, Will wouldn't betray me with her, he *wouldn't*. The more I think about it, the more I know that there must be a reason for what

I saw last night. There *is* a perfectly reasonable explanation, I can see that now.

Mum shakes her head and reaches towards me but I sit back in the chair, out of her reach.

'I can help you, Layla, if you let me.'

'I don't need help, I'm fine. Once I've spoken to Will, he'll explain it all, he doesn't want *her,* he wants me. It's just a blip, that's all.'

Mum bites her lip.

'Honestly, Mum, don't worry, this is nothing like before.'

'Darling,' she says hesitantly. 'I know you say that this is different from before but are you sure? I mean, you didn't *do anything*, did you, last night, when you saw them?'

I stare at her.

'Don't be angry with me.' Her mouth is set in a tight line, her expression grim. 'I'm trying to protect you.'

I shake my head, refusing to speak.

'Layla.' Mum looks at me with concern. 'It's okay, if you've done something bad I can help you, but you need to tell me *now*.'

CHAPTER NINETEEN

Mum's gone out. Lorna, the village gossip, picked her up in her car and took her to the community hall to meet up with all of the other Women's Institute members. They've all been baking like mad and it sounds as if they're having a bit of a tea party. Mum tried to persuade me to go with her but I flatly refused so then she said that she'd stay at home with me. I lied and told her I was meeting up with Jack in town but I'm not sure she believed me.

I seem to be lying a lot, lately.

I could tell that Mum didn't want to go but I told her that everyone had baked cakes in her honour and how would it look if she cancelled at the last minute? She hates to let people down or seem ungrateful so she couldn't really argue then, she *had* to go.

I'm trying very hard not to be angry with Mum for what she said to me. This is *nothing* like what happened with Darius Curran or Mr Evans, nothing at all. I don't have a silly crush on Will, it's love, and obviously this isn't one-sided because Will feels the same way about me. I'm sure there's a logical explanation for what I saw last night; maybe Lucinda got Will drunk and threw herself at him or perhaps she wraps herself around him like that to sleep but that's it, that's all. Anyway, Mum must realise that it's not a crush because she knows that I've been spending the night with him in his cottage so I just don't understand why she's saying such things to me.

When she asked me if I'd done something bad, for a moment I thought she meant if I'd had sex with Will. I would have thought it was obvious because we're hardly going to spend the night together and sit and talk, are we? Then I realised that of course she didn't mean that, because she wouldn't think having sex was a bad thing. She asked if I'd done something bad, *last night,* when Will and I weren't even together. Honestly, I think it's all got a bit much for Mum and she's getting confused. I've never done anything bad. Mum's getting it all mixed up in her mind and has obviously forgotten that it was Darius Curran who picked on me and I was only defending myself just as anyone else would. He's going to lie and say I started it, isn't he? Because it doesn't look good, does it, starting a fight with a girl?

And I wasn't charged, so that just proved he was lying. As for the damage to Mr Evans's car, that was mindless vandalism by persons unknown and nothing whatsoever to do with me. Mum knows that, too, despite the rumours that were circulated by my so-called school friends. I mean, really, what did she think I might have done? I may have felt hateful towards Lucinda but I've kept that totally to myself, so I don't know why Mum would even *say* such a thing to me.

Obviously, the week Mum spent in hospital has been more of a strain on her than I thought.

Coupled with me finding out about my birth mother and confronting her about it, I think it's all become too much for her and she's not thinking straight. All I can do now is try and shield her from any more stress so she can recover fully from her surgery and get back to her old self. An afternoon with her WI pals will do her the world of good.

I cross the lounge and look out of the lounge window for what seems like the hundredth time to see if Lucinda's car is still parked outside their cottage; disappointingly, it is. Why doesn't she go out or go running or something? I need to talk to Will and I can't wait until Monday so she needs to fuck off, right now. Anywhere will do, just as long as she goes. If I sit by the window all afternoon, I'll be sure not to miss her if she does leave the cottage. I'm just settling down in the rocking chair, which has a perfect view of the lane, when my mobile rings. I grab it quickly from the coffee table and am immediately crushed to see *Jack* on the screen and not *Will*.

'Hi Jack.' I try to sound upbeat and normal, but I'm not sure if I succeed.

'Hey. Can you talk?'

'Of course,' I say.

'There's no one listening?' He sounds serious, not like Jack at all.

'There's no one here except me, I'm in the house on my own. Have you found her? My mother?'

'What? No not yet.' He sounds distracted. 'Look, I asked Marcus and he'll find her for you no problem. He said you could probably find her yourself if you tried. No, it's not that, it's the other thing.'

I'm puzzled for a moment and then realise that he means Dylan. 'Okay.'

'Marcus is a bit twitchy about it, 'cos he doesn't know you. I've persuaded him to do it as a favour for me, but he needs insurance.'

'Insurance?'

'Yeah. Because if you change your mind or try to back out, he's the one taking all the risk. If the police come sniffing around and you get the shits and decide to shop him, he'd be fucked because it'd be his word against yours. And the police never believe anything he says anyway because he's got previous and once they start digging, they're going to find something on him. So, you need to do something that puts you in the mix if you want it to go ahead, so that if the police come sniffing around, you'll be implicated as well as Marcus."

'What?' I ask. Although I'm not sure now that I do want to go ahead with it. It's starting to seem too real.

'Write this number down.'

'Can't you text me it?'

'No.'

I get up and cross the room and pick up Mum's crossword book and pen. Of course he can't text me it because then Jack would be incriminated.

'I'm ready.'

Jack reads me the number and I write it on the corner of the last page of Mum's crossword book. I read the number back to him to make sure I've written it down properly.

'It's a burner phone,' Jack pauses. 'You send him one message and that's it, nothing else. Ever.'

'Okay.'

'You only have one day to do it, so you need to make your mind up. Send him the full name and address and picture if you can. Do you have a picture?'

'No, of course not.'

'Be better if you had a picture but too bad if you haven't. Name and address should be enough, maybe describe him, too. That's all, nothing else. Send it and then delete the message. Don't save the number to your contacts and make sure you destroy the paper you wrote it on.'

'What's the point of sending him the message if I delete it all from my phone?'

Jack sighs. 'Just 'cos you delete it, doesn't mean the police can't prove you sent it. You have to make it look as if you were trying to hide it. Like I say, it's insurance.'

'Okay, okay. And that's it? That's all I have to do?'

'Yeah, that's it. Be sure though, Layla, before you do it, because once you send that message there's no going back. You won't be able to change your mind.'

'Okay.'

'Right, gotta go. See you next week.'

I say *goodbye* and end the call. I notice that Jack never referred to Dylan by name and it all seems very cloak and dagger and slightly ridiculous, as if he's playing a prank on me. I wonder if he is, because he hasn't given me my mother's address, yet he told me it would be easy. If it's so easy to find someone, why hasn't Marcus found her yet? Surely Jack wouldn't play such a joke on me, would he? He's my friend.

Or at least I think he is, I'm not sure of anything anymore.

I carefully tear the corner of the page with the phone number on it out of the book and fold it up. I take off the plastic cover on the back of my phone and put the piece of paper inside and then clip the cover back on. I'll think about it later, I have too much other stuff on my mind right now to be bothered with it. I glance through the lounge window just in time to see Lucinda opening the driver's side door of her car. She tosses several empty *bags for life* onto the back seat and climbs into the driver's seat and pulls the door closed. I hold my breath, waiting to see if Will is going to join her. I hear her start the car up and I breathe a sigh of relief as I watch her drive off down the lane towards the main road. I jump up from the rocking chair and Benny looks up hopefully at me from his basket. I bend down and stroke him and tell him *later* and with a sigh, he puts his head between his paws. I go out into the hall and pick up my keys from the shelf and let myself out of the front door.

I walk quickly up the lane, past the tree where Will and I always meet, and then into the fields that run along the back of Will's cottage. As I walk through the grass I check my watch; two-fifteen. If Lucinda has gone to Chiverson's or Tesco's on the outskirts of Wellerton, she'll be at least a couple of hours because the roads and the shops will be busy on a Saturday afternoon.

When I reach the end of their garden, I walk slowly along, looking for a gap in the hedge. Just behind the shed I spot a way through, and I bend down and squeeze through the hedge and step over into the garden. I'm not quite sure why I came this way instead of walking across the lane, and I'm trying to ignore the part of my brain that's telling me it's because I don't want Will to see me coming.

In case he decides not to answer the door.

I'm being stupid and catastrophising, of course Will wants to see me; the only reason he didn't come last night was because of *her*. She stopped him, I know it, he would have come if he could. I walk up the garden towards the back of the house and when I reach the back door, I put my hand on the handle and press it down.

It's not locked. I open the door and walk in.

'Forgotten your purse?' Will calls out from the lounge.

I walk through the kitchen and into the lounge to see Will stretched out on the sofa, remote control in hand, watching TV.

'Layla,' he says, looking up at me. He looks surprised, shocked even, and swings his legs off the sofa and onto the floor.

I cross the room and sit down next to him but he moves away from me. I long to throw myself into his arms but there's something about him that's stopping me, he's not his usual self.

'I waited and waited last night,' I say. 'And I messaged you so many times but you never answered. What's going on, Will?'

He sighs, and leans forward and puts his head in his hands, raking his fingers through his hair. I wait. I could tell him what I saw last night, but I don't. I want to see if he'll tell me.

'I'm sorry, Layla.' He turns his head and looks at me.

'Did you oversleep?'

'What?' He looks confused.

'Last night? Is that why you didn't come and meet me? You fell asleep?'

'No. I didn't meet you because we need to stop seeing each other.' His voice is cold and he won't look at me and my worst fears are confirmed.

'Please don't say that.' My voice comes out as a whisper.

'I'm sorry, we should never have started it, *I* should never have started it. We need to finish.'

'No!' I almost shout and Will looks at me, alarm on his face. 'When Lucinda's better the two of us can be together properly.'

'WHAT?' he demands, as if he doesn't know what I'm talking about.

'I know you said she'll never let you go but she can't hang onto you forever, can she? She'll either get better or she'll have to face facts, won't she? She has to realise that you don't love her anymore. We can make this work, Will, I know we can.'

Will shakes his head and takes hold of my hand.

'Layla, listen to me.' His voice softens. 'Forget about me and move on. You're young, you have your whole life ahead of you and you'll meet someone your own age, not an old man like me.'

'Forget about you?'

'Yes, forget about me. We've had fun but all good things come to an end, don't they?' He grins and I stare at him unbelievingly.

'Fun?'

He caresses my hand with his fingers and smiles at me.

'It was fun, wasn't it? The whole clandestine meeting thing and keeping it secret made it exciting for a while, but you know I'm married, Layla, you've always known I'm married.'

'I love you, Will, and you love me.'

'Love me?' He looks stunned. 'We barely know each other.'

'Time doesn't matter, Will. I love you so much and I know you feel the same way.'

'No, no, no, Layla, I never said I loved you. I *never* said that.' He sits up straight and attempts to move further away but the arm of the sofa prevents him.

'But you said you were obsessed with me, you said you couldn't get enough of me. You said it, Will, you *said* it.'

'Oh, Layla.' Will shakes his head. 'I'm sorry if you got the wrong idea, it was just a bit of fun. A couple of weeks of fun, that's all it was. We're both adults and we were just enjoying each other. I'm a hot-blooded guy and I need a lot of sex. I'm not going to lie, you're not the first and you won't be the last. But it was just sex, Layla, that's all, nothing more. Honestly, I never would have got involved with you if I thought you wanted anything more than that. I never promised you anything. I *never* lied to you.'

I stare at Will in disbelief.

'You think I make a habit of jumping into bed with married men?' I demand.

'Well, yeah, since you put it like that, I do. Lots of girls do and there's nothing wrong with that, is there? Consenting adults and all that. And I didn't have to exactly force myself on you, did I? I mean, come on, we didn't actually do much talking, did we? And don't pretend that you didn't enjoy it as much as me because you were always up for it. And you were the one who chased after me, Layla, you were the one parading around in fuck all in front of your bedroom window.'

'But it wasn't like that,' I say. 'You're making it sound so sordid, Will.'

'Hey, it wasn't sordid.' Will smiles, and looks at his watch. 'There's nothing sordid about two people enjoying each other and it was great while it lasted but it has to be over now, Layla. It's for the best.'

'No.' I shake my head. 'I don't want it to be over. I love you, Will. Please don't say it's over.'

Will gets up from the sofa and looks out of the window.

'I'm sorry, Layla, but I don't love you and I never said that I did. I *never* said that and you know it. And you can't love me because you barely know me. I never promised you anything so don't make this difficult.' He looks at me coldly. 'You need to go now.'

I start to cry and I hear Will sigh, impatiently.

'Maybe I'll just stay here until Lucinda gets home,' I say, through sobs. 'And then I'll tell her about us, and who knows what she'll do then.'

'What?'

'She's not stable, so who knows what will happen.' I don't know why I'm threatening Will, because he doesn't want me, so why don't I just leave?

'Not stable?' Will says. 'What are you talking about?'

'Her illness! Don't you care what might happen if she walked in right now?'

'Nothing would happen. Lucy's not ill.'

'But you told me she was ill, you said if she found out you were seeing me you were frightened of what she might do.'

'Oh, for fuck's sake.' Will laughs. 'Don't pretend that you actually believed that. It was all part of the game and you knew that, Layla, you knew. It was what you wanted to hear, and I obliged. You were into the whole role play thing so don't pretend you weren't. It made the sex a bit more thrilling but we both know it wasn't real. You told me you were a virgin because you knew I'd love it and it would turn me on but it was just make-believe, a sexual fantasy.'

I stare at him, unable to believe what I'm hearing.

'It was fun while it lasted but we're done now, so please, don't humiliate yourself anymore. You're a gorgeous girl but we're over. Just go home.'

'I was a virgin,' I whisper.

'Oh, come *on*.' He laughs. 'You're nineteen, Layla, who the hell's still a virgin at nineteen?'

I stand up and face him.

'I will,' I say. 'Tell Lucinda. About us.'

Will starts to laugh and then stops abruptly.

'Go right ahead if you want to totally humiliate

yourself,' he says, nastily. 'She won't believe you; she thinks you have a massive crush on me.'

'I'll tell her the truth, I'll convince her.'

'Will you, though? We met in secret, nobody knew, except us. She thinks you're a love-struck kid with a crush on me, Layla, *because that's what I've told her.* And your behaviour when you saw us that day, in the supermarket? That convinced her even more. So if you want to make a complete fool of yourself, knock yourself out.'

I step towards him and put my hand on his cheek but he steps backwards, away from me, as if I've burned him.

'Please, Will,' I beg. 'Forget what I said about love, just don't finish with me. We can still meet, have sex, whatever you want.'

He stares down at me without smiling and I feel such total shame for begging him.

'Go home, Layla. Just go home.'

'Just tell me why, Will, why you want us to be over. What did I do wrong?'

'Oh, I don't know.' Will looks up at the ceiling, as if he's looking for something. 'Everything has it's time-limit, I suppose, doesn't it?'

'Does it?'

'Yeah.' He stretches his arms above his head, as if he's just got out of bed.

'Time-limit?' I echo.

'Yep.' He yawns. 'And maybe,' he adds. 'I was getting a bit bored.'

CHAPTER TWENTY

The time immediately after I left Will's cottage is a blur to me; I went home but I have no memory of doing so. I do have some memories of that afternoon; snapshots of crying and sobbing uncontrollably and trying to understand why Will was being so cruel. I know that there were also moments of pure rage; rage at Will for doing this to me, for his lying and for making me believe that we had a future together. He did lie, no matter what he says, and he knew that I believed what he told me about Lucinda. The anger and rage were all mixed up with love and the terrible heartbreak of knowing that I'd never be in his arms again, that he'd never hold me close, that he would never speak to me again, except in passing. It would be as if we'd never been together at all.

By the time Mum came home from her WI event it was gone ten o'clock and I was lying on the lounge floor in the darkness. I was curled up in a ball on the rug with my arms wrapped tightly around a bewildered Benny and I have no idea how long I'd been lying there. I'd stopped crying by then, but my throat was raw and my eyes were so sore and puffy that I could hardly open them. When I looked in the mirror later that night before I went to bed, the whites of my eyes were so pink and the eyelids so swollen that I looked as if I had conjunctivitis.

Mum gently helped me up from the floor as if I were an invalid, and sat me on the sofa and wrapped the furry throw around me. I was shivering, even though it was a warm night, and I sat on the sofa whilst she bustled about, making me tea and toast. I made no attempt to stop her because I was spent and exhausted.

When she asked me what had happened, I told her everything, leaving no detail out. I felt humiliated when I repeated the things that Will had said to me but I wanted her to know. I wanted her to see how bad it was and to know every single thing that he'd said. I could see the anger in Mum's eyes, even though she tried to hide it. I even told her how I begged him not to finish with me and offered sex as a way to keep him, I held nothing back. Mum listened without speaking and when I'd finished, she hugged me and said that although I felt terrible now, it would pass, it was just a matter of time. She said that Will was a cold-hearted bastard and I'd had a lucky escape. I was shocked with the way she spoke about him because Mum *never* swears and there was such coldness in her voice when she said it.

The next day, even though it took every bit of effort that I possessed, I made myself get up, get showered and dressed because I knew that I couldn't spend my life pining for Will. I knew that if I gave in to it, that would be the end of me. Mum and I took Benny out for a walk and he loved it because I've neglected him lately and walks have been few and far between. I felt bad about that, too, and realised that since I met Will, everything has been about him. All I could think about was Will, even with Mum being ill I'd selfishly put him above everything and everyone.

Not anymore.

We took Benny into the fields at the back of our house, going through the hedge at the end of our garden so that we could avoid going past Will's cottage. We stayed out for several hours and by the time we came back we were all worn out. It took all of our effort to cook dinner and then slump on the sofa afterwards and mindlessly watch TV. We did the same thing when we got up on Monday, although I couldn't stop myself from looking out of my bedroom window at Will's cottage when I was opening the curtains. Lucinda's car wasn't parked out the front, so she'd gone to London as usual. It seemed unreal that only a week earlier,

Will had turned up at the door to end things but had changed his mind when he saw me. How stupid was I to think that he loved me, that he couldn't live without me, when all he actually wanted was sex.

A week ago, I believed that I had a future with him.

What a fool I've been.

As Mum and I walked around the fields, she could see how preoccupied I was and I made the decision then that I had to move on, hard though it would be. I won't make a mistake like Will again. When I told Mum this, she said that the mistake wasn't mine but Will's, and that karma would pay him back one day. She made me think of Jack when she said that, because that's what he said about Ron. Only it wasn't karma that got Ron, it was Marcus. I then started thinking about Marcus and for some reason this made me feel uncomfortable, but I'm not exactly sure why. I had a feeling that I need to remember something but every time I tried, the memory would disappear like smoke.

Maybe Lucinda will cheat on Will, Mum suggested, and that would be karma because then he'd know how it felt to be thrown aside as if he counted for nothing. Maybe she'd be cruel to him and say unforgiveable things and then he would know the pain of loving someone who didn't love him back.

We both wondered then if Will really cared about Lucinda or if she was just convenient and useful, because she had a good job. He cheated on her before he met me and he'll do it again, because he said he would. As Mum says, Will is not a decent person, because decent people don't behave in that way. But even knowing that, I still can't help loving him, because when we were together, he made me feel loved, even if it was all a lie. There's a small part of me that hates him, too, so I know that I will get over him eventually, it's just a matter of time. I want to wish the months away so that I can be over him. I wish I could go to sleep and wake up in six months' time and he's a distant memory and I don't love him or hate him anymore, because those emotions are exhausting. I want to feel indifferent to him, to not even notice he's there, to be able to pass him in the lane and feel absolutely nothing. Then, I'll know I'm over him. As I said to Mum, it would be easier if he didn't live opposite us, easier if he wasn't there and I didn't have the fear of seeing him every time I step outside the front door. But it is what it is; he's not going anywhere and I'll just have to deal with it.

I feel as if I'm waking from a dream in a strange sort of way. My life has changed so much in such a short time. The strain of discovering the truth about my birth mother, meeting and then losing Will, the veiled threats from Dylan. It's all been too much.

There are blank spaces over the last few days where I can't clearly remember what I was doing or where I was. Mum thinks that I have a form of post-traumatic stress and my brain is struggling to cope. I think she might be right. I'm trying to be honest with myself, especially about Will. Did I throw myself at him? Did I pursue him? Maybe I did, because I didn't exactly play hard to get.

But that was because I loved him.

Will can pretend that it was just sex but he must have known that it wasn't for me. Why tell such a lie about Lucinda being ill? Why the hell would he tell a lie like that? He knew exactly how I felt and chose to play on my feelings because it suited him. He can call it a game and fantasy now but he's lying, he knew it wasn't a game for me.

I don't think I'll tell Jack the truth about Will, even though he is my friend. It's too humiliating; I know he would sympathise but I couldn't bear for him to look at me with pity.

It's over, and Will is gone from my life and it's only a matter of time before I no longer care.

At least that's what I keep telling myself

* * *

Jack and I are standing at the end of the smoking shelter and Jack is puffing away on a cigarette as if his life depended on it. It's our break and we only have fifteen minutes so there's not enough time to go to our favourite spot at the end of the car park. Besides, the weather has broken and it's raining. Hard. I move closer to Jack in attempt to stop the splashes from the rain landing on my hair.

'Is your Mum back to normal now?' Jack asks.

'Pretty much,' I say, dodging a massive drip from the shelter roof. 'We've been doing lots of walking and getting lots of exercise and fresh air, trying to get out and about. Poor old Benny's worn out. We went out for a pub lunch yesterday for a change which was nice, we haven't done that in ages. Good job the weather wasn't like this while we were sitting in the pub garden.'

It was nice, too. We sat and chatted and the sun was shining and it was a lovely day. We people watched a bit, too, because it was busy for a weekday, and I realised when we got home that I hadn't thought about Will for nearly two hours. So that was progress, of sorts.

'You've both had a shit time of it lately.'

'All over now, though.' I've already told Jack about Will; I kept it brief, said that we were done and I was fine about it. I told him that I ended it because I couldn't see Will ever leaving his wife, no matter what he said. I also said that I thought Will was too old for me and the age gap was too big. I felt pleased when I said it, because I was being spiteful. And then I thought about it and I realised I was right, he was nineteen years older than me, twice my age. When I'm thirty he'd be nearly fifty. I don't know if Jack believed me but he didn't ask any questions and I was relieved about that because I'm not sure I could have kept up the pretence.

'So,' Jack says, lighting yet another cigarette,

even though we have to go back to work in exactly three minutes.

'What about that streak of piss? You seen him?'

'No, not at all.' I've not even given Dylan a thought. I haven't felt as if I'm being watched, no tingle on the back of the neck, nothing. But maybe I've had too much on my mind to even notice. Today is the first time that I've been out on my own, without Mum. Although, technically, we were together this morning because Mum dropped me at work so she can have the car to deliver her paintings to the galleries in Wellerton. I have a feeling that Mum was just pretending to go to the galleries so that I didn't have to drive to work on my own. She's so over-protective although I've tried to tell her I'm fine, or I'm going to be fine. With all that's gone on I haven't even thought about Dylan.

'That's good,' Jack says. 'Maybe he's got the message.'

He doesn't ask if I sent a message to Marcus's burner phone and I remember what he said about Ron; the less he knows, the better. I have that uncomfortable feeling again and I can't quite put my finger on why; it's as if I've I forgotten something important.

'And that other thing you asked me? I've got you an address.'

I look at him blankly for a moment before it sinks in that he means my birth mother.

'You have?'

'Yep. I was going to text you but thought I might as well wait and give it to you as I was seeing you today.' He reaches into his trouser pocket and pulls out a piece of folded up paper and hands it to me. I slowly unfurl the paper and read the address.

'Not far from here,' Jack says. 'Only about thirty miles.'

'Thanks, Jack. Thank you so much.'

I refold the paper and tuck it into the zip up pocket of my jacket, although I don't need the paper to remember the address because it's now imprinted on my brain along with everything else that I know about her. I know where she lives, her name and what she looks like, I have everything that I need to find her.

And most of all, I know what she did.

My mother wasn't a victim. She wasn't the woman called Janice Caddell who I read about in the newspaper clipping. She wasn't murdered whilst her baby slept upstairs in her cot.

No, that woman wasn't my mother.

My mother was called Tamsin Greenton and she was the person who beat Janice Caddell to death.

CHAPTER TWENTY-ONE

As I reverse the car off our driveway, I can't help glancing over at Will's cottage. His car isn't there and neither is Lucinda's. I haven't seen Will at all this week and I wonder if he's deliberately staying away so he can avoid me. I know that he had to go to London on Wednesday but I've not seen him since and it's now Friday. He'll be staying in London with Lucinda, sharing her hotel room with her, spending the nights with her, sleeping with her.

My insides twist and I ram the car into first gear and tear off up the lane. I'm not going to think about him; I'm not going to allow the images of him with Lucinda to mar my day. If I don't think about him then I'm fine, and I'm getting better at not thinking about him as each day goes by. But I know that it's too late now; because I've stupidly let him in and now he's in my head. Will and Lucinda in bed, Will making love to her as he did to me, whispering to her, loving her, caressing her. An overpowering longing to be in his arms hits me like a physical force.

Oh God, I miss him so much.

Panic fills me and I want to howl and cry like an animal and force him to come back to me.

I want him so badly, it hurts.

I tell myself that I'm getting better each day, that I'm getting over him. And I *am* getting better at not thinking about him; I can go for hours at a time but once I let him in, the same longing comes back. It's no use lying to myself; if Will changed his mind and wanted me back, I wouldn't hesitate for a second, no matter how badly he might treat me. Just for a moment I allow myself the luxury of remembering how we were; the feel of him, the memory of his body entwined with mine, the way he made me feel.

I was getting a bit bored.

His words come back to me like a slap in the face and I force all thoughts of him from my mind. He's a bastard, just remember that, Layla, he's a heartless bastard and you're well rid. The blast of a horn makes me jump and I slam my foot on the brake when I realise that I've reached the roundabout and am making no attempt to slow down. The car screeches to a juddering halt and I stop half-way onto the roundabout, cars veering around me, blasting their horns at me.

Concentrate, Layla, before you kill yourself or someone else.

I fix my eyes on the road and push Will from my mind and when a gap finally opens in the traffic, I pull away and continue on my way to work. I *can* forget about him; I just need to give myself something to think about instead of him. This is how I spend my days; forcing myself to not think of him and then letting him in, just for a moment, so that I can remember how wonderful it was, and then forcing myself to forget him all over again.

I can get over him.

I will.

I arrive at work and park the car up in the car park closest to the store and hurry across to the staff entrance. After my shift today, it'll be the weekend and it stretches miserably ahead of me and I try to think of something that I can do to fill the days. I never used to feel like this before I met Will, I was content to while away my days helping Mum with her art stuff and keeping house, reading and pottering around. I seriously need to get some more friends and something worthwhile to fill my time. Maybe I should go to college or university, start planning for my future instead of waiting for life to happen to me.

Live life on your own terms.

That's what Mum always says and maybe she's right. I should start thinking about what I can do with my life instead of relying on one person to make me happy. Waiting for someone else to be solely responsible for my entire happiness isn't healthy, is it?

This is going through my mind as I walk quickly through the supermarket and out into the warehouse area at the back. As I continue on through to the staff lockers, the idea begins to take root that I need to look to the future and *do* something. If I start to plan my future it will give me something to focus on because I have my whole life ahead of me and I can't drift through it like a ghost. I start to feel slightly optimistic as I walk and I remind myself again that *I can do this* and then feel foolish when I realise that I've spoken aloud. Luckily there aren't very many people around as the store doesn't open until eight o'clock. As I emerge into the locker area, I'm surprised to see Jack is already in and at his open locker, stuffing his backpack inside.

'Morning mate.' He slams his locker closed, snaps his padlock shut and slips his bunch of keys into his pocket. The lockers originally had combination locks but most of them are broken and nearly everyone brings their own padlock and wedges it through the handle to keep it secure. We're supposed to leave our mobile phones in our lockers but no one ever does; not least because several of the lockers have been jimmied open, padlock or no padlock.

'Hi, Jack.' I unlock my padlock and slip my lunchbox inside and then close it. 'You're early.'

'Yeah, I know.' He rolls his eyes. 'Dunno how that

happened. Won't make that mistake again.'

'You'll be after the manager's job next,' I say, with a smile. Maybe if I smile and pretend that I'm happy, eventually I will be happy. Fake it until I make it.

Jack makes a snorting sound.

'I'm going out for a fag, too early to start work yet, I'm not giving them any time for free. You coming?'

'I'll come out and watch you smoke,' I say, glancing at my watch to see that it's only a quarter-to-seven. I follow him out through the back entrance and we stand at the end of the shelter. It's a beautiful morning, only one tiny, solitary, fluffy white cloud floating across the pure blue sky. Much too nice a day to dwell on things that I can't change.

'I was thinking about going back to college,' I say, as Jack lights up a cigarette.

'Oh, yeah?' Jack looks at me in surprise. 'To do what?'

'I don't know.' I shrug. 'There are hundreds of courses to choose from, there must be something that appeals to me. I just think I should do something instead of drifting around waiting for something to happen. Take control of my life. Can't do any harm, can it?'

'Makes sense.' Jack takes a deep drag. 'Because you're wasted stacking shelves.'

'So are you. You could come, too.'

Jack looks at me, frowns and then looks around

to make sure that we're alone.

'My reading and writing aren't up to it. I'd look a dick. A thick dick.'

'I could help you with that. It wouldn't take long either because you're clever Jack, and you're quick.'

He shakes his head. 'Nah, it's not for me. I've told you; I've had a different life from you. I'm not like you. I live in a different world.' He looks down at the ground and sucks furiously on his cigarette.

'Maybe you could change that, too, Jack. Maybe you could be a different person. Change your world. Have a different life from the one you think you have to have.'

We stand in silence and I watch as Jack smokes; I can see that he's thinking about what I've said. I've made him think.

'Think about it, there's no rush to make your mind up,' I say. 'Don't just say no.'

He shrugs but he doesn't say no, so I'm hopeful, because it suddenly seems very important to me that Jack has a life, a proper life. He doesn't have to be like Marcus and live in Marcus's world, he can break away from him and start again.

'I suppose we'd better go in,' I say. 'It's nearly seven o'clock.'

Jack inhales from the butt end of his cigarette one last time and stubs it out in the overflowing ashtray.

'Hang on a sec,' he says, pulling his phone out of his pocket. 'Better put this on silent or else I'll have some arsehole frogmarching me out of the store to put it in my locker.'

He looks down at his phone screen and then looks up at me.

'What's up?'

His eyes are suddenly huge and his face has turned pale.

'Jack, what's wrong? What's happened?'

He doesn't reply but slowly turns his screen towards me and I lean forward to read it. Before I've finished reading, the words start to jump around on the page and they won't keep still. The light seems to be fading and everything is growing darker and darker, as if night has fallen at seven o'clock in the morning.

* * *

Brenda the supervisor didn't want me to drive home but I insisted that I was fine. Jack offered to come with me but I wouldn't let him; I just wanted to get away, to get home so that I could try to process what's happened. I don't feel fine at all but I don't want anyone with me, I need to be alone.

The next thing that I remember after Jack showed me his phone was sitting in the staff cafeteria on one of the horribly uncomfortable metal chairs with a cup of tea on the table in front of me. I don't remember walking there and thought I must have passed out but Jack told me that although I went as white as a sheet, he grabbed hold of me and somehow, I managed to stay upright. I'd held onto him and we'd walked into the store and into the canteen. I have absolutely no recollection of doing so.

I never did drink the cup of tea and when a suitable amount of time had passed, I went back to my locker and picked up my things and left. Jack told Brenda that I wasn't feeling very well and had a virus and had come into work when I should clearly have stayed at home. I didn't ask him to lie but I'm glad that he did. The truth would involve explaining too much and the gossip mill would start spinning. I would have become known as the girl who was having an affair with a married man who was twice her age.

A married man who was now dead.

Will is dead.

The words echo through my head and I grip the steering wheel even tighter and try to concentrate on the road. I definitely shouldn't be driving because my brain is refusing to concentrate. I'm not safe and could easily have an accident.

Like Will.

When Jack pulled his phone out of his pocket to turn it to silent, a news item flashed up and it was this that I saw when he showed me the screen. The headline was *Local man dies in tragic accident* and underneath was a picture of Will; a picture that had been taken on his wedding day.

Will died after falling onto the tracks at a London tube station whilst waiting for a train. The station was very busy and Will was standing at the front of the crowded platform when there was a sudden surge forward as the train entered the station. Will stumbled and fell onto the tracks. One of the witnesses who saw him fall, said that there was a brief moment of eye contact with Will as he lay on the tracks. The witness said that he wanted to jump down onto the track and help him up but it was too late, the train was already in the station. Even though the driver attempted to brake, there was no way that the train could avoid hitting Will at speed.

The blare of horns echoes around the car and I realise that I've just run a red light and have narrowly avoided hitting a car coming from the opposite direction. I open my eyes wide, as if this will make a difference and continue along the road, my hands wet with sweat, until I see the roundabout before our lane. I drive carefully around the roundabout, double checking that the way is clear before pulling into the lane. I drive slowly along, past Will's cottage, and then pull up onto our driveway. I pull the handbrake on and turn off the ignition, my hands shaking so much that it takes me three attempts to turn off the ignition.

I rest my head on the steering wheel and close my eyes. A vision of Will lying on the tracks pleading for help as the train is about to hit him fills my head and I open my eyes again. I wish I didn't know that part, I wish the witness had kept that to himself. Surely, he must realise that what he's said will haunt Will's next of kin forever?

Although I'm not his next of kin, am I? Lucinda is.

I feel suddenly exhausted and desperately thirsty and I wish now that I'd drunk the vile tea that was given to me in the canteen. The lucid part of me knows that I'm in shock and also that I was in no fit state to drive. I should never have driven home but for some reason it seemed important that I could be alone so that I could think.

I can't believe he's dead.

I regret now, that I wanted to avoid seeing Will so it would make it easier to get over him. I cannot bear the thought that I'll never see him again. I would do anything to see him again, even though he doesn't – didn't - want me anymore, the fact of his death floors me completely. To think that he's no longer in this world is more than I can bear.

A tapping on the window gradually enters my consciousness and I drag my gaze to the window to see a face staring in at me. I scream when I see who it is and, on some level, I'm aware that the front door of our cottage is opening and Mum is running towards the car. As she reaches the driver's door, Dylan steps back out of the way and pulls the car door open. I can see both of their mouths moving as the door opens but I can't hear anything over the rushing noise in my ears. Dylan's mouth is shaped in a perfect O of surprise as Mum speaks to him. It's as if I'm watching a silent movie only it's not funny, not funny at all.

I feel Mum's arms around me as she helps me get out of the car and she holds me around the waist and walks me up to the front door. My legs feel as if they're made of cotton wool and I feel mildly surprised that they can manage to hold me up. Dylan hovers, taking the keys from the ignition and shutting the car door and I hear the bleep of the key fob as it locks. Some part of my brain registers that Dylan's car is parked on the lane in front of our cottage and I wonder why he's here.

Mum takes me into the lounge and lowers me onto the sofa. The rushing sound is quieter now and I can hear Mum as she tells Dylan to go to the kitchen and make hot, sweet, tea. I attempt to talk and tell her what's happened but she shushes me and tells me that *she's seen the news.* I allow her to tuck cushions behind me, place a throw over me, lay me down like a child. I'm shivering and I can't stop shaking, but I know it isn't cold, because it's a beautiful day outside.

Dylan appears in front of me. He has a mug in his hand and I want to tell him that it's the wrong one, it's the mug I never use because I don't like it. The mug is made of black pottery and tea doesn't taste the same from it, but I don't say anything.

Because there's something that I have to remember, something important that's been circling my brain since last Saturday, since Will told me we were over. Something that's been niggling away and making me feel uncomfortable whenever Marcus's name is mentioned.

Something that I'm not sure about; something that I'm not sure if I actually did or if I just thought about doing because I was so angry.

Something bad.

Something really, really, bad.

CHAPTER TWENTY-TWO

I spend the day lying on the sofa while Mum bustles around making me cups of tea that I don't drink and sandwiches that I don't eat. After bringing me the mug of tea, Dylan disappeared and I assume he went home. I want to ask why he was here but can't summon up the energy. Besides, I don't care. We spend most of the day like this until eventually, Mum goes out into the kitchen and makes dinner. We eat it in the lounge, sitting in front of the TV, or rather, I push the food around my plate until it's cold and Mum takes it away.

We don't talk very much, because what is there to say? Will is dead and there's no changing that, he won't be coming back. A kind of inertia has settled over me and as evening draws on, I wonder if I'm even going to be able to drag myself off the sofa and walk up the stairs to bed. Benny has clambered up onto the sofa with me and I lay, with my head resting on his fur, staring unseeingly at the TV. Mum insists that we watch a film all afternoon and it's only later that I realise it was because she wanted to avoid any local news programmes. Because the news about Will would be on there. Which is laughable when you think about it, because it's not as if I can forget it's happened so what does it matter if I see it on the news?

At ten o'clock, Mum suggests we go upstairs to bed and I somehow manage to drag myself up off the sofa. Every part of me aches, as if I've been working hard all day or running a marathon, not lying around doing nothing. We climb the stairs and when we reach the landing, Mum grabs hold of me and hugs me and asks if I want to sleep in her bed, as I did when I was a child. I tell her, no, that I'll be fine and I'm sure that I'll sleep because I'm exhausted. She makes me promise that I'll wake her if I need her or if I can't sleep.

I get undressed and put my pyjamas on and go into the bathroom and brush my teeth. When I go back into my bedroom, before I pull the curtains closed, I look out into the lane, across to Will's cottage. It's in total darkness and I guess that Lucinda is still in London. Maybe she'll stay there now and never come back. I look at the darkened windows of the cottage and remember the heady excitement of our trysts in Will's bedroom, the feel of his arms around me, his lips on mine. Did our secret meetings by the oak tree at the end of the lane and our love making in the field really happen, or have I imagined it all? It all seems so unreal now, as if I've dreamed it.

It feels like forever ago, a lifetime ago when I was a different person.

I pull the curtains closed and get into bed. I could pull the quilt over my head and shut out the world, pretend that Will isn't dead and dream that we're still together. Live in a make-believe world where everything is perfect and Will is alive and still loves me. Not loves me, no, because he never loved me and dreams have to have a semblance of reality in order for them to work. Wants me, then, a world where he still wants me even if it is only for when he feels like sex. Maybe this is why people take drugs, because they can't face real life. I wish I had a pill right now that would make the reality go away.

But that's not possible, and I have to face up to the fact that Will is dead but more than that, I have to face up to what I might have done. I can't put it off any longer; the thing that I've been trying to avoid thinking about all day. I pick up my mobile phone and look at it, aware that once I've done this, there is no going back.

Do I really want to know?

No, I don't, but I have to find out because otherwise I'll go insane. And there's still the faintest glimmer of hope that I might be wrong.

I carefully prize the case from my phone and hold it in my hand.

It's empty.

There is no piece of paper with Marcus's phone number on it inside the cover, there's nothing at all. Which means that I took that piece of paper out and sent a message to the number on it, because why else would I have removed it? The number that Jack gave me for Marcus's burner phone that I wrote on the corner of Mum's crossword book. The number I had to send Dylan's name and address to so that he could be *taught a lesson* or *disappeared*.

I scroll through my phone and check my sent messages and calls. There's nothing to an unknown number, but there wouldn't be, would there? Because I would have deleted all records, just as Jack told me to. The message was insurance for Marcus, so that if I had a sudden attack of guilt, I would be implicated, because all messages leave a trail for the police to follow. But not for me; there is no trail for me to follow and I have no way of knowing what I sent because I deleted it.

I lie back on the pillow and search my memory, trying to remember what I did in those hours after Will told me we were over. I have no clear recollection of even coming home, it's a blur. I remember snippets of it; crying and howling like a wounded animal and rage, too. Screaming at Will for lying to me, for treating me so badly, even though he wasn't here to hear me. And somewhere underneath it all, I have a vague memory of taking the case off my phone as I did just now, of unfolding that tiny slip of paper and tapping the number into my phone. I'm sure that I did that, because the slip of paper with his number on is gone, so I definitely took it out of the case. And I must have thrown the paper away, because Jack told me to. I wouldn't need the number again because I could only send one message.

But the real question is, what message did I send to Marcus?

Because Dylan is very much alive and Will is dead.

Did I, in my fury at Will, send a message to Marcus to make Will *disappear*?

* * *

Three days have passed since I learned of Will's death, that's how I count time now, the time since Will died. Although strictly speaking, although I learned of his death on Friday, he'd already been dead for two days.

That first night, Friday, when I realised what I'd done, I thought I would go mad. I didn't sleep at all that night and I spent those hours trying to decide whether I was going to give myself up to the police or not. By the time the sun rose, I still hadn't decided but I'd exhausted myself with thinking about it and fell into a deep sleep. When I woke again, it was nearly two o'clock in the afternoon. My head felt clearer and I knew that in reality, despite my noble intention to go to the police and give myself up, that I wasn't going to do it. If I confessed, the guilt would ease but I knew that the relief I felt would be only fleeting. I would face a long prison sentence but worse than that, I couldn't do it to Mum.

Because she would blame herself, she would think somehow, that she should have known and stopped me, even though she couldn't. Of course, Mum wasn't the only reason, because the truth is that I'm a coward, and I don't want to spend the next twenty years in prison like my mother. I could envisage the newspaper headlines of *like mother like daughter*, once the truth of my birth mother emerged. And the truth would come out, because journalists can smell a story a mile off. My mother is a murderer and I am too.

My mother is a free woman now; released from prison after serving eighteen years for murder. My mother was having an affair with a married man and she murdered his wife. The married man was also my father; he refused to leave his wife and questioned the paternity of me, but rather than kill him, my mother chose to beat his wife to death whilst her child slept soundly upstairs. She tried to call it a crime of passion, saying that she lashed out at her in a jealous rage but the facts told a different story. She beat Janice Cadell dozens of times, not the one blow that she admitted to, and there were numerous defence injuries showing that Janice Cadell tried to defend herself. My mother's barrister used the fact that I was only six months old at the time as a defence. He said that my mother was suffering from post-natal depression but there was no medical evidence because she had never visited a doctor about it. That and the fact that she purchased a baseball bat – the murder weapon - the day before the murder, sealed her fate. Janice Caddell's husband - my birth father - didn't help by stating that my mother was prone to violent rages when she didn't get her own way. He played the part of the confused husband tricked into bed by a conniving woman to perfection. He even managed to find some sympathy in the media stories that were in all the newspapers, no doubt helped by his good looks and willingness to pose with his now motherless daughter. I was rarely mentioned in the newspaper reporting and certainly never by name, once my mother was found unanimously guilty by the jury, I was swiftly adopted and given a new life. My father didn't want me and I can't say I blame him. What man would want to bring up a child whose mother had murdered his wife?

So although I may not have actually killed Will myself, I murdered him by cold-bloodedly arranging for someone else to do it.

I'm no better than my mother.

But honestly, what would be gained by telling the truth? My life would be ruined, deservedly so, but so would Mum's and Lucinda would find out that her husband was a cheat and a liar and she would carry that with her always. No, much better that everyone believe Will died in a tragic accident rather than murdered by a jealous mistress.

Having made that decision, I felt marginally better, not least because the fact of Will's death felt slightly unreal. And because we had finished and he no longer wanted anything to do with me, it struck me that to all intents and purposes, he was already dead to me.

I sound cold-hearted, don't I?

But that's what being a murderer does to a person; makes them hard. I'm a murderer and I have to live with that, I have to bear the guilt for that and there's no one to help me because I can't possibly confide in anyone, except, possibly, Jack, who I know wouldn't betray me. But I'm not going to do that to him, I'm not going to lay my guilt on him. I'm just going to get on with life and hope that in time, one day, I'll be able to forgive myself for what I've done. I know it's not going to be easy but it's all I can do. And although Mum knows about Will and I, no one else really knows, except Jack, and he doesn't know the whole truth of it. Which means that I can't be the grieving girlfriend because Will was just the neighbour across the road and I can't be seen to be in mourning for him. I'm going to have to behave as if everything is okay, and in time, if I keep doing it, it will be.

Mum said she didn't tell Dylan anything about Will. He thinks I was ill, she says, and he was only here by chance, dropping off surplus produce from his father's allotment. I'm almost certain that Dylan knew about Will and I, because he'd been spying on me, but he can hardly say anything without outing himself as a peeping tom.

I told Mum that I felt that I had to move on and that the less we talked about Will the better, because crying and wailing about him wasn't going to get me anywhere. Somehow, we got through the weekend, and even managed to behave quite normally, taking Benny for a walk, going to Tesco's to get some shopping, cooking dinner. Normal, mundane things. And every time I felt overwhelmed by the thought of Will being dead and it all being my fault, I would push the thought from my mind and think of something else. The nights, of course, were another matter, but I was alone then and no one was there to witness it. In time, I tell myself, it'll get better.

I hope.

I just have to carry on.

At breakfast this morning, Mum asked me what I wanted to do today. I told her that I'm going into Wellerton, to have a look around the shops and possibly treat myself to something new. She tried, unsuccessfully, to hide her surprise, and asked if I wanted her to come with me. I said that no, I was meeting Jack, and she should get back to her painting. The bit about meeting Jack was a lie but I knew that if Mum thought I'd be on my own, she would fuss and insist on coming with me and I need to be my own person, to grow up.

I got dressed and tied my hair up and even put some make-up on because I have to get back to normal, whatever that is. There was a moment when I got into the car where it all came rushing back to me; Jack turning his phone screen towards me, sitting in the staff canteen trying to take it in, the drive home on Friday in a complete daze. I sat there for several moments, unable to move or breathe, and I thought, *I can't do this.* And then I felt, rather than saw, Mum at the lounge window. I knew then that I had to carry on so I took a deep breath, started the car and reversed off the drive. I drove carefully into town, concentrating on the road and refusing to let any other thoughts in and by the time I parked the car I knew that I was going to be alright. It's not going to be easy, but I can do it.

Because I'm much stronger than I thought I was.

I looked around the shops, and bought some new make-up and perfume because I need to do the things that someone my age does. And it was all going well until I felt that tingle on the back of my neck and I just *knew* that I was being watched. I was walking down the high street and there weren't many people about because it was still quite early on a Monday morning, but I definitely felt that tingle. I looked to the right and the left but couldn't see anyone looking at me and I started to feel panicked. I stopped dead in the middle of the street and the person behind me practically walked into the back of me. I swung around in shock and came face to face with Dylan. He looked as alarmed to see me as I was to see him.

'What are you doing? I demanded.

'Nothing,' he lisped. 'Just minding my own business. You should watch where you're going.'

I took a step back from him and stared up at him in shock. One eye was puffed and nearly closed, blackened by bruises. His lip was split and swollen and there was a cut on his cheek.

'Oh my God, what happened to you, Dylan?'

He looked afraid for a moment and then stepped quickly to one side to walk around me.

'You *know* what happened,' he said, backing away from me. 'And I've got the message so just keep away from me.'

CHAPTER TWENTY-THREE

Mum and I never went to Will's funeral. It was held in London a few weeks ago and as Mum says, we were just neighbours, not friends, so no one would expect us to go. If the funeral had been held here, it might have been different, maybe we'd have gone.

Or maybe not.

Will and Lucinda's cottage is up for sale now, for a higher amount than the price they paid despite still needing loads of work doing to it. Such is the way of the housing market; a few months go by and it's possible to make a fortune. We've not seen Lucinda at all since Will died, and Lorna-the-gossip informed us that their furniture is still in the house getting dustier and dustier and no one has been to collect anything. She had no news of what's happened to Lucinda, though, and I imagine Lucinda spending all of her time at work and never leaving the office. Mum says she's young and pretty so she's sure she'll find someone else, someone better than a *low-life cheating bastard*. I actually laughed when Mum said it, because she never swears and the words sounded strange coming out of her mouth.

It's incredible how different a few weeks have made me feel. I never imagined that I'd be able to say this, but I'm over Will, now, *really* over him. Mum's right and I don't think that it was love at all, but infatuation. I think I've grown up a bit and I've realised that it's not possible to truly love someone when you've only known them a few weeks. I *thought* it was love, but quite honestly, I didn't *know* Will because we were only together for a few weeks. I projected the person that I wanted him to be onto him but in reality, he was nothing like that.

Mum is right, he was a low-life cheating bastard.

I'm still so glad though, that I had nothing to do with his death and that I don't have to feel guilty about him dying. Will's death was nothing to do with me because as soon as I saw Dylan in Wellerton that day, I knew. Dylan had been *warned off* and whoever did the warning off told Dylan why and to keep away from me. That's why he looked so afraid when he bumped into me, because he was trying to avoid me and walked into the back of me by sheer chance. As I watched him practically run down the high street away from me, I knew that Dylan was the name I sent to Marcus and not Will. The relief was overwhelming and when it had sunk in properly that I had nothing to feel guilty about, I felt lighter and loved Will a little less, somehow. And then it wasn't very long at all before I realised that I'd never loved him at all.

I *did* feel a little guilty about what had happened to Dylan, though. Because he did look quite battered, but I consoled myself with the fact that his black eye would heal and his cuts and bruises would disappear in time. And he got the message, didn't he? Now he'll leave me alone and I no longer have to worry about him stalking me and I can see whoever I like without worrying about him. It might make him think twice in the future about how he treats women, so in a way I'd done a good thing.

My life is looking up now and I'm feeling very positive about the future. I'm definitely going to enrol at college and I've almost persuaded Jack to do the same. I think that by the time enrolment opens in a couple of weeks, Jack will be coming along with me. I've *almost* decided that it's going to be some sort of art and design course, but it's not set in stone yet so I can change my mind if I want to.

As to my birth mother; I have no desire to meet her at all, or my birth father either – although I'm quite sure he wouldn't want to meet me. I'm not sure if I ever did want to meet her, actually; I think I just wanted to know the truth.

If I've learned one thing – apart from avoiding married men – it's that always knowing the truth is overrated; sometimes, a lie is better, and kinder.

Right now, Mum and I are getting ready for a little holiday to enjoy the last of the summer sunshine because we need a break after everything that's happened. It's a bit of a celebration too, because Mum's health is good and the cancer scare was just that – a scare. We're treating ourselves to a week at the seaside in an apartment right on the seafront and Benny is coming with us, too. The weather forecast looks good but we're going to enjoy it whether it rains or shines, because it'll be a change of scenery. I've already packed and have put my suitcase in the car but Mum is upstairs, still throwing clothes into her case, because she's a last minute Larry and always has been. I'm sitting on the sofa in the lounge because I know that even though Mum says she's nearly there, realistically, it could be another half-an-hour. Benny is sitting on the floor next to me and he's slightly agitated; he knows that something is going on but he's unsure quite what it is. He's sticking to me like glue to make sure that he's involved in whatever it is that's going on and isn't left behind. The clang of the letterbox from the hallway tells me that the postman has just been and I jump up from the sofa and go out into the hallway, closely followed by Benny.

There are a handful of pizza leaflets and one envelope lying on the door mat. I pick them up to see that there's an official looking letter addressed to Mum. I'm about to throw it onto the dresser for her to open when I pause and look more closely and realise that I know exactly what it is. On the day that I found out Will was dead, I drove home from Chiverson's in a daze and I went through a red light. This, I'm sure, is the fine for that; I must have been picked up on camera. Even though I'm the one at fault, the letter has come to Mum because she's the registered owner of the car. I wonder if I'll have penalty points as well as a fine, or maybe even a ban. I look at the envelope and I'm sure I can see the top of the letters of the car registration number underneath the transparent window where Mum's name and address are. If I leave it for her and she opens it, she'll fret. She'll imagine that I'm not capable of driving safely anymore and every time I go out in the car, she'll be worrying. It'll be much better if I just open it and pay the fine and tell them it was me and she need never know a thing about it. I can hear Mum bustling around upstairs and then the sound of wardrobe doors closing which means she'll be down soon so I have to make a decision. Before I start over-thinking it, I quickly rip open the envelope and pull out the flimsy sheet of paper that's inside.

As I unfold it, I see straightaway that it is a fine, a penalty charge notice. I start to read and discover that it's not for running a red light, as I thought, but for failing to pay the London congestion charge. I look at the notice in puzzlement; I haven't even *been* to London, so how can it be a congestion charge? I read the details carefully, already planning in my mind how we're going to contest it. Surely all I need to do is prove that the car was here and they'll have to withdraw the fine. I look at the date and know with certainty that I was working in Chiverson's on that day, because it was the Wednesday that Will died. I didn't know that he was dead until the Friday but he definitely died on the Wednesday. I've thought about that so many times since; that he was already dead whilst I was still trying to come to terms with the fact that he'd finished with me. The car was parked in the staff car park for most of the day so it couldn't possibly have been in London. Someone must have cloned our number plate in an effort to avoid paying; I've heard that this is a common ploy to avoid paying the congestion charge. I fold the notice back up and am putting it back into the envelope and thinking what a nuisance it is to have to contest it, when it hits me.

I never drove to work that day.

Mum gave me a lift so she could have the car to take her paintings to the galleries in Wellerton. Yes, it was definitely that day. I remember that I had to wait around in the staff car park after I finished work because she was late picking me up. When she eventually arrived, she was a bit flustered and said that she'd been held up in traffic.

On the day that Will died, Mum had the car.

Mum.

I recall the day I first met Will, Mum and I standing in his kitchen with the tray of tea as he tried to pull the old curtain rail down. How I stood gawping at him, in awe of him, tongue-tied and frozen with shyness, as Mum and Will chatted as if they'd know each other for years. They talked about London and Will told her where he worked and Mum said she knew it well; it was the next street to where she'd worked for years. I remember their laughter when they discovered that they'd often used the same café for lunch and what a *small world* it was. How Mum grew up in London and how she occasionally still missed it but not enough to consider moving back there. I remember wishing that I could chat to Will as easily as Mum did.

Mum knew exactly where Will worked.

And she knew he was going to London on the day he died *because I told her.*

Karma.

The anger in Mum's eyes when I told her the horrible things that Will had said to me.

Cold hearted bastard.

Low-life cheating bastard.

Mum hated Will for what he did to me and she told me, didn't she, that karma would get him. Mum loves me and would do anything for me, she would do anything to protect me, to save me from being hurt. A feeling of calmness settles over me and I know with sudden clarity that Mum killed Will. She followed him to the tube station on the day that he died and she pushed him onto the tracks, her actions hidden by the crowds of people on the platform.

Do I care?

The thought is there before I can stop it; do I care that Will is dead and Mum killed him?

I cared when I thought that I was the one that caused his death, but that was guilt. Does a part of me think that Will deserved to die? Maybe; because some people do deserve that fate. Ron, who was a vile, vicious, homophobic bully deserved to die and maybe Will did, too, because he wasn't a good person. He didn't treat me well, or Lucinda, although she didn't know it. When Will first died I was desperate for him to be alive again, to be back in the world, but now, honestly, do I care?

'Nearly ready, darling,' Mum calls from the top of the stairs. 'Two more minutes and I'll be down.'

No, quite honestly, I don't care. When I think of Will now, I feel only indifference. I consider what Mum has done and I feel no anger towards her, only love, because she's always put me first.

Mum killed Will because she loves me; she did it for love.

And now the question is, do I tell Mum that I know? If I show her the penalty charge notice she'll realise that I know what she's done. What will be achieved by telling her? It'll always be there, the thing we never talk about, forever, and we'll never be able to get past it or forget it. And really, what's the point of the truth if it causes pain?

No point at all, because I was told a lie for all of my life and my only regret about that, is that I learned the truth.

'I hope that I've remembered everything,' Mum says, bumping her case down the stairs. 'Although it's only a week, isn't it, so I've probably massively overpacked.'

I turn and she's there behind me, her cheeks flushed, excited and breathless and looking forward to our holiday.

'Okay, darling?' She smiles. 'Has the post been, any letters?'

'None,' I lie, as I slide the envelope into my pocket. 'Just pizza leaflets and junk mail.'

'Nothing exciting, then,' she says, with a laugh.

'No, Mum,' I lie, taking her case from her. 'Nothing exciting at all.'

THE END

Printed in Great Britain
by Amazon

22028116R00155

FREDDY TUYIZERE

WHERE THE COW-GRASS GROWS

PLANTING FAITH AND HOPE IN BURUNDI

WHERE THE COW-GRASS GROWS:
Planting Faith and Hope in Burundi
By Freddy Tuyizere

ISBN: 978-0-692-89382-1

Edited by Eleanor Perry-Smith
Design & Layout by Jonathan McGraw

DEDICATION

I dedicate this book to my family, my supporters over the years, the youth of Burundi, and Annabelle and David Sudreth who encouraged me to write my story.

CONTENTS

Testimonies 7
Chapter 1: The Meaning of Tuyizere 21
Chapter 2: A Tough Beginning 27
Chapter 3: Schooling in the South 31
Chapter 4: Moving to the City 39
Chapter 5: God's Protective Hand 45
Chapter 6: Teaching Trials 53
Chapter 7: Ministry Amidst Genocide 59
Chapter 8: The Chapter of Fire 65
Chapter 9: Marie Josee (Mama Jo) 71
Chapter 10: Immortal Ministry 75
Chapter 11: Dreams Awaken 81
Chapter 12: Burundi Youth for Christ is Born 87
Chapter 13: Studying in South Africa 93
Chapter 14: Roots in Gitega 101
Chapter 15: Cow-Grass 107
Chapter 16: Masenga Takes Shape 113
Chapter 17: Amani's Story 117
Chapter 18: Breaking Ground in Cibitoke 121
Chapter 19: City to City 127
Chapter 20: Always Dream Big 131
Chapter 21: Gitega International Academy 137
Chapter 22: The Year I Matured 143
Chapter 23: Hope for Burundi 151
Acknowledgements 157
Photographs 159

TESTIMONIES

JEAN BAPTISTE MUGARURA

National Director of YFC Rwanda:

In 1998, God laid upon my heart the burden for the youth of Burundi. As the National Director of Youth For Christ in Rwanda, I knew many people, but I knew of no one to send to pioneer YFC in Burundi. Besides, I did not have the financial resources. But the burden was so overwhelming that I decided to go there to see what God was calling me to do. I did not have enough money to pay for my accommodation, food, or bus transportation. I did not know who to meet on this trip, but I eventually went.

After several days of meeting and talking to various individuals and Christian leaders, I came back to Rwanda disappointed. Of the many candidates who came to me as prospective pioneers of this ministry, none wanted to work with YFCI because there was not enough money to pay their salaries and all ministry related costs. No one wanted to engage in fundraising, or in a journey of faith believing God will provide.

One year later, I organized a conference in Kigali for Christian Youth Leaders from the Great Lakes Region of Africa. I invited participants from Rwanda, Uganda, DRC/Congo and Burundi, and the main facilitator was Reverend Dr. Thomas Resane from South Africa.

From Burundi, all the delegates were people I had never met. Among them was Freddy Tuyizere. During one break, Dr. Thomas Resane came to me and told me that for some reason, he kept thinking about Freddy as someone who could pioneer the ministry in Burundi. Freddy continued to come up in Thomas's prayers. I told him that we would pray about it, and if Freddy is God's choice, who knows what the Lord may do? Some dialogue started with Freddy, whom I believe God was already speaking to about the ministering to the youth of his country. Before Freddy left Rwanda, some decisions had already been made. And as they say, the rest is history.

For anyone who sees the results of Youth For Christ Burundi today, I need to mention, that as someone who watched this growth, God used Freddy and his wife Marie Josee, Euphrate, and his wife Charlotte in a miraculous way. These two couples sacrificed a lot. They sacrificed their careers and their properties as they set out on an adventurous road on their journey of crazy faith. It has been a journey of belief and "God who called us is faithful." I have seen God provide for Freddy and Euphrate in a way that mesmerizes us and confounds non-believers. The sweets of today came from the sweat of so many. It came from the dedication of Freddy and his team, and above all, it is from the grace and faithfulness of God whose mercies never cease and are new every morning. I praise God for YFC Burundi.

EUPHRATE NDAYIZIGIYE

National Director of Burundi Youth for Christ:

In 1998, Mugarura Jean Baptiste, the leader of Rwanda YFC, came to visit Burundi on a mission to share the vision of Youth for Christ. I gathered together with other fellow Burundians who had been assembled for this cause. I was asked to attend this meeting but I was not sure whether I'd be involved in the future.

I joined Youth for Christ Burundi at the beginning of the ministry in 2000. Prior to this, a team led by Freddy Tuyizere began the process of creating a constitution for the ministry. I knew Freddy from our high school years. At the time, I was working for the government dealing with statistics. Freddy shared the vision of Burundi Youth for Christ with me and asked if I would be willing to be a part of the ministry.

Freddy and I went around preaching to young people while I was still working in the government. It was hard juggling both responsibilities. I experienced the challenge of giving my best, in terms of time and investment, in a satisfactory way. We had Bible clubs that ran between noon and 2 p.m., but coming back to my usual work schedule almost always made me late.

I pondered many times over my priorities and wondered where my heart was. I would ask myself many questions of whether it would be appropriate for me to quit my job and continue with what brought me so much joy—transforming the lives of young people for Jesus. I had a passion for evangelism to young people ever since my high school days when I became saved while studying in grade seven. Up to this point, my ministry mainly involved activities in the Bible clubs where I had the opportunity to lead in different high schools. These were my humble beginnings of ministry, which explained why I was so passionate about being a part of Burundi Youth for Christ.

I was still racking my brain on how to balance work and ministry, though on the inside my heart was at peace with the decision to resign from my job and take up full-time ministry to young people. It was a coincidence then, that when I was preparing to announce my resignation, Freddy was about to leave to South Africa for his studies. He needed someone to step in and take up the mantle until he returned. Knowing that this kind of decision would involve the agreement and support of my wife, Nyandwi Charlotte, I shared this opportunity with her. I asked if she would be willing to support me as I resigned from my job to work in full-time ministry.

I was anxious as I shared the news with her. This was a great woman whom I had loved so deeply, taken care of, and shared the best things in life. We could afford to live well. But all that was about to change, and provision was about to be needed in a much different way. It would all depend on our trust in God. Her response to my question has stuck with me to this day: “I know you love me, and I know you would not do anything to hurt me. Do the ministry. We shall believe God will provide for us.”

Knowing that I had her support energized me. There is a great blessing in having your wife stand by you and trust you to do things well under God’s leadership. You know you are well-covered and whatever happens, you both shall withstand it because of your common faith in God.

I drafted a letter of resignation the next day, asking that I be allowed leave the job for the next three years. This would be the period in which Freddy would be in South Africa pursuing his degree in Theology. Questions were raised, especially from my boss, as to my reasons for leaving my work in the government to go and work with the youth. It was hard for them to understand how I would leave a paying job for a job with no salary. But in response, I shared that my reason for change was not about money but my passion for something else. When you are driven by passion, money will be the least of your worries. Especially when you know that trusting God wholeheartedly is the gateway to experiencing more than just material blessing. I knew God was going to provide. I trusted Him to take care of my family and I, as His word asks us to put His kingdom first.

I finally received a letter authorizing my resignation. To date, I still keep it in one of the files in my office. My face beams at the sight of it. I am reminded of where I have come from, the journey I have taken, and the great things I have experienced whilst being a part of Burundi Youth for Christ. God has been using us to grow and expand His work in Burundi.

Freddy left for South Africa, and we had very little finances to start up the ministry. This money had come from the sale of Freddy's cows. We had been renting a small office that Freddy's pastor gave us. In that small office, we had only a table and two chairs which Freddy's family had given.

I managed to compel a carpenter to help us make four chairs and one table that we could use. I had only 24,000 Burundi Francs, which had a value of around US$24 at the time. Fortunately, he accepted it and designed the furniture for us. It was a small step in the right direction, but it felt like no accomplishment at all compared to the dreams that we had for the ministry.

Before Freddy left Burundi we began sports evangelism. This attracted a few young people with whom we shared the gospel. While engaging in this, I played around with the idea of beginning an English club. I approached Freddy to get his thoughts, and he greatly supported the idea. He linked me up with Surpeace Ndayizere, a young man who had been in Kenya for about three years. It was a matter of getting him on board and having him teach English to the young people we reached out to. So I called him, and asked him to come and meet me in my office. Ndayizeye had initially thought I had called him to offer him a paying job, but I unfortunately burst his bubble when I stated that we were looking for a volunteer to teach English. Though disappointed, he accepted the offer, and in 2001 we began the English clubs. We went to different quarters of Bujumbura advertising it and checking to see if there were any young people interested in learning English for free. We attracted so many young people who eventually improved their English greatly.

While deeply engaged in this, a man named Simon Guillebaud came to visit me in my office. He brought me a guitar. I had earlier mastered some basic elements of playing, but I did not understand at first why he brought it to my office. Nevertheless, I accepted it, and to make use of it, I went out again advertising to interested participants to come and join a music club. Almost six months down the line, another lady gave us a small keyboard which we integrated in the music club. The young people were always eager to learn something new. Slowly, perfecting each lesson, they were good enough to be considered a choir. It is this team that partnered together with us when we visited churches and schools for ministry. We sang songs and shared the gospel together with them.

Still, my problems screamed for my attention. It was not easy learning to live without a salary after coming from an assured place of receiving one at the end of each month. I was still renting a house and my thoughts raced on how I was going to manage to pay for it with no money at hand. Miraculously, someone walked into my office interrupting my considerations one day, and offered to pay my rent for the entire year. I was in utter shock and disbelief, but overwhelmed with so much joy, knowing that it could only have been God answering my unuttered prayers. My wife was earning a small salary, but still God's hand was on us. This I can say with confidence, remembering how those with whom we would share the gospel with would send us food from upcountry. I never lacked a meal in my house, instead, I was blessed with more than enough such that I could share with my neighbors.

Later, we received the help of a young woman named Jacky who had access to a computer which was connected with internet. Jacky helped us get connected from time to time, as she used to print and type emails between Freddy and I. He encouraged me all the time, despite the challenges I was facing. He shared books with me, and brought equipment for the office too. I am grateful to God that while Freddy was away, he always kept in touch.

God has been good to us all these years. He protected us in June 2003, when the biggest attack in Bujumbura happened. That was during the time an American woman named Jill Vaughn and her friend Susan Molinari from Oregon were with us ministering to street kids. Susan and Jill worked and played together with the kids in ways that allowed them to understand and appreciate the love of Jesus. They also supported us financially and spearheaded the ministry of Burundi Youth for Christ. Our ministry became known around Burundi in most of the provinces, but best of all, children got to know Christ, which was our main mandate.

When Freddy and his family returned to Burundi in December 2003, the ministry and the situation in the country somehow began to stabilize. Being the vision bearer, we were able to receive his direction on what projects we would undertake in the future. Freddy and I have been together for all these years and I'm grateful that we still continue to grow, mature, and experience life together building God's kingdom here under Burundi Youth for Christ.

TED BOSVELD
Founder and President of Villages of Life:

My journey with this Mighty Man of God started back in June 2006.

The peace agreement must have only just been signed in Burundi, but I was totally unaware of this, as I was in Africa for the first time in my life volunteering on a building project in Rwanda. I was assisting in construction of an orphan village just outside of Kigali as part of a program called "100 Days of Hope." It was a project from Australia that brought hope and healing to a nation that had suffered the most horrendous genocide in 1994.

It was late afternoon when my phone rang. On the other line was a man making the most natural conversation. He asked what I was doing in Rwanda and requested in the most humble, yet very direct and confident way, if I could come to Burundi to assist with Youth for Christ.

I knew nothing of Burundi at this stage. As I later learned, most of the rest of the world didn't know about Burundi either. They didn't know that it had only just emerged from 13 years of civil war and genocide. It was the exact same thing that Rwanda had been through, albeit in a less intense timeframe, but over many more years. Burundi's results were just as damaging. They needed support for the same reason I was Rwanda, being a part of bringing hope and healing to a nation.

After my return to Australia, this conversation with a man I had never met, in a country I had never heard of, with a request I knew in my soul was way out of my comfort zone, beyond anything I had ever imagined doing, challenged me for many sleepless nights. It was a request to go to the world's poorest country to help house and feed orphans.

I grappled with this for many months without ever communicating to Freddy my inner unrest. Finally, in December of 2006, I emailed Freddy explaining all that had been challenging me over that past months since we had spoken on the phone. His reply was quick. He explained that he and his YFC team had been praying every Wednesday for a man named Ted from Australia, a man they had never met, from a country most of them had never heard of before. They were believing that God would move and do the miraculous. They believed that God would send someone from Tasmania, Australia, which is about as far away from Burundi as you can get. They were believing the impossible, as I was being challenged by the impossible, from a God to whom *nothing* is impossible.

Following this conversation, I got in touch with YFC Australia who was linked to YFC Burundi through YFC International. We had a meeting in February 2007 in which I discussed with them the request from YFC Burundi. I asked if there was any way we could work together from Australia to assist YFC Burundi. This meeting went for approximately an hour-and-a-half, and at the end, YFC Australia and World Relief Australia, who was also sitting in on the meeting, revealed that some four years earlier they had set up an international aid organization to do aid work in third world countries, but they had never had a project to do. They had set up a tax deductible international aid organization and it was handed to me. Their comment was, "We have never had a project to do, looks like we now do."

After that short meeting, Villages of Life was birthed and ready to go fully tax deductible. God had prepared ahead of time everything we needed to proceed with haste. Three months later, in May 2007, I was in Burundi for the first time on a scouting trip to see what YFC Burundi was doing and how we could assist from Australia.

That trip is a whole other story for another time, but from that trip a bond was made that God had put in place, a bond that to this day has totally changed my perspective on life. It's a life full of love for my family and home country, but also a life that had a lot of adjustments along the way that turned into a passion for a country called Burundi and a man named Freddy. I say a lot of adjustments along the way, because at times this journey was all-Burundi, and family and home at times was second in line, but by the grace of God I now have balance.

This all started with a phone call from a humble man with faith in a God of the impossible who dared to ask, "Please come, we need your help," who then, with his team, got down on their knees and prayed.

Today, more than 30 people have joined me on the journey to Burundi. In Cibitoke, through Villages of Life, there are now seven homes, a community centre, the best ranked school in Cibitoke with 380-plus students, and sustainability farming project that all form a "Village."

DR. KELEBOGILE THOMAS RESANE

Pastor and Mentore:

It was in Rwanda in 1999. The conference venue was Scripture Union Conference Centre in Kigali. As a guest speaker, one prays daily for participants. The figure of this tall, slender, and handsome young man kept coming to my mind as I prayed. After few days I went to him during breakfast and asked to talk with him sometime during the day. My heart was overwhelmed with passion for him as he gloriously reflected quality and potential leadership.

In our conversation, after learning of him, his family, and ministry, I said, "I'd like you to trust the Lord with me. I want to take you and your wife, together with your little son, to an English-speaking country and put you in Bible College for three years. After that training, I'd like you to go back to Burundi to serve in YFC." He spoke through tears in his eyes and struggling English, then walked away like Zachariah after encountering God in the temple.

Communications and protocol followed, and in 2001, Freddy and Marie Josee entered Evangelical Seminary of Southern Africa in Pietermaritzburg. Challenges came all the way, such as their sponsor passing away on the eve of their arrival in South Africa, limitations of English as the medium of instruction, culture shocks, etc. But within record time they both graduated in 2003, and as promised, traveled back to Burundi to do this amazing ministry.

They made it through because they trusted the One who called them. The DNA of God was deposited in them, which is the motto of my life: "When He calls, He equips, and He provides!'"

MARIE JOSEE KARERWA

Wife of Freddy Tuyizere:

I knew that my husband Freddy would one day be in full-time ministry because he would go on and on about it during all our conversations, way before we even got married. He had great zeal for Christ (still does) and that was one of the vital things that drew me to him—his passion for God and ministry. Back then, he joked about me resigning from my teaching job to come and join him in becoming a fisher of men. I thought to myself, "This man is insane, how he could possibly think in such a manner?" But I chose to follow him anyway, because I loved him and still do.

From Him, I have learned the true meaning of walking by faith and not by sight. I was among the many who, unfortunately, considered most of his dreams and visions unrealistic and crazy. But in total surrender to God and utter submission to him, I realize the importance of exercising our faith by being audacious in our Christian walk.

Faith is real to those who know their God and His ability. I trusted God concerning my husband and his endeavors. God, on the other hand, has rewarded me and our children with admirable leadership in Freddy that I still never regret following. I follow him as he follows Christ. And there is no greater joy than serving the Lord with a God-fearing, faith-filled man like Freddy!

CHARLOTTE AND PASCAL KAREMERA

Board Chairman of YFC Rwanda:

In 2001, the Economic Society of South Africa left the key for Flat No.5 and told us that a family from East Africa would be coming over that weekend as new students. When Freddy's family arrived, we had dinner together and immediately became friends. Freddy has constantly been a strong Christian believer. He is hardworking and passionate about Youth for Christ Burundi. Under his leadership, we have witnessed remarkable growth of YFC Burundi and transformation of young people. We hope this book will inspire many people.

SIMON GUILLEBAUD

Director of Great Lakes Outreach:

Freddy's story is a remarkable one. From the humblest of beginnings he has grown into one of the most influential leaders in Burundi. During the war years, I was convinced we were going to die together as we rode around on my motorbike preaching throughout the country. He said that there was no way God would let us die—there was too much to do in Burundi! So far, Freddy has been proved right, and he has indeed accomplished staggering things in Jesus' name. As I look back and imagine that little shoeless boy walking ninety minutes each way to school ever day, I see it as a beautiful testimony to the "God of the impossible" that Freddy is who he is today, and has been used by God to achieve amazing things in such challenging circumstances. Read his story and be inspired to dream big and persevere in following Jesus wherever He calls you!

CHAPTER ONE

The Meaning of Tuyizere

With every step taken along an unknown path, a path of darkness so heavy you can feel it pressing your skin, one should always be content to move forward rather than back. It doesn't matter much where you are headed, but that you have begun the journey to somewhere else. Some call this kind of determination crazy; I call it reckless faith. I stand amazed at the work God continues to do in, and through, my life. I marvel daily at my place among those chosen by God, and willingly submit to His call.

For years upon years, I have harbored the encounters that would eventually become the transformation I witness today. When I look back over my life, I see a mix of triumphs, defeats, and major lessons—all coiled up like a ball of colored thread. To unravel it slowly and knit together a masterpiece is not as easy as I thought it would be.

Retrieving memories from the archives of my life and playing the tapes in my head is proving difficult. However, with the help of several pictures, and the people around me who remind me to count my blessings each day, I am now able to share my story of faith. It is the story of my life.

I come from a small village in Commune Songa in Bururi Province, exactly at a hill called Gaharo. I was privileged to be born to Christian parents. Both still live as I write this story. They were among the first generation to hear the gospel when Swedish missionaries came to Burundi and started the Swedish Assemblies of God church in the south. My parents became believers, fell in love, got married, and had eleven children. I am their firstborn.

They named me *"Tuyizere,"* which means: *"Believe in Him."* Him meaning God. People have come to know me as a man of faith. It is fitting, as belief in God is not only what I am called, but also what I was called to do.

Culturally, there is a naming party just after a child's birth. The entire family, friends, and neighbors come together and they choose a good name. There is no such thing as a family name in Burundi. The name is chosen according to the prevailing situation, or what the family wishes for their particular child. We have a saying in Kirundi: "Izina ni ryo muntu," meaning, a person is what his name means. Even when a woman gets married, she will keep the name that her family gave her at birth. (This would eventually cause some confusion in my life in cultures outside Burundi. I had to once convince my seminary school that my wife was indeed married to me.)

After I was born, my parents had two more sons. They then desired a little girl. It would help break up the monotony of so many boys. My dad was especially excited for a girl. Not too long after the birth of my second brother, we learned that Mama was expecting. It became clear that a baby girl was on the way. Excited, nervous, and full of anxiety, we waited in hope for this little, not-a-boy bundle. The day came, and Mama indeed gave birth to a beautiful baby girl. But our joy would not last. Two weeks later my sister passed away. It was a painful season, full of questions and agony.

My father, like others who have endured the loss of a newborn, was especially devastated. This was his first daughter. She was the little one he had hoped for, and believed would one day call him Papa.

Death can be numbing. Its shadow can linger without end. Needless to say, prayer and strength, that came from God alone, carried us through this period. My family never doubted that God was with us. We believed that through the storm, as a famous Hillsong Church melody says, "He is Lord, and Lord of All."

Mama was so strong. A woman of valor. She kept hope that we would eventually welcome a girl into our home. True to her belief, she was soon expecting once more. The day came, and our sister was born. The news spread through our village that my parents had a daughter. The next year brought another daughter, then another...and another. God not only answered Mama's prayer, but also fulfilled His promise to do "exceedingly, abundantly, over and above" what she had asked. Four beautiful girls in total balanced the ratio of boys in our family.

My childhood was spent mostly at home in our hut. As the firstborn, it was expected that I learn to take responsibility at an early age. I engaged in domestic duties around our home, including helping Mama take care of the rest of my siblings. I learned the art of homemaking, but looking back, I think that even in my ignorance this prepared me for leadership in the future.

I often did the work of most women in the village: carrying babies on my back, keeping them quiet and calm, while exerting myself in other household responsibilities. I cooked, not as a top chef, but well enough for digestion. Fetching water, too, was a daily task. Trekking shoeless, miles and miles away down a slippery hill I would go, down to the nearby river to carry back water on my head in a clay pot. I'd slowly wobble up the hill back home. The pot weighed heavy on my head. Sometimes I managed just fine, but other times I got to watch my effort as it rolled back down to the river. My ego was fragile and I was hard on myself, so whenever I dropped the clay pot, I'd refill it, then wallow in tears on my way home.

Nevertheless, there were still opportunities to prove to myself that, surely, I must be good at something.

Aside from water, my brothers and I would fetch firewood for cooking. This did not require much skill. The main idea was to collect pieces of wood that would easily catch fire. Wet wood was a disservice, as it would make it hard to light fire for both cooking and the late night bon fires.

I had several cousins who lived in my village. Most of my friends weren't Christians, but we all played together nonetheless. The only way to have fun was to play football (soccer). We used to make our own balls from the dried skins of banana leaves.

My family clan continued to grow, completing itself with a double blessing. Mama gave birth to twin boys who put the final touch on our family.

By the time my youngest twin brothers were born, I was helping support the family financially. I paid the hospital bill when Mama delivered them. I was so embarrassed one day when a hospital clerk asked if the woman delivering was my wife.

It was a very difficult ordeal for Mama, as she had already passed the normal age for giving birth. She spent many days recovering in the main hospital in Bururi Province. Eventually, the doctors told her that it was difficult for them to help her, so they sent her to Bujumbura, the capital, where there was more hospital equipment.

Mama was my biggest fan. She cheered me on as I continued to help her around the house. Occasionally she cracked jokes, wishing out loud that I was a girl, simply because everything I did aligned with society's beliefs that women were meant for housework and taking care of their families. Boys were believed to be hunters and gatherers. They would be out in the far fields, taking care of the flocks, trotting after cattle, and protecting the homestead. I had broken the norm by working domestically. And Mama always seemed to believe that the limiting factor to me doing more around the house was due to being male and not female.

We Burundians have a joke that was used back in the olden days. It states that if you were a girl and you happened to spend the night in an isekuru, a traditional vessel used to grind flour, then you would be transformed the next day into a boy, and vice versa. Mama sang this joke every other time we made flour, knowing her wish would probably never be granted. All the same, she greatly appreciated having a son who supported her.

As I recall this today, it brings laughter to my soul. Back then, deep down, I knew that all I wanted was to be supportive of my mother. I consider her a trooper for managing to take care of us all.

Life was simple back in those days. In my innocence, our status seemed normal. I never envisioned life to be different than what I had already experienced. My entire world was exactly where I was, and thinking beyond it was inconceivable. I was content in my ignorance. I was a simple village boy and that was all I knew myself to be. I did not dream of who I wanted to become. My only dream, per se, was to be able to help Mama take care of the rest of the family.

Little did I know that with growth comes change. This change would eventually alter my perspective on what to expect in the days ahead.

CHAPTER TWO

A Tough Beginning

In our days, hot showers, proper diets, and school transportation did not exist. I look at the demands some children make today, and I ponder deeply on how we were forced from sleep in the wee hours of the morning to trek barefoot several kilometers to school.

My children are living a totally different kind of life today. One of my sons asked me the kind of car my dad used to transport me to school. I had to explain to him that the first time my dad ever sat in car was when I drove him, instead of him driving me. Another time we went as a family to visit my parents in the village. My son refused to use the available toilette. He was very scared. He asked me, "How I am going to flush?" He only knew of a toilette with water. It's not like what we use in the city. In villages, people use latrines, which are just holes in the ground.

I was only six when I started first grade in 1976. We didn't have kindergarten or preschool. Five of us from my village started primary school at the same time. Before us, just one person from our village attended school each year. I was the youngest of the five.

My first school was owned by the Catholic Church. At this time, there were distinct divisions in the church. In the south of Burundi, we had mainly Roman Catholics, Anglicans, and Pentecostals, each with their own established schools. Nobody really had the liberty to learn outside their religious backgrounds.

The closest school was Tagara Primary School, which was Anglican, and different from the Pentecostal background that I came from. The Pentecostal church that my parents attended had no school to its name. So I was given the order to go to a faraway destination called Rumeza Primary School. This did not seem logical at all to my parents. However, none of my extended family members were born-again Christians, which would make my acceptance at the nearby school difficult. After much deliberation, and influence from my father's youngest brother, who went to a Catholic school, it was finally decided that instead of being in an Anglican school, I would be transferred to the Roman Catholic school at Rumeza.

The trip to and from school was a three-hour journey through sandy and occasionally muddy trails. There was so much wind, especially in the mornings, as we walked over the hills. Uniform clothing was available sometimes, though shoes were never part of the package. With empty stomachs most mornings, we jetted off, six days a week. The only difference on Saturday was that classes ended at noon. There were so many strict rules, and going against them resulted in big punishments.

On one occasion, I witnessed a student lose consciousness from hunger. It was not too surprising, as many of us were regularly sent to school hungry and spent the entire day there without eating. But this was an especially serious incident, so school leadership decided to make a rule that students were now obliged to bring their lunch meals. Those who were somewhat well-off could afford to carry their lunches nicely packed with plates. Others, like myself, would make use of dried banana skins to eat my lunch atop. The important thing was that administration made sure we all had food—whether packed in pots or wrapped carefully in skins—food for the stomach and God for the soul.

From then on, our classroom window ledges would be decorated with different lunch packages belonging to each child who managed to bring a meal. We all had the eyes of a hawk, jealously guarding our beloved pack from a distance, just in case it should disappear. We were oblivious about many things, but never about our food. To a poor, hungry child, even a piece of meat that he owns is considered a treasure. With satiated stomachs and innocent pride, we would sit straight up in our chairs together with curious minds, drinking from the wells of wisdom that poured from those teaching before us.

Breakfast and lunch in our household were rare, but Mama always worked hard to have a decent meal for dinner. We all knew, that one way or another, we could afford at least a meal a day, and so dinner it was. I thanked God every day, knowing well that many in the village had nothing to eat at all. Being in a Christian family and having parents who worked with missionaries came with some benefits—one being access to dinner ingredients. Nevertheless, our extended family was more than two football teams combined, thanks to my Grand Papa's many wives. I lived with many of my cousins on the same compound, which meant that the food portions would always be minimal. Needless to say, I am grateful to God for how far I have come.

Food was a high priority, as I needed all of the strength I could get to face the Iron Lady at school. Mrs. Anesie was the Iron Lady and my first grade teacher. I was among the many victims of her wrath. Hell surely revealed itself whenever she was present. It was common to feel trickles of sweat beneath my collar when her rage thundered. Her disciplinary method for a failed exercise was to turn the class into a wailing room. With no escape route, we endured senseless beatings, which remained etched on our skin for days as a reminder of her doom and gloom.

I got my fair share of the torture one day when I failed to present my father's registration book, called Igitabo c'ikori. Before the second republic took hold in Burundi, every male over the age of 21 was required to pay tax. This book provided documentation that my dad had paid each year. He was away from our village with his book the day I needed to present it to my teacher. He was out searching for small jobs with his acquaintances near a place called Rumonge, now the new southern province of Burundi. I returned home that day in excruciating pain, still wailing from the beating I had received due to the absence of the infamous book. I fell at Mama's feet, a frail boy covered in open wounds. My mother was taken aback, mourning together with me over the torture I had just endured. Full of holy anger, she escorted me to school the following day for a serious discussion with the Iron Lady. She explained the situation to her, but it could not erase the pain that my skinny, hungry body had to withstand.

As luck would have it, I passed first grade and lived to tell about it.

I also passed my second and third grade years with no struggle at all. Many of my fellow students were forced to redo their years in order to qualify to move forward.

I never quite understood intelligence until my friends and family commended my efforts and noted my outstanding results. They told me I was a smart boy. Despite being ill with chronic nose bleeding, I managed to emerge top of my class and didn't have to retake those first three years.

CHAPTER THREE
Schooling in the South

The year 1980 was significant in my schooling calendar. With little notice, all current schools, including those begun by missionaries, were officially declared government schools. As I was graduating into fourth grade, the original five students from our village, myself included, were moved from Rumeza Primary School and sent back to Tagara—the closer Anglican primary school.

At that age, I didn't quite feel the difference it made, and continued unquestionably with my schooling. My ultimate focus was to study hard and remain at the top of my class. But the hits kept coming.

The dry season during the months of June and July was a dreadful one, especially for me. During this period my nose bleeds worsened, occurring frequently during my school days. I was often admitted to the clinic to watch for improvement. Sometimes, they seemed to diagnose correctly. On other occasions, they didn't have the means to help me at all. My parents were understandably worried and restless. This cycle continued year after year during the same season. My health condition worsened just before the examination period, and I was forced to redo fourth grade. I tried hard, and passed the fourth, then the fifth grade.

In grade six, we had to sit for the national examination called Concours National. This test was taken annually by all grade six students in the entire country. There were few available positions in grade seven, which was considered the beginning of secondary school. Secondary schools in Burundi were mostly boarding public schools. This exam was extremely competitive; I knew one of the boys in our same village who had to sit six times for the same examination.

I failed the examination on my first try.

We had over 54 students that year at Tagara, but only one passed the Concours National. But there was only one classroom at the school for the sixth grade. There were many who had to redo the same year, but grade five had to move in. As a result, there was no place for me at Tagara. Mama had to find somewhere for me to redo grade six. This being the case, she had to take me to a farther school called Muzenga in another county where her older sister lived.

Going to this new primary school was a big challenge. I had to leave my family behind and reside with my aunt and her family. Once a month, I was allowed to go back home to my family and see them for the weekend. I was walking to-and-from, three-to-four hours. Fortunately, I was there for only one year. The pains and pangs of being far from my family were felt every day—whether in school or in my new home. Nevertheless, I had high hopes to excel this time around. I was eager to proceed to the next level of my schooling.

The time came for us to retake our examination, and this time I passed the national test. There were more than 50 boys and girls in one classroom, but only nine of us succeeded.

While awaiting the next step during summer, I was in constant prayer and supplication for a good secondary boarding school. My eyes were set on being a part of what I considered a prestigious school called Lycée Kiremba-Sud. I admired the school greatly. It sat on large piece of land, and was predominantly Christian, built and run by the Swedish missionaries who started the church that my parents were attending. I had been baptized in Kiremba and had witnessed the manner in which its students carried themselves with such godly poise and dignity. They would sometimes come to visit our church to share the gospel, and when they did, I pictured myself being a part of their elite group someday.

As I reflect on this moment, I count it as one of those in which I encountered the favor of God upon my life. Normally, Burundi's government is authorized under the Ministry of Education to select a school for those who qualify for secondary education. Miraculously, as I continued to pray, God answered my prayer. Out of the nine of us who qualified, I was the one selected and sent to my dream secondary school: Kiremba (then known as École Normale de Kiremba). In that instance, I strongly believed that God had a plan for my life.

With immense joy in my heart, I could not wait to begin my secondary education. My family managed to raise some money to facilitate my tuition fee. Additionally, my extended family joined the cause, contributing to my other school necessities. It was a huge accomplishment for us all, especially given that I was the firstborn. My secondary school acceptance was the pride and joy of the family.

On the first day of secondary school, I was set. I had put everything in a big bag that had been purchased for me. I carefully placed it on my head and balanced it all the way to school. It was a three-and-a-half-hour journey. But unlike other school trips, this one was going to end at school. I wouldn't be coming home at sundown. Kiremba would be my home for the next three months, with no access to close friends and family. Just God and my books.

This was a brand new start. With great expectations and excitement came my yearning to grow. I wanted to learn more about who God is and what it meant to have Him as a necessary part of my life. I was determined to continue the things I had done back home, which was ministering in song and sharing the word.

On my first evening, I arrived at the school premises with the other new students. This was it. A village boy about to fulfill a simple dream of attending his coveted school. The sight of many students both male and female greeted my eyes. Everyone seemed to know each other. I didn't notice people walking alone. There was lots of chattering, laughter, and ongoing commotion on the school grounds. Many were catching up on the latest gossip after being apart for a long time during the summer.

The new students were then assembled before the rest of the school. The welcome was not very comforting, but rather intimidating. The returning students from all sorts of backgrounds were looking at us like we were aliens that had landed from a distant planet. Some students appeared friendly, others seemed the opposite. The resident manager then gave a stern warning against bullying.

I had a lot to learn about the student culture here. I soon realized that not everyone who attends a Christian school aligns themselves with Christian beliefs. During my first year, there were many cases of bullying. Whenever the school assembled, a case of bullying was always addressed. The school staff seemed to know how to contain the situation. After all, they were Christians, and they took what the good book states seriously: "If you spare the rod, you spoil the child." Some learned from this punishment the first time, but for others, punishment became their identity.

The school routine was easy enough to adjust to. Early every morning, we would gather in a big hall and spend about half an hour in prayer and Bible study. I enjoyed this, so I made it my discipline to always be present and never miss a session. Likewise, in the evening we engaged in the same study before going to sleep. On some weekdays, there were Bible clubs. We were spiritually well-fed by some gifted senior students or staff member. They broke down the word of God for us in ways we could understand. Ironically, these lessons made us hunger more for God, rather than feel satisfied. It was thrilling to be amongst young brethren who were like-minded in "seeking the Lord while He may be found."

In the course of my spiritual growth, I decided to join and faithfully attend the music club where I learned to play the guitar and trumpet. I felt really good about myself. I felt as though I was exactly where I was supposed to be. I also enjoyed playing basketball. Noticeably, not many Christians were involved in school sports. They spent their time in prayer and deep meditation of the Bible. I guess in my innocence I pursued a balance of school, Bible study, and time off for playing. It became a great hobby during my high school years. Everything at Kiremba felt right and fulfilling. I owe it all to God, who in His mercy made a way and guided me down its path, equipping me for a future He had already prepared.

I wasn't as smart in class as I was back in primary school. I got to learn that even among the best, there is still competition. No one is at the same level. Still, I challenged myself to work hard and be diligent in my studies. I prayed and studied, making the most of my current season. Through it all, I can attest that God's hand was on me. His promise was true, that, "Never will I leave you, never will I forsake you." (Deuteronomy 31:6)

In time, I had group of Christian friends. We were a squad of five faith-filled boys who shared the same values and views regarding the things of God. We had a burning desire to grow, keep away from all kinds of evil, and lead worthy and pleasing lives for God. We remain friends today. We are all married, with our own careers and families attached to our blessings. God had ordained and mapped out our lives, reserving us for Himself and His work.

The first semester quickly passed, and so did another before the next summer break. I was doing relatively well in school, both academically and socially. I formed true bonds, and as a result, I had the opportunity to learn, grow, and enjoy my high school days all at once. During the summer break, I proceeded back home to help my parents with work. It was a time for rest for many of the students, but for me, this was a time to engage more in church activities.

I spent most of my time at the church, preaching to the locals there. My pastor was fond of giving me the platform to share God's word at my tender age—and I did with God's enabling grace and strength. This was the same church I attended long before I had begun my studies in secondary school, when I used to admire the Kiremba students. Now I was one of them.

The trust and investment my pastor awarded me was humbling. Our relationship was like Paul and Timothy. He mentored me, encouraging me to inculcate a spirit of love, power, and a sound mind. I gleaned from his wisdom, shared his platform, and won the favor of both him and his congregation. It was a blessing to have such a leader who trusted me and invested in me from a young age.

It was the summer after graduating grade eight that I felt the strong presence of God over my life. In my heart of hearts, I knew He was up to something and was calling me into ministry. At that time, I didn't have a clear understanding of what that meant, but looking back, I can say that was indeed the summer when God's voice was clear. He was telling me that I would spend my life leading His people and drawing many to Him.

That summer, I shared what I sensed with my mother while in the fields, harvesting sorghum. I poured out my heart to her, making it clear what exactly I felt the Lord was leading me to do. She did not support me right away, but she looked at me with affirming eyes and spoke, "Continue with your studies, continue praying, and as you grow, it will all become clear."

At the time, my understanding of who a minister was had to do with those in the government. I was a bit confused, not really comprehending why God would call me to work in the government. A minister working in the church sounded absurd. But as I grew, I finally learned to accept the terms "minister" and "ministry" for what they really are in the context of the church.

Sunday was the day designated for spiritual matters. The community liked to address it as "God's day." The day of the church. Everything had to be spiritual, including the clothes in which you adorned yourself. It was as though the spirit searched the clothes too. We had what we call kanisa clothes that were selected for Sunday service only. My friends and I would put on ties to make us look special every Sunday. Everyone would know that we were headed to the church when they saw our clothing. Church was a short distance from the school, so walking there was not much of an issue.

Sometimes I'd visit my friends at home during the summer break. My parents would also host my friends coming from the Kiremba school. My pastor would allow my friends to preach and sing in the church. We had the freedom to interact with girls as well. I was sometimes embarrassed when girls would visit and find me in our traditional grass house, cooking in a cloud of smoke. I always prayed for a miracle that our family would someday get a nice house to live in.

CHAPTER FOUR

Moving to the City

After my graduation from Kiremba, the government instructed me go to Bujumbura, the capital, to study to become a teacher. I would be taught the ropes for three years at Ngagara teaching school. I took this as a challenge to help me grow in servant leadership, because that is where my heart was.

I rode in a public bus from the south of Burundi to Bujumbura. Once again, I was on my own. I had to meander through the newness to figure out for myself what worked and what didn't. No one had really told me about life in the city. I had a vague idea about it, but no guide book that could teach me the basics of what to do, when, where, or how.

I arrived at Ngagara and my first observation was that the students were predominantly female. It had been under the management of Catholic nuns for many years. As a result, the number of male students was few, but that was no cause for alarm.

Living in the city was a great culture shock for me. Here I was, coming from a big Christian school with good morals, and being integrated into an environment where the majority were not Christian. They knew about God, but they paid Him no serious attention whatsoever. I felt like an innocent sheep dumped into a den of wolves.

Fortunately, before my arrival, the Christian Union of my new school in Bujumbura received news of my coming. Of course, they were eager to have me join them, and I too really needed some authentic Christian friends. I was not ready to leave behind the habits I acquired of fellowship with brethren, teaching the gospel, and spending time in prayer and study of the word. Once I got there, the team received me with open arms. I felt safe for some time. I knew that I was set to transform into an even better individual. Without wasting time, I officially joined the Christian Union. Together with like-minded members of the group, we would participate faithfully in ministry. We would pray together, share testimonies, preach, teach one another, and as the good book says, "Spur one another to good works."

School was not as stressful once I found my community. It was one that allowed me to continue the faith-filled life I enjoyed. I was in my element, and I felt God had his hand on me, preparing me for an even greater assignment. As to what it was exactly, I did not know. Still, I was convinced that I had been called to ministry and to be a part of those leading God's people.

Two weeks into the semester, I was quite excited and already active in most of the ministry activities in the school. The Christian Union soon held elections for new leadership. To my astonishment, I was selected to be among those fit for the position of Chairperson. Many votes were cast and a majority voted me as their new chair. I gladly accepted the responsibility, and for three years I led the Christian Union.

Having been accustomed to leadership back home, I knew that I had to be properly prepared for ministry. Preaching, teaching, mentoring, and encouraging others was familiar, but all the same, it was a great challenge to become better and wiser in my position. News had spread widely about me coming from Kiremba and what I had been doing at my home church. Many got to know my love for Christ and the seriousness in which I took my Christianity. Souls were being saved, many were being baptized and experiencing discoveries in their new life with God. There was a great revival taking place in the school. It was as though we had received a great awakening. In fact, among those who were saved during those three years is the woman who is now my wife and best friend, Marie Josee. She was one of the students who I mentored when teaching the baptism course.

The school was small, so everyone knew each other. My ministry became known by almost everyone on campus, from the principal to his subordinates. My associations through Christianity made it hard for me to hide from it if I ever wanted to. The reality of Christianity comes into play when those around you place you on a pedestal. Their expectations are of the image you portray, rather than who you really are. It was difficult to always maintain this image—being a staunch Christian 24/7. The struggle was real back then as a young Christian leader, and still is today as a grown man with even bigger responsibilities.

Regardless, I was engrossed in my work of preaching and teaching. The group of believers that I led was very diverse with different spiritual backgrounds. We had Anglicans, Baptists, Methodists, and others from independent churches. I had been ignorant all the while of them, and their beliefs, given that my background rarely allowed me to intermingle with other denominations. I was oblivious, thinking that my church had the only existing Christians. I now had to comprehend that there were others who professed to the same God, but spoke in a different way. Given the position that I had, I had no choice but to step out and make connections with other denominations.

I started to visit other churches. With every encounter, the blinders fell from my eyes and I began to see things from a different perspective. Salvation was not just for a selected few, it was for all of us. Even those whom I thought were not a part of us were still qualified, like any other Christian from our church, to meet with Jesus someday in heaven. Church was not just a selected denomination, it was not just the congregation that met back home in my church at the south of Burundi. Church was going on all over in many places around the city. It was not just the Pentecostals who were on fire for the Lord. There were other people just like us called into the ministry to fulfill the great commission. I was freed from my mental slavery. From then, henceforth, I walked with a sense of awareness of a grand world with different people being used by God to fulfill His desire. And His desire is simply to bring all men and women to salvation.

Different churches sang the same songs and hymns that we did. They taught from the same scriptures that we did, maybe just in a different way. They targeted the same world that we targeted. Surely, it was about time that I accepted that anyone who was willing could be used to share the love of Christ. The more my physical and spiritual eyes were opened, the more knowledgeable and sensitive I became to God and His work.

I spent most of my time studying His word and getting to know Him for myself, and later on shared with various congregations what I felt God wanted them to know when the platform arose. My ministry kept soaring, but with every elevation comes a challenge, one in which your faith is tested.

One morning, the student body had become restless dealing with arising issues in the school. The entire school resorted to going on strike, airing out their frustrations and demanding solutions to their problems. It had been reported that the food being provided by the school was unsatisfactory, and thus, the students had opted to go on a hunger strike. Students flooded the middle of the school field and sat next to one another, refusing to go to class or eat the meals being provided.

As a leader of my fellow Christians in the school, my instincts could not comprehend or justify the reasons for striking. I thought it best to try and dialogue with the school management rather than have the students resort to acts that would interfere with the routine. I opted not to join the strike, and so did all the members of the Christian Union. Those leading the strike were apprehensive of my decision. They tried by hook or crook to convince me and the rest of Christians to join them. It became a serious matter when the leaders of the strike decided to fight me. But along with the other Christians, I stood my ground. Miraculously, none of us were touched. For some strange reason our unwavering commitment to our faith spared us a painful ordeal. It had been known that there was a group of Christians who were committed to their Christianity and there were those who, though professing to be Christians, were known to be on the edge. The latter were easily persuaded into the camp of those in the strike.

I learned great lessons on that day. For one, Christianity is visible to all. Everyone sees what you say you are and is watching your actions to prove your professed Christianity either real or fake. It is not about who you say you are, it is what comes out of you that validates who you say you are, and people around you will know by what they see.

CHAPTER FIVE

God's Protective Hand

In 1991, there was an attack on Bujumbura by a rebel group called FNL who were trying to take over the government. On an unexpected night we were greeted by the sounds of gunfire not too far from our school. The shooting was intensely loud, practically deafening, and continued into the next day. The FNL rebel group had attacked the police camp that was situated just next to our school. It was one of the worst nights of my life.

At some point during that next day, the situation seemed to have subsided. With my heart and mind convinced to keep with routine, I left the dorm and set off for the library for some reading. It did not occur to me that the current situation was still too fragile for me to risk being seen walking around or visiting any place outside the confines of my dorm. I was not alone though, a couple of students were also out. I settled down to do some reading for the day when, suddenly, loud gunfire precipitated over the room.

I was numb, paralyzed with fear and confusion. With little sense in my mind, I was still able to detect that the shooting was not too far from the school grounds. It was just a stone's throw away and could easily spread to where I was in one of the classrooms. I could hear the screaming of frightened students from afar and it seemed that many were in search of a safe haven.

The shooting was between the rebel group FNL and the government's army. While the heated exchange continued, some of the rebels found their way into our school trying to escape the army. The intensity of the gunfire grew rapid and drew closer and closer to where I had sought refuge.

At this moment, my fellow students were disturbed and wondering where I was. Almost everyone else was hiding inside the dorm and they feared that I was already dead, given the sights that they had witnessed during the battle. Meanwhile, I was strategizing ways to keep myself safe, while at the same time mapping a way out of this fiery menace. I was flat on my stomach, laying stiff with fear on the ground, in hope that somehow, someway, God would watch over me and keep me safe until the erupting drama had dissolved. In my fear I whispered silent prayers as I moved carefully out of the classroom, then hurried toward the dorm in which my roommates where hiding. When they saw me they were full of joy, debriefing the horror they thought I had undergone.

As dawn approached, the curtain closed on this petrifying ordeal. Though some of us couldn't contain the traumatic experience, we were all filled with gratitude in our hearts, knowing that no student had been victim to injuries, or worse, death. We had been covered under the shadow of the Most High.

I soon continued with my normal activities of preaching and teaching. While at it, an invitation came for me to be part of an event bringing together representatives from every Christian Union in Burundi's universities and beyond. I got the opportunity to interact with delegates from different countries, including the Democratic Republic of Congo, Rwanda, and other French-speaking nations. The event took place at the University of Burundi up the hills, which is known as Kiriri Campus. Fulfilling, and somehow outdoing my expectations, this event fed me with daily bread from God's word. There were excellent speakers who challenged me and the other attendees.

One of the speakers, I remember, shared a great prophecy over us and over Burundi. He said that there will be a generation of young people in Burundi who move from one country to another sharing the gospel of Jesus Christ. They will move from plane to plane preaching the gospel to other people.

I took this prophecy with me and prayed in agreement with it. I asked God to allow me to be among those who would fulfill this prophecy by going around the world, country to country, from one plane to another, sharing the gospel. I hoped then that someday I could attend Bible school to learn the scriptures. Many times, I envisioned myself doing this, and the more I thought of it, the more excited I became, and the more determined I was to see this come to fruition. I remembered the call to ministry that I received when I was 16 and had told my mama about in the fields.

After the conference, we went back to school for a new year. I was ecstatic about what had taken place during the conference and was eager to share my revelations with the rest of my counterparts. Each and every day, I would talk to God in prayer concerning the prophecy I received. It had become the cry of my heart—one I sincerely wanted God to answer for me. I shared the prophecy with my friends, informing them of the great sense I felt of God leading me into ministry. I was eager to go to Bible school and learn more about the things of God. I longed to go out and study this great gospel, then come back and give what I acquired to my beloved country Burundi.

I still remember the assumptions that some of my friends had about where I would go. However, I barely knew my way around the European map, so I couldn't even call out a nation to step into by faith. The only thing I was certain about was the ministry that God had called me to and the training I would have to undertake. Frankly, I think that was all I needed to know at the time. The rest were ingredients to be added later.

I soon had another challenge. A girl became very interested in me at Ngagara. She told the world that she loved me, but I had little to do with it. She was not saved, and couldn't understand my faith. This happened as I was trying to share the love of Christ with her along with other students. To make matters worse, this happened during the year when boys and girls were sharing the same dorm. I had my own room, and I knew that others with their own rooms had a tendency of hosting their girlfriends to have sex with them.

This girl who was obsessed with me thought my Christianity was a mockery of my true manhood. It was difficult for her to accept the truth that I was different and immovable by her taunts. I would not compromise my values. I continued to share the message of Christ with her, but nevertheless, the Spirit didn't seem to move her at all. It was like trying to tell a stone to melt into liquid.

She was resilient. She was adamant. She was certain that I was for her and her alone. On several occasions, she threatened to take her own life unless I agreed to be with her. She became obsessed. In my mind, I had become the 21st Century Joseph beneath the overwhelming pressure of a duplicate Potiphar's wife. In my naivety, I promised to pray for her, which only made her more possessive. I told her that God would console her. I reminded her of the Christian values I held, and how costly it would be for me to sin against God.

On the last night of school, she was on a tirade, and I had to flee and seek refuge behind the locked door of my room. She was going to do anything to get to me, even if it meant breaking down my door. I was confused. What manner of obsession was this? My confusion turned into worry as I wondered what the rest of the school would think if they came and saw her pounding on my bedroom door. Would they be for me or against me? Would my Christian friends believe me? I had to think and fight this battle "like a man." I was not ready to involve anyone else, but neither was I willing to give up like a wimp and not deal with this menace of a young woman. While deliberating what action to take, I felt God soften my heart toward her. It was for people such as her that Christ had come—the lost. It was then my responsibility, in wisdom, to lead her to the giver of all good things. After hours and hours, she finally gave up pounding and went to bed. She left the next day not having seen me. I was glad to have missed her and that God was in control of the situation the entire time. I don't know whether the "flirt to convert" policy can be considered a legitimate way to draw men and women to Christ, but I doubt it.

I'm not sure to this day if anything I said presented itself as flirtatious. All I know is, by maintaining my stance, a girl once obsessed with me became a woman who later gave her life to Christ. She instead became obsessed with God who lives within her. What this lady needed was not me, it was the enabling power of the Holy Spirit that gives us the ability to reflect Christ. This rings a bell, reminding me of the verse that so clearly illustrates how people see Christ in us: "They will know you are my disciples by the love that you show." Had I given into temptation, we might both have stood at the gates of hell if the rapture took place at that moment. But by sharing the love of Christ unwaveringly, it allowed God's grace to flow through me to touch this woman.

My final days at Ngagara were full of reminiscing. While winding down my season at that school, I found myself reflecting over what I had been able to achieve, but more so, the better man I had become, and was still becoming. I was in my element, though still under God's refining fire. He was gracious enough to give me opportunities to share who He is and His love, whilst still teaching me that same thing every day.

Just before we closed our final year, the school organized a trip for Ngagara's students to go all around Burundi. The trip would give us a clear and up-close look at our country. Many of us had studied different places in Burundi, but never got the chance to see these remote places in our lives. On the day the trip began, both students and teaching staff boarded the bus with excitement. I was entrusted with the responsibility to handle the finances of the trip.

We are instructed as young people to enjoy our youth, and during this trip, many took that advice too far. The third night of our trip remains as clear as the activities that took place in my life just yesterday. A majority of the travelers, both staff and students, had one too many drinks. Drunk men and women surrounded me, and being the only sober one, I had no choice but to try and direct people back onto the bus. It was embarrassing for me. The worst part was seeing teachers who weren't able to control themselves. Some of the other students still sober enough could also bear to witness the shame that the teachers brought on themselves and on the name of the school. It was a horrible sight.

I had never tasted beer or alcohol in my life. I couldn't imagine seeing myself in such a state. (Never would I be convinced to indulge, not even by taking a sip of alcohol, because of the lingering image of those teachers in my head.) It was an image of dire shame. When we got back to school after the trip, the teachers were especially overcome with indignity knowing I had witnessed their unruly behavior. In my years of leadership, I had experienced divine favor with the teachers at Ngagara. Especially the school's leader. I recalled many times when he consulted me for godly advice on various issues. That night was an embarrassment for us all.

After graduating, I was asked by the leader of my school in Ngagara to stay and work for him. I still have the recommendation letter that he signed for me to take to the Ministry of Education. Unfortunately, that very year, major changes in the government influenced the posting of graduates in different work stations. The government sent me back to the south of Burundi to work there instead.

After many years, I still travel back to the school in Ngagara. I was later elected as the alumni president. I found myself leading my former teachers and students. To this day whenever we meet, I request for us to pray before we can do anything, and they respect that. We organize meet-ups to catch up with one another, allowing our bonds to grow. I am full of joy doing this for the people who molded me into who I am today. Ngagara was foundational for my key attainments and developments in life. It is the place my life was reformed and transformed. It was there that I met my lovely wife. It is there that I continue to invest my time and energy. I support them whenever I can by giving balls, books, and anything else I can help donate.

It is not every day that you get into a position where, as a follower, you have to lead your leader. Taking charge and trying to contain the situation of that drunken party challenged me to gather courage to stand up for what is right at all times. To me, that was God giving me a taste of the journey ahead. He was showing me the kinds of people He would have me lead. He was preparing my heart to deal with them like He would. He doesn't cast them away, but rather He embraces them, as shameful as they are. He rises up, covers their shame, and cares for them. That would be my mission—to be Christlike. I would lead like Jesus, and to lead like Jesus would mean to become a servant of all.

CHAPTER SIX

Teaching Trials

After leaving Ngagara in Bujumbura, the government sent me to teach in the south at a school in Rutovu County. I was asked to teach the final grade of primary school, which was the class that prepared students for the national exam.

To be honest, I disliked the school. Something about it struck a wrong chord in me. The environment was not friendly at all. My colleagues were all about drinking and merry-making, which was against my values. I persevered for a few days, though in my heart I knew this place where I'd been planted was one of doom and gloom, rather than bloom. I did not want to risk losing my sanity, so I quickly opted to resign and head back to Bujumbura to pray and look for another place to work.

It was easy for me to leave, as I was still awaiting government confirmation to work in the position at Ngagara. I had a feeling that things would turn around somehow. Finally, I got a letter. But it was not the outcome I had hoped for. The Ministry of Education posted me at a boarding school called Lycée Matana in Bururi Province.

At Mantana secondary school, I received a rude shock upon arrival. The principal greeted me poorly. I did not think much about him, but he clearly disliked me from the get-go. He told me that the school staff was full. There was no vacancy for any more teachers. I felt betrayed. Feelings of rejection overwhelmed me.

Was I ever going to find a place in which I could thrive and possibly build my ministry? Was this how things were going to unfold in the coming days?

I felt my cries were falling on deaf ears, but little did I know that I was close to a breakthrough.

My friend Enoch called. He and I had organized many gatherings together during our secondary school years at Kiremba. Like any other graduate, he was stationed as a teacher, but in a different school called Lycée Rubanga within the same Matana County. We spoke and prayed over my situation. Interestingly enough, his coworkers had also heard about me and what I had been involved in before. They were eager to have me work alongside them. Enoch managed to convince his boss of my qualifications. Enoch's boss had never met me before; nevertheless, he took my papers with him to Bujumbura to plead my case with the Ministry of Education in order to have me stationed at his school.

There were a lot of strings to pull, but one miraculous day in September of 1993, I was accepted to work at Lycée Rubanga. It would become my home from September 1993 until June 1996.

From the very first day of work my job was an experience of unmerited favor. I was diligent in my responsibilities and became the principal's pet, given the quality of work I produced. My coworkers, including Enoch, who I believe God used to make a pathway where there was none, gave good testimony about me. It did not raise my ego; if anything, it humbled me. I realized that God might still see fit to use me and fulfill my mission to share the gospel. He was leading and guiding me. It was a process that equipped me for other assignments to come in the future.

After one month teaching at Lycée Rubanga, big changes began taking place across Burundi. The government seemed restless about something, and their every act affected us all in some way. Whether it was in terms of finance or security, many of us were uncertain and fearful whenever changes took place.

During a youth camp at Lycée Rubanga, I shared a prophecy I received. It was perplexing yet hopeful. It was that the country shall be covered by a dark cloud which will bring tears and sorrow to every individual. But after the dark cloud, the sun will shine again over us, and Burundi will be a source of light to the nations. Many people will come to Burundi from other places to see what God is doing. The emphasis was on the passing away of the dark cloud, giving way to the sun shining over Burundi.

I began to preach and got involved with the Christian Union at our school. I was elected as chaplain, and with no delay, I began to deliberate how we were going to run the Christian Union in that big school.

My idea then was to engage people with the basic disciplines such as prayer and reading God's word. We implemented a program of morning and evening devotions. At six o'clock in the morning we would sing, pray, and read the Bible for half an hour before going to breakfast. The impact of this was evident from the growing number of students who attended the sessions.

The evening session filled up quickly. Both the saved and the unsaved made their way to these sessions, and many felt welcome whenever they came to fellowship with us. Many unsaved students enjoyed our songs, and that became their entry to join the fellowship.

As a result, several new students received salvation and the Christian Union became a revolution that was hard to ignore. The ministry grew so big that I was soon invited to go and minister in neighboring schools, including Lycée Matana—the school that rejected me and left a bitter taste in my mouth.

Among the things I came to appreciate was the small stipend provided as a salary. It was nothing to write home about, but it allowed me to go from door to door, school to school, fulfilling the great commission of making disciples.

Despite my efforts, the Lycée Rubanga school is well-known for all the wrong reasons. It was a public school, thus hosting people from all walks of life with different religious beliefs. That's why no one to spoke up when things went haywire in the heart of Burundi.

It was Thursday, October 21, 1993 when the President of Burundi, who was from the Hutu majority tribe and had been in office for barely three months, was murdered by soldiers from the second tribe, the Tutsi.

I received this news while I was teaching. I recalled the earlier prophecy I had received, that the country shall be covered by a dark cloud which would bring tears and sorrow to every individual. But after the dark cloud, the sun would shine again over us, and Burundi would be a source of light to the nations.

The genocide was ongoing. For two months, the normal school program was halted. It was not possible to go home. No one could leave the compound or come to be collected by family or friends. We were all trapped like prisoners, forced to listen to the teachings of one Mr. Freddy Tuyizere.

In all seriousness, we took authority to pray against the forces of darkness and committed in prayer for our families. I taught and preached many times throughout the day, and trained students to do the same.

The environment was unsettling. Tension was growing amongst students as reports of missing parents began trickling in. Worry was at the heart of every student in every minute, and understandably so. The news bearers did not bring good tidings of great joy. Stories of parents being killed in different villages reached our premise. Many students cried in anguish, while others feared for their own lives. I used my small salary to help those who had been orphaned while at school.

Eventually, the school became unsafe for all of us. The fighting came so close that the headmaster of the school had to run away, and a number of teachers from the Hutu tribe as well. Classes stopped completely. At the age of 23, I was responsible for taking care of the lives of others. Frightened children needed encouragement, comfort, and words that would at least carry them through this trying time.

I felt compassion for these little ones. They had to endure this great struggle at their tender age. I could only imagine what their minds comprehended and how it would later affect their view of life. We all heard the sound of crying babies and children beyond the school walls. They had been abandoned, unattended, and left so vulnerable to all the dangers that could possibly reach them. Others amidst this turbulence fell sick. We needed help, but desperately, we needed God himself to step in and come through for each of us.

Healthcare was nowhere near, so we turned to the only great physician we could think of, and that was God. We prayed for the sick, claiming their healing in the name of Jesus. Day in, day out, we practiced faith, relying fully on the Spirit of God to come through and touch every sick child. Many received their healing and were whole again. In some cases, we had to cast out demons, and through the enablement of the Holy Spirit and prayer, those who were possessed got delivered. Many of those freed are involved in the church to this day.

It may sound unnatural, but at that particular time, it was the peace of God that flooded my soul. Christ calmed my fears, even when I thought I would be among those wiped out. My courage was shaken severely, but I kept hanging on to the promise that someday Burundi would shine. God promised it, I received it, and I waited expectantly to see it come to fulfillment. I kept repeating this vision and preaching it to many of my students.

CHAPTER SEVEN

Ministry Amidst Genocide

In spite of, or because of, the times, our Christian Union continued to grow. When seasons of peace prevailed, we resumed our usual devotions and ministry activities in the school. On one occasion we invited a good friend of mine, Pastor Maxime Ntazinda, to speak. He was a favorite of many of the students. He shared the word in such a relevant and relatable way. Through his ministry, many other students received Christ and were eager to develop their relationship with God.

We continued to see God's hand upon our ministry despite the turbulence that we endured. Another time, one of the Burundi's best gospel artists, known as Apostle Apollinaire, was among those I invited to the school. Again, many were saved during that weekend.

One unforgettable moment was when a girl named Georgette Kaganwa was saved. She was a Rwandese refugee living in Burundi. She was also Miss Popular in the school, well-known for her dancing expertise. Everybody loved her and her name was on the tip of everyone's tongue. When she made the choice to accept Christ into her heart, a majority of the school community was completely shocked. But she had decided to follow Jesus, with no intention of turning back. Her lifestyle changed completely, and rather than making her own name famous, she was now among those hungering and thirsting for God. She was a committed Christian and her transformation spoke to many who looked up to her.

As the message of salvation continued to spread across corridors of the school, the love for Christ and the transformation it brought raised bitter concern among some staff members. Slowly, colleagues turned into enemies. A few felt the ministry was more of a threat than a benefit to the school.

One night, while I was deep in sleep, one of our staff members snuck into my room, drunk. He held a pot full of hot food. He poured the food all over me in a bid to provoke me to fight him. At that time I was indeed angry, but my strength and sanity could not bring me low enough to the point of revenge. I did not see the value in putting up a fight. I knew why he did it. He and other staff members were displeased with the sudden change of mind in students, like Georgette, who became Christians. These students had abandoned all of their previous behaviors, including being involved in relationships with staff members. The other issue was that people believed that I was taking people from the Roman Catholic Church and turning them into Protestants.

But I had favor with a number of students, students who believed in the principles of hard work, self-respect, and loving God with their whole heart, mind, body, and soul. Of course, there were some students who were against my way of doing things, but as we have always been told, "You cannot please everyone."

Besides, we had bigger things to worry about. During my time at Lycée Rubanga, some students were killed in the genocide. One night haunts me still.

It was a Tuesday. I had finished preaching at the Christian Union and said goodnight to a group of young students. It would be the last time I ever spoke to one of them. He was one of eight boys living in a dorm. Someone came later that evening while everyone slept and threw a grenade through their window, killing all of them on the spot. Others were injured. When the sun came up we saw their dead bodies. The army showed up and tried to contain the chaos.

I cried endlessly that day. I was angry and asked God why He allowed all of this to happen. I loved those boys. Their lifeless bodies were the worst thing I had ever seen. My heart was heavy as I tried to console myself in prayer. My strength failed me. I just couldn't see myself teaching anymore. The same act was done in schools nearby, and in another instance students killed their headmaster. Killings became prevalent during that time. Life became very uncertain. Fear surrounded us. Some nights my colleagues and I couldn't sleep at all. We had to watch over the students so that they wouldn't fight against each other, as they were from the two main tribes.

The country was no longer safe. Going anywhere became a risk. Because ours was a public school, the government stationed a group of soldiers to look after it. One of the soldiers was an acquaintance of mine and other staff members.

The soldiers would go fight in the villages during the day and come back to the school at night. They told us of the people they had killed from the other tribe. A few times I saw fresh blood on the knives attached to their Kalashnikovs. Their descriptions were horrifying.

I continued to pray though the genocide became intense in the country. I still shared the gospel and sometimes found time to take walks and talk with God. I had several opportunities to share the gospel in different places, which resulted in people getting saved, while others received healing.

In one particular instance, a girl was brought to us so we could pray for her healing. From the onset she looked unconscious, and many believed that she was actually dead. But we prayed for her. We believed that God would bring her back to consciousness and raise her back to life. It takes a whole lot of trust in Jesus for Him to perform such miracles before your very eyes. We were not seeking recognition; we simply hoped for her resurrection. It was the only thread we were hanging onto. True to our belief, the girl opened her eyes and got up. It was a very big miracle. One I'll never forget.

I saw many miracles during those dark years. I spent all of my time and energy in ministry, and the bright moments came through the people I met. So many demon possessed people were delivered as we continued to pray for them.

My time at Lycée Rubanga was a preparation stage for long-term ministry. God confirmed my heart for young people. My name had spread beyond the walls of the school, and I had the chance to know many believers. Through ministry, I met a friend named Philip from Congo who had lived in Rwanda. He taught science at Lycée Matana. He was a Christian, and we became good friends. I met another man named Gerard, who was a student leader in Lycée Rutovu school. He used to invite ministers of the gospel and choirs to share the message of Christ there. Gerard invited me to preach together with my friend Maxime.

Today, it is a joy today to see the fruits of our labor when we see those people who gave their lives to Christ. Many remained very active in ministry or became full-time pastors in Burundi and beyond. Unfortunately, Gerard later died in a moto accident, but his legacy of leadership lives on. He rallied young people to pray and be involved in God's work.

With the genocide slowing down at last, a time came when I sensed the need for youth camps in Lycée Rubanga. Scripture Union was the first facilitator of youth camps that came to mind. They were known for hosting many kinds of large Christian events. So I wrote them a letter requesting their help to get a youth camp set up at our school. The letter was well-received, and we had the first camp shortly after. When Scripture Union came, I was able to gather other schools to come over and join us for the camp. It was the first event of its kind and a successful one at that. We held summer youth camps for two consecutive years partnering with Scripture Union. It was a huge miracle to have many young people from schools around the country visiting a public school such as ours to learn about Christ.

My relationship with Scripture Union grew after that. They eventually elected me as their leader for the southern zone of Burundi. It was a volunteer position and their headquarters were in Bujumbura.

I realized I could no longer contain myself in Lycée Rubanga. I felt a deep passion to step out and do exploits around Burundi, not just in the school. I felt a burning desire in me to do bigger things for the Lord. I prayed about it, considering the effect it would have on my family, given that they were still living in a mud thatched house. So I asked God for a miracle. I asked Him to build a house for my family. I swore that if He helped me, then it would be a clear sign that He wanted me in full-time ministry. I promised I would quit my teaching job and serve Him, wherever he wanted me to go.

Soon after my prayer for a house, I got a call from my friend Philip. He was from Congo and had been studying theology in England. Philip sent me some money saying that he simply wanted to bless me. The amount was not big, but big enough to kick-start building my family a house. Indeed it was a sign. God had answered my prayer. I asked for permission from work to walk home so I could help my father get workers to prepare the land for construction. I left the money at home. God soon provided other utilities for building the house. It was completed during summer break in 1996. This was the moment I was waiting for.

In September 1996, I resigned from my teaching job. I went ahead to pursue my passion. Scripture Union was the only organization with access to public and private schools with youth. I felt I had already built a rapport with them. I would have to move from my family in the south of Burundi back to Bujumbura.

I said my goodbyes, not sure when I would again have the money to travel back and see them. But I had peace because I was off to do God's work. When you mind God's business, He takes care of yours. "Seek ye first the kingdom of God and all his righteousness, and all these things shall be added unto you." (Matthew 6:33)

It was hard for my family to understand why I was giving up my job to volunteer for free. I had been their support, having contributed financially for years. Plus, we were a family of eleven siblings, not to mention my parents, uncles, aunties, and cousins. We had many needs. My church family couldn't understand what I was doing either. But I had made up my mind, and it was time for me to step out and do what God had called me to do with all of my strength.

CHAPTER EIGHT

The Chapter of Fire

From my village in the southern hills of Burundi, I descended to Bujumbura to begin full-time ministry. Like Levi, I left everything I knew behind to follow Christ himself, vowing to do what He had called me to do. I knew that volunteering at Scripture Union would help me fulfill my calling. But first, there were essentials that needed to be handled, such as accommodation in Bujumbura, which was very difficult because I had no money for rent or food.

Living in the capital with no income at all was one of the hardest things ever. I had no place to lay my head. I knew three young men who were renting a one-bedroom house and I decided to join them. With four of us living in that wretched house, I quickly learned survival of the fittest.

It was every man for himself, and God for us all. Each one dealt with his own issues, minding his own sufferings, and hustling to make it through each day. At the end of every day we felt fortunate to be alive.

I now had accommodation, but no means to cater for my food. There are two things a man should not live without—food and hope. The latter is most important, as you can survive days without food, but you'd kiss this world goodbye in an instant without hope.

I had a lot of experience to draw from, but it wasn't helping me just now. I was smart and could argue intellectually, but still, my self-confidence was slowly dying away. I was enduring an entirely new chapter of life. I called it my chapter of fire.

Most of my humiliation was caused by my housemates. I couldn't defend myself against their taunting. Even if I were able, I did not have the right. It was not my house, and it was as Zambian singer Pompi once sang, "You cannot demand respect in a house that you never laid a brick in."

The house was in a place known as Buyenzi. It was a largely Muslim-dominated area in Bujumbura. It had very cheap restaurants so sometimes I had access to a meal a day, but there were often days with nothing. I didn't eat at all.

Sometimes I had to borrow money from some friends to at least feed my rumbling stomach. A cup of tea and a small piece of bread were quite cheap back then. That small meal managed to get me through a couple of days until I could find another source for my next meal.

After settling my living situation, I asked Scripture Union if they would accept me as a volunteer working with young people. I would go to their offices every morning to watch their routines. I watched how they studied the word of God *(umusomyi wa bibiliya)*, and I asked them if I could join their ministry. I thought I had gained their trust, but after weeks they put out their list of volunteers who would go and share the gospel, and I was not included. I was shocked. There was nothing I could do at that moment, but I was persistent. I was determined to be involved with them and ignite my passion for the youth through ministry. I did not give up. I continued visiting their offices for three months. At last, they noticed my interest in what they did.

Prayerfully, I would attend their sessions. I kept asking God to make a way for me. This was my heart's desire. Not only that, but it was God's assignment for me. It would not make much sense for me to leave and go my own way simply because I had been ignored the first time.

At last, I was officially asked to sit with the director. I asked him if I could work as a volunteer for them. He was more interested in knowing my means of survival rather than my desire to work with the organization. He said they had no money to pay me. I replied that I wouldn't be asking for an allowance to work with them; and as for my survival, I trusted that God would provide. It was as they say, where God guides, He provides. I had confidence that God was the one who sent me to work with Scripture Union. It was not my choice, but His calling, which I followed in obedience and absolute surrender of my will.

The director was not convinced and asked me again, "How will you survive?" Again I responded with confidence, but in humility, "Sir, the Lord will provide."

"If He does not, then how will you survive?"

To that I responded, "Sir, I am convinced that God has called me at this particular time to serve His people, especially, the young people. If He does not provide, then I am ready and willing to die in His hands, and that will be His fault."

My confidence scared me a bit, but I remained steadfast. This is what God said He wanted me to do. My task was to ensure that I did it. Period.

The director and I went back and forth for the next couple of days about the same issue of my survival.

Finally, he had heard enough of my answers, so he allowed me to be part of those reaching out to the youth. Step one accomplished!

I was right where I knew I was supposed to be, doing what I was supposed to do for the One who had appointed me and set me apart for such a time as this. It felt great to head out into the schools and churches during the weekends. We also got to go up-country where we would teach, preach, and equip young people with the knowledge of Christ.

I confess that the visits upcountry were my favorite because during the trip food was provided. I never missed Bujumbura when I left for upcountry. I always dreaded coming back to the confines of a one-bedroom house and continuous humiliation from my roommates. The weeks dragged along. Monday to Friday felt like eternity. The hours felt like days, and at times it seemed as though I would collapse and die in the middle of the week.

One day, Scripture Union sent me to go show a film somewhere in Bujumbura. I had not eaten the previous days. I was starving and had become very weak. It became evident that if I had no access to food or drink, then my survival rate would soon hit zero. I could not tell anyone. I did not see the need to act like a beggar with the confidence I had portrayed in God's ability to provide. So I went along, agreeing to show the film at the school. It was a day school, so the best time to show it was before dark. Scripture Union sent me with a car full of equipment and dropped me off at a school called Lycée du Saint Esprit. The film was two hours, then someone would come back to pick me up once it was done.

While the film played, I whispered a plea to God in my famished state. I asked Him to attend to my desperate cry for food. I needed a miracle, or at least the strength to pull me through the movie so I could head back to Scripture Union without dropping down dead in front of everyone.

I managed to show the movie to an attentive audience. At the end of it, I had to muster the energy to get up and make an altar call for those who wanted to receive Christ as their Savior. I almost collapsed the moment I stood up. I remember praying, "Lord Jesus, help me." Nobody knew what was going on, and I managed to finish the altar call with strength I believe only God had provided. I went back to sit as people were dismissed.

While still in prayer, but as weak and dry as a dead leaf, I managed to put the equipment together and found a place to rest while awaiting my transport back to Scripture Union. Due to dehydration, I began getting dizzy and my vision became blurred. My breathing was unusual. I tried hard to keep calm. The car came, we loaded the equipment and headed back to the office. Upon arrival, I asked a worker if it was possible for me to get a soft drink. Their response was heartless. I was told that it was not part of the budget. I had been a full-time volunteer with no pay, so I couldn't understand why compassion had to be a budget item. It didn't make sense. I left in agony, pleading that someone would have mercy on me.

In my weak state, I still managed to walk toward home. This must have been the hand of God. Under such circumstances, without food or drink for days, one usually passes out or dies. But I am certain that it was my hope that kept me going. It wasn't much hope, but the little that I still had caused me to persevere through this unbearable hunger and thirst.

On the walk back to my house someone spotted me stumbling and offered to give me some food and drink. I was immeasurably grateful. That in itself was God's provision. But when I got home to my one-bedroom house, I felt hopeless once again. I was so dejected that I couldn't hold back my tears. I moaned and groaned, asking God why he had brought me here to suffer. I pictured ministry to be exciting, not excruciating. I had believed and trusted

Him. I had obeyed, and yet, I felt abandoned and all on my own. Was God really present?

In this dark pit, I managed to gather strength. Like the King David in his time of sorrow, I encouraged myself in the Lord. I continued to serve at Scripture Union. I stayed actively involved in their missions. On one similar mission to show a film, I was blessed with 5,000 Burundi Francs, which in 1996 was the equivalent of about US$5. I was so grateful because for a while I didn't have to worry about my next meal. I could afford a decent cup of tea in the morning for survival, which to me was better than nothing.

As the days continued to pass I became nostalgic. I was homesick, craving and longing to feel the warmth of family again. I could not go back home because I could not afford to travel. If I asked for support, then those who helped would ridicule me. But I missed the village life. The city had become a den of lions, and I was a vulnerable sheep. But that is where God wanted me.

I had to keep reminding myself of that—to keep my eyes focused on He who sent me. I did not have much of a social life. In fact, I had none at all. Finances were the broken bridges between friendships, extended family in Bujumbura, and well-deserved leisure time. Not to mention the fact that people believed I was crazy to come to the city following the so-called will of "God." He had never made sense to most of my family.

CHAPTER NINE

Mama Josee (Mama Jo)

Perhaps I really must have been crazy, because during this trying time, I managed to pursue a girl named Marie Josee. Unlike me, she was working and prepared for marriage. I was a skimpy, malnourished, poor young man with nothing to offer that could sustain her. I did not qualify myself as worthy of a girl like her. Still, I wanted to propose. I wanted to marry Marie Josee. Crazy Freddy, I tell you!

I did not quite have my eye set on the future because my eyes were fixed on Christ and his work. Marie Josee was two years younger than me, but as I got to know her, my heart and soul felt that there was something different about her. We had met years before while at teaching school. It was strange because she never once hinted at any interest in me. Our interactions were platonic, and anyway, my inability to fit her social status would not allow a relationship to form. Or so I thought.

As my feelings for her grew, I decided that I would wait for her for five years. She was student, and I didn't want to interrupt her learning. Besides, we didn't know each other very well.

After some time, she was sent off to school in another province. It was no ordinary move. While we were apart, absence made our hearts grow fonder, as they say. I thought of her often. She was thinking about me too, but with her own doubts that I would ever be interested in her.

She was beautiful, and of course had a big heart to have fallen in love with a wretched man like me. She was reserved—a safe full of secrets. I loved the mystery in her. We kept in touch, and when she came back to Bujumbura we spent more time together. But we barely spoke about her family as our relationship grew. It was understandable, because her family was having major issues at the time…with me. They had big dreams for their daughter, and none of them involved marrying an unpaid volunteer. Volunteerism was a new phenomenon in Burundi, so no one really knew what it entailed, except that it didn't make you rich.

I was not the only one after Marie Josee during this time. There was stiff competition. It should have been enough to make me drop out of the race to her heart. I was the least qualified. Although I was determined to be with her, I couldn't manage to tear down the images of my flaws. They haunted me, making me feel undeserving of her future. What could a simple village man like me offer?

Still, after four years and eleven months of knowing her, I gathered my courage and embarked on a visit I knew would either make me feel like a conqueror, or else break me into a million pieces. I had spent numerous months in prayer, pleading with the Lord to keep her for me. But I didn't want to mess up our friendship, as she respected me from the times I helped her spiritually. It's my nature to love success, and I feel terrible when I fail, so this was an intense time. I asked two friends to continue praying for me while I was gone.

I presented myself at the doorstep of her cousin's house where she was staying. When Marie Josee came to the door, I made my intentions very clear.

It felt like a century leading up to this moment, but opening my heart now felt just right. My exact words, according to her, were these, "I did not want to disturb your studies. I prayed for you, and I knew if you were mine, God would keep you for me. I waited for a time like this when you'd be working."

I remember the look of bewilderment on her face (it was expected). But like a gentleman, I vowed not put any pressure on her, giving her time to think through my proposal. I was ready to wait for as long as she needed. I had kept the secret inside my heart for four years and eleven months, so what was a few more weeks?

I was patient. After four months and twelve days, she came and confirmed to me that she had prayed and felt peace about agreeing to my proposal.

Touchdown. I had won. I had conquered the impossible. I had received favor in the eyes of a queen who had every reason to push me away and choose someone else. I had been granted my heart's desire. But now, I had one more hurdle to cross in the near future—her family's approval.

While we were engaged, Marie Josee's sister was admitted to the hospital in Bujumbura for an emergency. It was across town, and I had no means of getting to her by bus or taxi, so I took the *"footsubishi"* way and trekked on my own two feet. Those watching me pass by thought I was exercising with others who took aerobic walks after work hours. But I was on a mission to get to the woman whose heart I was after and comfort her in her time of need. I arrived at the hospital in record time. We spent the afternoon together taking care of her sister, who was recovering, and enjoyed fellowship with one another.

After I left, her sister bombarded her with questions concerning her association with me. My appearance and occupation at the time disqualified me from her younger sister. Marie Josee later told me all this in gentle and polite way, trying hard not to hurt my feelings or wound my ego. But she had made up her mind about me. She loved me despite my current situation. This was true, unconditional love. And though our journey would entail entering the narrow gate of her family's expectations, we would walk the road together. Their view of me did not deter my love for my work, my mission, or my calling. I continued doing what I loved, and Marie Josee supported me. I went home that day and continued to hope and trust in God, despite my lack.

We were married on December 13, 1997 at Bujumbura Pentecostal Church. The wedding was simple, yet elegant, and some say pretty expensive at that time. We had set a high standard for weddings. Many came to celebrate with us, including a large number of high school students that I had mentored in the course of my ministry. I remember they ministered in song while dressed in their school uniforms. It was a glorious event.

The Lord is, and shall continue to be, our instructor. We now enjoy life with our precious three sons. We have seen God provide at all times. When asked her views on being a part of the ministry today, Marie Josee answers with a smile: "Today, seeing where the ministry is, I don't regret being a part of it. I feel humbled and honored to contribute to God's Kingdom supporting my husband's part in Youth for Christ."

In time, the Lord taught us how to balance ministry and family. Among the verses that my wife loves that has carried us through many years of love, adventure, obstacles, faith, and life's great lessons is Psalms 32:8: "I will instruct you and teach you in the way you should go; I will counsel you with my loving eye on you."

CHAPTER TEN

Immortal Ministry

On the day the foreign missionary arrived, I was busy out preaching to young people for Scripture Union. The director called me in to his office for an introduction. He wanted me to be the right-hand man for this missionary and help translate from French into Kirundi, our local language. This English missionary had arrived in Kigali, Rwanda then drove down to our offices in Bujumbura. His name was Simon Guillebaud.

I was seated upstairs in the waiting bay, anxious to meet someone I supposed would be quite a great man. I was with the director's secretary, who was as anxious as I was to meet this guest. When she saw him through a nearby window, she called me quickly to get a glimpse of him. Looking mortified, she uttered, "Is that the person we were waiting for? He's a poor missionary. We were waiting for a rich muzungu." Muzungu means white man. She was hoping this would be a wealthy benefactor who would help our organization, which was bankrupt.

It was true, the man's normal appearance betrayed our expectations. But in the following days, we saw God use him in a mighty way as a source of financial support for the organization and all its inhabitants.

I took up my responsibility, helping Simon translate his message whenever we shared the gospel. This became my full-time endeavor. We enjoyed ministering together in different parts of Burundi, though they were some of the most unsafe years that our nation went through. God protected us at all times. Simon was prepared to die any moment, but we kept faith that God had a purpose for us. During these dangerous times, I became a father to my first son Elvis P. Tuyizere.

Simon and I formed a true bond, and we ended up going around the country doing ministry together for years. It was always funny to see people's expressions when they saw a white man for the first time. They would run up to him to see if he was a real human being. We took the opportunity with these curious ones to share the gospel. Simon would share his word and I would assist him in translation. At the time we took most of our trips on a motor bike, which drew audiences wherever we left a trail. It was a very old bike and produced the loudest sound.

All this time, insecurity in the country had reached a very risky level. Safety was becoming a luxury, and all we could do was pray that each day that we lived was not our last. But what if it was? Well, then we would be happy to meet with Christ. For as Paul said, "For me, to live is Christ and to die is great gain."

Each day we were walking by faith. Steadfast faith. It was unshaken. It does not waver but stands the test of time, through every fire and storm. Ours was a solid, crazy faith. Simon and I called ourselves "The Immortals." Sounds like a hit movie, doesn't it? But that's how audacious we were, facing whatever life threw at us with an is-that-all-you've-got attitude. As we continued in our ministry, we had moments of sharing our hearts with one another. Simon's friends back home didn't believe that he could ever survive in a place like Burundi. And for sure, anyone listening to the reports of flying bullets and senseless deaths taking place would likely opt for safety rather than engage in the community to speak God's love.

How do you share a message of love to people staring death in the face each day? How relevant is the love of God, or the message of salvation, at a time when many are mourning the passing of their loved ones? We needed God's grace and His wisdom in order to compel his people to accept Christ Jesus as their savior, should the worst happen.

Every day before embarking in ministry, we would take hands and spend time in prayer. We prayed for the ministry and our safety. It was impossible to explain our mission to others. But after every prayer, there was a blanket of peace over us. Within, we felt a calm sense of God's presence. It gave us courage to step out and let God show His strength through us. The hungry crowd motivated us to continue doing so much more. The people were in search of something—encouragement. They were looking for the next thing to pull them through this devastating and seemingly unending crisis. There was need for hope, for a future to look forward to. Being used by God to direct them to the source of strength was humbling, yet inspiring.

When I wasn't off in the countryside with my friend Simon, Scripture Union asked me to run their small bookstore. This job was not my cup of tea.

I would arrive and basically sit through the day, unless someone came to purchase something. I felt confined. I had been squeezed into a box and forced to fit, even though it was not where I belonged. My evangelism fire was flickering in vain in that quiet room with some books, a few pens, and some pencils. I was so sad watching wasted days go by in that shop. Eventually, I got the opportunity to share my distress with the former director. He did not take it well, and so began our sour relationship.

Nevertheless, I still got time to move around the country with my friend Simon. We experienced a life of serving God's people together and shared great moments harvesting souls for Christ. Burundi was still at war. The genocide was ongoing, and people were killed daily. Every radio station broadcasted death. No positive news ever made it through the airwaves. We wished broadcasters would filter all the negativity and preach a message of hope that would encourage people who were so defeated. Burundi was a land of dead men and women walking. Many had no hope and began waiting for the day when they, too, would be killed. It was a heartbreaking sight.

But despite these things, we still had joy. We had passion. Joy is within. Either you have it or you don't—and boy, we had it. We were full of it. It was our only strength. It kept us doing what we were both called to do: preach the gospel, win souls, and share the love of Christ with His people.

One weekend we went to Makamba, in the south, to show the Jesus film. Thousands had traveled from distant areas to come and see it. After the movie, my friend Simon preached, then gave me the opportunity to pray for those who wanted to give their life to Christ. There were hundreds upon hundreds who raised their hands to receive Him. I was a bit skeptical, not expecting so many people to answer the call. So I made the request a second time, clarifying what it meant to be saved. And again, hundreds upon hundreds lifted their hands. I asked them to take one step forward before receiving prayer, and many did. I was blown away. I could not imagine that one day I would witness that many people so hungry for God. I realized that although many of them may not have fully understood the call, they all wanted something better. And Christ himself was the solution.

If we all lived our lives wanting nothing but Christ alone, then I believe Christianity would be much more appreciated. The Bible says, "Blessed are those who have not seen, yet believed." (John 20:29) God calls us blessed, meaning we have what we need. We may seem insufficient, but who we are in Him makes us whole. His call and presence in our lives makes us whole. We are provided for. We are catered for. We are able. We can live with confidence. This is what that multitude of people had agreed to—being called the blessed and chosen ones of Christ.

We were encouraged and continued showing the film across the country. On another mission trip, we set off to show it in Ngozi, up north. The location was at a boarding school, so we had to wait for the students to wrap up their dinner session, then help set up the room in which the film would be broadcasted. The film ended late in the night, around 11:00p.m. Simon and I left the school to drive back into the nearest town. It began raining. Driving in pitch black, through mud, down the mountains was not necessarily the safest thing to do. But we were tired and eager to rest, so we kept going.

We drove with caution and didn't see anyone else out on the roads. Eventually, we saw some policemen roaming with their dogs and guarding the road blocks. We were stopped at one of the barricades. The police asked us who we were and where we were coming from. I responded to their answers in Kirundi, explaining every detail. One of the policemen interrogated us without mercy. He refused to believe anything I told him. I remained calm and gave him the same information over and again. Tired from the conversation, he instructed them to lift the barricade and allow us to pass.

We got to the Ngozi City Centre. All the shops were closed and there was nowhere to fill our stomachs. We desperately needed a place to stay, so we went looking for somewhere to lay our tired heads. We were fortunate to find a small room at an Anglican Guest House. Exhausted and hungry, we set down our bags in the room. But there was only one small bed. Simon and I shrugged and laughed at each other, too tired to care. The bed was tiny for two grown and differently cultured men, but exhaustion outweighed all of our problems.

My time on the road was difficult for my family. Marie Josee was still working her teaching job and taking care of our son while I was gone. She also feared for me, as the rebels had intensified their mission, fighting against the government's army. In the following weeks, my friend and I were halted at more road blocks and had to field many questions. I felt pressure from all sides.

CHAPTER ELEVEN

Dreams Awaken

My time at Scripture Union was not meant to last. The former director and I could not see eye-to-eye. My transition began to take place when he received a letter from Scripture Union's regional office in Nairobi, Kenya. He, along with a board member and two selected people who worked with the youth, were invited for a special training at their headquarters. At that time, I was working with the youth and I also helped with the young children occasionally. I had been with the organization longer than most, but my efforts were overlooked. Sadly, the director chose not to invite me. He went on the trip with three others, while I was left behind.

My heart could not come to terms with this rejection. Disappointment was written all over my face for quite some time. I did not understand how someone could have the heart to treat others in such a calloused way. I had given my best, and I was still treated like an outsider.

After their trip, I got word that I was a topic of discussion with the Burundians who went. They asked the director for concrete reasons why I was not allowed to be part of the team. It must have felt difficult for him to hear this from his colleagues. Upon his return, he maneuvered indirect apologies to me for his actions.

As a result, the director sent me to Rwanda's Scripture Union office for one week to learn the ropes of children's ministry. I took a bus on my own to Kigali; the capital city of Rwanda. I was well-received by the team. There were eight of us Burundians amongst Rwandans and some Ugandans. They treated me as one of their own, and I hadn't felt that included in some time. During my visit, I got the chance to meet the director of Youth for Christ Rwanda. He was renting a small office in the Scripture Union building.

He shared his vision of Youth for Christ Rwanda and Youth for Christ Africa. As he spoke his dreams aloud, my heart swelled with excitement. I felt as though this was my own dream being relayed to me. My purpose was being confirmed, and my assignment was about to be handed to me.

I asked him more about this thing called Youth for Christ, in terms of its history and background. At that moment, I knew full well that this was why God had allowed me to miss out on the Nairobi trip, so I could be sent here to meet these exact people. This was the position He had in store for me all along. He had been preparing me all this time.

At our gathering was a speaker from South Africa named Dr. Thomas K. Resane. He was the Deputy Director of Youth for Christ in South Africa. I could tell he had passion for youth and a strong calling to raise a generation of godly leaders for our African region. While he spoke to us, he was open with us and mentioned that God had spoken to him. He had received a dream of Youth for Christ being established in Burundi, and someone was to be called to lead the organization. Thomas said he was ready to help that person.

My joys were compounding. The following morning, Thomas announced that he felt a call from God that he should help someone from Burundi attend Bible school and start Youth for Christ in Burundi. For seven years, I prayed for the opportunity to attend Bible school. I was reminded of the time I told my secondary school friends of my dream to travel outside Burundi for seminary. Dr. Thomas was the answer to my lengthy prayer. That was a huge miracle, as I had no uncle, mentor, or pastor to help me; it was God Himself making a way.

I was able to get one-on-one time with Dr. Thomas after the discussion about YFC and seminary. He asked me a simple but very direct question: “Freddy, is it you who wants to go to Bible school?” He asked if I also had a call to ministry. I could not speak to answer his question. Tears burned my eyes, almost rolling down my face from my overwhelming joy. At last I found my voice and shared my story. I told him about my deep desire to attend seminary. I had previously applied to Daystar University in Nairobi, but I never received a response from them. I could not have afforded the education and accommodation even if they had accepted me. After hearing my story, Dr. Thomas gave me the option of choosing between pursuing my studies in Nairobi or going to a similar seminary in South Africa, where he lived. This was a milestone for me. I was on the brink of beginning my mission and achieving my lifelong dream.

I got access to a phone so I could tell this good news to my dear wife. She could not believe it and kept laughing on the other line. I teased her, telling her to go get a passport. She knew the struggle I had undergone, enduring tough days just to get this far. Indeed, God was never asleep, neither did He slumber. He was “working all things out for my good.”

After the week in Rwanda, I got back to Burundi full of hope. I was not yet accustomed to the internet, and so things like sending emails were foreign to me, and to most Burundians. However, I found one spot that offered internet services to the few who knew what it was. You just had to pay a bit of money to send emails. I did this many times in order to communicate with Dr. Thomas. He started to look for ways via family and friends to support my funding to study in South Africa.

At that time he resided in Johannesburg, but spent most of his days traveling around South Africa doing work with YFC. One of the places he used to visit was Pietermaritzburg in Kwazulu-Natal, which is 600 kilometers from Johannesburg. While there, he met a Burundian couple. They were studying at the Evangelical Seminary of Southern Africa (ESSA). Dr. Thomas talked to them about me, and the couple suggested it was best to have my family with me at the seminary in Pietermaritzburg. Dr. Thomas kick-started the application process for Marie Josee and our son Elvis to stay with me at the seminary while I took classes.

The document process went smoothly until I had to start speaking in English. It was a new language for me. I could understand just a little, though speaking it was very difficult. I managed to get someone who knew English to help me go through the application process.

We then had another issue to deal with. In Burundian culture, there is not a single family name. Married couples, unlike other cultures, do not share a surname. Each one is referred to by their original name. This caused some hesitation in the seminary, because they could not believe we were a married couple without sharing a name. Parents always choose all the names of their children in Burundi. Names carry a particular meaning in our culture depending on what the parents want to express, or the circumstances the child was born in. But we were finally excused once they understood the cultural difference on naming, and my application was well on its way.

After that pivotal trip to Kigali, I also kept in touch with the director for YFC Rwanda. I learned that he had visited our country in the past in hopes of gaining people willing to partner with him to start the organization in Burundi. But his mission was unsuccessful due to lack of funding. No one was willing to pioneer Youth for Christ in Burundi. But I was eager to take this on, so I reached out in a big way. Without wasting any time, in faith, I got together a few friends who I managed to convince to help me, and we began the process of obtaining and filling in the necessary documents to file with the government. We then drafted a constitution for Youth for Christ Burundi at the end of 1999.

CHAPTER TWELVE

Burundi Youth for Christ is Born

Things were changing quickly, but they were changes I had desired for years. I soon heard from the Youth for Christ Rwanda leader, and he told me that a conference was scheduled to be held in Nairobi, called the National Directors Institute (NDI). It was an annual conference, and I had the privilege of an invitation in May 2000. I had to take a bus from Bujumbura all the way to Nairobi. I will never forget about that grueling trip as long as I live.

Financially, I had peanuts. I could barely make it to Kigali where I was hosted by the leader of YFC Rwanda. He, too, was unable to afford a flight to Nairobi. So we set off on a cheap bus to Kampala, Uganda, where we would then take a final bus to Nairobi.

We had been forewarned about pick-pockets and thieves on the bus, so my friend and I had to take turns sleeping to keep watch over our luggage. The bus was a nightmare. It was ragged and worn down from the inside out. All of us travelers were compacted together on broken seats. The seats were held together with rope for stability. One seat had to be retied by the driver, as only he knew the knot sequence that kept it from falling apart. We looked like potatoes stuffed into torn sacks. It was a miracle that we managed to get to our destination in such a state.

I had spent over 25 hours on buses and was weary when we arrived early in the morning in Nairobi. We had just enough money left to take a cab to the guest house where we would be staying. When we arrived, we were drained and hungry.

Fortunately, good things were in store. From the moment we stepped foot in the guest house, and all throughout the conference, we experienced nothing but sheer joy. For one week we could leave all our troubles back home and enjoy treatment that we considered luxurious. We had all that we wanted upon request, and got to meet with like-minded people who had the same vision for God's work. The environment was uplifting and stress-free.

When I saw Dr. Thomas, he greeted me with arms open wide and such warmth, calling out, "My son, my son." He lifted me up and spun me around with so much joy and excitement. I was overwhelmed and touched.

During the conference, I was honored to be amongst people from different cultures. There were leaders from Africa and the United States of America. I took down notes from different sessions that were important to me. They were lessons that carried me through to this day.

While interacting with friends and fellow leaders, I met a man called Graig Lockhart. (Graig became a great friend would end up supporting my ministry for the next sixteen years, and counting.) During a break in the conference, we went shopping in downtown Nairobi. Many of the Americans hadn't heard of the nation of Burundi, and so we decided to buy a map so we could point out where Burundi is located. Sadly, the map we found didn't even have Burundi on it. That was strange to note, given that we were indeed an existing African country. It helped me understand why a majority of the people I met with had never heard of a country called Burundi.

Before the conference ended, we all participated in a symbolic act of washing one another's feet. This practice was derived from the passage of scripture in John 13 where Jesus Christ washes his disciples' feet to display humility and servanthood. The leaders from the US who organized the conference washed all of our feet. I thought about how I was still volunteering with Scripture Union, and pioneering Youth for Christ at the same time. Though in that special moment, I decided it was time to resign from Scripture Union and devote all of my time to Youth for Christ in Burundi.

We headed back to Rwanda on the same long route we endured on the way in. I finally arrived back safely in Burundi. Soon after, I sat down and drafted a letter tendering my resignation from Scripture Union. It was not easy. It was a meaningful organization, and I would miss ministering with my friend Simon. Fortunately, it was summer and he was in England, so it made the transition easier. But I ensured that the news got to him regarding my resignation.

Youth for Christ Burundi began at a gathering in an Anglican guest house near the president's office in Bujumbura. This first meeting was held on July 23, 2000. I managed to gather 12 people. Among them was my friend from secondary school, and now colleague, Mr. Euphrate. I also invited two sisters who were my neighbors in Buyenzi. They were Emelyne and Rosine, and were still quite young at that time. I invited people who I knew were passionate about evangelizing to young people. I did not know how to formally run the meeting, nor did I have documents to explain what YFC would be all about. I didn't have a PowerPoint presentation to illustrate the vision, mission, core values, and strategy we would use to build YFC Burundi. All I had was a calling and some knowledge acquired during my training in Rwanda and in Kenya. I abandoned my will to the Holy Spirit to guide my words before these people I had gathered.

A few of them agreed to stick with me through the process of making the YFC Burundi dream a reality. And so we dug in, giving the vision what we could with our knowledge and skills. We began without financial support, which we urgently needed if we were going to move any further than just a name of an organization.

I had nothing else except faith that the One who called me was going to provide. Youth for Christ was not yet registered with the government, and in those days, the systems were full of corruption. My pastor at that time graciously offered us a room in his church office that we could use for Youth for Christ Burundi. It was nested under the name of his own ministry called Minister Chrétien de la Délivrance (MCD). The church couldn't provide furniture, so I took a few chairs and our landline phone from home. I also owned two cows, and I had to sell them to obtain money to get us off the ground. I assembled the furniture in our YFC room and we got to work.

We began our ministry in a small way, setting off to high schools with a Bible in-hand and the Holy Spirit guiding us all the way. We initiated Bible clubs in schools that Scripture Union had not yet set foot in, so as to avoid confusion.

My friend, and now colleague, Euphrate, also got on board with our work. He was working for a government department handling statistics, but he opted to join our other volunteers during his lunch breaks.

During this time of building, the war had still not quite subsided. Several camps had been set up for displaced people. Many were orphans who lost their parents at tender ages. They walked aimlessly on the streets, malnourished, and with tattered clothes. It was heartbreaking. I knew I had to do something for these special ones. I believed they too had a future, if only we could help them gain the opportunity to see it and live it out. Together with the team of 12, we brainstormed ways to get these children off the streets. We realized that in the physical realm, we had basically nothing. But we had Jesus Christ, and Christ, we believed, would be enough. We set out to be Christ to them. We decided to go out into the streets and talk with many of the children. When we spoke, many of them had hope written on their faces.

Others were physically hungry, but mostly hungry for love and comfort. They wanted someone to be there for them and live life with them—whatever that may have looked like. We were happy that some of the children listened to us and understood our belief in them. We knew from the smiles on their faces that Christ was at work in their lives. There was hope.

Chrissie Chapman, a fellow missionary who has been in Burundi for more than two decades, said this in her book *The Night the Angels Came: Miracles of Protection in Burundi*, "It is a fact that people can live without food for quite a long time. You can even live without water for a few days. But people do not survive without hope." And it was our responsibility, by the grace of God, to lead them to the Source of all hope.

But words were not enough for their desperate needs. We had to do more than tell them about Jesus. We decided that we would use our rented office building to cook basic meals for these kids. We would call them in from the streets and invite them to have a meal. We also sent out requests to families to help donate clothing. This became a ministry in itself, taking a form that we did not expect. Our ministry grew at a rapid rate. We witnessed many more children coming in for emotional and physical help. Some were psychologically traumatized and needed a place to debrief from the chaos that might swallow them alive.

During this time, yet another miracle began to unfold. A lady by the name of Jill Vaughn from Oregon, USA heard about the ministry we were engaged in with the street kids. She found out about us via a Swedish internet prayer network. Jill was, and still is, a prayer warrior. After praying for Burundi for months, she believed that the Holy Spirit spoke to her about the needs of Burundian children, especially street kids. Jill then decided to email the Swedish person running the prayer network. She wanted to learn how she could get connected with the person sending out prayer requests for Burundi.

One day, the prayer network in Sweden sent an email to connect me with Jill so that we could talk directly. Jill started to share with me how the Holy Spirit kept directing her to pray for Burundi. I continued to give her updates on Burundi about the war situation and the suffering the children were going through. She made plans to come help us as soon as she could.

Although YFC was helping in small ways, I felt we were not making much of an impact on the country in terms of raising up godly leaders. That was the ultimate goal of YFC Burundi, but it had not yet begun to take place. We could only focus on the current weight on our shoulders—ministering to the basic needs of these street kids. It was difficult to get them accustomed to living normal life, as opposed to the one they had been used to on streets. As I said earlier, many of them had been traumatized by all they had seen during the war, and so we had to be careful how we handled each of them. There was much work to be done.

CHAPTER THIRTEEN

Studying in South Africa

Meanwhile, Dr. Thomas Resane was spreading the word about my family, and my desire to study the Bible in South Africa. He was helpful making connections with supporters and a host family for us.

Marie Josee, Elvis, and I prepared ourselves to leave Burundi for the next few years. I put some systems in place and handed responsibilities to the team we were leaving behind at YFC Burundi.

We hoped to entrust the organization to Euphrate, who was still working at his government job. It was not an easy decision for him to step down from his paid position to take over leadership in YFC where there was no paycheck. Marie Josee and I scheduled a meeting with Euphrate and his wife to discuss this possibility.

I described the ministry's vision in detail. I explained the value of my schooling in South Africa and the urgent need for a new leader to take over Youth for Christ. Euphrate's wife was concerned at first and had many questions regarding the ministry. We held a lengthy discussion. Of course it was a challenge for her to allow her husband to quit his job to attend to YFC on a full-time basis. In humility, she submitted and agreed to support her husband's decision to become the leader while I was away. It was a big leap of faith on their part. At that time, our YFC budget was a total of 50,000 Burundian Francs, which was around US$50.

In January 2001, my wife, son, and I left Burundi for South Africa. We had to go via Nairobi to access the South African embassy where we could apply for a study permit. I got in touch with Youth for Christ Kenya to facilitate our accommodations. A proper place to stay would give me time to take care of the issues regarding my application without stressing about my family's wellbeing. We spent more than a week in Nairobi waiting for a response from the embassy. Finally, on a Friday afternoon, we were granted our study visas and quickly informed Dr. Thomas in South Africa.

He then had to look for finances to pay for our tickets, which he managed to do. The next day, we were on the plane heading down to Johannesburg. We got there in the evening, which made it impossible for us to go directly to the school. Dr. Thomas welcomed us in his home.

This was the beginning of many culture shocks that would greet us in the days ahead. We met Dr. Thomas' wife, and once she realize that we could not speak English, she became very worried. She was concerned about our survival at the English-speaking seminary if all we spoke were French and our native language Kirundi. But Dr. Thomas was a man of great faith. His wife's concerns did not shake his confidence that we would manage well in the school. To him, learning in an English school with a French background was possible, and he was excited to see it happen. Once that was settled, they treated us to a sumptuous dinner, and then we called it a night after our long journey.

The next day we prepared ourselves and piled in the car to head to the Intercape bus station. Fortunately, Dr. Thomas gave us 200 Rands (South African currency) for the bus that would take us to the school in Pietermaritzburg. Dr. Thomas had also arranged with Pastor Dennis Solomon from the Assemblies of God church to meet us at the bus station.

We arrived late in the afternoon. Dennis had a description of our appearance so that we could be identified at the bus stop. As we descended from the bus, he came and shook our hands, then drove us to the evangelical seminary. There was a church service that was about to take place, and we were invited to attend. We agreed to it, and at that evening we stepped foot into the grandeur of the church. Everything was so new to us, but we enjoyed being part of a different culture's service.

We found a host family from Rwanda. Pascal, his wife Charlotte, and their four boys took us in. We shared a meal together that first night in Pietermaritzburg, sparking a friendship that remains strong to this day. Their home in Rwanda is like our home whenever we are able to go and visit them.

The following Monday morning, Marie Josee and I had to attend classes. We were a week late because of the visa situation. It was bound to be an interesting day. Our greatest challenge was the language barrier. Plus, we had to take our two-year-old son with us. We had nowhere to keep him and no one to leave him with, so he had to endure the whole day with us.

Our first class involved computer skills where we were taught how to type. Elvis thought the computer was a TV to watch. He was curious and would not stop putting his hands all over the screen. Occasionally, he became restless and wailed, so we were forced to take him outside to calm him down.

The stress of being in a foreign culture, caring for a toddler, and learning new skills at the same time took a toll on my dear wife. The next three months were very unsettling. We all missed home. Marie Josee was on the verge of giving up the training to head back to Burundi. I watched her cry many times, feeling helpless that I was unable to ease her burden. What had I done? Was it right for me to bring her along with me? Many questions ran through my mind, weighing me down. This grand opportunity turned out to be perhaps the worst experience we would ever have as a young family.

I needed strength, not just for Marie Josee, but for me too. I would not reveal it to her, but I also needed comfort and encouragement. I needed someone to be there for me. But I held it all in and pushed myself to be there for her, hoping and praying that she would find peace of heart and mind.

Among our strenuous problems was our lack of finances. Dr. Thomas had found someone from Texas who wanted to help us financially, but unfortunately, this American sponsor passed away on Christmas Eve. Dr. Thomas withheld the information from us for a while, fearing that it would add to our discouragement. He hoped that the family would still support us, but that was not meant to be.

We needed finances soon, so my friend and host, Pascal, took me to an internet café near the school. I sent a short email to some friends of mine. I explained my situation to them and asked for their prayers and financial support. Among those who received the email was my English missionary friend Simon back in Burundi. He forwarded this message to other friends, including Yvonne Buckner and her husband, Peter, who were in Johannesburg at the time. Yvonne replied, asking me to open a bank account so that she could assist me financially.

The seminary gave me a supporting letter to help open an account, and Pascal assisted me with the process. That very same week, Yvonne and Peter put 800 Rands in my account. They provided for our needs at a difficult time and continue to support my family today.

Life became easier now that we had some financial support. I could go to class without worrying. My wife and I committed to learning the language, so I tried to be attentive and capture sentences that would improve our vocabulary.

The ministry of Youth for Christ Burundi continued while we were away. Euphrate was doing what he could and sent us email updates. Once in a while, I would top off my phone and get to speak with him. I encouraged him as best I could, challenging him to continue the great work that he was doing for the street kids.

I also got word that at last, Jill Vaughn from Oregon and her friend Susan Molinari would be coming to Burundi to help YFC for a while. I flew back home briefly to meet Jill and Susan and we ministered together. While we were there, Bujumbura experienced one of its most dangerous times, as it was heavily bombarded by two rebel groups, the FNL and the CDD-FDD. So many young people were killed during that week. Marie Josee was still in South Africa and didn't know if I would ever to return to her and Elvis.

However, I saw the hand of God in many ways during our years in South Africa. One time, our sponsor Yvonne encountered a situation at work and had to pause our financial support. It was a hard pill to swallow, as she had been such a faithful donor. I sent a distressful email to Dr. Thomas concerning this issue. I did not know how we were going to carry on without her support. Thomas wrote back to me with the following words, "Relax, God will provide."

True to his word, God did provide. I did not lack once. I always had just enough to keep both my family and my studies moving along. We built up some debts at the school, and again I sent some of my friends requests for financial assistance. We got word that Valley Church in Cape Town was going to support my friend Simon, but Simon requested that they support me instead. He gave them my information, explaining how we worked together in difficult situations in Burundi.

Not long after that, my family and I we were invited to the Valley Church in Cape Town to share our story before they committed to supporting us. So we organized ourselves and took a 24-hour bus trip to Hout Bay, Cape Town from Pietermaritzburg. During that journey, my wife fell sick. We later learned that she was pregnant with our second son, James.

The church received us well, with love and care. They took us sightseeing to the tourist spots in Cape Town. We spent a few days there being spoiled like kings and queens. They served us different breakfasts, lunches, and dinners each day. Our visit was an amazing experience, and we enjoyed it so much.

Before leaving, we also got to share our dream for Burundi and what we intended to do once we were done with our studies. Before we left, the church paid the debt we owed to the school and agreed to support us monthly. They were faithful donors to the end of our studies in South Africa, and that church has been our great supporter to this day.

I completed my studies, and the time came for us to head back to Burundi. Before heading home, I reached out to friends and family all across the globe, asking if anyone desired to chip in to aid our return. God's people graciously helped us. Our plane tickets were provided, and we were given an amount to get us back on our feet in Burundi. We had given away most of our belongings before coming to South Africa, and so we felt blessed, knowing God had provided a fresh start for us with little, if no, struggle at all. We also had some savings that we had managed to keep aside. With the money accumulated, we were able to purchase our first car and a plot of land in Bujumbura. The car we bought became the very first car for Burundi Youth for Christ.

Marie Josee was on her third trimester with our middle son at the time, making it risky for her to fly back home. We got a doctor from Ghana to do a checkup, clearing her for travel. We showed the doctor's slip to the travel agency, and to the plane attendants as well. Unfortunately, there were no direct flights to Burundi because of insecurity from the war. We landed in Kigali, then took a small jet back, setting foot at home on December 4, 2003, three years after leaving Burundi.

The next month, I resumed my position as the National Director of YFC Burundi. We moved our office to a new bigger building. We have since grown and transformed this ministry to touch lives in ways we never could have imagined. I can only attribute it to this one thing: faith! Crazy, unwavering faith. That is what it took to make a dream become a reality.

But first, we had to claim land for the Kingdom.

CHAPTER FOURTEEN

Roots in Gitega

My motto in life is a scripture in the Bible. It is 2 Corinthians 5:7, which says, "For we walk by faith, not by sight." (NKJV) As simple as it may sound, I have not seen many people practice this. It is easier said, and in this case, easier quoted, than done. Although, each of us travels a different journey when it comes to faith.

As I have grown in my walk with the Lord, I have learned that in most instances, I exercise my faith by dreaming, envisioning, and consulting with God. Then I evaluate whether I have peace in my heart about what I want to do. Peace has always been the determining factor in my ventures. If I have no peace, then I believe that God is probably not going to be present with me. This is the reason I ended up doing what I have done with nothing but faith, and total trust, in God's providence.

I have come to love a song called *"Imana ni Nziza"* which means God is good. It is a simple song:

Imana ni Nziza, Halleluyah (Oh God is Good, Hallelujah)
Imana ni Nziza, Halleluyah (Oh God is good, Hallelujah)
Imana ni Nziza, ni Nziza cane
(Oh God is good, He's so good to me, Hallelujah)

This simple chorus became our YFC Burundi anthem. I sing it all the time with my colleagues during devotions, or when we have visitors come from across the globe. I sing it at home with my family all the time. It has been our testimony from the ancestry of Burundi YFC.

The beginning of our organization sprouted from a few people coming together to partner in the vision, bringing what little we had. We abandoned our minds and hearts to the ministry, and God Himself led the way. Tangibly, we had nothing to call our own. Finances were scarce and we relied on well-wishes to support a dream that looked impossible at first. As I mentioned earlier, we began reaching out to secondary schools, forming Bible clubs that would help in the students' spiritual development. We also opened up a ministry for street kids that eventually took up most of our time, as it grew rapidly.

However, we were not quite satisfied because our initial vision looked different from what we were doing. We had gone down an important road, but we still felt the need to fulfill the vision of raising godly leaders to positively transform Burundi. We were not going to stop what we were doing, but rather work our way around it.

Years before, the Lord had given me a vision about Gitega; the central province of Burundi. It is right at the center of our nation, just as Burundi is central and known as the "Heart of Africa." I figured if Africa is in the center of the world, and Burundi is the heart of Africa, and Gitega is at the heart of Burundi, then this place must be special in God's heart.

I had no idea how I was going to obtain a piece of land in Gitega. Nor did I know anyone who could help me. But a few months after my return to Burundi, I got an opportunity to visit the USA for the first time. I intended to raise money to purchase land and build an orphanage in Gitega. I also planned to build a school, a clinic, a training center, and anything else we might need to raise a generation of leaders. I landed in Denver, Colorado at the Denver

International Airport for the first time in March 2004 and was welcomed by a man named John Bastian. John is a staff member of Youth for Christ International.

There was a lot to process at the airport. I took note of the high speed at which things operated. It was a beehive of activity, and everybody seemed to be running after something, someone, or the next flight. As we drove away from the airport, I did not see anyone on the streets. Back home, there would have been people walking everywhere. I noticed several cars but most of them were transporting just one person. It baffled me, seeing more cars than people. I turned to John a bit confused and asked him, "John, where are the people?" He was surprised at my question, but responded that people were either in their houses, in their cars, or at work. I came to accept how different our lifestyles were. I hailed from a culture where people always did things together.

Later that week I flew to Oregon where my new friends and supporters Jill Vaughn and Suzan lived. While in Salem Oregon, they took me to a new kind of restaurant for me. A "buffet." I had never seen so much food in my life. Jill and her husband John told me to feel free to help myself. I smiled sheepishly because my mind could not comprehend the amount of food I was witnessing. I gave myself allowance to sample each dish. In one serving, my plate was full. Back home, our plates would not amount to even half the food I had. But here was a mountain of edible color. I had a little bit of everything, with the option for more if I wanted it. I felt guilty at a certain point, but I enjoyed my meal with gratitude. I guess I was unsettled because my main aim was getting funding for my projects back home. I did not manage to do so. I came back home empty-handed.

Back in Burundi, I thought and prayed about how I was going to establish the orphanage. While in the process, a woman named Jacqueline Kandava got a hold of me. She was one of the ladies

I met in a church I used to visit. She used to live in Gitega before she got married. She came to me and suggested the possibility of getting the land for free from the government. I wondered if that was a good idea, and whether it would work. She said she was willing to help me if I was open to it. I did not know anyone else in Gitega, so finding someone to help was divine intervention. We planned a day and drove up together.

Jacqueline had a few friends in Gitega. One of them worked in the same building with Gitega's governor. His name was Mr. Bosco. He helped us get access to the governor, and Jacqueline and I were soon scheduled to meet with him. At our meeting, Jacqueline and I explained to the governor my vision for the land.

Over the year, we had many more meetings with Gitega's governor, who happened to be Muslim. We met again and again to negotiate the land, and after lengthy talks, he signed the documents for Youth for Christ Burundi to own ten acres.

Right before the governor signed the documents, he looked at me and asked, "Sir, do you have money to build on this land?" According to Burundi's constitution, it states that once land is gifted, a structure must be built, or in-progress within six months, or else the land is taken back by the government. Knowing this, I still answered him without hesitation: "Yes, I do." I remember thinking to myself that I had just shot myself in the foot. Here I was, declaring I was able to have a structure on this prime land, yet without any money. What in the world was I thinking? To this day, I still don't know where my firm "Yes" came from.

But I had faith. Crazy faith that pushed me to speak with such conviction. I believed that indeed we would have a structure built on this plot in good time. I had nothing else but God. God had said He would provide. I believed it, and now I was waiting for Him to fulfill it.

I left the office with the signed documents and a huge smile on my face. I was so excited and could not wait to share the good news about the land we had just received. As I left the office and continued to think, pray, and share the news, someone gave me 80,000 Burundi Francs, which was an equivalent to US$50 back then. It would help us to kick-start the orphanage, but it was merely peanuts in the grand scheme. However, big things grow from small seeds.

CHAPTER FIFTEEN

Cow-Grass

We didn't have the means to build, so we pitched a tent where we started caring for five children. Our first child was Theogene. Then Blaise. Then three more. The children would keep coming. But at first, there was just the tent and lots of hope.

After a few months, the Holy Spirit dropped an idea in my mind. I wanted to gather those living around Gitega who did not have jobs to help dig the land. I inquired as to the wages one would be paid for this work. I found out that it would be at least $1 dollar per person, per day.

My goal was to dig the land and plant cow-grass. The cow-grass would then be used to feed cows, which would then produce milk. The milk would be part of the meal that we would feed the malnourished children whom we would host at the orphanage. This was what my limited wisdom came up with before venturing into building structures. It would be the foundation for greater things to come.

Upon inspection, the government was happy to see that we were busy utilizing the ground. The tent and planted grass was great evidence of use and helped us avoid the plot being taken back. This was just the beginning of what would eventually be known as the Homes of Hope orphanage in Gitega. We later managed to build Future Hope School and Shammah Health Centre on the same property.

Those who saw the work we were actively doing felt compelled to give donations towards the ministry. Financial support came in a consistent stream, which went into building structures for both the children and the staff who were taking care of them.

Before we began building and construction, I invited ten engineers from the US under the Engineers Ministries International (EMI) organization. Their headquarters are in Colorado Springs, Colorado. They came and spent two weeks with me as I shared the kind of structures I envisioned on the land. Seeing the possibility of my vision, they chose to prepare a document for me with the drawings of how the area would look. They also blessed me with a projector that still functions to date.

I used to take my visitors, both local and international, to that empty lot we were given in Masenga to pray. One of them was Auntie Joan Vetter from Pietermaritzburg in South Africa. She was a jolly 65-year-old. She came to visit me, so I scheduled time to go with her to Gitega. While there, I shared my vision and dream for the project in Gitega, and Burundi as a whole. She has never stopped praying for us since that day. She has kept in touch, informing us of the intercession she makes for our projects and the country of Burundi.

I also took a couple from Canada and showed them the empty land, pouring out my heart and the vast dreams I had for this place. They asked where I would get the money. Confidently, I looked up and pointed to the sky, and in the words of Dr. Thomas, I responded, "God will provide." After leaving Burundi, the couple went to Rwanda and happened to meet with my friends Pascal and Charlotte Karemera who had been our friends since we were in seminary in South Africa. They discussed my craziness for having such big dreams with no tangible financial support. The Canadians suggested that Pascal and Charlotte should check on me to confirm if I really had lost my mind. But they were not the only ones. Many who heard about my vision did not believe that I could achieve it. They thought it was too big a dream to consider implementing. To them, it all looked impossible in the real world. But things kept moving forward.

Another visitor from the USA came. He was the international board chair of Youth for Christ. He wanted to visit our organization in Burundi. I took him to visit the new land. He also suggested that I was dreaming too big. Despite his doubts, he believed in us and was among the first to send me US$5,000 towards executing my plan.

I took my friend Daniel Scott Mays from Australia, together with his pastor, Steve, to see the location. My friend Krista Von Stein, who was YFC Burundi's first volunteer, came too. That was the special day when we met our first orphaned child, Theogene. We call him Theo, while his nickname was Kadogo, which means the little one.

In Burundi's remote upcountry, people are always curious to see white people. Among those who came to watch Daniel and Steve that day was a local lady named Marceline. She was elderly, and she was carrying a baby that resembled a skeleton. He was very malnourished, weak, and wore no clothes. I asked Marceline about him, and she told me he was an orphan. I was very curious to know the reason behind the child's deteriorating health state, to which Marceline told us she had been unable to afford to take care of herself or the child. They had no food, no medical care, nothing.

Marceline had no money or possessions to speak of. She tried to look after Theo, but could only afford a bottle of beer most times, which she mixed with water and gave to the child to drink. She used a straw to feed him this mixture while we all stared in shock and sadness. Theo sucked his thumb when there was nothing to eat. Daniel and Pastor Steve felt as horrible as we did. Daniel asked if we could adopt the child into the orphanage once the building was done. I responded with a resounding "Yes." I hoped Theo would be the first child in the orphanage at Gitega, now called Gitega Homes of Hope.

We drove back to Bujumbura, but the image of this child never left my mind. He was glued into my heart, and I was determined to get the orphanage up and running.

Soon, the day came when we were ready to find Theo. Krista came with me, and we looked for him all over Gitega. At last we found the child and brought him to our land. He became the first child who lived in the small tent we were able to put together before we received any funding to build a normal house.

Our plan was to create a family situation for the orphans. We wanted small houses where a few of them would live with a host mother. Our first mom's name was Félicité. She used to live in a refugee camp near the land that we were first given at Tankoma in Gitega. She was a single mom, and we invited her to bring her son Blaise with her. So Theo and Blaise were the very first children to make Gitega Homes of Hope their true home.

We then invited at team from Youth for Christ East Africa to come and help us do some work. There were about 30 people from Kenya, 20 from Uganda and Rwanda, and many young Burundians. We made it our mission to help Marceline, the elderly woman who had cared for Theo. She needed a proper home, as I saw once when I went to visit her when she had fallen ill from exposure. I will never forget what I saw when I entered the kind-of shelter Marceline was living inside. I was taken aback to see that for a bed, she would lie down on banana leaves and cover herself with a piece of old kitenge, a fabric, which also served as her only clothing. She was almost naked because her fabric was not long enough to cover her body while she slept. She had no shoes, no underwear, and no other pieces of cloth. Marceline was extremely poor. She had nothing except a big heart to help orphans with what little she had.

I took her to the clinic together with Krista. We found out that she had also been badly beaten up by her daughter-in-law. She had been chopping a piece of wood to sell in the market so she could buy something to eat. Marceline's daughter-in-law came and found the wood, which she then claimed as her own. Things got heated during their confrontation, and while trying to fight for it, Marceline was brutally beaten. It was so bad that she could not move her neck. Her bones had been damaged and some of her teeth were broken.

We paid for her medical bill and the clinic took care of her for a week. After her recovery, she went back to the home we had built for her. To this day she keeps in touch with me, asking me to thank the white person who saved her. She was referring to Krista, who had helped carry and transport her to the hospital during her time of need.

Krista and Marceline are still great friends, and as for Theo, Krista supports him financially to this very day. Marceline became a friend of Burundi Youth for Christ and we make a point of visiting her home. We buy clothes for her from time to time. We also sponsor her son, Eric, who is now studying at Future Hope School. Marceline's other son called Mbuji became one of our first workers.

CHAPTER SIXTEEN

Masenga Takes Shape

We then started to build our first home for the orphanage.

I have witnessed many lives transformed on that piece of land. Many who could not afford a day's meal are now employed with the school or the orphanage. Children who were abandoned now have a place to call home.

I remember the first set of children we received. They were extremely shy. They had fear in their faces, and more often than not, they refused to smile back or look into our eyes. They were impoverished, sickly, and traumatized. Many of them had never seen so much food, and would gobble down everything they had on their plate in such a hurry that they vomited it all back out. We did not judge their actions at all, because most of us, myself included, knew what it felt like to starve, then be presented with abundant food. They would eat, thinking that this would be their only chance to fill their tummies. But as they continued to stay with us, they realized that the food was not going away. There would be more for the next day, and the days after that. They were home. This home would be the place that never ran out of meals.

It takes roughly two weeks for a child to begin showing signs of improvement. They get more flesh on their bones. Their smiles get brighter, as evidence from dimples in their full cheeks. Their minds open up, and socially they begin to interact with one another in song, dance, and games.

Faces of gloom began to bloom. I daresay we have the happiest children alive with us. They are ever-smiling, and it is those smiles that open your heart wider to give all the more. We are able to feed and nurture them, and give them a chance at life. But above all, we are able to lead them in the ways of the Lord. We attribute our success daily to the enablement of the Holy Spirit. It is through these kids that we are able to experience God in such a real way. In Burundi, people who now want to start orphanages come to us to learn our secrets for success.

It is from my encounters with precious people that I came to understand why God had us move from our initial plot in Tankoma to Masenga in Gitega. We would not have met these needy people otherwise. These people were the beginning of many more to come that would benefit from the love of Christ poured over them.

The Masenga community has played a big part in the growth and expansion of YFC Burundi. We have seen neighbors and passers-by voluntarily assist in building our houses. They had no building skills, but were open to learn something. We managed to pay them, which makes them feel appreciated. It is a win-win situation for us all. We provided the opportunity for some people to do small jobs, and in the process we got to share the word of God with them.

We also had international guests who came to assist us. During the initial stages, we struggled a lot due to a lack of electricity and water. These two essentials made it hard to care for the little children who were vulnerable to every kind of disease.

We used to walk down a hill to fetch buckets of water until we got someone to install a water pump for us. We had only one strong man who could work this humongous, old, Chinese water pump. Whenever he was not around, or if for some reason he woke up on the wrong side of the bed, we would not get to pump water for the day. It taught us to be humble and respectful to one another. Given the vitality of this natural resource, we invested and managed to get another water pump, but it broke soon after.

We received a team from South Carolina that witnessed our struggles with fetching water. They were compelled to raise funds so that would get the help of an organization called Water Mission International based in Charleston, South Carolina. The organization came and installed a brand new water system for us that also had a solar purifier. It still works perfectly. We rarely run out of water. It now flows in abundance so that we can supply it to the community. Not only that, but we are also now supplied with city water. Every project in Masenga is covered when it comes to our water supply.

Our power supply has evolved from candles, to paraffin lamps, to solar. Our friends from YFC Edmonton in Canada sent solar panels that we now use for electricity at night. Due to the growing center, the solar cannot provide light for too long, but everyone can at least enjoy electricity for a few hours from 6 p.m. to 9 p.m. Henry Rempel, a friend from Edmonton, sent us extra solar panels that serve the Shammah Health Centre plus the guest house at Masenga. There have been many changes and improvements at our Gitega center over the years.

Our second and third homes on the campus were supported by friends who did a cycling marathon around England to raise funds for our project. Miraculously, many other people got on board. We had several visitors come to us. They helped with construction. Whenever we set out to build a new home, we would gather around and take time to pray over the foundation. Each house that has been built today stands on prayer. We wanted God to be the center of each home and His presence to manifest in those who would dwell inside.

As the number of children continued to grow, we were compelled to begin teaching elementary classes. We built Future Hope School and hosted about twenty kids on the first day of class. It then grew into a second class. An organization called Fields of Life contributed a huge donation by building an entire block for the school. Today, Future Hope School stands as the best primary school in the Gitega region. We now have two campuses and our students score the best marks in the national examinations.

When I look back over the years, my heart swells with gratitude. I am amazed by the things God can do with nothing. When a little hope is put in God's hands, He works in His own ways to make it grow bigger and better. I never would have imagined seeing all that I see today. I dare not boast that it was I alone who has done all this. Far be it from me. It has been God. He works all things for good. It has been His faithfulness that has been great, not just to me, but also to Youth for Christ Burundi as a whole. We are at a glorious stage right now, where we see the promise of life in abundance.

Today, there are several structures standing on our land in Masenga. We have different buildings that house several children and the workers who live with them as host parents. We also have the Shammah Health Centre—a clinic that is used by locals in the area. Our Future Hope School now has close to 600 children who attend. The property is home to a farm full of cows, goats, pigs, rabbits, and many other domestic animals.

From simple cow-grass has come homes, schools, and a health center. There are many other projects we intend to do in the near future. Who would have thought that God would transform a simple ten-acre plot of cow-grass into a lighthouse for a city, and beyond?

CHAPTER SEVENTEEN

Amani's Story

We have had several encounters with all kinds of children during the life-changing ministry at our Gitega orphanage. I often travel to YFC Burundi's centers to see the progress of the children we have taken responsibility over. Though most times my visit turns into fun rather than a formal visit. Children have an innocence that draws you in. They also challenge you to be Christlike, if you are keen enough to read between the lines of their words.

One child especially fills my heart. I met him one night as I was lingering after a showing of the Jesus movie in a village near our Gitega orphanage. We showed the film outside on a small court where local people play football (soccer). It became very dark after we shut down the small generator we were using. While wrapping things up, I felt someone tugging my leg in a bid for my attention. He called out at me, "Director. Director." I looked for the source of the voice, and peering down I saw a small boy about knee-high.

I could not see him well, as it was very dark, but I could tell from his voice that he was eager to tell me something. I asked him who he was, and he responded with confidence: "My name is Amani." Amani is Swahili for "Peace." I was curious to know more about him as he had captured my full attention. His confidence made me believe he was a smart boy. He was of small stature, but spoke like an adult. Amani and I went to the bus I had traveled in and sat together. We began a conversation that would eventually change this boy's future forever.

He shared his story with me. He was a street boy with no one to take care of him. My curiosity grew deeper, as I wanted to know why he ended up in the street. Given that it was late, around 11 p.m., I took him with me to the orphanage. We shared a meal together, and I gave him a place to sleep. I was scheduled to leave the next day, but I promised to get in touch with him on my next visit to Gitega.

As we became acquainted with one another, I learned how he ended up homeless. Both of his parents were still living, but they had divorced and each married different spouses. His mother had initially wanted to bring Amani into her new home, but her new husband's older children refused to take him on as another responsibility. So I sought out Amani's mother. She told me that her new husband and his children refused to take in Amani as her family lacked enough food, and they feared that he would ask for an inheritance when he grew older. Amani had nowhere to go, and so the streets were all he had to call home.

This world can be pretty cruel, and it did not spare Amani its suffering. He survived as a street beggar. There were good days, but most days he did not obtain much at all. I witnessed his struggle when I would go to Gitega.

From time to time, I would see him sitting near bars and restaurants hoping that someone would give him food or a beer. On a few occasions, I was able to give him some fresh clothing and food whenever he heard I was at the orphanage and came to visit.

The amazing thing about Amani is that he often helped an old blind man who lived in a run-down house by the road on the way to our orphanage. Amani helped this man get water to drink and sometimes shared the little food he got from begging. He was a homeless child, but he had the compassion to care for another.

I went visit where Amani resided. The conditions of his little premise were extremely bad. It explained the state of his body. He was perhaps ten, but did not grow from malnourishment, so he appeared six. His feet were jigger-infested, which caused deep holes. He could only afford the clothes on his back, which were dirty and torn. Bathing was not in his vocabulary as soap required money. I had to do something. His needs were great, and I could not just sit and watch this little boy's life go to waste.

I couldn't bring Amani into the orphanage while his parents were still alive, due to the policies concerning orphaned children. But I had no peace about leaving him on the streets.

I questioned Amani's mother again, and I found her reasons for abandoning him strange. They did not sound quite convincing to me. We talked more, and eventually I requested that she find a way to convince her husband to accommodate her son while Burundi YFC would take care of his education. She found the offer reasonable and promised to go and ask her new husband's family, although she implored me to talk to them also, as she believed they would give me respect and listen to my point of view. It was then clear to me that this lady had tried to get her son accepted in her family but had not succeeded.

As I'm not always at the Gitega orphanage, I sent my colleague, Regis, to go as my representative. He met with her husband and discussed the issue at hand. Surprisingly, he agreed to the offer, but his other children were still stubborn. By God's grace and wisdom, Regis managed to convince them to take Amani in. Regis had to sign a document proving that Amani did not plan to ask for any land as inheritance. Miraculously, one of the Burundi YFC supporters decided to buy some land for Amani so that he could happily continue his studies without worrying about the schemes of his step-siblings.

We were more than happy to support Amani, keeping in mind the condition put in place. Our ultimate goal was to give this young boy, with so much life ahead, a chance to live it out to the fullest.

These days, Amani has accommodation in a proper house close to his mother. He is receiving attention and affection, the essential needs of every child. We still cater for his schooling. He is now attending Future Hope School in Gitega with a bright future ahead of him.

CHAPTER EIGHTEEN

Breaking Ground in Cibitoke

As Gitega continued to grow over the year, a man I had never heard of began corresponding with me. His name was Ted Bosveld. He was an Australian visiting and serving in Rwanda. Ted sent me an encouraging email, and I responded asking for details about who he was. His explained in second email and sent me had his phone number. So rather than continue this back-and-forth, I opted to call him directly.

I introduced myself and shared the work I was currently doing. In the process, I asked him to consider assisting and helping out in Burundi. He declined my request politely, stating that he had committed to a five-year term in Rwanda. He was not sure whether he would be able to take on anything else beyond that.

This was a familiar scenario. Many people had heard about the genocide in Rwanda and were interested in helping them recover. But few had interest in Burundi, or even knew that we'd experienced a similar genocide. We received very little international attention. We were still at war and needed as much help as our neighboring country.

After the phone call, instead of frustration, I felt God's peace in my heart. I was moved to pray for Ted. Along with my intercessory team, we began a time of prayer and fasting. We prayed and believed for a harvest of laborers. This prayer season lasted weeks.

Three months later, I received an email from Ted. He reminded me of our phone call and said that our conversation kept recurring in his mind. He asked me to pray for him to see if God would allow him to come to Burundi. I mentioned that we had been praying for that last three months, and maybe God was the one prompting him to make a move. We continued to talk over emails and he suggested that he could at least come visit Burundi. I gladly welcomed him. We planned the trip, and he flew down to Burundi in February of 2007.

Ted came with his friend John who was a camera man. I drove them around Burundi and showed them the Gitega project. One afternoon, while driving back from Rumonge in the south, John wanted to get out and take a good shot of the lake. I took him up to a place called Mutumba that has a beautiful view of Lake Tanganyika. It was about 4 p.m. John got out with his camera and began taking shots, while Ted and I waited by the car for him to finish his expedition.

Suddenly, we saw a group of people coming swiftly toward us. John quickly took the memory card from his camera and hid it in his sock. The man at the head of the group turned out to be the county administrator. I could tell that he was not thinking straight. He looked drunk. When he got close to us, he asked me several angry questions. He wanted to know who we were, why we had come to Mutumba, and why we had a video camera. He was furious with us. Chills overcame Ted and John. Because of his anger and intimidation, Ted was afraid that this man might try to kill one of us. He managed to sneak close to me while all the fracas was taking place. In his anger, the county administrator took my car documents, telling me that I would end up in prison.

I could not go anywhere without my documents. I pleaded with him, explaining who we were and the purpose of my friends' visit. He refused to listen, leaving us for a nearby bar with his group so they could continue drinking. We stood there hopeless and afraid. We had little chance of retrieving my documents.

A local stranger who had seen it all happen approached us. He said that he knew the administrator. He was convinced that there was a way of getting my papers back. He said he knew a man who chaired Burundi's anti-corruption department. I asked the young man if he could help me and he willfully accepted. I asked John and Ted to wait in the car as I walked a couple of kilometers to meet this influential man.

I knocked on the government chair's door. A man opened it, and I felt small before his haughty, untrusting eyes. He let me inside, and I quickly tried to identify the government official. I spotted him. It was obvious from his posture, physique, and nice hat that he was a man of high status. He welcomed me and offered me a beer. I declined, but humbly requested to see him in private. He accepted and listened to my ordeal as I explained what had just happened. Generously, he came with me back to my car, and I pointed out the bar where the county administrator who had taken my papers was drinking. I nervously waited for the outcome. In less than five minutes, this angel-man came back outside with all my documents and released me to go.

Relieved, I jumped into the car and sped off. It was getting dark. I knew my wife and colleagues would be getting worried given that the war was ongoing and nighttime was never safe. Road blocks were normally put up by 6 p.m. When we reached Bujumbura, I thanked God for our safety. My visitors were traumatized, but in spite of it, this began my long friendship with Ted.

Back in Bujumbura, I dropped Ted and John back off at their hotel. As I drove away, I thought of the place they were staying. It was known as Ubuntu Residence Hotel. The concept Ubuntu means a lot to us in Africa: "I am because you are; you are because I am. You and I, we are interconnected, we are one."

When I took them to the airport later, I thought of this saying and it prompted me to ask if they were interested in funding my projects in Gitega, especially the secondary school I wanted to build. Ted said he would pray about it and get back to me.

After about two weeks, I emailed Ted and asked if he was ready to help. He said he would help me, but he would not be able to help in Gitega. He offered to help me start another orphanage. However, I was not quite ready to start another center because my responsibility was in Gitega. I said that I would help him find another Burundian to work with, but for now I would continue to focus on Gitega. The reason Ted couldn't help me continue with the Gitega project was because in order for him to be able to get funding and to offer tax deductions to Australian donors, the charity had to be an Australian-run organization. Therefore, it had to be under a new name and project. Plus, Gitega center was already moving along with financial support from the UK and USA.

Ted and I continued emailing back and forth in the following weeks. I brought the board of Burundi Youth for Christ together to discuss the option of opening another orphanage. They suggested that we find a way to initiate this project with Ted, but with a few conditions. These conditions included a full salary for the person who would run the project, as well as a car for the new project, because there are many errands to run to keep an orphanage going. Ted completely agreed to these terms, and next thing I knew, YFC Burundi now had two mission homes for street kids.

We got to work thinking about this new project. My colleague Euphrate said he was in contact with Pastor Isidore, the pastor of Living Church in Cibitoke, in the west of Burundi. Cibitoke was a very hungry place. In this region especially, many children were in desperate need of love, care, nutrition, and spiritual development.

We began by organizing a kid's Bible camp. We planned for 150 kids. Over 200 needy children showed up on the first day of camp. We fed them and shared Bible stories with them. The children continued showing up, and on the last day of the camp over 900 kids were present. We realized that although Cibitoke was among the most dangerous places in Burundi, it was where we felt the need for an orphanage must be met.

In previous years, Pastor Isidore had been given a piece of land that he had not yet worked on. He was ready to partner with YFC Burundi in order to utilize the land, as his church didn't have the money to build anything. We realized we needed a bit more land and had to take another step, asking the local government for help. The governor of Cibitoke province cosigned 10 acres for us.

Ted was concerned about the stability of the new orphanage, given the insecurity evident in the area. But we had been praying, and we knew that this blessing of land was nothing short of confirmation from God. Ted came out to survey the land, and as they say, the rest is history.

In Cibitoke, we now have the best school in the province, an orphanage, a medical clinic, a farm, and more.

Working in Cibitoke has brought transformation in the community in general, not only to the people in our center there. For instance, we continue to train local pastors in collaboration with friends from North Point Church in Texas. We have seen transformation among the pastors from different kind of churches. Previously, there had been division among them due to competition for congregations. They harbored anger, bitterness, and deep rage toward each other. But healing has been evident and restoration of relationships is ongoing. We are all amazed by what God is doing through Burundi YFC in Cibitoke.

CHAPTER NINETEEN

City to City

Towards the end of 2013, I prayed, asking God for a gift for the new year.

In the beginning of 2014, I took some of my colleagues and headed to the south of Burundi. I informed them that we were going out to pray over the country. We would stop at different places, pray, and ask for available pieces of land to start another new center for YFC Burundi.

We left from Bujumbura and toured the entire south region. We met with many officials and other people that we knew. When we reached Makamba, we met an individual who introduced my colleague Japheth and me to the governor of Makamba Province. We shared with him what our organization had been doing in other parts of the country. To our surprise, the governor asked us why we had been involved in all these projects, but had done nothing in Makamba yet. We realized that he already knew about Burundi YFC projects, especially our good schools. We told him that we would come, and if we got a piece of land, then we would establish the same projects as those in other provinces. He asked us to write him an official letter asking for a piece of land in Makamba, and we proceeded forward from there.

Back in Bujumbura, I drafted the letter, and in response the governor helped us get 12 1/2 acres.

As always, when the Burundian government gives away a piece of land to an organization like ours, that land has to be built on within six months to one year, otherwise it can be taken back. So we needed another miracle. We needed money. This one didn't take long. Shortly after we got the land, God used his people to allow us build so that we could secure our place in Makamba.

We established a beautiful primary school project just like the ones in Gitega and Cibitoke. As we continue to receive favor and blessings in abundance from God, we see it as our responsibility to continue branching out to the unreached parts of Burundi.

As I write this book, our next target is a province called Ngozi, on the northern side of Burundi. We hope to gain ground there and establish the love of Jesus Christ. The urgent need for Ngozi is a nice school. The region is one of the most populated provinces, but they lack a school that is at the quality level of ours. Many people have come to the realization that Burundi Youth for Christ is running some of the best schools in the entire country. We continue to receive people who ask if we can build a school in their area.

So although we had planted YFC in locations across Burundi, we still needed a permanent place for our offices and a training center headquarters in Bujumbura, the capital city. We hoped to get a place while prices were still affordable.

Burundi is organized in such a way that every good thing has to start in Bujumbura. Since we started YFC, we had been renting offices in Bujumbura. We had to relocate many times from one place to another, which wasn't helpful.

It was another big dream to own a building in the capital.

A friend of mine mentioned to me that the Japanese Embassy in Nairobi offered grants to fund grassroots organizations like ours. However, he was not sure if they granted funds to Christian organizations like Burundi YFC. I got the Embassy contacts in Nairobi and emailed them. I heard nothing for a few months, but they eventually responded. I described our current mission and future goals, and they wrote back saying they'd contact me again soon. As I was waiting, I kept praying.

On a Sunday morning, just after church, I got a call from an out-of-country number. When I picked it up, it was the assistant to the Japanese ambassador. She had just landed in Bujumbura. She was on her way to her hotel and hoped to meet with me the next day. She gave the details of her hotel and the time when we would meet so she could hear more about my work. Our discussion resulted in funding worth US$83,000 to start the construction of a training center in Bujumbura. It was such good news that I could not contain my excitement.

As we started construction, the big building drained us financially, but we got assistance from England, Canada, and the USA. This took almost two years, but standing tall today is the two-story building containing a number of offices serving as headquarters for Burundi YFC, plus six classrooms where we train young people as we continue raise up godly leaders.

CHAPTER TWENTY

Always Dream Big

I love to dream. I love to dream big. And I love experiencing the adventure of making a dream into a reality. I have learned that pursuing dreams can be done by anyone. However, staying consistent, diligent, and persevering through hindrances is done by very few. To achieve a dream, one must be willing to face adversity, even from those closest to you. Then at some point, the dreamer must wake up and work at making it all a reality, despite what the cost may be.

Due to the uncertainty in Burundi, it is understandable to dream small, if at all. The natural thing would be to simply surrender to the oppressive realities. With a majority living with hopelessness even today, very few can attempt to be imaginative. Few can come up with ideas that might revolutionize this country, let alone their own lives. It is hard to hope in the midst of adversity, uncertainty, and suffering.

Although Marie Josee and I had different coping tactics during the tough times, we believed that trusting God to come through for us was not a request, but a necessity. Any time we felt we needed something, we always prayed and trusted God, even when our inner voice whispered, "Impossible. Impossible."

During our time in ministry, Marie Josee and I began pondering over the possibility of owning our own home. This was her grand idea, as she had become concerned about her future and the future of our children, of which we now had three. We had no home of our own, and due to my rather daring faith that led me to different places despite the war, she said she felt vulnerable, never knowing when I might pass away. I found it hilarious to hear her train of thought, but I knew that behind it all was a sincere cry. She was thinking and planning for the future as a mother. What then would she be left with if I died? What would our boys inherit and call their own?

Securing a home for my family was a process that spanned many years and just as many miracles. Way back in our final year at the seminary in South Africa, we were able to save some money that we intended to use while in Burundi. Together, with the financial assistance from friends around the globe, we were able to accumulate funds for a plot in Bujumbura. This is how it occurred:

When we returned that year from South Africa, we met a man at our church named Pascal. He networked for people on where to buy property. In Burundi, they are known as *"Commissioners."* He came up to me after preaching in a service one Sunday and asked if I was interested in buying a house. I told him that I couldn't afford it. We spoke again later on, and he mentioned to me that there was a piece of land that was available for sale in a prestigious area called Gasekebuye.

He kept coming to me, as he believed that I had a lot of money because my family and I had just returned from South Africa. We were struggling financially, but this time I agreed to his suggestion. I made the decision of buying this particular plot, though I had only the general idea of the location. I understood the general region of Bujumbura but did not know the specific area of my plot. I learned that this land belonged to someone in the government with a large plot. He wanted to sell off his land into smaller pieces. The land owner had the documents; however each of them were in his name, which would make the process of signing it over difficult. At last, the time came when different plots were divided into smaller plots, and Pascal took me to the exact location of our land.

When I saw it, I had nothing but joy. It was the kind that swells your heart but only exudes a calm smile on the outside. It was one of the best plots. It was situated on a large hill and had an exquisite view of Bujumbura. As my eyes took in the beauty and potential of this piece of land, I sensed a peace within that I reckoned confirmed God's pleasure in giving me what I had asked for.

At that stage, Burundi Youth for Christ had vehicles that we would use for ministry. I also had my own car, so I sold it and managed to get $1,500, which was so small, really nothing in comparison to the amount we needed to build a home. Again, I walked by faith and not by sight. With this small amount we started to build, and then money started to come in. Soon, another $5,000 was donated by a family from Charleston, South Carolina.

Our prayers were being answered at Godspeed! We could not believe what had just happened. In awe of God's provision, we responded to this lovely couple from South Carolina, telling them how grateful we were. The miracles continued one after the other.

There was also a young lady named Kaitlin Woody who had volunteered with our ministry in the past and stayed two months with my family in our rental house. When she heard about our quest to build a home, she immediately wanted to contribute. She was about to get married, and as she was planning for her wedding, she realized she had more than enough money. So she sent us part of what she had been given for her ceremony. That was another US$8,000 into our account for the continued construction of our new home.

Another couple who had visited us from England in the past also heard our story and contributed UK$7,000 towards the house.

Years before, Marie Josee and I had visited a church in Portland, Oregon. The pastor requested that his congregation contribute to our ministry in Burundi. Many people came forward and gave generously. Others prayed over us. While we stood up front, the pastor kept encouraging the church to come and donate. A couple named Melissa and Anthony came forward toward the end of the service. They put a piece of paper in my hands. On that paper they wrote that they were praying for a miracle regarding their business, and if the miracle happened, then they would send us ten percent, not for the ministry, but as a gift specifically for my family. We came back to Burundi with that piece of paper and continued to pray over it for a year. The couple got in touch with us and sent money, specifying that it was set aside for my family. It was US$4,500. At the same time, a former colleague from Scripture Union approached me and mentioned that there was a piece of land for sale in an area in Bujumbura called Kanyosha. I took the $4,500 and bought that piece of land in 2005. At the time, it served poor farmers who grew and harvested small crops. But five years down the line we sold that same land for five times the cost of what we purchased it for. This amount helped us greatly with the construction of our house.

Another day, our supporting church from Cape Town sent us a large donation that we could not believe. I hinted to my wife that it was a sign from above that we ought to build a bigger house; a house that would hold not just my family, but also visiting friends from other countries. It would also give us space to minister to our local people if they needed a place to stay for a while. I went ahead and changed our plans to add a second story.

Building this house took time, as we relied on incoming finances. However, we did our construction bit-by-bit until we were able to see the fruit of many years.

We moved into our house in November of 2008 before the first floor was even finished. There was no water or electricity. The necessities of life became a luxury for a long period of time. But through it all, we did not complain much, because we knew we were getting closer to realizing our dream. It was a lesson on how to be content with what we had, and how to trust the Lord for a better future ahead.

But as the days kept going, our social class kept rising. Our area of Gasekebuye became the hub of respectable Burundians, influential in various sectors, both public and private. It was more than I could have hoped for. I could now have a safe home to call my own, a home in which I could easily watch my boys grow and take over one day. I did not want them to grow up saying that my choice to do God's work left them in desperate need.

Today, my three boys are safe and secure in our home. We managed to build a basketball court where they are free to play with their friends from the neighborhood. We have fruit trees too. Our neighbors come for Bible study and fellowship on a weekly basis. We continue to marvel at the way God has continued to bless us beyond measure.

My wife and I have also been so blessed to travel the world. It has been amazing to see so many groups of people and cultures. We have stayed in so many homes, and people have been so good to us. We always share our stories and the calling the Lord has entrusted to us. We tell these stories of changing lives in Burundi wherever we go.

God's people have contributed many prayers and finances to our ministry. We have also been blessed to host so many people in our home. We love to share our lives with God's people wherever they come from. We love to sing *Imana ni nziza* with different groups of people in preparation for eternity. We plan to continue to host God's people in our home. We believe we are one big family, and we shall spend eternity together in heaven. So why not practice now?

CHAPTER TWENTY-ONE

Gitega International Academy

Our vision was to raise up a generation of godly leaders who would transform our society, so it didn't seem right when educated Burundians sent their children out of the country for better schools. Many of those young people who studied abroad never returned to help their home nation. Even I had to send my oldest son Elvis to a Christian school in Rwanda for a while because of poor schools in Burundi.

So, being the dreamer that I am, I dreamed to build the best school in Burundi. I wanted to give students the education they were looking for so they would stay here and elevate the prosperity of our country.

Once again, I figured Gitega would be the best location for such a school to attract young people from all the corners of Burundi. I started to look for another piece of land aside from what we already had. I went to the department in charge of land for the country and they soon gave me the first piece of property, which was around three acres.

I used to ask friends and visitors to come and pray with me on that empty land, with faith that that we could build and open a school there by 2012. One time, a family of four from Denver, Colorado visited and prayed for the land. They were the Perry-Smiths. Their oldest daughter, Olivia, was living and serving in Burundi and her family came to visit her. I took them to pray for the yet-to-be-built school called Gitega International Academy. While we were praying, Mrs. Debbie got inspiration from the Holy Spirit for the four of them to pray over the four corners of the land back-to-back. They called in funds to build, but also called students from the four corners of Burundi to come and study there.

For a while, I had wanted to seek the help of Builders Without Borders, an organization based in Fort Myers, Florida in the US. I knew of them because they had built a building for Rwanda Youth for Christ. But timing and planning had never worked out. This time I had something to show them.

When their leaders came to see our new piece of land there at Gitega, they told me that the land was too small if they were to help me build the school of my dreams.

Upon hearing this, I went back to the government and they allowed me to buy their last piece of land in Gitega, which was almost the similar size to the first piece of land YFC Burundi had gotten from the government.

Still, the land wasn't big enough for a boarding secondary school. Unfortunately, the government had already sold the other pieces of neighboring land to our two plots. Then, I got the idea to investigate who owned the land around ours, and see if they were open to selling.

I managed to find out that there were two people who owned the pieces of land that I needed. The first one wasn't difficult to persuade, as he needed money. We paid him, and he soon signed the ownership papers. Now we had three pieces in total.

But we needed the fourth and final piece of land next to ours move forward. After investigating, I learned that the owner was Burundian, but he was a member of the East African community, so he was always on the move around the region for meetings. He would be a difficult man to get a hold of.

I asked a friend of mine to help find his contact information. My friend went to a friend of his friend, to yet another friend, and finally got his phone number. When I called this man for the first time, I had lots to explain. He wanted to know who I was, what I was looking for, and where I got his phone number. The questions went on and on.

It took a long time for us to finally sit and discuss face-to-face. When I told him that I wanted to buy his land to build a school, he told me that he wasn't ready to sell it. I begged him. At last, he finally asked me if I was ready to pay him 1,000,000,000 Francs, which was around US$500,000 at that time. I was shocked. I simply smiled, as I had no answer to give him. I had nothing other than faith and patience.

I scheduled many more meetings with this land owner over the following months. I kept trying to explain and convince him that what I was planning would help the children of our country.

Often times I had to track him down in bars. I spent many hours there with him and his friends as they were drinking. I cannot drink more than one soft drink a day, so I would have to just sit there and wait for him.

At last a day came when I finally persuaded him to sell at a fair price. We bought his land for US$25,000, which was donated by a businessman from Edmonton, Canada.

My colleagues and I had to work hard to combine the four pieces of land into one big piece so that we could build on one campus, and be able to get one title deed. So, at last everything was in order.

We had the land and we needed to find ways to start building this dream school.

At this time, I called back the Builders Without Borders to come and help us begin construction on the best school in Burundi. They came in 2011 and got to work.

On September 10, 2012, Gitega International Academy was launched. My friend Pastor Sallie Liefeste of Northpoint Church based in New Braunfels, Texas connected us with Joshua D. Hill, a member of the church, who became the very first headmaster for Gitega International Academy.

Edmonton Youth for Christ was also very instrumental in the construction of GIA. I received a lot of donations from them to help build.

Today, influential parents are now bringing their children to GIA; everyone knows that it's a Youth for Christ school where the gospel is preached and the Bible is taught in the classroom. Still, non-Christian parents, Muslims, politicians, and top business people all around Burundi send their children to GIA for a better education. GIA is the very first English Christian boarding school in the entire nation of Burundi. As far as we know, we are the only school teaching leadership from grade seven onward.

The unique thing about GIA is that these young leaders are not only receiving a quality education, but are also going through a coaching and mentoring process so that they may become servant leaders who will transform our nation.

In the few years of GIA's existence, we have seen a lot of transformation in the lives of our students. They come to us with no English skills and some have never attended church before coming. They are now growing intellectually and spiritually. They are also becoming the best leaders to transform Burundi and beyond.

My dream has always been to give the best training and best exposure to the young men and women we are discipling. We are preparing them to study abroad, to return to Burundi, and positively change the history of our needy nation. This is why we are busy looking for colleges in the US. We want our graduates to have the best education and to return to help Burundi when they are done.

CHAPTER TWENTY-TWO

The Year I Matured

The manner in which you start Christmas tends to influence the way you spend the coming year. The year 2015 held more challenges than successes for me. In December 2014, just before Christmas, I was called and informed that my mother was in the hospital. She had been involved in a serious accident. A motorcycle hit her and broke her leg. She was in so much pain. We took her into our home, so we did not celebrate Christmas as usual. Then Marie Josee and our children all got very sick, making my burden heavier.

As if that were not enough, YFC Burundi had internal disputes that required sound leadership and advice. There had been disagreements that I had not been informed of among team members. I received an email from staff members requesting endorsement for plans regarding the ministry's leadership. Since I had not been informed earlier of the issues, I was taken aback. I hoped that someone would have brought these things to my attention before they unnecessarily became mountains.

I declined signing any consent, which led to expected friction between staff members. It was not easy in this particular season, trying to juggle all the responsibilities of being a priest of the home and a shepherd of the ministry. I couldn't understand why things were transpiring as they were.

Then, the week between Christmas and the New Year, my best friend and I had a disagreement that threatened to end our friendship.

Now more than ever, I needed a shoulder to cry on, an ear to listen, and an encouraging word that would nourish my soul. But the hits kept coming.

On January 1st, my wife received an unusual call in the wee hours of the morning. She couldn't ignore it, because more often than not it was happy friends expressing their well wishes for the New Year. Upon answering, she was informed that her mother was very sick and on the verge of death. It required that we get to her, in some miraculous way, before she passed.

Without delay, we gathered a few things, got in the car and speed off upcountry. When we arrived at the clinic, Marie Josee's mom was in a coma. We could not accept this sight. She could not communicate at all. Piece by piece, our hearts began to break. Our strength was dilapidated.

Trying hard to be strong, I gave quick instructions to have her put in our car so we could rush her back to Bujumbura for treatment. We arrived in the city at a hospital. I remember running up and down the halls, trying to find a hospital bed and a ward where they could check her in. It took a while before they found one, but they eventually got a place for her late in the night. The days after felt like an eternity. Each morning we walked into her room hoping that she would wake up and say something. Silence from a loved one never felt so loud. Darkness never felt so real. The world never felt so unbearable, and we have never felt so small and helpless. It pained my wife and me to see her in such a state, but the greatest pain was having to endure all this on top of the frustrations erupting with family and ministry.

Marie Josee's mom spent less than a week in hospital. On the 6th of January, my mother-in-law passed away.

While all of this was happening, our personal bank account in South Africa had been locked since we had not personally been in the country for years. We couldn't access any of our money.

The year had begun on a somber note. I had my fears and doubts. I wondered what the rest of the year had in store for me if death had set the tone. The future did not look as bright any longer. I wandered through my days with blurred vision, but thank God, not blind. I still had hope to keep my mind set on things above.

Resuming my duties, I received an email indicating that our ministry could not access the outside funds that our donors had sent us. Could this be true? No funds for the family, and now, not even funds for the ministry? What was going on?

For the first time in years, I had to borrow money for myself to facilitate my mother-in-law's funeral. All these misfortunes happening at such a rapid speed in such a short amount of time led me into discouragement. I needed strength to tackle every issue that reared its ugly head. I had been a pioneer, a hero. But even heroes need a hero sometimes.

It was one of the darkest times of our lives.

The enemy continued to shoot his arrows. I received an email from one of our biggest donors stating his intention to end funding for Burundi Youth for Christ. He believed our ministry had grown and matured plenty, and he wanted to support other projects. I was surprised. He had been one of our faithful donors for over ten years, and all of a sudden, he wanted out? Something was not right somewhere. Things had reached a point where nothing made sense to me. While processing what had just transpired and how I would come up with a quick solution, another email came in from another donor stating the same thing—they were stopping their funding of Burundi Youth for Christ.

The discouragements became a trend from then on into the next year. Several donors cut off their support for Burundi Youth for Christ. My strength was weakening. I needed a needed a lifeline to cling to. At this time I remembered the story of David, how he nearly came to his end after losing several battles in opposition with King Saul. The Bible says that despite his state and the unbearable circumstances, "David encouraged himself in the Lord." (1 Samuel 30:6).

In the year 2015, I also saw hell break lose in Burundi. The country had been gearing up for peaceful elections in hopes that a new government would be put in place. Businesses and schools were going on as usual, but tension began simmering underneath.

Operations at YFC were ongoing, until April 25th. On that day, the ruling party, CNDD-FDD, named their candidate who would run for the presidency. The better part of the country did not take this lightly, and tension began to bubble even stronger than usual. This continued up to April 26th. Bujumbura became impassible; citizens took to the streets protesting the running of President Pierre Nkurunziza for a third term. We heard that the protesting was not only taking place in the capital city, but other major towns in Burundi as well.

During this period, the welfare of the staff members became my responsibility. Some of them had grown fearful of the future, and understandably so. Rumors spread like wildfire. The radio stations had plenty to say to a nation that was curious to hear what was coming next. Burundians are attached to their radios. We have a culture of believing everything that comes out of their speakers, whether positive or negative, but mostly negative.

Many streets had been blocked, and transportation was paralyzed. It was impossible to attend to office duty, or any kind of duty, for that matter. I remember I had to walk my middle son to his school to sit for his grade six national exam. Unfortunately, he could not take his exams because of interruptions caused by protestors.

The situation continued to deteriorate. It got so bad that on the 15th of May, there was an attempted coup. It became impossible to function in the city. All of our schools, as well as our ministry, had to close down due to the insecurity.

A cloud of panic and great fear hung over all the stakeholders of Burundi Youth for Christ. Concerned parents came to collect their children from our schools. Our staff was worried as well. Most of them were from other countries and had been given warnings from their embassies to evacuate the country.

Gunfire became the order of the day as the fight to conquer the nation, and national radio, was on. Within 48 hours, the coup failed.

I prayed all along, asking God how to handle the current situation. Donors had pulled out, and some staff members took flight. There were still a good number remaining, but how were we to pay them if there was no money? I was between a rock and a hard place, realizing that whichever decision I made, there were going to be painful consequences in the end. We decided to reduce the number of staff members. It was a desperate situation, given that Burundians rely greatly on employment to sustain them.

I remember having to make painful calls to some of our staff members, asking them to remain home until the organization recovered well enough to pay them. I was the only one able to make the calls, because my colleagues did not feel confident to relay the news to their coworkers. It was a distressful season. There were many tears, plus feelings of anger and betrayal brewing in the hearts of staff members at our different work stations.

In Gitega, the issue turned ugly when one of the employees we had to release opted to tarnish the name of Gitega International Academy and the ministry as a whole. He gathered a group of 13 people and they opened a court case against Burundi Youth for Christ. We were then summoned in the court of justice. A lot of negativity surrounded this case, the ministry, and my name. Accusations and malicious comments spread over the internet, which made it visible to all my partners and friends overseas.

The man who started this was not going to stop at anything. The harder he persisted, the weaker we felt, and the stronger he seemed to become. There were only a few who chose to look beyond the surface and asked me what was going on. But as soon as the lies were spread, a majority chose to believe everything they heard.

Even the airline I had used since 2004 became a financial burden to my travel plans and ministry. I had flown with them for years, and with that came the privilege of gold member status for my long flights. However, in 2015, I had to cancel most of my trips because they had taken away all my privileges and discounts. I was reduced to blue member, meaning I had to go back to long lines and extra fees.

I was on the verge of a breakdown. My prayers became less frequent and my words became few. My strength was draining away and I could no longer find it in me to face anything or anyone. I felt alone for a long time. I questioned whether God had left me on my own. Out of anger, I began planning to start another business aside from the ministry. It was a temptation so sweet, because then, it was hard for me to understand how God would allow trials on every side to refine my faith. I began my plans slowly, but with much less enthusiasm than I had begun YFC.

It took only a few months before the side-business collapsed and I was back to square one. I was back in my world full of anger and feelings of defeat. In humility, I had to repent and ask for God's forgiveness for making Him small and for going against His call and agenda for my life. I knew He understood what I felt, but I still felt I owed Him so much more.

I thank God when mercy meets us in these messy situations. Psalm 103:11-13 is a great encouragement when we feel we have gone astray and wandered our own way. When we come back to our Heavenly Father, we are reminded of this:

> *"For as high as the heavens are above the earth, so great is his love for those who fear him; as far as the east is from the west, so far has he removed our transgressions from us. As a father has compassion on his children, so the Lord has compassion on those who fear him."*

Slowly, but surely, I managed to rise from the ashes. Our ministry has seen God turn everything around for our good. Practically speaking, it was necessary to bring in our auditors to come and work on the entirety of Burundi Youth for Christ's Ministry, so as to clear up any confusion, and also inform us where we stood.

We have now expanded our territories. We built a second campus for Future Hope School in Gitega. We have witnessed God's provision overflow our borders. We watch the lives of children transformed daily.

One of the biggest lessons that 2015 left me with is to not get offended any longer. I learned that people will always be people, and God's work is done by people. Once a missionary friend got me thinking about people. I met him at the Bujumbura Airport, and I asked him: "Jim how are you? And how is God's work for you?" He turned at me with a very serious look and answered, "I am fine

Freddy. God's work is always good, but it would be fantastic if wasn't being done by people." Then he got into his car.

I have been pondering what he told me for many years now. How can we do God's work without people?

CHAPTER TWENTY-THREE
Hope for Burundi

Over the years, many people have asked me, "How is Rwanda?"

Normally I am flabbergasted and somewhat appalled by this question. I manage to contain my irritation and embrace an attitude of humility as I correct them in love about my nationality as a Burundian. It also surprises me how many people from our neighboring countries are clueless about the existence of a country called Burundi. This is when I realize that our time as Burundians has come. It is time for us to shine and be the light of the world, a city on a hill that cannot be hidden (Matthew 5:14).

Allow me to blow the trumpet just a little bit: Burundi is a country on the map. It's a beautiful nation covered with so much vegetation resulting from rain that pours for close to nine months. There are green, beautiful, serene hills that you get to enjoy as you drive through the countryside. Many beautiful fruits originate in Burundi. In addition to that, we grow delicious coffee.

Burundian drummers are considered some of the best in the entire world. Recently, UNESCO declared Burundian drumming as part of our cultural world heritage.

Burundi is host to the second deepest lake in the world, Lake Tanganyika. The lake is the southern source of the Nile. It is home to a delicacy known as *mukeke*, a type of fish that is only found here. If made well, you will be licking your fingers and indulge it with either some fried potatoes or *bugali* (maize flour baked with hot water) and a sauce.

We have the most hospitable citizens. Visitors are considered important people. Those from far places are labeled "carriers of wisdom" who come to share ideas with the people of Burundi.

However, struggle is written on the faces of many people. They carry the weight of the past events, pondering endlessly on the losses and trauma they have incurred over the years of violence. But this does not outshine their beautiful smiles. Burundians are generally happy people and love to enjoy life together. They are very communal and value family as well.

The trials of 2015 proved to me that though I was lonely, I was never completely alone. God was present for me and for Burundians in need. He was a Father who was constantly encouraging me to keep going. He was guiding me through every situation. He held my hand through it all.

A great hymn that I love by Andrae Crouch comes to mind whenever I look back over the past years. The chorus is a summary of the lesson I carry with me:

"Through it all, through it all
I've learned to trust in Jesus, I've learned to trust in God
Through it all, through it all
I've learned to depend upon his word."

God has taken me from a small village in the south of Burundi—a country that very few people have even heard of, and allowed me to travel to many powerful nations of the world. I have been hosted by many successful families in the USA, Canada, Australia, Europe, South Africa and many other nations in Africa…all for God's kingdom's sake. I was honored as one of the few Burundians to represent our nation in the third Lausanne Congress held in beautiful Cape Town. I am also reminded of the time I got the privilege of meeting Bob Kruger, who was the US Ambassador to Burundi during the genocide years. I remember sitting in his office in New Braunfels, Texas. After sharing my vision with him for my country, he signed a copy of his book for me called *From Bloodshed to Hope in Burundi.* I was very encouraged to meet such a man who still sees hope for Burundi despite all the challenges going on.

I trust God for my nation and for the future of Burundi Youth for Christ. I am only a steward, entrusted to care for what has been given to me. Ultimately, it all belongs to the Lord.

The year 2015 remains fresh in our memories. Many of our colleagues and friends fled the country, never to return again. The economy dropped to such low levels that we need God's mighty intervention for restoration.

Being classified as one of the top five poorest countries in the world in 2016 was a grieving statement to hear. Knowing the great potential that this country has, I refuse to believe that we are poor. We have untapped wealth. That does not make us poor.

Burundi has so much potential that many people cannot see. Eleven million of us speak the same language. We live in a country where more than 90% of people can survive just by digging the land and growing crops. There is drinkable water in most of the country. It's possible to drive to the four corners of our country in just one day. Burundi is such a beautiful land with so many sights that are still unknown to the rest of the world. You can spend your day on the beach by the lake, or up in the cool, misty mountains where waterfalls flow.

I do pray and hope that the situation will change. My heart grieves especially for the future of our young people. It is my hope that they will step up and be part of slow but steady development. I hope that in their future, they will be able to enjoy a peaceful land flowing with milk and honey. I pray for quick recovery and restoration. I believe we will have a generation of Nehemiahs who will come back home to rebuild the walls of the heart of Africa.

I continue to believe the prophecy given years ago. I believe that many from this nation will be sent out to make disciples. It will come true in our time. Burundi shall be a blessing to the nations. Nobody who comes to this land leaves the same way. There is always a change of heart or perspective once you have landed here. We like to tell our visitors: "When you come to Burundi and Burundi gets under your skin, you never leave again." I pray that Burundi will one day be recognized as a destination of peace, warmth, love, and above all, a place you can come to encounter God Himself.

Yes, there is hope for Burundi. We have an entire generation of young people who are tired of the ethnic divisions and cycles of revenge between our two major tribes, the Hutus and Tutsis. Burundi's problems are now more political than ethnic, contrary to the past, which is a very positive change. It's no longer a Hutu vs. Tutsi problem; it's more fighting for a piece of the small pie. The day we get more businesses into Burundi is the day our people will get busy finding ways to eat without entering politics for survival.

If God can use a village boy like me, then He can certainly use you.

God enabled me to start Burundi Youth for Christ from nothing and make the big organization it is today. As of this year, 2017, Burundi YFC counts five schools, three orphanages, two medical clinics, land ownership in different parts of the country, a farm, livestock, and many other small projects. Every day our staff of 216 makes an impact in lives of 1,300 young people and children.

God can surely use anyone to touch lives for Him.

I am personally ready to continue to do His work in Burundi, reaching out to more young people and discipling them to become godly leaders. I am in His hands. I will be happy to go wherever He takes me. He just has to make it clear.

As I write this book, I have invited all my friends and supporters from across the globe to come to Burundi and celebrate with us the many miracles God has done for, and through, Burundi Youth for Christ over the past 18 years.

June the 17th is a very big day this year. It will mark the graduation of our first class from Gitega International Academy. It is a time when we will look back and thank God for the amazing journey that He has taken Burundi YFC on. We are all amazed by His provision.

I have learned that the biggest impact on ministry is your *calling* from God. I have understood that if God calls you, then it doesn't matter who you are or where you come from. God can use anyone from any kind of background for His kingdom's sake.

If God can take a poor village boy this far, then how far can he take the rest of us struggling in Burundi?

Let us find hope, and find out.

ACKNOWLEDGEMENTS

Special thanks to the following:

My wife and our three sons for being there for me at all times. I spent many busy years pioneering Burundi Youth for Christ, and you were always patient with me.

To my parents for sending me to school although they needed me at home to help raise my many siblings. Thanks, Mama, for your support and unceasing prayers.

Pastor and friend Zachee Ndayisenga, who believed in me while I was still a small boy. You encouraged me and allowed me to preach while I was still in primary school.

Simon Guillebaud for many years of ministry together in dangerous Burundi, and for connecting me with many of your friends and supporters.

Dr. Thomas Resane for investing in me and mentoring me over the years since we first met in Kigali, Rwanda in 1999. Your love and support has kept me focused.

Friends in South Africa, including Valley Church at Hout Bay in Cape Town for your financial support over the years, and my friend Cori Weilenga in Pretoria for the long years of support, as well as Yvonne and Peter Buckner.

All my colleagues at Burundi YFC, especially Euphrate for being so faithful to the vision and for your commitment since the beginning.

Eleanor Perry-Smith for editing this book for me.

Thank you as well to all the friends and supporters of Burundi YFC wherever you are. Surely, we couldn't have done the work without your love, support, and prayers.

My wife Marie Josee and I at the Youth for Christ International general assembly in Colorado Springs, Colorado in 2005.

Theogene on the first day we met him. He was the first child to call our Gitega orphanage home.

The very first building for Burundi YFC where we raised the first five orphans. It was just a tent covered with grass to reduce the heat during the day and to keep warm at night. Two small cooking stoves sit in front of it.

Workers plant cow-grass on our first land.

The first plot of land we got where I planted cow-grass as it currently looks.

The Perry-Smith family praying on the empty land at Karera in 2010 before any money was given to build Gitega International Academy. It was launched in 2012, a huge miracle.

The campus of Gitega International Academy.

Karen Korineza, an 11th grade student at GIA, reads her winning poem on Martin Luther King, Jr. at the US Embassy.

Students point to the original vision statement for Youth for Christ Burundi.

New Building: Our newest building at GLA where we will hold the very first graduation on June 17th on the top floor. It seats up to 800 people. God has done wonders.

22470925R00092

Printed in Great Britain
by Amazon